THE RISE OF 3V1L

THE RISE OF 3V1L

MAGICAL GIRL UNDERGRAD – BOOK 3

Aest Belequa

Podium

Podium

THE RISE OF 3V1L

PART ONE

1

Arrivals and Departures

SUNDAY, AUGUST 31

[Flight Delay: Act Three in Progress]

A pink-and-blue streak followed my sailboard through the air as I dove toward Tokyexico International Airport's white cloth towers. If I was right, the plane carrying my girlfriend and sidekick, Bianca, had just touched down, so I only had a few minutes to finish this ridiculous Episode. I gritted my teeth, slid through the gap in TIA's false roof, and crashed through the glass below it.

I'd been fighting this little-leaguer for almost an hour. He wasn't particularly tough; I'd only had to shift forms for defense twice, and once to get a **[Rejuvenation]** charge. But Solarbeam just *wouldn't* give up, and he wouldn't stay still.

Right now, he was sprinting toward the duty-free shop with flaming feet. I rolled my eyes, **[Quick-Time Changed]** into Copy Cat, and **[Leaping Leopards'd]** to close the gap, but as I jumped, he disintegrated into a pool of light, then reappeared a few feet away, still running.

[Flashy Fitting-Room! +1 Flamboyance Point]

"Come *on*!" I shouted, gritting my teeth in frustration. I didn't even know what the guy wanted at the airport, just that when my ride dropped me off, the first thing I saw was a **[Casting Call]**. At this point, it was just personal. I shifted back to Magical Girl Understudy, taking the extra time. It'd take me seconds to catch up, but if Solarbeam just dodged all my gap-closers, I'd be better off with solid ranged damage.

I needed to move fast, though, so as I finished spinning and summoned **[Starwave Sail]**, I plotted a course that'd catch me up to him. Then, the magical windsurfer shimmered into being below me, and I took off.

I wove through the old pre-Launch Day planes hanging in the airport, ducked through a biplane's wings, and narrowly avoided a fighter jet's pointed nose. Then, as I closed in, I lowered my wand and said, "[**Starlance**]!"

I'd gotten the upgraded version of [**Stellar Ray**] from my signing bonus for the minor leagues. Instead of a bright white beam, [**Starlance**] was a bolt of pinkish-white light about eight feet long. Its main advantages weren't helpful here, but I'd discovered that in addition to hitting harder against armor and high-HP supers, it had a little guidance built in.

So, as Solarbeam shifted places again and started his own attack, my lance turned just enough to clip him. He spun in place, and his beam went wide, bouncing off a silvery aluminum airplane fuselage and fizzling out midair.

[**Dramatic Damage! +1 Drama Point**]

I winced. Part of me felt bad for the villain. He hadn't expected a minor-league hero like me at the airport. Then again, I hadn't expected a little-league villain. Unlike him, though, I was ready. Also, unlike him, I was on a time crunch.

He started running again, blinking from spot to spot. In another couple of years, he'd be a threat. But right now . . .

"Solarbeam, this is Magical Girl Understudy. For the last time, this mess is inter-rupting my *personal* life, so if you surrender now, I'll drop you off somewhere. We can forget this ever happened," I said.

"[**Beep!**] you!" the villain shouted, raising a red-gloved finger at me. He kept running. "I just wanted a jet, but you can't let me have that, can you?"

"No. You're endangering people." I fired another [**Starlance**] his way. This time, he waited to blink until the last possible second, and I missed.

I grimaced. I'd been bullying him all day, and only some crazy grit powers were keeping him in the fight. I did *not* want to fight this guy in two or three years.

Heck, I didn't want to be fighting him in two or three minutes.

He kept running, and I kept chasing him, watching the digital clocks change. The concourses had emptied out as Extras fled the fighting, and I didn't have to worry *too* much about collateral damage, but I didn't want to break up any planes if I could help it. As another of Solarbeam's attacks scorched the floor below me, I let [**Starwave Sail**] go, quickly found the flights from Tortuga West, and cursed mentally.

She'd landed. The plane was offloading passengers already. If I didn't wrap this up, I'd be too late to meet her at baggage claim, too.

It was time to take the kid gloves off. I spun, aiming at Solarbeam's retreating back, and used [**Bit-Part Barrage**]. It still fired the classic [**Stellar Ray**] barrage, but I hit the first shot and stunned the villain. The rest of the rays thudded into him one after another, and I smiled as he collapsed.

[Episode Finished!]
[Episode: Pilot: Flight Delay - PG]
[Penalties: N/A]
[Episode Finished! +5 of each Style Point]
[Winner Winner! +3 of each Style Point]
[Role Focus: Drama + Flamboyance - Goal Met! +10 Focused Style Points]
[Alias - Understudy] [Archetype - Magical Girl] [Community Rank - 219/523]
[HP 11/11]
[Styles and Skills]
►Archetype Skill - Transformation Sequence
►Combo Skills - Power-Weaving
►Badass (27)
►Cunning (24)
►Drama (55) (Skill Roll Available)
►Starlance 1
►Bit-Part Barrage 2
►Flamboyance (53) (Skill Roll Available)
►Signature Skill - Adaptive Armoire 3
►Stored Costumes: (Rainy Day, Copy Cat, Lab Assistant Panic)
►Starwave Sail 1
►Quick-Time Change 3
►Hog the Limelight 1
►Grit (17)
►I-Frame Transform 3
[50 Drama Credits Used. Rolling Skill!]
[50 Flamboyance Credits Used. Rolling Skill!]

I rolled my skills even as I stared into the camera. "Day or night, justice is watch-ing!" Honestly, I was going through the motions to get the whole process over before—

Something hit me from behind like a tsunami, wrapping around me in a gigantic embrace. I struggled and turned toward a head of black, curly hair. For once, Bianca Marino didn't smell like green apples; I got the whiff of stale airplane air and deodor-ant. She looked comfortable in her shorts and spaghetti-strap tank top, though. "Thank you so much for saving the airport, Magical Girl Understudy. I was *so* scared!"

I struggled not to roll my eyes since the camera was still watching. The overly thankful college girl didn't have to worry—she wasn't facing it, and she gave me a big, painfully obvious wink as my skills came in.

[Skill Upgrade! Starwave Sail 1 > Solar Wing: Choose between a rideable vehicle and highly maneuverable personal flight]
[Rank-Up! Thunderhead 1: Storm builds faster for quicker combos]

"Uh, no problem, citizen. Now, it's curtain call for this Episode," I said, extricating myself from Bianca's embrace. She let me go, and I fled the cameras and still-emerging onlookers. My phone buzzed three times before I finally found a place to untransform in private, and I popped out of the bathroom stall in a pink T-shirt and jeans.

<Hey, I thought we said no Episodes - Fursona 3:45>
<You owe me one - Fursona 3:46>
<I'll see you at baggage claim. You can carry some of my bags - Bianca 3:37>

I rolled my eyes and shot back a pair of texts, one on each of our chats.

<It just kind of happened. Oops - Understudy 3:48>
<Sure. Let me take your luggage - Annie 3:48>

"You should have seen it, Annie," Bee said as I dragged two oversized rolling duffels along the sidewalk. I didn't have a superpower to carry lots of stuff, and I was out of my Costume, so that was the best I could do. "Understudy whooshed out of the sky and fired all these wimpy-looking magical rays at Solarbeam, and then he was like 'whoa' when the first one hit, and the others all flattened him. It was amazing!"

I wasn't sure whether to be annoyed that Bianca was doing this to me, thankful she wasn't giving up my secret identity, or relieved that we'd almost made it to our waiting ride. Either way, she seemed like her old self—bubbly, goofy, and ill-mannered. As if to prove the last thought, she wiped her mouth on her sleeve to clean the pretzel oil off.

I jostled and shoved until all my girlfriend's bags were safely in the car's trunk, then hopped in, activated the privacy screen, and shut the door.

"I'm sure it was. What classes did you end up signing up for?" I asked.

"Well, I *tried* to get English 201, Ilneat Culture, and a few science ones, but there's a hold on my profile. They won't say what it is, but I *know* I passed everything with flying colors. What about you?" Bee pulled out her phone and started texting.

"Same. That's weird. I wanted some more theater, and I'm supposed to take another couple of history courses to set myself up for the prelaw stuff, but I'll have to talk to my advisor and figure out what's up. Either way, I'm glad to see you. It's been way too long."

<The holds got something to do with the Superpower Studies program - Fursona 4:26>
<Yeah. Wonder what's up - Understudy 4:27>
<Dunno - Fursona 4:27>
<Oh, you hear about Theseus? - Understudy 4:27>

"So, no classes. Still got your Walnut Tower place?" Bianca asked.
"Yeah. You going to move in?"

<No, what about him? - Fursona 4:27>
<I heard a rumor he dropped out - Understudy 4:28>
<No way - Fursona 4:28>

"I'll think about it," Bianca said. "I've got a lot to do in my own space, though."

"Well, you're welcome any time," I said, trying to hide my disappointment, and probably failing. "I've got plenty of space for all your stuff."

I did, too. I'd just loaded it all in the trunk. Unlike me, Bianca had moved out of her ground-floor room at the end of the year. They had an up-and-comer moving in, and conveniently, an opening at the top of Hickory Hall offered near-Walnut Tower levels of roominess. If she had offered, I'd have been tempted to move in with her. She hadn't, though. And the place in Hickory Hall had other implications. It meant Ikenga had graduated. That was a blow to the Tokyexico University Student Superhero Association, for sure. I texted Fursona back.

<Why'd he quit? - Fursona 4:29>
<I heard he got an offer he couldn't refuse, but Gourmet isn't talking - Understudy 4:30>
<So weird. He was career focused - Fursona 4:30>
<The offer must be real good - Fursona 4:30>
<I bet a big shot vil saw his potential - Fursona 4:31>
<Maybe - Understudy 4:31>

"Su-Bin's been texting. She wants us to go to another of those weird APPEAL meetings. I guess she's president now, or running, or something," I said.

Bianca made a face. "As long as Avan's not there, I can tolerate one more meeting."

"Good, because I was thinking about superheroes over the summer, and I'm a lot more curious about what's going on with other people's lives. Superheroes are cool, but what about the people they end up displacing?"

"Don't tell me you see the appeal of APPEAL," Bianca said. "I couldn't stand it if you went and joined their club—and bought their merch. Ugh."

"No, I'm not thinking about that. But I do want to know more and be more open-minded about them this time," I said.

<Heard from VV? - Fursona 4:32>
<No. Don't expect to either. He's gotta figure the new him out - Understudy 4:33>
<Yeah. Point - Fursona 4:33>

"Hey, let's swing by your place," Bianca said. I looked at her questioningly. "I want to pick up your keys again."

I rolled my eyes at her.

Bianca blushed. "Uh, if that's cool, I mean. If not, I get it. Maybe you want some space or something—"

"No, no. I only just invited you to move in. Of course, you can have the keys."

We chatted for a while longer, in person for regular stuff and through text for the superheroics. Then, as we pulled up outside Walnut Tower and told the driver to wait, Bianca slipped her hand into mine. We rode the elevator—the public one, not my super-secret superhero one—up to the thirteenth floor, and stepped into 1301 Walnut. My apartment hadn't changed much, and Bee flopped onto the couch. "It's good to be back at TU."

2

Back at TU

MONDAY, SEPTEMBER 1

It turned out that TU was excited to have us back, too. When I woke up, an email awaited me.

> *Subject: Reminder: Superpower Studies Meeting*
> *To Magical Girl Understudy,*
> *Dr. Mays here for the TU Department of Superpower Studies! This is a reminder that today (Monday, September 1), the department is having an all-students meeting in the training room from 11:00 to 12:00. If you are currently enrolled as a super student, whether hero, villain, or vigilante, your presence is requested. Subjects to go over include:*
> *1. TUSSA and SSS presidency vacancies*
> *2. The Orientation Episode*
> *But wait! There's more!*
> *3. New educational opportunities at Tokyexico University.*
> *Refreshments will be provided. Don't miss out on this exciting beginning-of-semester informational meeting! Now yours for just one easy payment of showing up!*
> *Dr. Mays*
> *Head of Superpower Studies*
> *Tokyexico University*

I looked at the clock. 10:15. I'd slept in, and I loved it. I most likely wouldn't get another opportunity to, and I wanted to enjoy it. I thought about crawling back under the covers and skipping the meeting. Nothing about it said it was mandatory. But inside information on the Orientation Episode felt too good to pass up, so I dragged my butt out of bed.

<You going to the meeting? - Understudy 10:18>
<Already dressed and ready - Fursona 10:19>

<Okay. Be there in 25 - Understudy 10:19>

I grabbed Tails and transformed into my pink, pastel-purple, and gold-filigreed magical girl Costume, then checked to make sure the tiara and tights were on perfectly. I'd been suited up the day before, but this was my official public-facing debut as a minor-leaguer, and I wanted to make the most of it. Once I was satisfied that I'd checked all the boxes and looked my best, I headed through my secret base behind the maintenance door.

It was much the same as I'd left it before heading to Riverside—and later, to Tortuga West—for summer break. The spatial-warping hero Fang Swee's power kept it pristine, and the only real changes since last year were a pair of new TV screens. One showed a completely blank list, with four slots and empty spaces for information, while the other showed a map of the University, Mid-Town, and Poudre districts of Tokyexico City. I had an area of responsibility now, but I couldn't say what the list was for.

I jogged up the stairs and then opened the door to the roof. **[Starwave Sail]** had upgraded into **[Solar Wing]**, and I wanted to see what it could do in a noncombat situation. The sailboard had never been *too* unmaneuverable, but it sounded like **[Solar Wing]** outperformed it on that front.

I spread my arms, said, "**[Solar Wing]**," and jumped off the roof.

Within a second, I could feel the difference. The two pink-red wings popped from the red, off-the-shoulder sleeves on my dress, and they shifted in the air with my every thought. I swung my wand around a few times to see how sudden arm motions disrupted them, sure they'd be thrown off, but they flexed and adjusted every time I moved to keep me mostly flat in the air. When I tried to stop, they beat slightly, hovering me three hundred feet over Walnut Tower's roof.

I pulled a couple of loop the loops, did a barrel roll, and then steadied out.

<Make that 5. New power is flashy - Understudy 10:31>

Below me, the Mister Felsic statue loomed, and I ducked down toward it. A familiar supervillain stood there, eating an apple and watching me. Gourmet. The big woman snorted as I landed and popped the uneaten half of her apple into her mouth, chewing. "Snack, good to see you. I was worried you'd gotten too high up for us."

"Nah, I'm in it to graduate," I said. "Theseus bailed, though?"

"Yeah. He got an offer from some corp. 'Be our supervillain, solve our problems, test out our prosthetic weapons!' I couldn't believe his studio let him go, but I guess it's not that different than me and Gourmet's Glutton Hour. You never gave me back my Costume piece. Keep it. Just don't use it in any Episodes, okay?"

"Sure. Thanks. So he's still out there?" I asked. "Like, in town?"

"Yeah. Hi, Wombat," Gourmet said.

"Still Fursona," my sidekick said from inside her kangaroo fursuit. "What's up with Theseus?"

As Gourmet repeated herself, looking annoyed, we headed inside, past the theater classroom where we'd taken Superpower Ethics, and into the training room. Super students filed down the stairs into the arena itself, and we followed. I saw Punch and Grapple, the melee-focused super-twins. Grapple nodded while Punch glared at me and turned away.

I shrugged. You couldn't win every battle.

Almost every super student, from Flare and The Crumb to Springlock and Milo, plus three or four I didn't recognize, stood packed into the arena, mumbling and talking with their neighbors. Tensions flared, a few arguments got heated, and Punch started walking toward me.

"Dr. Mays here with some exciting news!"

The whole room froze—not because the metapowered professor had stopped us, but because he was talking and we *weren't* frozen. He grinned. The four superpower studies professors stood on a low stage: Dr. Mays in his button-down shirt and khakis, Dr. Jackson in a pantsuit, and Tennyson and Mindstorm in a silver super-suit and black-and-white-spiraled catsuit, respectively.

"Thank you all for coming. I see a few faces missing, so I'm counting on you to spread the word to your friends and associates," Dr. Jackson said. "Welcome to TU's 2042–2043 school year. We've got a busy year ahead of us, some students more than others, so let's jump into it. Tennyson?"

Tennyson took the mic. The poetry-reciting, teleporting superhero grinned widely as he started talking. "Yeah, exciting news on the student superpower clubs front. Ikenga and Monologue, the presidents of the Tokyexico University Student Superhero Association and the Student Supervillain Society, respectively, graduated in May. That leaves both clubs without leadership, so elections are in order. I'm taking over sponsorship of both clubs since Dr. Mays is stepping into a new role, and I think we should have elections on September 24th. Any disagreement?"

The crowd buzzed. I could already see Tearjerker and Iron Fist, the top two student villains on campus with Monologue out of the picture, sizing each other up. I didn't envy either of them *that* challenge; running the SSS sounded incredibly thankless—or super-lucrative, based on Monologue's theft of a hundred students' book money last year.

On the other side of the room, Springlock nodded at her boyfriend, Milo, as his fingers flew. She'd make a fantastic president for TUSSA, and as far as I was concerned, she had it in the bag. The only possible competition, Sara-N-Dipity (whose power wasn't luck), couldn't compete. I could already see the battle lines being drawn for TUSSA. Punch, Grapple, and Sara against Milo, Springlock, Fursona, and me. If the incoming freshmen split their votes evenly, the best girl would win.

And it'd be Springlock.

"Wonderful," Dr. Tennyson said. He clapped his hands. "September 24th. That's a Wednesday. We'll know who the club presidents are on the 29th. I'm looking forward to sponsoring both organizations, and I know that in the aftermath of the conflict-heavy interclub rivalry of the last few years, we can cooperate."

"We're going to need it," Mindstorm muttered ominously.

Dr. Jackson took the mic. "Next, some incoming freshman information. Tuesday is Orientation Day. As you all know, it's an opportunity for us professors to corner the incoming freshmen, register them, and remind them that on-campus superheroics are a step up from their small ponds."

I winced. That'd been me last year, convinced I was hot stuff because I was coming off a big victory in Small Town Super. It hadn't gone well, and I couldn't imagine it'd go better for most of the incoming class. At least they'd *have* powers to use, even if they lost quickly.

"So," Dr. Jackson continued, "I want to go over a few ground rules so we're all on the same page. First, try to keep massive property damage to a minimum. Tokyexico University wants to maintain its beautiful grounds better than last year and needs our help. Keep destructive powers under control.

"Second, remember that this is a minor-league-leveled Episode for a reason. We *want* the freshmen to bite off more than they can chew by getting involved. It's meant to be a challenge for them, one that they almost always accept, thanks to the brain worm. Don't take it easy on your fellow supers here."

Iron Fist cracked his steel knuckles loudly enough that the microphone picked it up, sending a squeal of feedback across the room.

Mindstorm grabbed the mic, looking bored. "And third, do not take shots at the professors. We all have our roles to play. Villains, you're making problems. Heroes, you're solving them. Tennyson, Mays, and Jackson are the evac team. And I'm . . . here to keep the professor team safe so they can . . . do their jobs. Make my day, vils. Just do it."

She handed the mic to Dr. Mays as an uncomfortable silence descended across the room. Dr. Mindstorm could *absolutely* carry out that threat. She could almost certainly beat TUSSA and the SSS if they fought her *together*. I shivered, remembering that she'd been in my head last year, and the ill-fated attempt to fight her in this training room. What a disaster that'd been, and she hadn't even been using mind control.

Mays waited for the room to refocus. "And now, the big news. You've probably noticed that there were holds on your accounts. We've done that because we have an exciting opportunity we're hoping a few of you take advantage of. Dr. Jackson and I have been working on this for two long years, and as of today, I'm stepping down as club sponsor and abdicating all my noneducational responsibilities.

"Instead, I will run the Department of Superpower Studies as it expands from a minor-only program to one with an associate's degree! We've been working in tandem with several organizations, from the Mutual Assistance League and—until recently, 3V1L—to the Tokyexico Council of Heroes, and we've developed a two-year program that we all believe will prepare supers of all stripes for bright futures."

He held up a hand, cutting off the small smattering of applause. Fursona held her hands up, mid-clap. I hadn't started yet.

"The reason we put holds on your accounts is simple. We need at least twelve of you to step up and try the associate's program. The TU administration is hesitant about giving our program more of a presence; in the long term, this will mean hiring more professors. They're understandably concerned about the potential for possible Drs. Brick House and Father Thyme to carry on their rivalry on-campus if we hire them, so we need your help to prove this can be successful."

He handed the mic to Dr. Mindstorm. The supervillain seemed to stare directly at me, her eyes boring holes into my brain as she spoke. "If you choose to . . . pursue . . . the associate's program, your advisor will set your schedule. It will include three superpower studies courses per semester and additional courses in physics, psychology, acting, and . . . Ilneat Studies. Fifteen credits each semester, with must-pass pressure. This is a generalization. Older students may have already . . . covered . . . some of these courses."

"If you want to give it a go, please email your advisors as soon as we end this meeting," Dr. Mays said, taking the mic back. "Anything else for the good of the department?"

"Yeah," Dr. Tennyson said. "All four of us are willing to put extra effort into ensuring associate's degree students succeed. This does *not* mean cheating for our students."

He glared at Mindstorm for a moment. The villain didn't look embarrassed at all. I couldn't imagine her cheating to help *me*, but I didn't know who else had her as an advisor.

Tennyson cleared his throat. "Each of us will host rotating study groups once per four weeks. That means you'll have access to a different professor outside of office hours once per week. I strongly suggest you take advantage of that."

"And with that," Dr. Mays said, "I'm closing this informational meeting. Please email any questions so we don't waste the last days of summer."

3

The Last Days of Summer

Subject: Associate's Degree
Dr. Mindstorm,
I'm interested in the associate's degree program for Superpower Studies. Sign me up, please.
Thanks,
Magical Girl Understudy

I hit Send and watched as my hopes, dreams, and freedom zipped through the internet and appeared in Mindstorm's inbox. "We're both idiots, you know that, right?" I asked Bianca, who'd somehow sprawled across my entire couch.

"Yeah, well, we could un-sign up, but Mindstorm would kill you. I doubt Mays would be happy with me, either. I think you're right. We should give this a try. It's got a lot of potential to play well with the minor leagues. Think about all that we could—"

"Learn. I know. You're spitting my argument back at me."

"It's not my fault it was a good argument." Bianca stuck her tongue out at me.

I stood up and closed my laptop. "Speaking of the minor leagues, we need to meet with Rocko. Today. Like, now. They said we'd kick off in late August or early September, right?"

"Right. They're probably gonna be high-energy about getting started. Hopefully, they have some information about how minor-league Episodes usually play out. They said the ones we did were on the weak side, right?"

"Right." I really hoped the Ilneat wasn't too amped. They could be . . . a lot.

As we walked through my pastel-pink secret base to the door with the star and the Rocko Studios label, I tried to mentally prepare myself for the heat and humidity.

[Welcome to Rocko's Studio. System Disabled. Now arriving Backstage.]

"DuPont and Marino! Just the two I wanted to see! I've been waiting to get this whole thing kicked off, and boy, do I have a roster for you two." The Ilneat knuckle-walked on two thick squeezing hands and their feet while the other two grasping hands clutched the almost-ubiquitous cigar and a sheet of paper, which they waved. They grinned, flashing gorilla teeth, and ran a squeezing hand through their thick, otter-like fur. "Grab a drink and sit."

"I can't," Bee said. "You're blocking the way."

As Rocko maneuvered out of Bianca's personal space, a second Ilneat appeared from the Costuming department. They pulled a cigarette from a pack and lit it. "DuPont, got any new Costume pieces?"

"Kind of, Pataki. I'm still on the fence about Mom's suit. It's evil."

"Of course it is. I need parts for a new project for you," they said. "Marino. I've got something fresh in the cooker for you, though. I think I've cracked how the roo suit works with your powers. After Rocko's done, come see me."

Bianca nodded. "What do you have for us, Rocko?"

"Standard 'Minor-League Welcome Package.' Ahem." Rocko adjusted the paper and started reading. "'Welcome to the minor leagues,' blah blah blah. 'On behalf of the Ilneat Super Network, I, Rocko, would like to welcome you to the minor leagues. Your previous threats have been' blah blah. You don't need to hear most of this. Here's the quick version. Little league? Easy-peasy. Minor league? Neighborhood to city-level threats and problems. You'll see bigger powers, higher risks, more Extras in danger, and more pick-up heroes and villains. So, DuPont, I know you had a sort of rogues' gallery with Professor Panic. We're gonna expand that idea in the minors."

"Okay." I'd only had Professor Panic in my rogue's gallery because he was the only villain in Riverside. "Who's on the list?"

"First up, we've got 3V1L," Rocko said.

Bianca held up her hand. "Weren't they a major/minor threat last year?"

"Yes. But then Golden Goose fried the Three *V*s, and they're rebuilding. The One *L*'s struggling to get them going again, and a couple of minor-league heroes should be able to slow that down, leaving Stella-Lunar to deal with *real* problems. They're mostly henchman-swarms and low-threat minor-leaguers, but they love multifront operations, so you'll rarely get a clean win without help.

"We've also got Livestream. His gimmick is that he's an influencer."

"Seriously?" I asked. I knew about him, of course, but I didn't realize he was still active in Tokyexico City.

"Yes, seriously. If you fight him, be prepared to go live at a moment's notice. We're talking five-second-delay levels of live. He's unpredictable unless you realize he'll do anything for TV ratings. The perfect villain, really. Super jealous he's not one of mine."

"So none of these villains are Rocko Studios' villains?" I asked.

"I didn't say that. But correct. The budget's just not there for a villain." Rocko sucked on their cigar and exhaled a cloud of smoke. "Next up is Sister Sly. She's not really in this as a rival to you, DuPont. She's got a grudge against Marino. Any idea *why*?"

Bianca thought hard, looking nervous. After a minute, she shook her head slowly and sipped from her water. "No. I've never gone out of my way to piss anyone off."

"That's what you think. Sister Sly's gonna be your problem, Marino. And yours too, DuPont, as long as you roll together—which I *strongly* recommend. Splitting up in the minors opens you up to too much risk. You'll see what she's pissed about soon."

"But what's her power?" Bee asked.

"Can't say. Contractually obligated not to," they said. "The last vil's also got it out for you, Marino, so don't go telling me you've never tried to piss someone off. The good news is that he's the most professional minor-leaguer I've ever seen. The bad news is he's not with a studio."

"Theseus? Really?" I asked. We'd never beaten Theseus before. In fact, the last time they'd fought, Bianca had ended up in the hospital overnight. I wasn't confident we could handle him in a no-holds-barred minor-league fight. Then again, we'd grown a lot, and he'd always been minor league, so maybe we had a shot now. We'd have to find out.

"Yeah, really. He bailed on his producer and signed up with some robotics firm in Tokyexico. Apparently, he's the ideal super for testing prosthetics' potential, and all he asked for was, and I quote, 'phenomenal destructive power.' Thornberry was *furious*. They went straight to the System and tried to get him booted, but that damn thing's got a mind of its own sometimes, and they weren't in a negotiating place. Now it won't even talk to Thornberry, the idiot." Rocko did *not* sound like he felt bad for Thornberry.

"So, to sum it up, a villain organization, an influencer, a revenge-minded loony tune, and an old frenemy?" We could totally handle that.

"Loony tune, huh? Closer than you think. Yeah, that's your rogue's gallery, plus whatever bullshit the Student Supervillain Society gets into," Rocko said. "Now, to business."

Rocko only cared about business sometimes. "What do you need from us?"

"Easy. Two Episodes every week. No ifs, ands, or buts."

I shut my eyes and rubbed the side of my head. For some stupid reason, I'd hoped I'd be home free in the minor leagues. I didn't have ambitions for the majors—not *really*, at least. Those heroes and villains hit too hard, and the penalties for failure were brutal. I *would* be happy just floating on the bottom half of the minors. But Rocko wanted more.

"I'm in classes too, Rocko. That's not always going to be possible."

"Alright, I'm a reasonable Ilneat," my producer said. "I'm willing to do one a week, but that puts a ton of pressure on the studio. If we're cutting down that much, you *can't* run any little-league Episodes unless you get the minor-league one done first. Deal?"

"Deal," I said. A moment later, Bianca repeated me.

The second we did, Rocko relaxed. "Good, good, that'll give us a solid release schedule. Hopefully, we'll climb quickly. Gotta get you up in the ranks before . . .

well, that's a surprise. Now, with great power comes great probability of people dropping into your Episodes. I'm talking pick-up heroes and villains. You've done it to Magical Girl Honeycomb a few times, but it happens *all the time* in the minor leagues. The whole thing turns into a free-for-all. So, here's my advice. You get a warning that Stella-Lunar or Golden Goose is dropping in, you leave. Abandon the Episode."

"Won't that go against what you just said?" Bianca asked. "You want one a week, no matter what."

"Sure do. What I *don't* want is for the two of you to get killed in the crossfire. GG is a walking collateral damage machine. So, if she shows up, you don't owe me an Episode that week. I want you two alive. You're up-and-comers, and if nothing else, think of it as protecting my investment." Rocko took another puff from their cigar, and I relaxed. It'd be nice not to have to try surviving an enraged Golden Goose to get the win, even if she wasn't aimed at me.

"Besides, I'm sure you two would be willing to find another Episode out of the goodness of your hearts."

[**System Enabled**]

We walked the four blocks to Nico's Barbecue. Unless you counted the Orientation Episode as a day off, it was the last day before classes, and I had a feeling that tomorrow would be nothing but work. So, we were out on a date instead of planning out the future, figuring out our schedules, or trying to see what Sister Sly and 3V1L were all about. Bianca had picked the place—somewhere she could be as messy as she wanted without consequences. She'd be covered in barbeque sauce, but so would everyone else.

"So, I'm not saying they're wrong here. I'm just saying that for the next two semesters, we do the bare minimum for them and focus on locking down this degree. Once that's done, we'll have plenty of time to push hard, career-wise."

"That's shop talk, Bee."

"Shit. Okay, how about this? We get the barbecue, eat up, and then hit up Confluence Park. It's a train ride away, but it should have a pretty nice sunset between the towers. We can talk about you moving in with me." She grinned at me, obviously baiting me into a response.

It worked.

"You wouldn't even let me see your room, and you want me to move in with you? Unbelievable. Plus, Walnut Tower's the best room on campus. It has good views, not many neighbors, and you and I can leave from the roof! You should move in with me."

"Nah. Big glass windows are a problem for me."

I tried to pretend that didn't hurt, but Bee must've seen the look on my face because her arm was around me before I could say anything. "Sorry. That was out of line. You're working on it, and I need to be better about letting go. That's something Jessie said I had a problem with, too."

"It's okay. I know you didn't mean to." My mood was crushed. She might not have meant to, but it sucked so much that she could accidentally put all that guilt on me.

Then she kissed me, and the green apple smell got stronger. "I really don't mean to. If you want me to move in, we can talk about it later, but right now, let's focus on having a good last day of freedom. Orientation's going to be a pain in the ass, and I want to enjoy some Annie time before that whole mess blows up."

"I know. And I do want you to move in. We could use Walnut Tower as our main base and Hickory Hall as a secret emergency retreat. Plus, I sleep better when you're around, even if you're a space heater." I forced a smile. "There it is!"

The goofy, pig-shaped sign for Nico's Barbecue glowed a light orange in the dusk. Bee broke into a run, dragging me along. "I'm going to eat *so* many ribs!"

I trailed in her wake. The start of this semester already felt a lot different than the last one, and we hadn't even started the Orientation Episode.

4

The Orientation Episode

TUESDAY, SEPTEMBER 2

Mom and Dad waved the moment our video chat connected, then fiddled with their computer until the giant No Sound icon faded from my screen.

"Hi, Dot," Dad said. "Settling in okay?"

"Yeah, I'm doing alright. It's been nice to have a few days to get back in the big city mindset." I lay in bed in my PJs, snacking on leftover popcorn Bee had made before she left and trying not to get crumbs even more everywhere than they already were.

"Well, Anika, I hope you've got a good plan for the semester. Did you figure out that hold?"

"I did. I'm going for an associate's degree in superpower studies," I said. "It's a new program, and I've got a feeling it's going to line up well with my chosen career. If I work hard, I can be done by the end of the year, and it's a ton of good training for superhero work."

Mom's brow furrowed. I'd been worried about this. She started to say something, but I interrupted her. "I know it's not what you want, Mom. But I looked into the classes I'd be taking, and they all line up with going into superpower legal work, so if I get tired of being a hero, I can switch with a couple of years' worth of classes. I get what I want in the short-term without losing out on your long-term plans. Best of both worlds."

I stopped. Mom needed a moment to think, and I couldn't push her too far all at once—especially when I knew *why* she didn't like my superhero work and why she wanted me fighting on the legal side, not on television. Dad put a hand on her shoulder and whispered something in her ear. She stiffened, but nodded slowly.

"Well, congratulations on your choice, Dot. Wish we'd known earlier, though," Dad said. "What do you need help with?"

Right. Help. What *did* I need help with? I felt pretty much in control, but Rocko clearly wanted to get Heroics 101's minor-league series up and rolling quickly, and I didn't know what my class schedule looked like yet. Plus, I needed to make sure I spent time with Bee, not just Fursona. "I'm not super worried about anything yet," I said.

Dad snorted. "Super. Ha!"

"Shut up," I said, smiling. "Maybe Mom can help me with something, though. How did you keep your schedule balanced when you were working and taking care of me? I have a lot on my plate, and I need some help."

"Hmm. I'm not sure how much help I can be. I worked at the diner, but the managers and I worked out a deal so I only had to work when your dad had time off. We swapped you between the two of us for years. It worked out well, but I'm not sure that'll work for classes and a demanding job. How many Episodes a month does Rocko want?"

"One a week. I get to call out if the top-tier major-league heroes or villains interrupt one, but other than that, I'm committed."

Dad cleared his throat. "That doesn't seem like much, Dot, and if you know they're—"

"So, that means patrolling for Episodes, right? That could take hours before you find something viable for you, and I bet he wants you going after certain villains, right?" Mom said, all business.

"Right. I've got a rogue's gallery now."

Mom and Dad shared a long look, and then Mom shrugged. Dad cleared his throat. "Dot, you're treading new paths for the DuPonts. Neither of us went to college, and your mom was a supervillain for one Episode. We're not going to be good people to come to for advice. Support? Wholeheartedly. Unconditional love? Yep. But useful advice? Not so much."

An awkward silence descended. I'd known for a while that Mom and Dad weren't all-knowing, but the whole revelation that they'd known I was a superhero and that they'd been better at hiding Mom's secret identity than I had been mine had convinced me they'd be able to give me *some* good advice. I thought back to the Madame Shockwave Costume tucked away in my closet. I'd have to do something with it eventually.

As the quiet grew too long, I cleared my throat. "Well, thanks. I love you both too. Anything new in Riverside?"

We chatted for a while, but I hadn't been gone that long—only a few days—and Riverside . . . Riverside never changed much. It'd been a quiet summer. The moment I arrived, Professor Panic went underground, and he didn't start anything until I left. Supposedly, he had a lieutenant now, which was exciting since Collidus still didn't have a sidekick. The balance of power was shifting in Riverside.

Mom and Dad were busy with work and didn't pay much attention to the town as a whole. I didn't have much news to share on the Tokyexico front, though I told them about the battle at the airport the night before. Then, when we'd shared all we could, I cleared my throat. "Freshman Orientation is today, and I'm supposed to be involved, so I've gotta go. Love you both."

"Love you too, Anika."

"Bye, Dot."

After closing my laptop, I *should* have suited up right away. Instead, I stared at the screen. That hadn't been as helpful as I'd hoped, but I wasn't out of people to talk to about scheduling. I just didn't want to talk to the other people on my list. I knew I'd have to, though. Eventually.

Just not yet.

[Casting Call]
[Episode: The Annual Orientation Episode - PG-13]
[Role: Heroic Helper! Do you accept the role? (Yes/No)]
[Role Focus: Flamboyance + Drama]

The **[Casting Call]** came, along with several texts.

<Meet @ SUB, right? - Fursona 2:01>
<All TUSSA members loyal to Sara, rally at Mister Felsic in 5 - Sara-N-Dipity to Group 2:01>
<Springlock supporters to the TUSSA Cave - Milo to Group 2:01>
<Wait a second. This is political? - Fursona to Group 2:02>
<Everything is political - Sara-N-Dipity to Group 2:02>
<With me or against me! - Sara-N-Dipity to Group 2:02>

I transformed, threatening the villains with an exit stage left and everything. Excitement built inside me, and I tried to force it down, but I hadn't had my powers during my freshman-year Orientation Episode, and I was looking forward to getting some revenge on the SSS.

<Fursona and me are going to the SUB - Understudy to Group 2:03>

I accepted the **[Casting Call]** and headed for the roof. Truthfully, I wanted to meet up with Milo, Springlock, and Hephaestus, but Fursona and I had discussed our strategy beforehand. The Student Union Building and library had been the focus of the SSS's campaign last year; while I doubted they'd repeat the same plan without Monologue's ridiculous power, the building would be crawling with Extras—and with freshman heroes and villains looking to make a name for themselves.

[The Annual Orientation Episode: Act One in Progress]

It wasn't a long flight over to the Student Union Building, and [**Solar Wing**] made it even faster, but I could already see the Student Supervillain Society causing trouble on the long, wide sidewalk that ran down TU's center. I thought about blasting a couple of the villains. The Crumb, fighting a hero I didn't recognize, would have made a great target. But then the air shimmered, a group of four professors appeared in the middle of the fight, and I pulled up to avoid Dr. Mays's power.

I landed next to my kangaroo-shaped sidekick. "Any action?"

"Yes. Flare, Tearjerker, and Iron Fist headed inside about a minute ago. I wasn't ready to get rolled over, so I let them go, but now that you're here, we can try breaking their plan up. Looks like the whole leadership is there, so if we shut them down, it might end the SSS's strategy. Then it's just cleaning them up."

"Got a plan in mind?"

"Bomber-Roo through the window, then Variant Three Old Yeller on Tearjerker. We ignore Flare except for my [**Combo-Breaker**], and I keep Iron Fist off you while you take out Tearjerker."

"Sounds good," I said. I summoned [**Starwave Sail**], and we rocketed toward the wide bookstore window. At the last second, I fired a [**Starlance**] into the glass, and Fursona kicked off, landing on top of a very surprised Flare.

[**Badass Bomber! +1 Badass Point**]
[**Bull in a China Shop! +1 Badass Point**]
[**Dramatic Damage! +1 Drama Point**]

Books flew as Iron Fist rushed through the shelves toward me, steel fists oscillating up and down like jackhammers, but I was already airborne, using [**Solar Wing**] to fly until I almost touched the ceiling. He jumped higher than I expected, only to take a Fursona [**Double-Kick**] that knocked him off course and into a pile of chemistry textbooks, which scattered across the floor.

Extras were screaming all around us, but I only had eyes for one person in the room. Tearjerker whirled toward Fursona, but before she could point or open her mouth, I used [**Power-Weaving**] and opened up on her with [**Bit-Part Barrage**]. Variant Three Old Yeller was all about hitting a single target as hard as possible from range, and I'd come up with a combo that'd do the trick.

[**Dramatic Damage! +4 Drama Points**]

Even as the damage slammed into her, I was already [**Quick-Time Changing**], which triggered [**I-Frame Transform**]. The notifications poured in, and I grinned as the combo built up far faster than Tearjerker could react.

[Flashy Fitting-Room! +1 Flamboyance Point]
[Floating Points: 1 Drama]
[Steel Yourself! +1 Grit Point]
[Floating Points: 3 Drama, 1 Flamboyance]

Plus, I was ending on Copy Cat, not my usual Magical Girl Rainy Day transformation. As my brain and Tails's merged, I dashed toward the still-stunned Tearjerker. My claws lashed out, and a moment later, a nasty-looking set of scratches started bleeding through the goth supervillain's fishnet-covered calves. [**Cat-Scratch Fever**] had made contact.

[**Dramatic Damage! +1 Drama Point**]
[**Power-Weaving! +6 Drama, +3 Flamboyance, +1 Grit Point**]

Behind me, something crashed through a bookshelf, and I had just enough time to watch Flare fly across the room before Iron Fist's massive frame filled my vision. "I don't got him!" Fursona yelled.

I was still on top of the badly hurt Tearjerker. Tear tracks smeared her overdone mascara, and she glared at me, but I didn't have time to mess around. In the moment before Iron Fist slammed into me, I used [**Doom Ball**].

[**Badass Damage! +3 Badass Points**]

Tearjerker collapsed onto the bookstore's floor, surrounded by books on drawing naked people and landscapes. I breathed a sigh of relief; Variant Three Old Yeller had worked.

Then Iron Fist hit me, slamming into me like one of those damn white vans.

[HP 8/11]

I smashed through a shelf filled with art supplies, and I would have kept going if it weren't for a short, white-armored . . . kid.

That's the only descriptor I had. A kid. She wasn't more than five feet tall—maybe five-one in her armor, and she projected a pair of whirling blue tractor beams from her hands. One wrapped around me, and the other pushed against Iron Fist. "I can't . . . hold . . . him . . . much longer," she said through gritted teeth as she set me down.

Sure enough, Iron Fist was making headway against the tractor beams. He'd reach both the tiny heroine and me in a matter of seconds. "Fursona, send TUSSA a text. We've got one!" I shouted and used [**Leaping Leopards**], springing *toward* Iron Fist.

The villain laughed as I slammed into him, then swatted me aside and grabbed the white-armored tractor-beam heroine. She struggled in his . . . iron fist . . .

punching and kicking for everything she was worth, but couldn't break free, and before I could try to break her out, Iron Fist fled the battle of the bookstore with Flare in tow.

[HP 7/11]

I groaned and picked myself up. "I can't believe they're running the same plan, but they're probably heading for—"

Fursona interrupted me just as my phone buzzed with her text. "The ballroom!"

5

The Ballroom!

We left Tearjerker on the floor and followed Iron Fist and Flare. She was out of the fight for now, and whoever the tiny freshman heroine was, she'd need our help more than we needed to pin Tearjerker down. I transformed back to Understudy. If the villains got holed up before we could get there, it'd be entirely up to the professors to get Tractor-Beam-Girl out, and I wanted to do it myself.

My phone was blowing up. As we sprinted up the stairs toward the ballroom, I grabbed it and read some of the messages.

<Hold on. The Sara Squad is coming! - Grapple 2:12>
<I contacted the Drs. They're occupied. 3 minutes - Springlock 2:12>

"Okay, Sara's team is almost here, but we've gotta keep Iron Fist and Flare busy. I feel good about Kite Fight for me while you sit on Flare. Sound good?" I asked.

Fursona nodded, and a moment later, we crashed through the ballroom's double doors. "Shit," I muttered.

"Indeed," Fursona said.

The Kite Fight battle plan was *not* going to cut it. Flare and Iron Fist weren't alone. Lady Lockless was there, and so, to my surprise, was Gourmet. They had half a dozen hostages already, but most looked like panicky Extras, not supers. They'd be fine. Probably. I doubted we would be, though, not against that many villains. "Really?" I asked.

"Really," Iron Fist said. "Get them!"

"Let's do Choke Point," Fursona said, stepping back into the double doors. "You cover me from range. I'll keep them off you!"

"Deal! Don't let Lady L do her thing!" I fired a [**Starlance**] at the ballgown-clad villain, getting a familiar message as the bolt hit home, knocking her to the side.

[Dramatic Damage! +1 Drama Point]
[Double Damage! +1 Badass Point]

Gourmet snapped into a jerky stick, grew horns, and charged Fursona, who countered with a kick even as I fired another [Starlance] at Lady Lockless. Then Flare piled in, a fiery fist slamming into Fursona's pouch.

[Dramatic Damage! +1 Drama Point]
[Double Damage! +1 Badass Point]

The ballroom's windows blew inward, and I wondered if the school had special Orientation Episode insurance for the Student Union Building. Then Grapple slammed into Iron Fist, who dropped Tractor-Beam-Girl. A moment later, Punch joined him, and I stopped firing at Lady Lockless.

If those two were here, Sara-N-Dipity was, too. I pointed at the villainess. "Your counter's here. Not your lucky day, huh?"

"*Goddammit!*" Lady Lockless said. At the same time, Sara-N-Dipity walked up the stairs, copying her rival's tone and phrasing perfectly.

"Goddammit! It's *not* luck! It's not! I created a 95% chance the boys could get through the window and hit Iron Fist, and you're calling that luck!" Sara-N-Dipity said, her suit flawless. She tossed a card at Flare, then blew on it so it changed spin midair and hit the villain, perfectly predicting his dodge.

It didn't do much damage, but he sputtered at her. "My combo!"

"Yep. Your combo," Sara said mockingly.

A moment later, Fursona tackled the fire-themed villain, letting Sara focus on hard-countering Lady Lockless. This left me with . . . Gourmet.

The villain—and my friend—bit into her jerky stick again, sprouted horns, and charged me. I leaped into the air, letting [Solar Wing] catch me and boost me up to the chandeliers, then fired a [Starlance] down at Gourmet.

[Dramatic Damage! +1 Drama Point]

"Clever, but I've got something for that," Gourmet said. She whipped open a lunch box and took a bite from a spicy buffalo wing. A moment later, she grew two scaly wings and belched fire.

As she took to the air, I rolled my eyes and muttered, "Really? She gets to turn into a goddamn dragon? How is this fair?" I strafed away from her, and Tractor-Beam-Girl grabbed her leg, trying to slow her down, but it was useless; Dragon-Gourmet was too fast, and her fire breath was too accurate. She was going to shoot me down.

But before Dragon-Gourmet could make contact, the professors arrived.

[End of Act One: Act Two in Three Minutes]

"Dr. Mays here for Quanduct Ephemeral Piping Solutions!" The battlefield froze, and he walked toward Flare, holding a cardboard-looking box and reading as fast as possible. "QEPS are great for moving hard-to-contain liquids and gasses from one place to another. This villain right here? He's got a problem. His fire attacks don't travel far enough, and the hero he's fighting keeps dodging. But with a QEPS pipe, he can make that fire appear up to twenty feet away through the air. And that's not all . . ."

I relaxed, watching Dr. Jackson stroll through the battle. She grabbed Tractor-Beam-Girl, and the shimmering bubble around the metapowered professor expanded to cover the white-armored freshman. They argued, and while I couldn't hear their words, I knew exactly what Tractor-Beam-Girl was saying. After all, I'd had the same conversation during my first Orientation Episode.

But something *was* different. Last time, we hadn't hit an Act Break mid-combat, and Tractor-Beam-Girl wouldn't stop arguing and let the professors take her. Dr. Mays had been talking for almost three minutes, and he couldn't keep it up forever—could he?

No, he looked more panicked and less sure of himself. Dr. Jackson had already frozen and unfrozen Tractor-Beam-Girl a few times. They couldn't stick around. They had to leave soon.

I tried to look around because even with the delay, there shouldn't have been an Act Break right here. And then I saw the *real* reason why. A blue, curvy shadow was caught mid-leap, flying straight for Iron Fist.

As soon as the professors evacuated Tractor-Beam-Girl for registration, this fight was changing—a lot.

[The Annual Orientation Episode: Act Two in Progress]

When Tractor-Beam-Girl finally realized—at least I assumed—that her hero complex didn't mean anything, and Tennyson teleported the four professors away mid-Mays's speech, all hell broke loose.

Literally.

Dragon-Gourmet's flames whipped around me, scorching my Costume and wings, and I started spiraling toward the ground. Fursona **[Double-Kicked]** Flare in the face, knocking him out. Tearjerker burst through the door behind Fursona and yelled, "**[Cry for Me]**! Remember your goldfish? It's not at a farm!"

[HP 6/11]

And, of course, Punch and Grapple carried on trading punches and grappling with Iron Fist. Only now, they had a friend, because Springlock hit the villain in the stomach like a freight train.

A moment later, I crash-landed, magical wings disappearing, and slid across the polished ballroom floor. I started to pick myself up, only for Gourmet to land with her whole weight on top of me, driving the air from my lungs.

[HP 4/11]

If it weren't for superhero damage, something would have broken. She glared at me. "Don't move, Snack."

I nodded, but I was already calculating my next move.

Iron Fist shook off his three attackers with a roar, grabbed one of the Extras, and leaped through the broken window. "If you follow, he gets the iron fist!" he shouted, then fled down the road.

That was my cue. I used **[Quick-Time Change]**, doing the Itsy Bitsy Spider dance as best I could and getting a moment of **[I-Frame Transform]** immunity that ate most of Gourmet's dragon's breath. Then, as Magical Girl Rainy Day, I inhaled and used **[Wind Front]**. I'd learned the move as part of my minor-league signing bonus skills.

[Flashy Fitting-Room! +1 Flamboyance Point]
[Steel Yourself! +1 Grit Point]
[Badass Move! +1 Badass Point]

The wind slammed into Gourmet's outstretched dragon wings, lifting her off me and tossing her into the air. I thought about using **[Ride the Lightning]**, but truthfully, we had a numbers advantage. Even with Fursona locked down, Milo and possibly Hephaestus had to be on their way. It was time to leverage action economy and end this fight.

I **[Quick-Time Changed]** again, this time to Lab Assistant Panic.

"THE LAB ASSISTANT'S BACK, SHE'S UP IN THIS HOOD!
BUT WILL SHE BE EVIL, NEUTRAL, OR GOOD?"

[Rejuvenation Activated! HP 8/11]
[Flashy Fitting-Room! +1 Flamboyance Point]

TA-1LZ appeared on the floor, **[TA-1LZ New Head-Cannon]** already opening fire on the still-recovering Gourmet. Tasers bounced off her wings and caught her in the stomach, then stopped as the Melee Brothers jumped her, pinned her to the ground, and punched her in the face.

[Badass Bot! +1 Badass Point]

"Alright, alright, enough!" Lady Lockless shouted. "We know when we're beaten! We surrender!"

"Coward!" Tearjerker said. Her makeup had smeared, her face looked like hell, and my scratch had destroyed her bright green fishnets. "I'm not done yet!"

She headed for the stairs and fled. No one followed her. The rest of the villains slowly held up their hands. I didn't blame them. The SSS didn't stand a chance against seven heroes, including five minor-leaguers. I walked over to Gourmet and held out a hand to help her up.

"Thanks, I guess. What was *that?*" she asked, wincing and letting me take her weight.

"[**Wind Front**]. Pretty cool, huh?"

"Yeah, I guess. I think you're close to beating me one-on-one."

"We'll have to try that later. Training room sometime this week?"

"You're on." Gourmet grinned. I smiled back. Gourmet had never struck me as one of the *really* bad villains. She mostly just wanted to hang out on her cooking show, but the Orientation Episode was an all-hands-on-deck event for both TUSSA and the SSS. It sucked for the SSS right now, because they looked to be pretty outgunned.

Sara-N-Dipity walked over to Lady Lockless, kicked her cane away so she couldn't trap anyone, and then turned on Springlock. Her fingers flew faster than I could translate, and both women looked furious. A big red hand settled onto my shoulder as they signed at each other. I turned to see Milo shaking his head slowly. "I'm not getting involved in that mess," he said softly.

"No? Springlock's your girlfriend," I said.

He nodded. "And you've gotta know when getting involved will help and when it won't. Speaking of which, Fursona's about to snap out of Tearjerker's power. You should be there for them."

I nodded and turned. The kangaroo superhero sobbed quietly into her voice modulator. I walked toward her, then turned. "Milo, what are they fighting about?"

Milo's red face soured. "Politics."

"Ah." Yeah, no. I did not want any of that. I returned to the door, put an arm around Fursona, and waited while the kangaroo fursuit shivered and shook.

When it finally stopped, I wrapped my arms tighter. "It's okay, Fursona. I've got you. I bet you never even had a goldfish, huh?"

"N-no! I did! His name was Amarillo, and he was the best goldfish ever. I'm gonna make her pay!" She tried to get to her feet, and I pushed her back down.

"She's gone. We're stuck here for a minute while the campus police show up to deal with the SSS, but it's just her, Iron Fist, and whoever they didn't have here. I don't think it'll take long once we get moving. All of TUSSA's here."

"Yeah. This should have been a real ultimate showdown, huh?" Fursona said, trying to lighten up.

"Yep. We were so close to getting the win right here."

I looked up. Sara and Springlock continued to throw signs at each other, each woman glaring daggers as they went. Milo, apparently, had decided to do something, because now he, too, was signing, though from his body language, his goal was to get the other two to *stop*. "He's playing with fire," I muttered.

"What are they so pissed about? Aren't we winning?" Fursona asked.

"Politics."

"That'll do it," Fursona said.

Milo got between the two furious superheroines, and as things calmed down, I helped Fursona up. I didn't necessarily *want* to get involved in their drama, but if it was over, we needed a new plan to take the fight to Iron Fist.

[Tense Moment! +1 Drama Point]

I blinked. It was rare that I got points without using my powers, so whatever Milo had headed off, it must've been about to get nasty. The red, Greek-themed wrestler beckoned everyone over. Springlock and Sara-N-Dipity stood about ten feet to either side of him, each refusing to look at the other. Once TUSSA had assembled, he cleared his throat. "We were hoping to save this announcement until *after* the Orientation Episode, but it's gotta get out in the open so everyone knows what's going on." His hands flew as he talked, signing along for Springlock's benefit.

"Members of TUSSA, I formally present Springlock and Sara-N-Dipity, your club president candidates."

[**End of Act Two: Act Three in Three Minutes**]

6

Candidates

I stared at Milo, jaw practically on the floor. We already *knew* who was running, and there was an *Episode* going! "Don't we have other things to do? He's getting away!"

"No, he's really not," Sara said. The ballroom looked terrible. We'd trashed it, breaking windows and denting the walls. Defeated villains lay strewn all over the place. She cleared her throat. "We need to talk for a minute. Milo?"

"Yep, I got it. Last year's Orientation had pretty low stakes, all in all. Just the usual 'stop the SSS, collect the baby supers, and stay out of the professors' way' junk. But with Ikenga and Monologue gone, both organizations need new leadership, directions, and presidents. Springlock *should* have been a lock for president. We were all part of the leadership group together, and she'd be carrying on a lot of Ikenga's ideas." Milo's fingers moved as he talked.

"But TUSSA's been outmaneuvered for two years," Sara-N-Dipity said. She signed, too, though Milo copied her every motion, and Springlock watched him, not her. "We've lucked into a couple of wins in the last year, but mostly, they've been because of junior members or pure chance. And yes, I know I said luck.

"It's been frustrating watching a superhero who can literally predict the future fail to stop a bunch of villains because his ex is president. But now, I've got a chance to change the Tokyexico University Student Superhero Association and get us back on the right path. I don't have any ridiculous ties to the villains, and I've got power that's pretty similar to Ikenga's but much more flexible."

Milo interrupted before she could get going on a campaign speech. "Now's not the time for full-on speeches. The fast version is that this is sort of a job tryout for Sara, Springlock, Tearjerker, and Iron Fist."

"Then why were Tearjerker and Iron Fist working together in the bookstore?" I asked. Fursona nodded.

"The SSS has a consistent problem with large-scale cooperation—there are actually more villains on campus than heroes most years, but you wouldn't know it," Sara said. "I'd guess—not with my power, just a guess—that they're trying to prove they can work with their rivals to reach their goals. If the whole SSS united, that'd be real bad for us."

"So, who's got who?" Fursona shifted her head like she was trying to crack the kangaroo's neck.

"Iron Fist," Springlock signed. "We can take him easy."

"Fine. I'll track down Tearjerker with the boys." Sara turned on her heel, her coattails flaring behind her dramatically. "I'll see you all after the Episode."

As she left, I turned toward Milo and Springlock. "Plan?"

"She really should have picked Iron Fist," Fursona said. "Tearjerker's terrible solo, and she's out of the fighting at this point unless she can rally some villains somewhere or find a few henches. We've got more to gain here."

"Yep. So, here's the plan. Break into twos. Milo and me, Fursona and Understudy, Hephaestus, you and Forger," Springlock signed. "If you see Iron Fist, call it in and keep him pinned down. He's got a hostage, so don't let him escape."

I nodded, and Fursona and I took off.

[The Annual Orientation Episode: Act Three in Progress]

"I can't believe they're not taking the Orientation Episode seriously," Fursona whined as we threaded our way past parents, freshmen, and tour guides. With the fighting mostly calmed down, the Extras were wasting no time getting back to TU's Orientation process.

I nodded, staring as a dozen wide-eyed students passed by the Mister Felsic statue. The tour guide rattled off facts about TU's Superpower Studies program; most sounded like he'd made them up on the spot, but the kids looked impressed. I rolled my eyes and kept searching. Then I looked at Fursona. "What was Pataki working on for you?"

"New Costume," she said.

I rolled my eyes. "You steal my heart, you steal my apartment key, fine, whatever! But now you're coming for my gimmick! Unbelievable! What's the Costume?"

"Eagle."

"Ah." Fursona wasn't big on flying, so I could see why a bird Costume might throw her for a loop. Still . . . "It'd be handy right now. We could do aerial observation over the whole campus and catch villains out all over the place. Come to think of it, there aren't many supers with flight as a power, are there?"

"No. Not compared to how many you'd expect. The eagle Costume sacrifices a lot of the roo's firepower, too, and it takes a long time to change between them."

"Like a minute?"

"No." I couldn't see her, but I knew she was rolling her eyes inside the kangaroo fursuit. "Like manually taking the suit on and off. I'm not a Magical Girl. I can't just wave a wand and become something else."

"Fair. So, want a lift?"

"Nope."

We didn't have to search for long—or very hard. The Hemlock Building, where the chemistry and biology majors and a few other sciencey types hung out, was missing a window in a very Iron Fist-sized pattern. The glass had been pushed in, too. "Think he's still in there?" I asked, pulling out my phone.

"Maybe," Fursona said.

<Possible IF @ hemlock - Understudy 2:35>

With the message sent, I pointed at the building. "This is your space, right? You know it?"

"Yeah, I'll take the lead. Really glad I'm not a bird, though."

She stepped through the glass. A moment later, Iron Fist's massive fist slammed into her, and she flew across the classroom, shattering a desk with the force of her impact.

I pulled out my wand, sending a [**Starlance**] at the big Bruiser, but though it hit, he shrugged it off—and that's when I realized he wasn't the biggest problem.

[Dramatic Damage! +1 Drama Point]

A Magical Girl in fishnets, a red skirt, black top, and glowing red mascara disappeared further into the building, dragging a terrified-looking Extra behind her. I groaned, then dropped to the floor to avoid an Iron Fist punch. "Dark Girl Anima's got the hostage!" I shouted.

"I'm on her!" Fursona said, but Iron Fist closed the gap and slammed my side-kick into a cinderblock wall. Dust filled the room as the ceiling's panels bounced in their frames.

"I'll pin him down. Go!" I said, whirling in place and using [**Hog the Limelight**]. Spotlights flared all around me, and the rest of the room darkened until the only hero Iron Fist could see was my pink-and-purple shape shimmering in the light.

[Eye-Catcher! +1 Flamboyance Point]

"Come at me!" I said, beckoning him to attack, and he did. The taunt worked perfectly, his power focusing on me, and I used [**Power-Weaving**] and [**I-Frame Transform**], aiming for Rainy Day to control the fighting and land a big combo.

[Flashy Fitting-Room! +1 Flamboyance Point]
[Steel Yourself! +1 Grit Point]
[Floating Points: 1 Flamboyance]

The combo built as Iron Fist phased through me, my immunity and the taunt working perfectly. Then, as he caromed toward the window, off-balance, I shifted into Rainy Day and used [**Wind Front**]. The sudden gust burst out the rest of the window and shoved Iron Fist the rest of the way through it.

[Badass Move! +1 Badass Point]
[Floating Points: 3 Flamboyance, 1 Grit]

I followed up with a [**Ride the Lightning**], filling the air with tendrils of electricity that lashed out at him even as he tried to find his feet, but though the thunder cracked and lightning rushed into him, he pushed through it and started running around the building.

[Electric Lightshow! +1 Flamboyance Point]
[Power-Weaving! +6 Flamboyance, +3 Grit, +1 Badass Point]

A part of me wanted to chase the villain. He'd already been low on superhero damage from the fight at the ballroom, but I still wanted to be the one to bring him down. But the rest of me knew that he'd be long gone by the time I transformed into something that could catch him.

Besides, my phone had buzzed. Springlock, Milo, and maybe Hephaestus and his mechanical assistant Forger were on the way. He wouldn't get far, and I wanted to save the hostage more than I wanted to fight Iron Fist.

Unfortunately, that meant handling Dark Girl Anima, and her power was outstanding on defense—as I knew from experience. Plus, I already had a reputation for trashing science buildings. I couldn't afford to reinforce that—not this early in my minor-league career!

"Let's take it slow," I whispered, switching back to Understudy. "Anima's our target now."

[Rejuvenation Activated! HP 11/11]

"Got it," Fursona said. "Think she's got more of those catling-gun bots?"

"I don't know. I'd be shocked if we dealt with them all, and who knows what else she can animate? Actually . . ." I paused and looked at my biology-based girlfriend. "You'd know. Anything in here that'd be a problem for us if it somehow came to life?"

"Yeah, half the building's experiments from last year shouldn't be alive," Fursona laughed. "Let's go."

We crept through the halls while red exit lights flickered overhead and security cameras blinked above us. I knew, for sure, that Dark Girl Anima's powers were at work all across the building, but even so, I couldn't help but pretend to be sneaky. Posters with chemistry formulas that looked like math covered the walls, along with a few animal biome art pieces.

We rounded a corner, and a hulking presence vanished around a different one. "Was that?"

"Iron Fist?" I nodded, already running to try to get a shot off. I readied a [**Starlance**], but before I could fire it at the villain, a gold-chrome robot surged toward me, glowing red and rippling off a wave of tasers in my direction!

[HP 10/11]

The tasers hit me, dropping me to the ground as electricity surged through the wires. The cat-shaped robot bounded toward me and extended a wicked-looking knife, which crashed down on my stunned form. The blade punched through my superhero damage, but the shielding slowed and directed it so that instead of slamming into my shoulder, it sliced a narrow cut right above my sleeves.

[HP 7/11]

All the same, I couldn't stay in melee combat with the machine. As I regained control of my body, Fursona hopped into battle, slamming her feet into the war robot and forcing it to stagger. It stabilized and turned to continue attacking me.

I'd seen these before during the "Grant Building Dogpile" Episode. Back then, I'd been a little-league heroine, but now, Fursona and I were both minor-leaguers. We had more firepower, more experience, and a battle plan. "Try Bait and Switch!" I called and used [**Hog the Limelight**] again, burning my last use.

I braced myself as the room darkened and the spotlights centered on me. The vibrating knife sliced through the air with a wicked hum echoed by the cat-bot's Gatling taser spinning. I knew the knife was coming, so I ducked instead of using [**Quick-Time Change**]. It sailed over my head, and a moment later, Fursona's fists slammed into the bot, glowing as chunks of armor flew everywhere. It turned, shaking her off but exposing the spot she'd attacked.

I fired a [**Bit-Part Barrage**], spun in the air, and launched a half dozen rays.

[**Dramatic Damage! +4 Drama Points**]

The first shot hit, and the robot stopped moving as ray after ray found their marks. It wobbled, started to turn, and received a vicious [**Double-Kick**] from Fursona that knocked it off its feet. Then, before it could recover, I shouted, "[**Starlance**]!"

[**Dramatic Damage! +1 Drama Point**]

The robot started moving, then stopped. Smoke poured from the hole in its side, and a moment later, the reddish glow vanished, disappearing down the hall and rounding a corner. "Bet Anima's that way," I said, following the light. Victory was as good as ours.

But my heart dropped as I rounded the corner and looked at the wall of reddish light on the hall's far side. The Dark Girl stood behind an army of constructs—a few cats, but mostly just different experiments. "Good luck, Understudy. I don't think you can beat this," Anima said as Iron Fist stomped up next to her, hostage in hand.

"No," a voice said from behind me. "But we're not here to beat them. We're here to beat your ass."

I turned, half expecting to see Springlock and Milo. Instead, I narrowed my eyes. "Sara-N-Dipity . . ."

7

Sara-N-Dipity

Sara was *not* the superhero I wanted to see, and she was *not* the kind of superhero to be making threats like that. Even with Punch and Grapple in tow, I didn't see how the five of us could take on the swarm of machines. Sure, Fursona and I could handle one cat-bot, and maybe the three of them could fight another, but—

"What the hell?" Milo said, staring at Springlock, who glared at Sara-N-Dipity. "Did you text her, too?"

"Nope. She must've gotten lucky," I said, needling the probability-based heroine.

"It's not . . . dammit. No, I predicted with 83% likelihood that Iron Fist would be here," Sara said. "It seemed like a good enough bet, so after the boys wrapped up Tearjerker, we headed here to see if you needed help. And it sure looks like you do."

She pointed at the horde of red-glowing bots, science projects, and plants. "Anima's got a good defense, but she can't attack against all of us, especially when Hephaestus shows up with Forger. So, we're at a stalemate, and we need to break it."

Then, she gestured at the security camera overhead. "Knock those out. They're telling her what we're up to, and I have an idea."

"**[Starlance]**," I said, and the security camera popped and the reddish aura surrounding it disappeared.

[Dramatic Damage! +1 Drama Point]

"Great. Now, we're going to build a Springlockpult," Sara said.

I blinked at her. Springlock's fingers flew, and Milo interpreted. "A *what*? That sounds completely ridiculous."

"It's not completely ridiculous. You have massive control over your power, right? But even with that control, hitting Anima from this range isn't likely. She's got too many minions in the way. You *can* launch yourself that far, right?"

Springlock nodded, glaring at the suit-clad heroine.

"Great. Here's the plan, then. I'll aim you, or you can throw Milo if you think he can burst harder than you. That'll increase the probability of success. Whoever we throw will take out Anima with everything they have, and then the rest of you will rush Iron Fist and get the hostage. Good plan, great plan."

It sounded like a decent plan, but I saw a flaw right away. "Won't Iron Fist leave with the hostage?"

Sara considered for a moment. "Good point. Let's do Springlock *and* Milo, then. Milo can go for the rescue, and Springlock can—"

"Nah, send Springlock and me," I interrupted. "I've got a few rescue-based powers. Not much, but I can protect one Extra for a few seconds until a heavy hitter distracts Iron Fist, then I can set up a combo to help out."

"Got it. Are we in agreement?" Sara asked.

Springlock signed back and forth with Milo, then nodded slowly, still scowling at Sara. Milo cleared his throat. "Alright, Understudy. You've never been thrown, right? It's going to feel like pressure is building up. Grit your teeth through it, let it build up, and trust Springlock to launch you before it gets to be too much."

"Got it," I said, already gritting my teeth.

The pressure built and built, and I tried to look back to wink at Fursona, but I couldn't move. I gritted my teeth instead, feeling an ear pop. Then, suddenly, I launched through the air over the ranks of red-glowing animated experiments. Iron Fist's eyes widened as I slammed, boot-first, into his chest, and he dropped the Extra.

[**Bold Plan! +1 Cunning Point**]
[**Badass Damage! +1 Badass Point**]
[**Badass Assist! +1 Badass Point**]
[**Stylish Save! +1 Flamboyance Point**]

A half second later, Springlock sailed through the air like a blue lightning bolt, tackling Dark Girl Anima and driving her into a wall.

I whirled, skirt swishing as I did, and [**Quick-Time Changed**] Iron Fist's punch, shifting into Magical Girl Rainy Day again and activating [**I-Frame Transform**]. Then, as he recovered and sent another devastating blow toward me, I used [**Wind Front**] on the Extra.

[**Flashy Fitting-Room! +1 Flamboyance Point**]
[**Steel Yourself! +1 Grit Point**]
[**Badass Move! +1 Badass Point**]

The kid, who couldn't have been more than a sophomore like me, pinwheeled down the hall, away from the fighting, and hit a wall. It looked like it hurt, but I couldn't do anything about it since Iron Fist's blow connected and sent me crashing off the walls to join the Extra.

[**HP 4/11**]

As I shook off the impact, Iron Fist turned on Springlock, who hadn't gotten Anima down yet. Faced with his fists, she had to let the Dark Girl recover for a moment, and I couldn't have that. "Stay down," I told the Extra, and **[Quick-Time Changed]** to Lab Assistant Panic.

"EVERYONE STOP! THE LAB ASSISTANT'S BACK!
TIME FOR THE GENIUS TO START HER ATTACK!"

TA-1LZ appeared, already charging up her **[New Head-Cannon]** and aiming the spinning, sparking weapon toward Anima. The robo-cat shimmered and disappeared a moment later, but the constant barrage of tasers slamming into the Dark Girl revealed her position.

Not that it mattered. As she twitched on the ground, Springlock loomed over her and launched a bench toward the villainess. She stopped moving, and a moment later, so did her army of constructs.

I sat back and watched as the entirety of TUSSA, including Hephaestus and a crude-looking machine with a massive blacksmith's hammer, tore into Iron Fist. He lasted about five seconds before his hands went up in surrender.

A camera drone dipped down, mercifully focusing on Springlock and Sara-N-Dipity. They said something into it, and the end-of-Episode message popped up a moment later.

[Episode Finished!]
[Episode: The Annual Orientation Episode - PG-13]
[Penalties: N/A]
[Episode Finished! +5 of each Style Point]
[Winner Winner! +3 of each Style Point]
[Role Focus: Drama + Flamboyance - Goal Met! +10 Focused Style Points]
[Alias - Understudy] [Archetype - Magical Girl] [Community Rank - 219/523]
[HP 11/11]
[Styles and Skills]
▶Archetype Skill - Transformation Sequence
▶Combo Skills - Power-Weaving
▶Badass (48)
▶Cunning (33)
▶Drama (41)
▶Starlance 1
▶Bit-Part Barrage 2
▶Flamboyance (35)
▶Signature Skill - Adaptive Armoire 3
▶Stored Costumes: (Rainy Day, Copy Cat, Lab Assistant Panic)
▶Starwave Sail 1
▶Quick-Time Change 3
▶Hog the Limelight 1

▶Grit (31)
▶I-Frame Transform 3

We'd won. As Fursona and I headed for the exit, I blew out a long breath of air. I'd thought about catching up with Springlock and Sara-N-Dipity, but everyone had classes to get ready for tomorrow. The two candidates could email or text me if they wanted to.

Instead, we started the long walk from the Hemlock Building to Walnut Tower, on the campus's far side. "So, that went well," Fursona said.

"Yep. Think Rocko will accept it as a minor-league Episode for the first week?" I asked. "It meets all the requirements."

"I'm not sure we had enough of a starring role," Fursona replied. "Don't we need to be headlining?"

"Technically, TUSSA and the SSS are the headliners, right?"

Fursona thought about it as we walked toward a crowd of Extras. "I suppose . . . shit."

"Yeah, shit," I agreed. The Extras wore T-shirts with the words "APPEAL: For a Post-Superpower World" across the front of them, a picture of a fist behind a globe, and a slashed-out red circle over Mister Felsic's face. They held signs saying Our Campus, Our Safety, Our Voices, and as I winced, Su-Bin led them in a ridiculous chant. Nearby, a few more APPEAL members sat behind a table, helping freshmen fill out club paperwork. They'd clearly benefited from the Orientation Episode, too.

Scattered around their edges were other students. A few had Springlock T-shirts, one or two were wearing togas, and—to my absolute shock—a half dozen girls waved pink wands that looked a lot like mine. Fans. I had fans, and I was *not* ready to deal with them yet.

Luckily, they faced the Student Union Building, and even more fortunately, they hadn't seen us yet.

Unluckily, we needed to get through the crowd to get home and debrief.

"Do we . . . try getting through?" Fursona asked.

I shook my head. "Let's go over. It'll be so much faster, and I don't want to deal with Vice President Pak right now."

My sidekick shivered but nodded, and I summoned my sailboard under us.

We kept low as long as we could—I knew Fursona had a problem with altitude, and even though she'd toughed it out before, it didn't help to scare her if I didn't have to. Then, just before we reached Walnut Tower's concrete facade, I spiraled up, gaining enough height to put us even with the top of the tower. Fursona and I landed, and she half laughed/half sighed in relief. "Thanks. Let's get inside."

I nodded. We ditched our superhero personas, and I sat on the couch with my feet under me. Bianca left the bathroom and joined me, and I wrapped my arms around her waist. She let me pull her in for a good snuggling, and I sniffed. The smell of her sweat from the Episode mixed with the familiar green apple perfume. "So, our first Episode as minor-leaguers? I think we're off to a good start," I said.

"Yeah. I'm a little concerned about the APPEAL protest, though. Do you think the professors knew they'd be out in force today?"

"Probably not. They'd have warned us."

Bianca shook her head. "Su-Bin's going to get hurt."

"Yep. Not much we can do about it. She's made up her mind to be actively anti-super. All we can do is make sure we're not the ones that get tired of her. Speaking of getting tired of someone, though," I said and yawned.

"Annie! It's three o'clock! You can't seriously be tired."

"No, not really, but I *am* tired of Sara already," I said. Bianca looked shocked, and I continued, "I think Springlock would be a better candidate, and I know you do, too."

"I did . . ." Bee hesitated. I saw her look at the blank TV screen. Then she met my eye. "Look, Springlock's cool, but Sara's tailor-made for being president—and not just her suit. She's not a combatant, sure, but her power's got a lot of potential to . . . win Episodes out of nowhere. And, yeah, she's, uh, kind of bossy and full of herself—"

"Yep."

"—but she's also got more leadership potential than Springlock."

"Why? Because of the sign language thing?" I asked.

Bee rolled her eyes. "No. Because she took over the Orientation Episode and turned what would have been a nasty fight against the animated experiments and stuff into a cakewalk with her brains and her power."

I pondered that. "Springlock had some good ideas during the 'Grant Building Dogpile,' too. She's not dumb."

"No, not arguing that," Bee said. Her phone buzzed, and she grabbed it. "Schedules are in for the semester. The professors will have our books, so we don't have to go shopping. That's nice of them."

I untangled my arms from Bianca's waist against her protests, found my phone, and opened my emails.

Subject: Magical Girl Understudy Schedule, 2042, Fall Semester
To Magical Girl Understudy,
The following is your schedule for 2042's fall semester.
MWF 8:00–8:50 - Team Composition Symposium
MWF 11:00–11:50 - Stage Combat
MWF 3:00–3:50 - Psychology in Action
T/TH 10:00–11:15 - Superpower Legal Issues Forum
T/TH 12:30–1:45 - Extra Relations and Public Presentation
Since you're in my Team Compositions Symposium, please meet at the Mister Felsic statue. Dr. Jackson's Superpower Ethics class will be meeting there as well. I encourage you all to befriend and mentor the new super-students. They'll need help for sure.

Please be aware that, as associate's degree students, all these classes are must-pass if you want to graduate this school year.
Dr. Mays
Head of Superpower Studies
Tokyexico University

I finished reading and then swapped phones with Bee. Her email looked identical, and she grinned at me. "Guess we're doubling up this time around. Wonder if the professors know we're going to help each other with every assignment?"

"They're probably counting on it," I said. Then I stared at my phone. "I'm going to have to talk to Mindstorm, aren't I?"

"About your schedule?"

"Yeah. I need some help with the planning side of it, and before you ask, the whiteboard's not going to cut it."

Subject: Associate's Degree and Minor-League Help
Dr. Mindstorm,
Can we meet as soon as possible to discuss my schedule and how to balance everything on my plate?
Thanks,
Magical Girl Understudy

I gulped, sent it, and turned to Bee. "Hope she sees it tonight. The sooner I can get this figured—"

My phone buzzed.

Subject: RE: Associate's Degree and Minor-League Help
Magical Girl Understudy,
4:30 this afternoon. My office. You can bring Fursona. My advice will benefit both of you.
Dr. Mindstorm

8

Dr. Mindstorm

"Welcome . . . to my office hours!" Mindstorm said. She looked happy, which threw me off more than anything she could have done. In all the time I'd been a student here, she'd only been happy once; she'd smiled during our make-up assignment.

Still, there were two chairs in the dark office and no delivery food sitting on the desk, so I took that as a sign that this meeting would be on the fast side. I gulped, pushing down my worry about being in the same room with Mindstorm, and cleared my throat. "Thanks for meeting with me so quickly. I appreciate it," I said.

"You're more . . . interesting . . . than the current crop of incoming students. Such a typical load. Three super-strength Bruisers, a Magical, and a handful of Speedsters and Elementalists. The only interesting ones are the girl with the tractor beams . . . and one of the upcoming villains. He'll shake up the SSS power dynamics as he grows into his powers." Mindstorm stared at me, and I gazed back, literally unable to look away. "Tell me what your problem is."

"Okay. We're signed up for the associate's degree program. We have the same classes and everything, and that workload looks doable for sure. But we're also starting a minor-league career, and Rocko—our producer—wants us to focus on that. We could get the whiteboard out again—"

"That's where that went," Mindstorm said, and Fursona fidgeted next to me in her fursuit. "I . . . appreciate you coming to me. Let's talk about your classes first."

"Team Composition with Mays, then Stage Combat and Psychology in Action. Those are Monday, Wednesday, and Friday, and they're spread out, so it'll be hard to get Episodes in until the evening. Then, on Tuesday and Thursday, we've got Superpower Legal Issues and Extra Relations and Public Presentation, again spread through the day. So, my concern is that the weekends will be the best time to do Episodes since we won't be able to get away during the weekdays because of classes.

"Basically, I'm hoping for a strategy for balancing TU's needs with Rocko's," I finished.

"And making sure we're successful at all of it, ideally while having *some* downtime," Bee added.

Mindstorm looked at her, then, to my surprise, nodded. "I understand. Would you believe me if . . . I said the schedule was crafted with working supers in mind? We professors aren't clueless. Minor-league heroes—and most of the associate's degree students are minor league—start running into new problems and opportunities. You two are already . . . partners, correct?"

"Yes," Fursona said, slipping a paw into my hand below the table. I nodded.

"Then Team Composition will be theoretical for the most part, but with your power, Magical Girl Understudy, you should . . . pay closer attention. You represent either a one-woman team or whatever your teammate and Episode need, and you should listen to the professionals on how best to . . . take advantage of that. However, Legal Issues Forum and Extra Relations both work together with Psychology in Action and the acting class."

"Stage Combat is acting?" Fursona asked, sounding vaguely shocked through her modulator.

"Yes, Fursona." I rolled my eyes. "You said you took fencing, right? It's like fencing but for flair instead of efficiency. It'll be awesome."

"There are three ways to push from the minor leagues to the majors," Mindstorm said. "One is to be so . . . good . . . at what you do that they can't help but promote you. Another is to have a big hit in the high minors or against low majors. That'll catch eyes and move you forward. But for most heroes, including . . . your friend Magical Girl Stella-Lunar, the path to promotion runs through being good enough, but eye-catching for the . . . audience."

Her face darkened, and she glared across the desk. "For you two, I recommend the last way. It's the easiest path forward. It means paying attention in your theater classes, though, and there's a danger of getting . . . scripted. There are a lot of heroes on scripts whose producers watch their every move for maximum screen impact. You'd be surprised who they are."

I didn't want to be scripted. An actress I might be, but even so, the free-form nature of Episodes felt the most natural—not whatever The Narrator did with the kids. And I had other reservations about progressing upward. "Dr. Mindstorm, I don't *want* to be a major-league hero," I said.

"Oh? Interesting." Mindstorm brought her face into a perfectly neutral expression. It looked almost bored, and she looked at Fursona. "What about you?"

The kangaroo looked down, and her paw slipped from my hand. I tried not to wince, especially when she started talking. "I don't know. I feel like I moved through the little leagues really fast, and I could use the time to settle into my powers. The studio's Costume designer's figured out how to get me into different fursuits, too, so I'll have new powers to test out. I guess, uh, no for now?" She sounded hesitant.

Mindstorm steepled her fingers. "Would you mind if I . . . took a look at your powers? Both of you?" As she stared at me, I could see exhaustion warring with hunger. Still, she hadn't hurt either of us—at least, not outside of the Combat Styles training room. I slowly nodded, and Fursona copied me.

"Wonderful," Mindstorm said. Then, her voice echoed in my head. *[System Menu].*

Fursona and I staggered across campus back to Walnut Tower. True to her word, Mindstorm had taken a good, long look at our power sets. Then, without another word of advice, she'd ended the meeting. "I'll have . . . more personalized steps for you in an email, but I need to think it through," she'd said.

So, as the secret elevator to my base lifted us up, we leaned on each other. We didn't feel sick or headachey; we were just off-balance, and it was nice to have someone to support me. I'm sure Fursona felt the same way, too. Still, when we arrived in my pastel-pink hideout, Fursona's helmet came off, and she flopped unceremoniously onto the chaise lounge. I joined her, lying down on my couch.

"That . . . that sucked," Bianca said, eyes closed and face pale. "Does she do that often?"

"No. Just give it a minute. Hopefully, the room will stop spinning, and you'll be able to change the rest of the way once it does. That sucked—a lot. Did that meeting seem useful to you?"

"Yeah, actually. It told us a lot about what the professors are trying to do with the associate's degree program and why they chose these classes." Bianca lay unmoving, falling silent until I worried she'd fallen asleep in her fursuit. Then, just as I was about to try waking her up, she continued, "God, this is rough. I forgot how bad it was. All these classes work together. If we can figure out the core lessons each is teaching and how those relate to each other, it'll be easier to focus on *that.*"

"I see," I said, running through the classes. "Actually, I don't yet, but I will by Friday. How long do you think it'll take Mindstorm to send us that advice?"

"It'll either be tonight, in the next five minutes, or after classes have been going for a couple of days. It depends on whether she decides we need the class's context to understand her advice."

"Makes sense."

Bianca struggled to her feet and started pulling off the fursuit's straps. I untransformed, then helped her, still feeling wobbly. As I did, I got a good look around the room—especially at the new screens.

"Got something new here," I said, walking over to them. The screen that'd been a blank map of the city had been updated, with my three areas highlighted in different colors. The Poudre districts glowed red, and the word *3V1L* was scrawled across it in jagged letters, but a tiny dot in the top corner shone gold. There, an Old English script covered a tiny enclave labeled *Sister Sly.* It took almost a minute to track down the electric-blue dot for Livestream, and Theseus's green was relegated to a single building in Mid-Town, right next to the Council of Heroes building.

"We have maps of their locations?" Bianca said incredulously. "This is gonna be easy."

"I don't think they're up-to-date locations," I said. "Let's check the other screen."

This screen had way more information, and it made the other one's information more useful, too. Each of the four villains in my rogue's gallery had a section, including recent sightings. The ones for Theseus and Livestream only had one sighting each in the last twenty-four hours, so their last known locations were both more precise and more out-of-date.

Bianca narrowed her eyes. "Doesn't Livestream constantly stream his superhero work? It feels odd to have only a single location and sighting."

"Yeah. Lemme check something." I fiddled with my phone, then nodded slowly. "Looks like he takes Tuesdays off. Let's remember that. It'll help narrow things down for the future."

Sister Sly hadn't been active . . . ever. In fact, there was *no* record of her existing before a week ago, and even then, she was just a name. No Episodes, no history. Nothing. Fursona shrugged. "That's weird. Ideas?"

"Not really. We'll just have to deal with her when we deal with her."

And then there was 3V1L. Golden Goose had wiped them out during the spring semester last year, but they looked to be making a serious comeback. The map's bright red glow made sense; a full two-thirds of the screen was dedicated to news stories about their activities over the last twenty-four hours, along with forum posts claiming they'd seen 3V1L henchmen patrolling their neighborhoods. "They're . . . going to be a problem," I hedged.

"Definitely. We should patrol the Poudre district this weekend and try to keep them suppressed. Otherwise, they'll be the biggest threat in our gallery, just by virtue of being everywhere," Bianca said. She cleared her throat. "I think right now, our priority should be on them, homework, and classes. I don't think Sister Sly will be much of a threat. She looks outgunned by the others. And Livestream and Theseus are one-man shows. Not a real problem if we keep working on our teamwork."

"So you think we focus on the hardest target first?" I asked. "Theseus?"

She shook her head. "No. Theseus is a corpo villain now. He's probably not going to make huge waves—he'll just go after other corporations. And Livestream's got his thing going. He's been a vil for a while, and he hasn't seen fit to expand. He's Gourmet but with a little more ambition. So, really, it's 3V1L or Sister Sly, and 3V1L's proven it'll grow out of control. Think of our focus as pruning, not uprooting."

"Alright. Do you want to stay over tonight? We've got the same schedule, so I won't wake you up in the morning," I asked. Then I hesitated. "Actually, I'll totally wake you up, but it'll be for a reason, not because I'm singing in the shower or something."

Bee looked away, staring at the fuchsia-framed mirror. Then she nodded slowly, walked up, and wrapped her arms around me. "Yeah. Yeah, we could give that a try. Just don't sing too loud."

I started talking, but she stood on tiptoes and pressed her lips to mine before I could say anything. Then she pulled away. "But *only* because we've got the same schedule."

Her face looked deadly serious, and my heart started sinking. Then she winked. "So, what's for dinner?"

PART TWO

9

Composition

I didn't end up waking Bianca. It would have been funny, but neither of us was a morning person, and in the end, we'd settled on dual phone alarms, both of which required passwords to stop. That meant we both had to be awake, and as Bianca's phone squawked at me in some sort of birdcall and I tried desperately to get her to wake up, I regretted my choices. If she didn't want to be awake, it could be impossible to get her up.

After a minute of listening to the increasingly loud bird screech, I put the phone next to her ear and went to take a shower. She could deal with it herself. But the calls didn't stop the whole time I shampooed and conditioned. Not until I'd toweled dry and gotten dressed did she finally turn it off.

"Breakfast? I'm thinking the SUB for burritos," I said.

"Mfff. Whatever," Bee groaned into the pillow. "Clothes."

"No shower?" I asked.

"No time. Get me clothes."

I tossed her the tank top and shorts she'd been in the day before. "They'll do for now."

As she climbed out of bed and tracked down a bra, I stared, not bothering to hide it. She still had an athlete's build, but it had shifted from the more lean-muscled soccer athlete's body to something with more defined, bulkier muscles that rippled under her skin. She was still plenty curvy, though, especially her hips, which I admired for a moment even after she caught me looking. "Did you change your workout routine?"

"Yeah." She pulled on her clothes. "For the last month, I've been pushing hard— lots of weights, kickboxing for cardio, and practicing my fencing moves. I'm gonna try to stick with the club since it's a place where I can strive for number one as long as I don't enter any competitions. There are a few guys there who are *fast*, though."

"Well, you're carrying the muscles well." I grinned.

She hoisted her bag to her shoulder and gave me a quick kiss on the cheek. "Thanks, babe. Gimme five in the bathroom, then we can get moving. Lots to do today."

The door locked, and a minute later, her voice came through. It was muffled from the door and her toothbrush, but I pieced it together. I thought she'd said, "Do you want to try getting Tractor-Beam-Girl as a mentee?"

I thought about it, but we had a good thing going with the two of us. "I don't know. Let's at least see what classes are like first before we commit to another thing."

And speaking of other things . . .

"Besides, we'll be getting contacted by The Narrator soon. We owe her some time with the kids this semester. Maybe she'll let us be flexible and do just a little at a time," I said. We owed her because she'd given Su-Bin and me "free childcare" so we could pass Child Psych. A small part of me was looking forward to it. Unfortunately, that part was Rainy Day, and the rest of me knew it'd be a total waste of time.

"Yeah. I think Tractor-Beam-Girl could be a fun member for a trio, and Mindstorm said she was the hero with the most potential," Bee said. She'd finished brushing her teeth and came across much more clearly. A moment later, the door opened, and she posed for a moment. "How do I look?"

"Good. Breakfast. Let's go."

The Mister Felsic statue was crawling with supers, and the tension hung heavy in the air.

Flare and The Crumb were there; so was Milo, though Springlock was missing. Tearjerker had also decided to take the associate's degree path, and Sara-N-Dipity glared at her from near the statue's base. But though the older heroes and villains definitely had some conflict going, it was the freshmen I was most worried about.

Tractor-Beam-Girl looked like she was ready to kill Flare. On some level, I understood. Flare *was* very killable.

But on another level, she'd shown during the Orientation Episode that she wasn't a soloist—not unless her beams did more than just hold a target in place. And with two dozen villains and heroes standing around at the statue, things could get nasty if she went for it.

Fursona's plastic eyes looked at me, and I gritted my teeth and nodded grudgingly. "Fine. *Fine*, we can talk to her. Maybe we can calm her down or something."

We walked over just as she stood up and jammed a finger in Flare's chest. He charged up a fiery fist. "Bad idea, Tinkerbell."

"Hold on, hold on!" I shouted, pushing Flare back and grabbing Tractor-Beam-Girl's shoulder. Fursona cleared her throat next to the supervillain, who paled and let his flames die out. Clearly, he didn't want any of Fursona at this point.

Which still left the furious, tiny Tractor-Beam-Girl. She pushed my hand off her shoulder, shifting her glare to me. "I can deal with my own problems! I don't need you stepping in for me all the time!"

I held up my hands. "Okay, just trying to keep this from turning into something that destroys half the campus. What's your name?"

"Vicegrip," she said, blushing. I held my tongue as she scowled. "I'm going to be a star. On my way up the little-league leaderboards and everything, and I'm not scared of you or anyone."

Okay, holy shit. It was like meeting a tinier, angrier version of me. Vicegrip had all the confidence I'd had that she'd move up, and a giant chip on her shoulder. Something was going to kick her ass, though, unless someone intervened. I shot Fursona a *look*, then sat on the bench. "Where are you from?"

"Yorkston."

Oh. She *wasn't* just like me. She was from the biggest superhero city in North America, although Tokyexico had produced a few exceptional supers in the last decade. "So you know what you're getting into, then? You can handle all these villains by yourself? You didn't get kidnapped by Iron Fist yesterday?"

Vicegrip's fists clenched. "What do you want?"

"Just to give you some friendly advice. I grew up in a small town, and I thought I was hot shit when I got here last year. The thing is, everyone here's got a year of classes on you. Flare's got at *least* half of his minor-league kit, and he might have made it over the summer. I doubt it, but it's possible. I'm not saying keep your head down. Make a name for yourself, just maybe without starting a massive showdown on day one, yeah?"

She wilted in her white armor, then looked away, refusing to make eye contact. I turned to Fursona. "Okay, that went really badly. You still want to try after class?"

"I hope so," Dr. Jackson said, eying Vicegrip. "Magical Girl Understudy, thanks for getting in the way and keeping your composure. I'll email you later today, so keep an eye on your mail. You too, Fursona. We're heading down into the theater, new heroes, villains, and vigilantes. Superpower Ethics will prepare you for resolving situations like this."

As the freshmen filed down into the Department of Superpower Studies, Dr. Mays cleared his throat. "As for you older students, we're heading down as well. I've got coffee going inside, so hopefully, you're all ready for the boring Day One intro to the class. Room 105. We'll start in ten minutes, so get comfortable, use the bathroom, find something to drink, and be there at 8:10. And no, that's not going to be a normal thing, so don't get used to it."

I rolled my eyes and headed down the ramp. The coffee wasn't bad, but Sara kept trying to corner me. I avoided her until she gave up just before time was up and sat in one of the comfortable lounge chairs that dotted the room. It wasn't set up as a theater, but it could do it in a pinch.

I breathed a sigh of relief when the luckiest superheroine on campus finally decided to leave me alone, and thanked whoever was watching out for me that she hadn't used her power to pin me down. She clearly wanted my vote, but I was already committed to Springlock.

At exactly 8:10, Dr. Mays leaned over his podium. "Alright, several of you have partners, whether they're in this class or not. Either way, the class is pretty simple.

For the first half, we'll look at the different archetypes—Bruisers, Tanks, Speedsters, Elementalists, Geniuses, and Magicals—and work through their best duo, trio, and full-team compositions. We'll spend six weeks on each team size, splitting the time between the six archetypes as best we can. Then, when we're done, you'll have a standard test on the material. That's half your grade."

I yawned. All of this was on the syllabus, but every professor in the world insisted on going over it. Plus, I already had my partner in Fursona, a Bruiser with a hint of Speedster to her. We complimented each other well, and I couldn't see what good the first six weeks would do for us.

"The other half will be practical work outside of class time. You'll need to find a partner for the first six weeks, a trio for the second, and a full team for the third, then run at least one Episode with them. After that Episode, you'll need to write a three-to-five-page paper on how the pair-up went, what you learned, and how you applied what we've talked about to them. You'll also have a one-to-three-page paper due at the end of weeks two, four, eight, ten, fourteen, and sixteen."

Fursona groaned, fidgeting in her seat. I didn't blame her, even though it *really* wasn't that much of a workload. Everything added up, after all, and 8:30 wasn't the time you wanted to hear about a bunch of short essays. Still, they were short ones, so that was a small mercy, and other than the unit tests, there weren't any actual exams.

I flipped through the syllabus, following along as Dr. Mays blazed through it. When he finished, he cleared his throat again. "Speaking truthfully, there's not a single super in the TU faculty who can teach this class from experience. Jackson, Tennyson, and I formed the most successful trio in history, but our situation was unique. With two metapower heroes and a space Elementalist, we handled combat wildly differently from what you'll likely be doing.

"The big picture reasons for choosing Jackson and Tennyson as a trio, though, are things I think you can learn from. The fact is, when you're looking for long-term teammates, you can pick a bunch of people you like, like The Triad. They run two individually powerful heroes in Underdelver and Lightbeam, but the reason they work well as a team is the pure happenstance of Underdelver and Tele-Portal being friends and Lightbeam meeting them early in their careers. There's little synergy between Underdelver and Lightbeam without Tele-Portal."

"So, what's the other method?" Sara asked. Dr. Mays looked at her gratefully, and she grinned like it had been scripted.

"Instead of picking your partners based on who you like, think about what you bring to the table, and find heroes or villains who make that better—or who you make better. Synergy breeds success, and success creates room for showmanship."

10

Showmanship

Bee and I finished up a Ramsey Fieri lunch and changed into our superhero personas. We'd been through Stage Combat with, oddly enough, an ex-professional wrestler named Dr. Boulder Vicente and a room that was an even mix of drama kids, wannabe badasses, and students I strongly suspected were supers. That class sounded like it'd be awesome. After that was Psychology in Action, which turned out to be focused on how the brain reacted to intense situations.

Then, this morning, we'd been in Superpower Legal Issues. It felt boring compared to Superpower Ethics and Combat Styles, but I kept my eyes open as we discussed the various laws that'd been proposed to restrict supers over the last twenty or so years. The class gave me an opportunity, though; I could learn a lot about APPEAL here that I couldn't learn from Su-Bin, since she was biased.

And now—hopefully—was the highlight class for the semester. I wanted to shift from aggressive combat to working as a support hero with at least one Costume, and Extra Relations and Public Presentation looked like it'd be good training for that type of work. Plus, as a minor-league hero, I'd have more eyes on me before, during, and after Episodes, even when I was just fighting.

This class was going to be phenomenal, and I was ready to treat it like Superpower Ethics. Not the first few months, either, but the last ones, where we'd all gotten our shit together.

"Ready for this?" I asked as we worked our way down the secret tunnels below TU. Fursona nodded.

Dr. Tennyson stood in front of the class in his silver super-suit, writing on the whiteboard as we slipped into the room with minutes to spare. He'd piled textbooks in neat stacks, each about twelve books high. Flare, both the SSS candidates, and Sara-N-Dipity already had seats, along with a few other heroes and villains. I didn't see Springlock or Milo, though. Did they have multiple associate's degree tracks?

"Welcome. It looks like we're all here, so let's get started," Tennyson said. "This class is, in combination with Dr. Jackson's Superpower Legal Issues course, the most important class you'll take at TU. In her class, you'll learn how to handle the many legal issues facing heroes and villains. You'll become an expert on the arguments your lawyers will use when you inevitably do something that causes the legal system to look at you. And, as she no doubt said, you'll be informed about the big policies working their way through the North American government.

"In my class, you'll learn how to avoid all of that, so you never have to use it."

Tennyson clapped his hands. "Now, let's get to it. Class is divided into a couple of different tasks. First, the reading. Please come to the front and pick up one book from each stack."

Speechmaking: Dos and Don'ts, *How to Influence People* Without *Using Powers*, and *Public-Facing Personas*, along with a few others—this all looked like the kind of information I wanted. I scooped up the books and headed back to my seat.

"Okay, we'll have assigned readings from each of these books. The chapters we'll cover are in the syllabus. Normally, I know there's a huge resale market for textbooks, and you're all pretending to be broke college students. That's not as true for superhero texts. Still, these are solid references, so I recommend you keep them, and maybe even read the nonassigned page numbers," Tennyson said.

"Will this stuff be on the test?" Flare asked.

Tennyson laughed. "Yes. Speaking of the test, here it is. You will interact with the Extra population frequently in this class and report back to the class on your experiences. We'll have two different tracks of interaction—one for heroes and one for villains. I'll explain more after today's intro lesson, but the idea is to get you used to being public-facing, let you make the most common mistakes, and discuss them in a learning environment."

He turned to the board. "That brings us to the 'three pillars' setup for the class. Every day, starting at 12:30, we'll have twenty minutes of discussion about the previous week's interaction task. Then, we'll have twenty minutes to talk about the readings. The remaining thirty-five will be focused on new concepts, which the reading for the next period will reinforce.

"The goal of Extra Relations and Public Presentation is not to make you a star for the camera. It's not to change the personas you've been building as a little-league hero, or even into the minors. We're going to tune those personas, give you the skills you need to build rapport with Extras, henchmen, and maybe even other supers, and, of course, teach you how to handle situations that've gone wrong.

"So, since I'm in speech-making mode," Dr. Tennyson said and laughed, "here's the interaction task for this week. Find someone who hates supers and talk with them."

"What?" Flare asked, jaw almost on the floor. "How are we supposed to do that?"

"Don't be Flare," Dr. Tennyson said. When the class laughed, he held up a hand. "Not that your persona is grating, but this task doesn't *have* to be done as a super.

You can use your secret identity to make it happen. Your goal is to learn why your person is antisuper."

"What if I've already done this?" I asked. Actually, I'd done it twice: once with Su-Bin and once with Mom.

"Then dig deeper. People don't say it, but they often have deep-seated reasons. They'll say it's because crime is up, the world is more dangerous for Extras, or supers treat our job like a game. But there's almost always a personal reason to hate supers, and it almost always has a kernel of truth to it. Find that kernel, come back to class, and tell us about it."

For the rest of class, Dr. Tennyson talked about the common antisuper arguments and why they happened. The big one seemed to be "crime," which he said was symptomatic of a need for logic to take over from emotions. It was funny because, according to him, the emotional appeal of a personal story that happened to someone was more powerful than statistics, but somehow, the "crime" argument kept being a thing over and over.

For some reason, the other big plays were appeals to authority. A few antisuper candidates and celebrities were out there, so people tended to quote them incessantly. I remembered Su-Bin's parents. They'd been all about the Pherris Report, a show filled with antisuper rhetoric, and treated everything Pherris said like gospel.

By the time class was over, I had a feeling I'd be talking to Su-Bin soon.

Bianca sat on my couch, a cartoon running quietly on the TV from inside a nest of blankets and pillows. I cooked. I was cheating. Since I knew Su-Bin was coming at 5:30, I could be Ramsey Fieri until about 5:15. I wouldn't be able to **[Speed-Plate]** the meals, but it'd *taste* right.

We'd wrestle the truth out of Su-Bin, even if it killed us.

"You ready?" I asked.

"Yep. Got my list of not-so-prying questions right here," Bianca said. "How's the chicken?"

"Solid. Totally respectable. I've got a timer set for when it'll all be done. Nothing but sous-chef stuff now." I untransformed, stirred the pots, and flipped the chicken in its pan. It'd be easy enough to make the meal a success. I'd cooked honey lemon chicken, mashed potatoes, and asparagus because the combo felt like a homestyle meal but with a little more flair than the rotisserie and container mac and cheese Mom made. It was intentionally simple by Ramsey Fieri's standards, but pushed the limits of what Anika DuPont could handle in the kitchen.

I'd just turned off all three burners, mentally high-fiving myself over the timing, when the doorbell rang. "I've got it!" Bee shouted, leaping off the couch and turning off the TV in the middle of a badly animated 3D kid playing in a rock band.

"Hi, Bianca," Su-Bin said as soon as the door opened, peering at us through her dark hair and holding a huge drink. "Hi, Annie. I'm still incredibly jealous of your current room, but I've got a solo one this year!"

"No more annoying roommate?" I asked from the kitchen.

"No more annoying roommate," Su-Bin confirmed, sucking on her soda straw. She sat on the couch, right next to where Bee's nest lay scattered, half on the sofa and half over the coffee table.

I rolled my eyes. "Bianca, clean that mess up before dinner."

"Yes, *mother*," Bee said, matching my eye-roll.

"I'm disappointed," Su-Bin said. "I don't share a class with either of you."

"Nope. Busy schedules, and we're all starting to get into our fields' classes now." I shoveled mashed potatoes into a mixing bowl and carried them to the table.

Su-Bin waited until I was halfway through carrying the chicken. Then, grinning, she asked, "Is there anything I can do?"

"No, just sit down," I said. Then I hesitated, oven mitts heating up. "Actually, I think I saw you with APPEAL on Tuesday. What's going on with them? You were out protesting, but I don't remember that happening last year."

"Yeah," Su-Bin said as she found a chair at the table. She beamed, her smile from ear to ear. "Say hello to President Pak."

"As a sophomore? No way," I said. When she nodded seriously, I continued. "Well, congratulations. APPEAL is lucky to have you."

"Actually, it was super frustrating," she said. "I knew Erik was graduating, so I spent the whole summer gathering data on effective APPEAL protests in other places, how to manage a college-level club, and which supers were causing the most havoc in Tokyexico. Then, two weeks before classes started, the only other candidate dropped out suddenly. So, I became the president by default, and all my campaign material and information was totally wasted."

"That sounds rough," I said. We filled up our plates—Bee looked a little ashamed when I glared at her for eating early—and dug in. The food was solid—not Ramsey Fieri's usual top-restaurant quality, but better than anything the TU Student Union served. The chicken had a nice tang to it, the potatoes had been peppered and garlicked to perfection, and the asparagus still had a crunch that, so often, sauteed asparagus lacked.

"Last year, at the end of Spring Break, I asked you about why you were antisuper," I said once the eating had slowed down. Su-Bin stiffened a little, and I hurriedly continued. "I'm mostly trying to understand why because I'm taking some law classes that want me to dig into the reasoning behind protesters. If I can get a jump on the subject material, that might help me understand."

Su-Bin smiled sadly across the table, then shoveled one more bite of potato into her mouth. She chewed slowly, even though it was mashed potato; clearly, she was stalling. Then she shook her head. "I think I told you then. It's about crime rates and safety."

I hesitated. Then I nodded slowly. "I get it. I really do. My mom was antisuper for a long time, too. She watched a villain kill someone, and it stuck with her for a long time. Now, she doesn't care as much, but she doesn't trust the showrunners at all." It wasn't a lie—at least not technically.

"That makes sense," Su-Bin said. She ate another bite of potato, stalling once again. Then she nodded. "Okay. My parents wanted to move back to Seoul after Launch Day. They made plans and everything—spent a fortune on plane tickets, sold the house and everything. But the day before they were supposed to go, the Ilneats decided that Seoul wasn't recoverable, and they flattened it. It wasn't financially worthwhile to clean it up. Launch Day had done too much, and people were all relocated already.

"So, my parents lost their homes twice. Once to Launch Day, and once to trying to recover their first one. But that second one was the Ilneats' fault. Then, they moved into a smaller house near the outskirts of Thornton. They'd been living there for a while—and I was just a kid—when Man vs. Nature Four kicked off."

"Oh," I said, heart sinking.

"Yeah. They fought The Bear Lord in our neighborhood. After, they moved us into apartments while they MIRACLE'd up some new houses, but the program stopped working halfway through, and Thornton fell apart after." Su-Bin took a deep breath, shaking a little. "The supers who fought The Bear Lord didn't bother to follow up and see if Thornton recovered. It didn't. And we got stuck in the apartment."

Bianca stood up and offered Su-Bin a hug. The tiny Korean girl accepted, sniffling a little as Bee's arms wrapped around her.

I stood awkwardly nearby. "I'm sorry. That sounds incredibly tough, and it makes sense. Can I share your story with my law class next week?"

Su-Bin's eyes narrowed briefly, shining with tears of frustration and sorrow. Then they softened, and she nodded. "Yes. If it's for a class. Just keep it anonymous. I don't need APPEAL knowing everything. I've got a reputation for being logical and fact-based, and I can't lose it."

I smiled genuinely. "You can count on me."

11

Count on Me

SATURDAY, SEPTEMBER 6

My phone buzzed, and I slammed my Extra Relations book shut, happy for the interruption. It was the Magical Girl Understudy number, which was weird. Only Rocko called this number—them and a few other superheroes. But Bee was in the room with me, and she usually texted; Tele-Portal's number was in my phone, and TUSSA members used email or group texts.

"Magical Girl Understudy!" I said.

"Detective Rathburn, TCPD. We talked last spring about a henchman who'd been involved in a semi collision."

"Yes, I remember," I said. That Episode had been a real eye-opener about danger. "How can I help you? And can I put you on speaker? My sidekick's here, too."

Bianca narrowed her eyes at me slightly. We'd talked about the *S* word, but I'd forgotten. "Sorry. My partner."

"Of course." He paused for a moment to let me fiddle with my phone, then spoke again, echoing through the green room. "The Tokyexico City Police Department needs your help. I'm at a crime scene in the Poudre district, at the corner of Eighty-Fifth and Gold Dust. My partner and I know it's a supervillain—probably 3V1L—and that's a little past our pay grades. We talked with the Council of Heroes, who pointed us toward you. Something about your new rogues?"

"Yep. We've got a whole collection now," I said.

"Great. Glad their info was right. Could you come out in, say, twenty minutes? My partner's going back to HQ to check up on some leads, but I'll be around."

"Sure. We're on the case," I said after looking at a nodding Bianca for confirmation. "We'll bring our best Investigative Episode setups. See you in twenty."

"Thanks. Goodbye, MG Understudy." The phone clicked off, and I glanced at Bianca. She was already going for her backpack and the fursuit inside, leaving me to deal with my powerset for the Episode.

After some serious pondering, I came up with the following two changes. I cut **[Starlance]** for **[Check the Script]** and **[Hog the Limelight]** for **[Audition Notes]**, giving me two Cunning powers to drive an Investigative Episode forward. **[Check the Script]** gave me on-demand information and clues, while **[Audition Notes]** was a power I'd picked up during "Winter is Coming" and promptly set aside. It didn't fit in any of my builds so far, but for something like this, it'd be perfect.

[Alias - Understudy] [Archetype - Magical Girl] [Community Rank - 219/523] [HP 11/11]
[Styles and Skills]
▶Archetype Skill - Transformation Sequence
▶Combo Skills - Power-Weaving
▶Badass (48)
▶Cunning (32)
▶Check the Script 1
▶Audition Notes 1
▶Drama (41)
▶Bit-Part Barrage 2
▶Flamboyance (37)
▶Signature Skill - Adaptive Armoire 3
▶Stored Costumes: (Rainy Day, Copy Cat, Lab Assistant Panic)
▶Solar Wing 1
▶Quick-Time Change 3
▶Grit (32)
▶I-Frame Transform 3

The new setup didn't support sustained fighting, but I'd rely on Copy Cat and, shockingly, Lab Assistant Panic for that job. Both had the ability to fight sustained battles, Copy Cat in melee and Lab Assistant thanks to TA-1LZ and **[Science has Rules?]**.

I glanced at Fursona, then blinked. "That's new."

"Sure is. This is my Eagle-sona Costume. Pataki made it for me, and it seems more built for an Episode like this. Increased vision, a few talon attacks, a screech for ranged damage, and flight." She shivered. "I'm not sure about the flight. Heights aren't great for me, but maybe if I'm in control?"

"You'll be fine. You've got this. But let's take Bombing Run off our list of moves while you're an eagle."

"Nah, it can stay. But you can cover my dive-bomb runs. I don't think I'll be as effective in them, but I can do them at my own speed now." Fursona finished strapping on the helmet.

I nodded appreciatively at her Costume. It had "real" feathers, not plush, and it'd probably be less fun to hug, but she looked way more intimidating. Pataki had matched her colors, giving her wings and body a metallic-blue coloring and the Costume over the top orange stripes. She looked fast, and the eagle's eyes glared out at me. "It looks great!"

"Thanks. Let's get out there." She headed for the stairs, talons clicking on the floor, and I followed.

As we flew over the Poudre districts, I fired up the **[Casting Call]** for an Investigative Episode.

[Investigative Casting Call]
[Investigative Episode: The Gold Dust Avenue Mystery - PG]
[Role: Amateur Sleuth! Do you accept the role? (Yes/No)]
[Role Focus: Cunning + Drama]
[The Gold Dust Avenue Mystery: Act One in Progress]

I accepted, and so did Fursona. I didn't *want* to deal with an Investigative Episode, but it was a lead toward a minor-league one; Detective Rathburn thought it involved our rogue's gallery, and we needed to lock down an Episode for Rocko whenever we could. "We'll talk with Rathburn, then check out the crime scene and patrol from there!" I shouted over the wind.

"Got it!" Fursona said, feathers whistling in the wind. "I see him!"

A moment later, the detective came into view. He stood on the corner with a half dozen cops inside a taped-off intersection. He wore an officer's outfit, the dark navy shirt and pants marking him as part of the TCPD. While the other cops looked busy doing cop things, he seemed more occupied with giving orders. I dipped down and landed outside of the tape, then nodded. "Detective, Magical Girl Understudy and Fursona on the case!"

"Thanks, MG Understudy," Rathburn said. He pointed at the corner, where an officer had placed a familiar-looking helmet in a bag. "3V1L was definitely here."

"Yep," Fursona said. "That's a 3V1L helmet, alright. What do you have for us? Anything to get us started?"

"Officers responded to a call about a mugging gone wrong a couple of hours ago, just before dawn. When they got here, the victim was on the street. She's alive, but she's in the hospital, so interviews aren't an option. Supposedly, someone hit her hard enough to knock her out cold and break some bones. We dug around and found the helmet nearby, which told us we were dealing with supervillains."

I **[Checked the Script]**. For a moment, nothing lit up, but as I panned around the area, I caught a faint glow from a nearby apartment tower's roof. I pointed. "Detective, I'm heading up there. If there's anything else, Fursona can—"

Before I could finish, Fursona took off. "I've got this," she said, disappearing into the sky, wings flapping.

"Or . . . that. That's fine, too." I watched her fly away and turned back to the detective. "Anything else?"

"Yes. There's only one set of tracks leaving the crime scene. It was a solo attack, but that's not how 3V1L operates. They're always in a pack of henchmen, usually with one or two *V*s and a pile of lieutenants as support. They've been acting weird since Golden Goose cleaned them out last year, but this is too far out of their usual MO."

"Understood. So we're possibly looking for a solo 3V1L hench? Or do you think it's a setup?" I wasn't sure who'd be setting 3V1L up, but Detective Rathburn was right. This didn't feel like how the group had operated in the past.

[Good Thinking! +1 Cunning Point]
[Clever Assist! +1 Cunning Point]

Fursona glided down with something clutched in her talons. When she landed, I saw what it was: a rifle, complete with a scope. "This is weird," she said, dropping it.

"That *is* strange," Rathburn agreed. "It doesn't look rusted or weathered, so it hasn't been there long. Do you think they're related?"

"I don't know, but I want to talk to a local or two. They must've heard something." I headed for the apartment building's entrance.

"I'll check the other rooftops," Fursona said. "Detective, you might want to spread your people out and search for other clues nearby. This feels bigger than a mugging gone wrong."

As she took off again, I watched her go, then shook my head. I'd let her have this.

I knocked on a third-floor door. "Hello. Magical Girl Understudy on official super-hero business. I'm investigating a superpowered crime that happened here last night. I need to ask you a few questions," I said. I was getting good at the speech after the last six doors I'd randomly selected.

The door opened, and a balding man in a white tank top poked his head out. The air inside smelled like Rocko's Studio or my parents' double-wide, but worse. He nodded once. "Come on in."

I used **[Audition Notes]**.

[Informed! +1 Cunning Point]
[Audition Notes for John Deer: This Extra's not the cooperative type by default. Still, whether he heard or saw something, he knows something. What he does with that information, he's not sure. Does he tell the pig down on the street,

or does he keep it to himself until he can profit from it? John Deer is leaning toward profit.]

I grabbed a kitchen chair, spun it backward, and sat down as "John Deer" returned to a well-worn La-Z-Boy armchair. The TV showed a football game on mute, and he stared at it, almost ignoring me until I cleared my throat. "Last night, someone got hurt down on the street. We found evidence that someone was on top of the building. Did you hear anything?"

I already knew he had, but I hoped he'd tell me right away. Still, it wasn't a shock when he shook his head. "Nope. I was watching the game."

"You're sure? Because it happened right outside, you know?"

"Yeah. I'm sure. The window was closed, the game was on, and I was on my way to wasted."

The pile of bottles in the corner and the muted TV proved that. If he'd drank that much, he probably had a massive hangover. Still, I needed to find the truth, and this guy was the closest I had to a lead. I stood up and pointed at the chrome camera hovering overhead. "You know, I'm a minor-league heroine, and this is being filmed. That means you're being filmed. Now—what's your name, anyway?"

"Bob."

I struggled not to roll my eyes. Either his name *was* Bob, and he just had the perfect name, or he didn't want to say it on camera. "Now, Bob, you have the chance to be a hero and help keep the Poudre district safe. I just need to know a few things. Did you hear a gunshot last night?"

Bob rubbed his temples. The hangover seemed real enough, and I felt for him, but only a little. Then he opened his eyes. "Nope. No gunshots."

"Anything else?"

"Yeah. Someone went inside the building across the street, just after a fight started. Might check the basement. That it?"

[Persuasive! +1 Drama Point]
[Good Thinking! +1 Cunning Point]

"Yes, that's it," I said. I headed for the door, opened it, then turned. "Thanks, Bob. You've been a real help."

Then, before he could respond, I headed back outside with the drone following close behind. Fursona landed next to me, sniffing through her modulator. "Smells worse than your parents'—"

"I know. The guy was gross, but he said something about the basement across the way. Maybe we'll find something there." I nodded at Detective Rathburn, then pointed. "Could you keep a wide perimeter around that building? Cover the entrances and the sides. I got a tip that something went down in there last night, too, but it didn't get reported to you."

He nodded, and I continued, "Fursona, you're not equipped for a basement fight. Still want in?"

"Absolutely."

"Great. Let's head in." I readied my wand, opened the door, and headed down the hall toward the apartment building's basement.

12

Basement

I had no idea what Fursona's new Costume could do in a closed space, but we were still in an Investigative Episode, so I didn't argue when she took point. My heart pounded, though; if this really *was* 3V1L, we'd have our hands full soon enough, and I somehow doubted the eagle fursuit had the same staying power as Roo-sona.

Still, the basement was our best lead, even if I didn't know how Bob had known about it. And if he was lying, it'd be easy enough to shift our investigation elsewhere. So we crept down the concrete stairs and into a long, dark laundry room. I reached for the light switch and flicked it, but the fluorescents overhead didn't turn on. "Someone needs to get maintenance down here, stat!" I joked.

"Yeah. Listen to those machines," Fursona agreed. She walked over to a washer that kept thumping against the floor with every spin. "This place is falling apart."

"Yeah." I thought about shifting to Copy Cat, hoping Tails's cat eyes would be able to guide us, but then I had a better idea. **[Check the Script]** revealed the problem; a sparking glow behind the switch told me someone had broken the wire. As I looked closer, I realized that they had shot it out.

[Good Thinking! +1 Cunning Point]

"Okay, we may be dealing with more guns," I said, shivering. I had no idea how well superhero damage took a bullet. "And 3V1L probably came through here."

"Got it. Let's push on." Fursona started across the room, moving purposefully, and I followed in her wake. On the far side, a hallway led farther into the basement, and this time, when Fursona flipped the switch, the light flickered on. It wasn't much, but it *did* reveal a half-opened door ahead.

I started toward it, but Fursona held out a winged hand. "I can see better than you. Let me take a look."

"Uh, sure," I said. "I'll just wait here."

While I waited, she crept to the door, talons clicking slightly on the concrete, and peeked inside. Then she quickly pulled her beaked head back. "We've got henches. Lots of them. They're tearing the room apart looking for something. Devil masks. It's 3V1L for sure."

[Episode Finished!]
[Investigative Episode: The Gold Dust Avenue Mystery - PG]
[Penalties: N/A]
[Episode Finished! +3 of each Style Point]
[Winner Winner! +1 of each Style Point]
[Role Focus: Cunning + Drama - Goal Met! +5 to Focused Styles]
[Alias - Understudy] [Archetype - Magical Girl] [Community Rank - 218/523]
[HP 11/11]
[Styles and Skills]
►Archetype Skill - Transformation Sequence
►Combo Skills - Power-Weaving
►Badass (52) (Skill Roll Available)
►Cunning (47)
►Check the Script 1
►Audition Notes 1
►Drama (51) (Skill Roll Available)
►Bit-Part Barrage 2
►Flamboyance (39)
►Signature Skill - Adaptive Armoire 3
►Stored Costumes: (Rainy Day, Copy Cat, Lab Assistant Panic)
►Solar Wing 1
►Quick-Time Change 3
►Grit (35)
►I-Frame Transform 3
[50 Badass Credits Used. Rolling Skill!]
[50 Drama Credits Used. Rolling Skill!]

While I waited for my skill rolls to finish, I pointed at the door. "We should take the fight to them fast, especially if they have guns. Focus on anyone who's packing, take them out, and mop up the rest."

[Rank-Up! TA-1LZ New Head-Cannon 1: Gatling-taser replaced with rubber bullets in higher-league fights]
[Rank-Up! Hometown Heroine 3 Speed increase, allowing you to dodge more attacks and close gaps against quicker enemies]

Fursona nodded. The moment she did, I got a new Casting Call.

[Casting Call]
[Episode: The Root of All 3V1L - PG-13]
[Role: Super Sidekick! Do you accept the role? (Yes/No)]
[Role Focus: Flamboyance + Badass]

I accepted without thinking, but Fursona kept staring into space for a moment. Then she laughed softly. "What?" I asked.

"Nothing."

I read it again. Then it hit me. "Wait, wait, wait. *I'm* the sidekick here?"

"Looks like it. Alright, through the door, beat up the henches!" Before I could protest, Fursona flung the door open and screeched. The sound bounced through the door, and I heard a dozen people, maybe more, groaning and screaming.

[The Root of All 3V1L: Act One in Progress]

Then we rushed in.

The room was a long, wide space with dozens of doors around it, each packed close to the others and each with a lock on the outside. Some of the 3V1L henchmen had been trying to break into them, judging by the crowbars, hammers, and even a battery-powered drill they carried. But none of them had succeeded yet. Others held bats, heavy wrenches, and, in two minions' hands, pistols. One went off, but the shot went wild, slamming into the ceiling above.

I fired a [**Bit-Part Barrage**] at the shooter before he could pull the trigger again. My spin was a touch off, though, and the first shot missed, hitting a hench behind him. The second two made contact, and then the rest rocketed into the mass of henchmen. Three henches went down, screaming and cursing.

[Dramatic Damage! +5 Drama Points]

Fursona screeched again, and the whole group of henches covered their ears as the high-pitched attack washed over them. Then, before they could recover, she flapped her wings twice and slammed, talons first, into another gunman. They hit the ground in a whirlwind of feathers, claws, and fists, and the gun skittered across the floor. I kicked it, and it clattered under a locked door.

[Good Thinking! +1 Cunning Point]

The henches recovered a moment later. They rushed me, and I reached for my wand, then realized that Understudy's build was spent already. Instead, I activated [**Quick-Time Change**] just as the first hench reached me, mind-merging with Tails to become Copy Cat. The **[I-Frame Transform]** ducked a whole barrage of kicks, punches, and baseball-bat swings, but it only lasted a few seconds.

[Flashy Fitting-Room! +1 Flamboyance Point]
[Steel Yourself! +1 Grit Point]

I lashed out with my claws, scoring hits across a hench that sent her hobbling back and holding her shredded arm. Then I used **[Leaping Leopards]** to get some distance. Across the way, Fursona had finished off her gunman and was tearing into the henches on her side of the room. It looked like we were winning.

[Badass Move! +1 Badass Point]

BANG!

[HP 8/11]

The impact forced me back, and I staggered against the wall. I looked down at the bullet that'd punched into my arm, then at the gunman who'd pulled the trigger, blinking in horror. He'd shot me! But before I could use **[Leaping Leopards]** again, Fursona's screech filled the room for a third time, and she shredded the shooter with her talons, screaming obscenities at the top of her modulated voice.

I used **[Doom Ball]** on a nearby hench, ripping into her stomach and legs with a series of vicious scratches, then looked for another target.

[Badass Damage! +3 Badass Points]

There was one, but he wasn't a henchman.

The man wore a devil helmet complete with too-long horns that left his chin exposed, and a reddish cloak whirled around his body. He carried a vicious-looking sword in one hand. His other hand was raised in a wave, and he cleared his throat the moment he had my attention. "I propose a Neutral Field. Stand down, minions of 3V1L."

The henches didn't drop their weapons, but they lowered them, and I realized that two more had drawn handguns and pointed them my way. "Terms?" Fursona asked. Something felt off, but I couldn't place it. Was it the villain? Or something about how the Episode was going? I couldn't tell.

He cleared his throat before I could figure it out. "You're not who 3V1L is after. Truth be told, you're an inconvenience, but one that'd be expensive to clean up. So, we'll withdraw our henchmen from the area and then discuss what we believe is happening. Once that's done, you'll be free to resolve the problem as you see fit. My henches will wait in the laundry room, and if you choose to go your own way, you can continue through the door we came in. We'll switch sides of the basement."

The man's voice felt familiar—and slimy—and I shivered. "We shouldn't accept," I whispered, walking up to Fursona.

"But if we don't, the henches will gun us down, and they have supervillain support now. At this point, I think it's our best play," Fursona said. I nodded slowly. "We accept. Neutral Fields."

[End of Act One: Act Two in Three Minutes]

My fingernails dug into my palms, even through my cloth gloves, as the 3V1L henches filed out of the room, carrying their fallen comrades. *Everything* about this felt like a trap—the henchmen outside, the villain's confidence, and the setup that'd drawn us in here. Was Fursona crazy? I looked at her, trying to get her to change her attention, but it was too late. Whatever she'd set in motion, it couldn't be stopped now. We just had to trust 3V1L.

Meanwhile, the devil-helmed man smirked and sat on the floor, legs crossed and sword across his lap. Once the room emptied out, he cleared his throat again. "I am, for the moment, the Third *V*. You're here because, according to all evidence, an Extra was assaulted by one of our henchmen, correct?"

"Yes," I muttered, fists balled. How dare he condescend us like that?! He knew what we were after.

"Wrong. What you've walked into is nothing but a simple turf war," he said, grinning. "The assaulted Extra was, in fact, our henchman, and the attacker was— we believe—Sister Sly."

"I don't believe you," I said.

Fursona shot me a *look* with her eagle eyes, but the Third *V* laughed before she could say anything. "Frankly, I don't care what you believe. I don't need to talk you down from here. I can call in the henches, or we can keep talking. Up to you."

"Say we believe you," Fursona said. "What's your proof?"

"To be honest, I don't care to share the details. They'll compromise 3V1L's goals. In general terms, Sister Sly wasn't an issue for us a year ago. We were in the process of shredding the Mutual Assistance League's Poudre operations and making sure the districts were ours. Since then, she's come out of nowhere, and we've had to pivot to dealing with her. Golden Goose's murder spree made keeping her out of North Poudre much tougher. Otherwise, Sister Sly would never have gotten a foothold."

Something was *really* off here. It seemed like he was giving us too much, even though he'd said he didn't want to share details. I glanced at Fursona, trying to get her attention. When that didn't work, I cleared my throat. "So, let me guess? You want us to stop beating up your henchmen, hunt down your villainous rival, and beat her. In return, you'll . . . what?"

"Stop having my henches fight you, of course." The Third *V* laughed. "You'll have free passage through the Poudre districts today, and unless you interfere with our operations, my henches won't harass you in the University or Mid-Town districts from here on."

"A tempting offer," Fursona said. Then she stood up and stretched her wings. "What's the catch?"

"No catch. We both get what we want. You get to focus on your other rogues, and we get to solidify control of the Poudre districts before the Third Power War begins."

"I think—" I started.

"No," Fursona said before I could finish. "Of all the villains in our rogue's gallery, 3V1L is the biggest threat. Making a deal with *Theseus* would be one thing. We can trust him to honor it. But we can't trust you. So, given that it's two against one, we propose an alternative arrangement. We beat you, shut down your part of 3V1L, and then go after Sister Sly."

The Third *V* laughed. "I thought you might say that. So, my counteroffer. I fight you two and delay you while my henches swarm down the police outside and use them as bargaining chips. Then, we rediscuss this arrangement with different stakes. Henches, get them!"

[The Root of All 3V1L: Act Two in Progress]

13

Henches, Get Them!

A roar went up from the henchmen, and I could hear them rushing through the darkened laundry room. I dashed for the door, using **[Hometown Heroine]** to gain some speed. Behind me, Fursona screeched again as the Third *V*'s sword cut through the air with a hiss. I hesitated, looking back as the supervillain rushed my sidekick.

"Go!" Fursona yelled. She flapped her wings, shooting a jet of air at the villain and launching herself away from the sword at the same time. "I've got this!"

"No, you don't!" the villain roared.

A small part of me knew I should stay. But more important than beating the villain, Fursona was giving me a chance to do what I *wanted* to do. Or at least, what I'd *said* I wanted. If I hurried, I could save the police before the swarm of henchmen hit them. It'd be the right thing to do. But at the same time—no, whatever it was, it could wait. The cops outside probably couldn't.

"Hurry!" she screamed, using her wing to block a sword stroke. Sparks and feathers flew, revealing the frame inside her fursuit's arm.

This time, I started running, letting **[Hometown Heroine's]** brilliant blue aura speed me through the hall. A henchman turned to stop me, pistol in hand, but I gave him a **[Cat-Scratch Fever]** as I ran by, and the gun fired harmlessly into the floor.

[Dramatic Damage! +1 Drama Point]

Then I charged up the stairs, pouncing on another henchman with **[Leaping Leopards]** and knocking her cold. She hit the ground with a thud and then bumped down the stairs. I felt for her—she'd be covered in bruises when she woke up—but I didn't have time to deal with it. Gunfire and yelling from upstairs had my full attention.

[Badass Damage! +1 Badass Point]

When I rushed into the apartment building's atrium and looked into the intersection, the police and Detective Rathburn had hunkered down behind their patrol cars. Meanwhile, the henches had found cover behind some concrete planters on their side of the street. Neither side had clean shots, and the police were mostly firing to force the henches to stay down.

That meant I had a little time. I rotated to Rainy Day, doing the full Itsy Bitsy Spider dance as bullets bounced off the street and ricocheted into the air. Then, poking my head out of the apartment door, I activated [**Power-Weaving**] and used [**Thunderhead**].

[**Pause for Effect! +1 Drama Point**]

Truthfully, I didn't know if this would work, but it had to be worth a shot.

As the clouds built up, a henchman turned toward me and opened fire. Bullets ripped past my head, and I pulled back to avoid them, but one caught me in the shoulder and spun me around, throwing me to the street. A moment later, [**Hometown Heroine**] expired.

[**HP 4/11**]

I used [**Quick-Time Change**] and switched to Magical Girl Understudy. But when the Style System's message came in, I couldn't tell if [**Rejuvenation**] counted toward the [**Power-Weaving**] combo.

[**Rejuvenation Activated! HP 8/11**]
[**Flashy Fitting-Room! +1 Flamboyance Point**]
[**Floating Points: 3 Drama, 1 Flamboyance**]

I didn't have time to find out, though. The spotlights and orchestral music faded, and I spun again, dressed in my pink-and-purple dress and wand in hand. Then I pushed myself off the ground, landing behind the gun-toting henchmen, and fired a [**Bit-Part Barrage**] at them from the side—where they didn't have cover!

[**Stellar Ray**] blasts smashed into the gunmen, knocking them out of cover and scattering them across the sidewalk as the combo-infused beams hammered into one, then another, and then two more, hitting ridiculously hard from the [**Power-Weaving**] combo I'd built up.

[**Dramatic Damage! +4 Drama Points**]
[**Power-Weaving! +6 Drama, +3 Flamboyance, +1 Grit Point**]

The police stayed in cover for one beat . . . two . . . three. Then Detective Rathburn poked his head out from behind a car. "Attention, henchmen, surrender now!" he shouted through a megaphone.

I rolled my eyes. "Otherwise, I've got more where that—"

"3V1L made me," a henchman whined, hands going up. "I never asked for this!"

It was almost unbelievable. Every time a henchman got into a bad situation, they always used the same routine. As the police officers started cuffing villains, I took a deep breath and turned back toward the door. Fursona needed my—

BAM!

A gigantic eagle, battle-damaged and missing feathers on both wings and its tail, crashed through the door and into me! Behind her, the Third *V* stalked up the stairs, sword glowing a vicious, dark maroon color.

—help!

"Get to cover! Get to cover now!" Fursona screamed at the flabbergasted-looking cops. She turned and screeched again, bombarding the supervillain with sonic force that passed an inch from my head. Then she fought her way free from our tangled limbs.

"What's going on?" I asked. I hadn't expected Fursona to win solo, but she'd barely delayed the supervillain, and she looked like she'd been through the wringer!

She shook her head. "No time!" Then she dodged a sword blow, flapping into the air and sending another burst of air toward the villain. The cloud hid me from him momentarily, and I ducked behind a bullet-pocked planter to think through a plan.

There were, as I saw it, two problems.

Problem One: The Third *V*. He had super cool sword powers, and clearly, he was more than a match for Fursona's eagle Costume in close quarters. I *might* be able to handle him in Copy Cat, but I couldn't be sure, and I'd already used a few of my powers, including [**Cat-Scratch Fever**]. I thought Fursona had the right idea to hit him from the air, but she didn't have any firepower to stop him. That led to . . .

Problem Two: I'd stripped down Magical Girl Understudy to win the Investigative Episode, so I didn't have any ranged attacks I could use from the air. I could—

The Third *V*'s sword slashed toward me with a wicked hiss, air crackling, and I instinctively pulled back and used [**Quick-Time Change**] at the same time. The blade froze an inch from my [**I-Frame Transform**]-protected neck, and I shivered as '90s hip-hop music echoed in my head. I hit the ground, lab coat swishing and TA-1LZ already unfurling her cannon. A second later, the sword sliced through my neck and out the other side with no resistance, my power protecting me from both it and his follow-up stab.

[**Flashy Fitting-Room! +1 Flamboyance Point**]
[**Steel Yourself! +1 Grit Point**]

"Evil Breakdown at 45%!" TA-1LZ shouted through loudspeakers. Then her [**New Head-Cannon**] opened up on the villain, peppering him with bullets that bounced off instead of punching through his superhero damage.

I threw myself to the side, and a moment later, a gust of wind filled the intersection as Fursona gave me cover. I scooped up a pistol from the ground, popped the magazine out, and began fiddling with it, sprinting toward the police cars as officers scattered.

Right behind me, the Third *V* charged, doing his best to ignore the bullets slamming into his arms and legs. His sword swung down, cleaving through the flashing blue-and-red lights on top of a cruiser and into the caged back seat. While the villain wrestled his sword from the wreckage, I grabbed one of the light bulbs, yanked it free, then jammed it into the pistol where the magazine had been.

"By combining bright light particles and standard gunpowder-based explosives, I've created . . . a laser cannon!" **[Science Has Rules?]** activated, and a moment later, I pulled the trigger.

Bwoooonnnnnmmmm!

I'd been wrong. It wasn't a laser cannon. Instead, a riot of color erupted from the gun's barrel, blinding me momentarily and whirling around the Third *V*'s head. He spun and slammed into the ground, twitching for a moment.

[Pseudoscientific Mumbo-Jumbo! +1 Drama Point]

"Alright, it's a light taser, then. Cool!" I said.

Fursona dove from the sky, smashing the Third *V* into the ground and working him over with her talons, but she couldn't dislodge the sword from his grip, and as he recovered, he slashed across her chest, and feathers flew. She caromed across the intersection, out of control, and the Third *V* got to his feet and turned toward me.

Then, a moment later, a red, black, and white figure swung across the battlefield, slapping something across my face as it scooped me from my feet onto a rooftop. It slapped another device across my wrist, and I dropped my gun. Something slammed into TA-1LZ, and she shorted out.

I turned my head to the newcomer and blinked. Everything suddenly made sense in the stupidest possible way.

The new super was a fox fursuit, every bit as nice as either of Fursona's. Red-orange fur poked from the nun's black-and-white habit, and unlike Fursona's gender-neutral suit, this one was *definitely* female. A belt around her waist was filled with gizmos and devices, and though none of them were as intimidating as Professor Panic's bots, they seemed much more well-made.

She pointed at Fursona. "You've fallen into my trap, and so has 3V1L! I'm taking your sidekick, Fursona. If you want her back, come find me in North Poudre!"

"Oh god," Fursona muttered, gazing up at us. "Understudy? You've got this, right?"

"I think—"

The fox nun interrupted me before I could finish. "See you soon, Fursona!"

The new villain grabbed my wrist and tossed her grapple into the air. It hooked onto a nearby building, and a split second later, we both jerked off our feet. Before we reached the apex of our swing, the grapple retracted, and we plunged through the air.

I screamed, but the villainess laughed and tossed it toward another building. It latched on, and away we zoomed, quickly outpacing Fursona's eagle form. My heart plummeted as she banked, then turned around. My powers *worked* just fine. I didn't have anything to handle close-range grappling as Lab Assistant Panic.

A few minutes later, a System message I'd been dreading came in.

[End of Act Two: Act Three in Three Minutes]

We landed inside a broken stained glass window high in an abandoned church's tower. Organ music played as we hit the ground, and a single henchman in a monk's robes opened a door. The villain dragged me through and down some stairs, then into the church's main hall.

"Sister Sly, I presume?" I asked.

"Yep. Soon, that wannabee will know who's the best fursuit-themed super in Tokyexico! And even better, 3V1L will be weak while we take over Poudre!"

As she laughed maniacally, I tried to shift Costumes. If I could hit her with Copy Cat or Rainy Day, I could turn this around. But the moment I did, the device locked to my wrist activated, sending a shock through my arm.

"Nice try, but I do my research, and I developed that device specifically to keep you in your scientist getup."

"Well, then you know it's only a matter of time before I go full villain! You think you'll rule the Poudre districts, but I'm the future, Sister Sly!" I said.

"I think not." She shoved me at another robed henchman, who led me toward . . . a chair. A chair in the middle of a circle of steel plates. As he secured me to it, I got a bad feeling in my gut. The chair stood right on the dais, where the preacher's stand would have been, and I realized that Sister Sly was a Genius, just like my ex-boyfriend.

"Okay, you're planning and plotting, but what's your endgame?" I asked, turning in the chair to look at the fox-suited villainess.

The steel panels moved, revealing a tank with a real, 100% genuine Junior Florida maneater in it, circling twenty feet below me. Lasers fired from the ceiling, walling off the tank in reddish light, and I groaned inside as Sister Sly laughed. "Total domination by the time the Power Wars start, control of the Poudre districts, and no more Fursona!"

14

No More Fursona!

The whole damn thing annoyed me, to be honest. The alligator pit, the device that wouldn't let me switch off Lab Assistant Panic, and the laser wall, for starters. That all seemed really over-the-top, even by minor-league standards. There had to be a better way to contain an early minor-league hero, and a Genius like Sister Sly could certainly discover it, right?

But even more than that, this whole Episode felt weird.

The setup didn't make sense. Was Sister Sly making a power play last night, trying to frame 3V1L like the Third *V* had said? Or was it all a trap for us? With Power War Three on the horizon, were they clearing the battlefield for their power struggle or getting started early? That made more sense, honestly, except for one thing that kept bouncing around in my head. I tried to get rid of it as Sister Sly's monk-robed henches disappeared into the old abandoned church, but I couldn't.

This wasn't about 3V1L and Sister Sly. It was about Fursona.

Why? She was a sidekick, not a hero. She'd been doing this for a year, and yeah, she'd had a meteoric rise—minor leagues in one year was no joke! But . . . all this maneuvering and manipulation to beat her made no sense. Sister Sly had *issues*.

Still, it was up to her now. I couldn't do anything until Sister Sly made a mistake or Fursona created an opportunity. So, instead of stressing too much about the impending fursuit fight, I concentrated on preventing a villainous breakdown.

Secured to the chair, it wasn't hard.

[The Root of All 3V1L: Act Three in Progress]

Sister Sly braced herself, reaching into her bag, but nothing crashed through the stained glass windows, and the door didn't burst in under Fursona's assault. The villain's brow wrinkled, and then she glared at the back door and shouted, "Henches! Check the back! Report in—*don't* fight her if she's there!"

A pair of monks headed back, carrying gizmos and silvery bombs, and Sister Sly turned to me, a remote in hand. "As for you . . . I think we'll start the process early. Fursona will have to attack soon to—"

CRASH!

WHAM!

Glass shattered around Sister Sly as a gigantic eagle slammed into the fox nun. She rolled, and her hand closed on the remote, pushing a bunch of buttons. The platform my chair was bolted to started lowering toward the Florida Maneaters below, and the lasers began closing in. "Fursona! Help!" I shouted.

I wasn't worried about it. Nope. Not at all. She'd figure out a way to bail me out of my predicament.

Then her talons slashed out and caught Sister Sly on the arm, and the remote went clattering across the room. The two anthropomorphic animals both dove for it, but Fursona's talons wrapped around the device first. Sister Sly landed on her a second later, scratching and clawing at the eagle Costume. I really wished she'd run the kangaroo; Sister Sly's defenses wouldn't have had a chance against it.

But she hadn't, and the fox-nun broke free of Fursona's attempt to pin her. Spinning away, she reached into her bag and pulled out a silvery bomb, much like the ones the henches had taken. It went off with a hissing sound that filled the air with a sulfury smell and a choking yellow cloud.

It wafted over me, and while I coughed, the floor kept lowering toward the alligator pit. I still wasn't worried, though. I had six feet before I was gator chow and eight before the lasers hit.

"Fursona, hurry!" I screamed, and if a bit of panic got through, sorry. It wasn't my fault, though. Five and seven. Four and five and a half. Three and—

The floor stopped with a horrible screeching sound. I'd been lowered too far; I couldn't see the battle between Fursona and Sister Sly anymore. And I wasn't free from the chair, but at least it looked like I'd be late for my date with the Florida Maneaters. Where had Sister Sly even sourced those?

The fighting raged, and then, after an eternity of sitting there, twiddling my thumbs and staring at the camera drone while wondering how far my villainous breakdown had progressed, the chair slowly started to rise. Fursona's eagle head poked over the edge. "Hi, Understudy. Having some trouble there?"

"Yeah! Get me out of here, Fursona."

"One second. She's still up, she just dashed into a secret room after I kicked her ass." Fursona fiddled with the remote, and eventually, the armrest cuffs holding me in place released.

I transformed immediately, shifting into Understudy. "Let's go get her. She's a Genius, so we can't let her regroup!"

"On it," Fursona said. "She went that way."

We headed into the passage in the church's wall, which led to an enclosed garden area. Either Sister Sly had let it go feral, or it hadn't been taken care of the whole time the building was abandoned, because the trees needed trimming, the grass had grown almost knee-high, and weeds choked the sidewalk around a cracked but still running fountain.

"Think she's in this mess?" I asked.

Fursona shrugged. "Probably. If not, she's slipped through a different door."

A bomb appeared out of thin air, detonating with a familiar hiss and vomiting sulfur clouds into the courtyard. Fursona jumped one way and I leaped the other, then raised my wand. But other than swirling yellow smoke, I couldn't see anything.

Then a second bomb went off, and the sulfur burst into flames that disappeared almost as quickly as they'd erupted!

[HP 6/11]
[**On Fire! -1 HP every 10 seconds for 1 minute**]

I stopped, dropped, and rolled. Across the courtyard, Fursona's feathers were ablaze, the flaming eagle screeching as she took flight and then dove. I couldn't tell what she'd seen, but she hit *something* before she reached the ground, and both she and whatever it was tumbled away in a flurry of feathers and plush.

Had Sister Sly gone invisible?

[HP 5/11]

The fire kept burning. At this rate, it'd take out my superhero damage buffer before it stopped, and the elementary school stop/drop/roll technique had failed! I watched Fursona and the invisible fox-nun grapple with each other, lining up a shot and ignoring the fire for now. Then, when I was *pretty* sure I wouldn't hit Fursona, I yelled, "Duck! [**Bit-Part Barrage**]!" and spun in the air.

The beams sliced across the battlefield, making contact with *something* as Fursona flapped her burning wings and gained a few feet of altitude, putting her out of my line of fire.

[**Dramatic Damage! +X Drama Points**]

Plus X? I'd never seen that before. Then again, I'd never attacked an invisible enemy. As the flames spread across my Costume, I used [**Quick-Time Change**] and [**I-Frame Transform**] to dodge the damage, doing the Itsy Bitsy Spider. The whole courtyard was on fire—weeds burned, smoldering leaves blew in the hot wind, and it was only a matter of time before the church went up in smoke.

[**Flashy Fitting-Room! +1 Flamboyance Point**]
[**Steel Yourself! +1 Grit Point**]

"Understudy, can you deal with the fire?" Fursona asked.

I *wanted* to combo off, but instead, I nodded. "I've got a few tools for it! You get Sister Sly!"

She nodded, and I felt a pang of jealousy as she flapped into the air. That was it! I wanted to be fighting the villain, making the decisions—doing things that *mattered*. Not putting out fires that didn't threaten anyone. Was this important? Yes. Kind of. But no one was in danger, and Fursona needed help, too.

Another bomb went off, and the flames burned higher. I'd said I'd handle them, even if it delayed the fight's ending, so I started up a [**Power-Weaving**] combo. This one, however, was going to be different.

I used [**Virga**], filling the air with rain that healed Fursona, myself, and Sister Sly equally.

[Medic! +2 Cunning Points]
[HP 6/11]
[Doctors Without Borders! -1 Cunning Point]

The rain falling had two other effects. The first was obvious. As it fell, the flames covering the courtyard started to fade. It wasn't much, but it was a start.

The second, though, was unexpected.

An electric discharge filled the center of the room, near where Fursona was circling, and a shocked-looking Sister Sly flickered into view as her camouflage shorted out. Fursona didn't waste any time, and neither did I. The eagle dove on the fox, talons outstretched, and drove her into the ground, tearing her habit. A moment later, I followed up with [**Ride the Lightning**], building up my combo even as the remaining dozen fires fought against the rain and new ones started spreading.

[Electric Lightshow! +1 Flamboyance Point]
[Floating Points: 1 Cunning]
[X=12! +12 Drama Points]

The electricity ripped into the courtyard's center, slamming into the villainess, but she wasn't down yet, and my rain clouds were already fading. Fursona screeched, the sonic attack slamming Sister Sly into the ground yet again. The fox reached into her bag, but dealing with her was Fursona's job, not mine. Like it or not, I was the sidekick on this one.

So, instead of piling into the fight, I used the next part of my combo: [**Thunderhead**]. Clouds filled the courtyard, static building in the sky.

[Pause for Effect! +1 Drama Point]
[Floating Points: 3 Cunning, 1 Flamboyance]

Then, before Sister Sly could disrupt me, I used [**Virga**] again.

[Medic! +2 Cunning Points]
[HP 7/11]
[Doctors Without Borders! -1 Cunning Point]
[Power-Weaving! +6 Cunning, +3 Flamboyance, +1 Drama Point]

This time, the rain felt less like a calm drizzle and more like a hurricane making landfall. It blew in sideways from the storm, dousing the flames almost instantly. The clouds parted a moment before Fursona took off straight up, Sister Sly in her arms, then dove straight down. Bombs went off midair, filling the sky with a column of fire. But Fursona was too fast. She outpaced the blaze, which smoked and faded behind her.

Then they slammed into the grass with a sickening crunch.

I rushed over and tore at Sister Sly's bag, ripping it free from the fox-nun. It tumbled to the ground, covering the courtyard in bombs that, thankfully, didn't detonate. Disarmed and visible, Sister Sly quickly lost to Fursona's punches, screeches, and claws.

And just like that, the Episode was over.

[Episode Finished!]
[Episode: The Root of all 3V1L - PG-13]
[Penalties: N/A]
[Episode Finished! +5 of each Style Point]
[Winner Winner! +2 of each Style Point]
[Role Focus: Flamboyance + Badass - Goal Partially Met! +10 to Flamboyance]
[Alias - Understudy] [Archetype - Magical Girl] [Community Rank - 215/523]
[HP 7/11]
[Styles and Skills]
►Archetype Skill - Transformation Sequence
►Combo Skills - Power-Weaving
►Badass (14)
►Cunning (63) (Skill Roll Available)
►Check the Script 1
►Audition Notes 1
►Drama (38)
►Bit-Part Barrage 2
►Flamboyance (61) (Skill Roll Available)
►Signature Skill - Adaptive Armoire 3
►Stored Costumes: (Rainy Day, Copy Cat, Lab Assistant Panic)
►Solar Wing 1
►Quick-Time Change 3
►Grit (46)
►I-Frame Transform 3

[50 Cunning Credits Used. Rolling Skill!]
[50 Flamboyance Credits Used. Rolling Skill!]

The Style System's letters spun in the familiar slot machine cadence, text falling slowly into place as my two rolls started materializing. But I didn't have eyes for the process. Instead, I was watching a smoking Fursona talk to the camera drone. And even though I tried to push it down, I couldn't help but think it should have been me.

She waved at me, and I waved back, but I needed to talk this over with her when we got back to the green room. It wasn't a problem yet, but she needed to know how I felt—what I'd figured out about myself.

[Rank-Up! Virga 2: Healing increased on all targets]
[Rank-Up! Ride the Lightning 1: Lightning gains a ranged component, hitting a second target for half damage]

Both rank-ups felt suitable for my second-favorite Costume, though they didn't fundamentally change either power. It felt like I needed skill upgrades to really get power-changing upgrades; otherwise, they just gained a little more firepower or utility. I started walking over to Fursona as the camera drone took off.

"Good job, Understudy. We got her!" Fursona said. Then she yawned loudly enough to be heard over the still falling rain, the wail of sirens, and the still smoldering flames. Maybe right now wasn't the best time to approach things.

Maybe we needed some sleep first.

15

Sleep First

Bee went to sleep fast, but she woke up way too early, and even though she tried to be quiet, I still heard the TV flick on and the far-too-familiar Heroics 101 theme song playing. I dragged myself out of bed, pulled on a robe, and dragged a second into the living room, where Bianca perched on the back of the couch, looking like a goblin person as she stared at the TV, enraptured.

"Put this on, feral girl," I said, tossing the robe at her hard enough to knock her onto the cushions with a surprised squeal. "You're not decent. I don't mind *too* much, but if you're going to perch, get dressed first."

She untangled herself from the robe and pulled it on. Her excitement was contagious, and I sat down next to her to watch as she kicked Sister Sly's butt. "You know, you got a quick win there because she's a planning Genius, not an improvising one."

"So? I still got the win, didn't I? Fursona the headliner!" Bee said, smirking. Then she caught my look, and her face fell. "What?"

"About her? Or about me?"

"You," Bee said. "This was a big break for me, and you should be excited!"

I sighed and sat down next to her. "Babe, I am. I'm really happy for you. But that whole Episode, I kept feeling off. And I realized I don't want to be the sidekick."

"Oh—"

I kept going before I could lose momentum and backtrack. "When I got the **[Casting Call]** for the sidekick role, that bugged me. I've only ever been a sidekick on Episodes with people who outrank me, and it really threw me for a loop that this one was all about you. And then the cameras kept following you, and you did so many cool things, like fighting the Third *V* while I mopped up henches, or saving me from Sister Sly's trap. I bet it felt cool for you, but it felt like a downgrade for me, and that's not what I thought the minor leagues would be."

To my surprise, Bianca didn't get upset. Instead, she took a deep breath. "What *did* you think the minor leagues would be?" Somehow, the question didn't sound condescending like it would have from Rocko, Mindstorm, or anyone but Bianca—and maybe Dr. Ayers.

"Okay, I know I *said* I wanted to save people and play the support role, and I know I *said* I wanted to take it easy in the minor leagues, but I don't think we've got that option. The reality is that we'll get into bigger and bigger fights with 3V1L and the rest of the rogue's gallery."

"And?" Bee asked.

"And my **[Signature Skill]** makes me the obvious go-to as headliner. I can do it all, and I'm not that far behind the more focused heroes." I'd been thinking about this over the summer and again in our Team Composition class. At some point, I wouldn't *need* Fursona. If I could keep the Style Points coming, I'd be able to out-compete everyone, just like Rocko had said before I went to college. Magical Girl Understudy would only be more and more of a headliner as time went on until, eventually, I was the best—if I chose to be.

Or if Rocko pushed me into it.

"And?" Bianca asked again, brow wrinkling.

I paused. "And what?"

"And what do *you* want?" Bee sighed and shook her head. "Look, if there's anything you should learn from Madame Shockwave, it's that you don't *have* to be what the studios want. You can choose to walk away, and if you can choose that, you can choose anything. So what do you want?"

What did I want? If I could do anything, what would make me feel the most like a hero? I paused, jaw dropping. "You're *psychologying* me!"

"Guilty! Look, I don't get what you're upset about, Annie." Bee grinned sheepishly. "We're partners, right? I think that sometimes, the Style System's going to decide an Episode's all about me, and that's okay, because a lot of the time, it's about you. Besides, remember how you handed control over last semester, when Vigilant Vow took Tails? You did that without feeling weird about it."

"I don't feel weird about it. I just—"

"Liar," Bee said. "I could tell something was off last night. You seemed grumpy, and you were way too happy to get an early night's sleep. That's not like you, Annie. So you're upset because what? You don't want to be a sidekick?"

"Kind of? Maybe? Babe, I'm not sure. Being at full power and playing second fiddle just felt funny. And then you kept making choices that put you in front of the drones."

"Okay. Let's step back, because we need to answer an important question. If you can't answer it, none of the rest of this matters, Annie," Bee said. "What kind of superhero do you want to be? You could be Golden Goose or Stella-Lunar, sure. Or you could be Magical Girl Res-Cute or Tele-Portal. Honestly, I'm jealous. I wish I had half that many choices."

"You do? Do you not like Fursona?"

Bee laughed. "I love Fursona. But Annie, I've got ambitions, too."

Shit. I'd built this amazing fantasy around just hanging out in the minor leagues, but Fursona *would* want more. She'd always been competitive, and she wouldn't be content to sit still—even if she'd said she would be last semester when the Vigilant Vow situation had gotten bad. "You want to be number one, huh?"

"What? No. I want to be as high as possible without losing sight of what matters. I want to keep my friends outside of superhero work, be able to see my family when I want to, and be happy, but I also want to win, and that means moving up the Community Ranks. It means I won't be a sidekick forever, Annie," Bee said. "Shit, I'll say it again. It means I don't want to be a sidekick *now*. I want to be partners. What do *you* want?"

"I want to do everything," I said.

"Great. That includes sidekick work, support hero, and being focused on saving people, *not* fighting villains. That means I get to headline sometimes," Bee said.

"Just like that, huh?" I said, grinning. It really *was* that easy, wasn't it? I could still be the headliner sometimes—with my power, maybe even *most* of the time— but sometimes, the Episode *would* be about Fursona, and that was fine. Why hadn't I been comfortable with that? The more I thought about it, the more I realized why.

It wasn't that I wanted to dominate our team's Episodes. It wasn't even that I didn't trust Fursona to nail the role. It was just that I'd never *thought* about any of this before. "I'm sorry, Bee. I was being stupid."

"I forgive you, and you kind of were, but not really. Right now, in Rocko's eyes, you're the headliner, and I'm the sidekick. That was fine for the first year when I was learning, but let's talk about how things can change. We could run a duo with the same dynamics as The Triad."

"What do you mean? Tele-Portal's clearly the sidekick in The Triad."

"No, she's not. She's really not. If anything, she's the leader. She's playing to her strengths, but The Triad doesn't run a sidekick dynamic, and you know it. Bud Lightbeam covers the team's ranged, flight, and face roles. Underdelver acts as a heavy melee fighter and problem-solver. And Tele-Portal's entire powerset is built around supporting other heroes, but that doesn't make her a sidekick. That makes her oil for the team's gears. She can operate independently, but when they're on the battlefield, she's not fighting henches while the others go after the villain. She's right there with them. In fact, Lightbeam usually goes for the henches."

Bianca had once again done her homework. "Alright. She's not a sidekick by the definition you're setting up. How does that fit in with us?"

"Well, I fill a melee role as Roo-sona. That Costume's tanky and hits hard. And I can do melee and scouting/flight as Eagle-sona. What do you bring?"

"Everything."

"Yeah, maybe you should work toward a full support Costume?" Bee asked, standing and stretching. Her shoulders popped loudly. "You do everything, but if you run that, it'd let you excel at the role and let me shine as a headliner sometimes.

It'd also give us some seriously needed flexibility on Investigative Episodes and when we have Extras in play."

I nodded. "I'll work on it, partner."

"Thank you." Bee unpaused the TV, and the on-screen Eagle Slam finally happened. The impact was somehow even more bone-jarring on the screen than in person. Had Rocko added a little extra pop to it?

Either way, Bianca was thrilled. "Did you see that?!"

"Yes. Once when it happened and again just now. You hit her pretty hard." I pulled her back onto the couch, where she bounced up and down on the cushions.

Okay. Bianca was serious about this. I didn't necessarily *like* change, but this one was happening whether I wanted it or not, so I pushed down my jealousy as she signed off with, "The Talons of Justice have a long reach!" on the screen. Then I took the remote from her.

"Hey! I wasn't done with that!"

"Yes, you were. Rocko's got the master recordings, so if you want to watch them over and over, feel free, but it's breakfast time—and time to check our messages from yesterday."

"Fine." Bee pouted, and I quickly poked her in the side, making her squeal again.

Then I kissed her forehead. "Go take a shower. I'll have Ramsey Fieri whip up something nice."

She nodded and stood up, then walked to the bathroom, shedding the robe as she went.

"And put some clothes on!" I shouted at her retreating but cute butt as I transformed into the Magical Girl chef.

A much more decent, apple-smelling Bianca finished her ham and cheese omelet and leaned back in her chair as I took my last bite. I was still wearing my robe, but it was a Sunday morning, and I deserved to relax after cooking breakfast. So I sat in my chair, sipping coffee, checking my emails, and trying to figure out how to manage Bianca's newfound desire to lead Episodes.

In between a pair of fan emails—how had they gotten my superhero address, anyway?—I found one from Sara-N-Dipity.

Subject: TUSSA Elections
Magical Girl Understudy,
I'm 93% sure this email finds you well.
I know you're a Springlock loyalist, and I respect your right to vote how you'd like to, but I want to mention the reality of our powers and how they work. Springlock is a Bruiser/ Speedster hybrid. She's a fighter, not a thinker or planner. That worked well when Ikenga was president because he could see possible futures and maneuver the team into winning.

All probability points to his prediction of Power Wars coming true soon, and we'll need a strong leader—like Springlock. But even more important, we'll need a leader who can guide TUSSA through the coming storm. I believe I can be that leader in a way that Springlock can't. In fact, my powers are uniquely suited to the job.

Please consider changing your vote. We're meeting in a couple of weeks to figure out our roles, and it'd mean a lot to me if you chose correctly. That being said, I'm not using my powers to manipulate the election—but I could.

But I won't.

Thanks,

Sara-N-Dipity

"Did you get an email from Sara?" I asked Bianca.

"No." She looked over my shoulder. "She must think I'm a swing vote already, but not enough to get the win. She needs you, Annie. What are you going to do?"

I thought it over for a moment. "I'm going to do nothing. Springlock's my friend, and Sara didn't pick me when I needed her support. I'm not sure I can forgive that, but I'll keep an open mind until it's time to vote. She really might be the stronger candidate, but Springlock's so cool!" I returned to my emails.

Subject: Tottergarten and Babysitting Fees

Magical Girl Understudy,

This is a courtesy reminder that your repayment for watching your baby, [Cash], on the night of [April 22, 2042] is due this month. Please have your payment of [One Episode] in by [September 31, 2042] to avoid late fees.

Mrs. N

Tottergarten Day Care

"We Do a Super Job with Your Kids!"

"Time's up, Fursona. We've gotta do the Tottergarten job." I rubbed my eyes. Those kids gave me a headache, but at least it wouldn't be *hard* work. In fact, it'd mostly be interacting with the villains, giving moral lessons, and letting the Playpen Patrol use their powers in a safe, forgiving environment—which The Narrator was an expert at providing.

"Yep. It'll be . . . something . . . to see Kaiju Kid again. I wonder if she's grown out of her sugar problems."

"Probably not." I started typing up a response. "How about the twenty-fifth?" That'd give us all week to find an Episode that'll make Rocko happy."

"Sure," Bianca said. She stood up and shuttled our plates to the sink while I sent the email. The timing couldn't have been better.

PART THREE

16

Election Day

WEDNESDAY, SEPTEMBER 24

The TUSSA Cave was packed. The entire club had gathered, along with Dr. Tennyson, who was overseeing the club elections. That meant, for the first time, that I had time to meet with Tractor-Beam-Girl near the bar, where she sipped on something that Hephaestus had made. I hoped it was virgin, with the professor standing just ten feet away; neither Tractor-Beam-Girl nor I were old enough to drink—legally.

Not that that'd usually stop Hephaestus, but with faculty right there, it might be different.

Tractor-Beam-Girl was telling me about her time in Yorkston, where she'd been part of a youth supers group that was setting her on the right track for a quick rank-up. Her official superhero name was Vicegrip, but trying not to think of her as Tractor-Beam-Girl was impossible, especially when she refused to listen to older, wiser superheroes like me. Still, there was the hope that I'd be able to talk her down from her foolish ambitions, make her not jump Flare the next time she saw him, or *something*.

Still, she was about the most frustrating super I'd ever talked to. Apparently, her parents were big shots, too, if not in the super world, then in Yorkston's business circle. That explained so much. She wouldn't say who they were; no one said anything about their unpowered parents. It was too risky to let others know. That's how you lost your secret identity. But they were, apparently, involved in Yorkston politics, or MIRACLE planning, or leading the resistance against the New Gotham Accords. Or something like that. I had her on partial ignore, just nodding and saying "Yeah," when she paused.

It was a relief when Dr. Tennyson stood up, a glass in hand, and tapped a mic a few times.

"Okay, you all know your two candidates for Tokyexico University Student Superhero Society president. On the right is Springlock, with Milo interpreting. On the left is Sara-N-Dipity. They're going to give a quick speech, throw out their ideas for the club, and take things from there. Springlock, you're up first."

Springlock's fingers flew, and Milo started interpreting a second later. "Hi, I'm Springlock. I was vice president under Ikenga last year, and I've got a great idea of how TUSSA operates. Based on our recent performance in the Orientation Episode, we've got a major advantage against either a Tearjerker- or Iron-Fist-led Student Supervillain Society. Now's the time to press that advantage.

"So, I'm proposing we push the SSS hard this semester and see if we can make the TU campus safer for everyone. If we pressure them right from the get-go, we can force their operations into the Poudre districts, where they'll be competing with 3V1L. That'll force them to fight each other and take pressure off us. We can make it happen before finals this semester and avoid a result like last fall semester.

"Keeping our campus safe is the most important thing we can do, and that's what a Springlock-led TUSSA would be about. Thanks," Springlock finished, smiling in her blue catsuit.

Dr. Tennyson nodded as the assembled TUSSA heroes clapped. I thought it was a good speech, but something was missing. It took me a minute to realize what it was; the Third Power War was looming in our future, and she hadn't mentioned it once. Was she trying to run a business-as-usual campaign? Or did she know something we didn't? Either way, it felt like a big omission.

And it was one that Sara-N-Dipity capitalized on.

"I'm Sara-N-Dipity. Many of you think my power is luck, but it's not. It's probability manipulation. I've been running the numbers, and they keep coming out the same way. We're imminently due for the Third Power War. It's going to be messy, it's going to be violent, and we'll need insightful leadership to get through it intact. I can offer that leadership.

"With my plan, TUSSA will ignore the SSS completely. They're a spent force without Monologue's guidance, and we're in a position of power. If they choose to start something on campus, we'll deal with it, but we're not waging a full-blown war. Instead, I think there's an 80% likelihood that we'll be able to thread the needle between the warring villain factions and come out the other side completely intact.

"We'll do this by allying ourselves with the professors, working with off-campus super-groups like the Mutual Assistance League—or what's left of it—and The Triad, and cooperating with the Council of Heroes. I'll also reach out to the campus APPEAL club and try to come to an understanding with them for the duration, but that's got a 12% chance of success no matter how I slice it." She shook her head.

"My plan allows high-league students to participate in the Power War as needed, moves the bulk of the fighting off-campus, and keeps students on campus safe. Through teamwork comes strength."

More applause echoed through the room, but I didn't join in. Springlock was my friend. She and I had been through some things last fall, and when I'd needed help, she and Milo had been there for me at Cherry Creek High. But honestly, Sara's plan felt more like . . . well, a plan.

Then she kept talking. The slogan wasn't the end? "I've also just decided that if I'm elected president, I'll ask Springlock to be my vice president. She's not wrong in anything she's said tonight, and I think we can work together to meet both of our goals. She also has valuable experience in-office, and I want to rely on that as your TUSSA president."

"Thank you, Sara," Dr. Tennyson said. He clapped his hands. "Okay, heroes. You have fifteen minutes to get your ballots in. I'm expecting a tight race here, so every vote will count. Get your ballots from me, and return them to me when you're done. No voter fraud on my watch. And go!"

As I waited in line for my ballot, I struggled even more with who to vote for. Springlock's plan felt solid for a peacetime president, but I couldn't shake the feeling that Sara's would actually work if the Third Power War started tomorrow. What it really came down to was whether I thought the next Power War was *that* imminent. If Springlock had three months to plan and get ready, she'd be fine. TUSSA would be fine. Heck, TU itself would be fine.

But if not—if the Third Power War *did* start tomorrow—Sara's plan was probably stronger. She'd thought about more variables, and she was right. The SSS was a spent force. They'd lost more with Monologue than we had with Ikenga, and unless their new students were phenomenal, TUSSA could handle them with no problems. They also wouldn't be more than a bump in the road for a resurgent 3V1L.

I looked at my ballot. Springlock and Sara-N-Dipity's names were bolded, with little checkboxes next to them. I bubbled in a box, folded my ballot in half, and turned it in to Dr. Tennyson.

Springlock smiled at me.

But so, oddly enough, did Sara.

Subject: TUSSA Election Results

TUSSA Superheroes,

I'm proud to announce the results of the TUSSA elections.

Springlock - 46%, 11 votes

Sara-N-Dipity - 54%, 13 votes

With these results, Sara-N-Dipity will be president for the 2042–2043 year, with an option to continue as president next year should she continue taking classes at Tokyexico University. Springlock will be the vice president.

Expect a TUSSA meeting next week to go over priorities, policy, and formally take oaths of office.

Thanks,

Dr. Tennyson

I sat on my bed, Bianca curled up in a ball with her head on my leg. As I looked at the results, a pit grew in the bottom of my stomach. Sara had won. I honestly hadn't expected it, and the email below it in my inbox gave me an even worse stomachache.

Subject: Personal Thank-You
Magical Girl Understudy,
I used my power postvoting, and you were the most likely swing vote. I want to thank you for your trust and support. I assure you that I won't forget that you set aside my choice of sidekicks last year to make the best choice for the Tokyexico University Student Superhero Association.

I'd like to meet with you and Fursona in the next week or so to discuss my vision for your roles in TUSSA's new plan and offer you a thank-you gift for your trust and support.
Thanks,
Sara-N-Dipity
TUSSA President-Elect

Bianca lifted her head from where it was resting on my lap, looking at me seriously. "You stiffened up. Are you okay? Did I do something wrong?"

"What could you have done wrong? You're just lying there, playing on your phone, just like me," I replied. Then I took a deep breath. "No, I'm fine. Sara-N-Dipity won."

"Yeah, I figured she might. She has a better plan than Springlock, and she didn't blow off Springlock's possible help, either. Honestly, I'm surprised she didn't win by more, but then again, Springlock is *hot*. That probably swayed a few votes right there. It almost did mine." Bee wiggled up next to me.

I handed her the phone. "How did she *know*?"

Bianca read Sara's email, jaw dropping. "Wow, you're the traitor! Ha! This is great. I'm not going to tell Springlock, but you probably should. She really wanted this win, and you took a tie from her. Why'd you do it?"

"Honestly?" I paused, and Bee nodded. "Super-counseling. Dr. Ayers seemed to think the Power War was coming, and Ikenga thought so, too. If it does, Sara has a much better plan, and, whether or not I liked her, that was more important."

"So we're going to meet her, right?"

"Yes." I shut off my phone. "But I'm not worried about when. I've got a lot of other things on my mind."

"Oh? Like what?" Bianca batted her eyelashes at me, and I burst out laughing. She flushed and sat up. "Hey! Rude!"

"Oh relax. You know I've always got you on my mind. But right now, it's honestly the Tottergarten Episode tomorrow. You know, we've seen a bunch of the Anti-Nap League, but I don't think we've ever seen Felicia Fire."

"You mean Mindstorm?" Bianca asked. She looked slightly offended that I hadn't taken her bait, but she lay back down. "We saw her once, actually. I'm pretty sure she was The Present Pilferer in 'The Grinch's Christmas.'"

"Yeah, true. Okay, we haven't dealt with Felicia Fire for real, though, and we know she's our professor undercover. How are we going to deal with that?" I asked.

"Simple. We take revenge!" Bee laughed in an almost maniacal way. When she finally calmed down and flopped onto the bed beside me, she continued, "Seriously, though, this is a chance for us to get even with her for kicking our asses during the make-up assignment last year. All we have to do is figure out how to pin her down by herself while she's running whatever the Felicia Fire powerset is, and we can take her. Plus, with the kids around, we can't actually lose—The Narrator won't let us. It's the perfect crime."

"True." I pulled her in for a hug, then ran a thumb across her cheek. She pushed my hand away, then went in for a kiss before I could stop her, so I ducked my head, giving her a face full of hair and forehead. "Blech!"

I laughed and rolled over. "Let's shelf this Tottergarten conversation, Bee. Neither of us really wants it right now." Then, I stood up and pulled off my top. Bianca rolled off the other side and started undressing, too, and I couldn't help but sneak a look. She really was gorgeous in an athletic, firm way.

And for the rest of the night, I didn't think about Power Wars, the TUSSA election, or the Playpen Patrol.

17

The Playpen Patrol

THURSDAY, SEPTEMBER 25

Mindstorm was on fire.

So was the Tottergarten playground as she stood atop a slide, dressed like Felicia Fire in her smoke-gray and red Costume. We'd been teaching a lesson on fire safety, so naturally, Mindstorm's retired persona was the only choice for a villain. At the moment, she was lighting the playground on fire with jets of flame that shot from her hands.

This had to be a safety violation. Or twenty.

The Narrator would fix it all up when she was done, and the kids knew they'd be totally fine, so in a way, managing them was harder than dealing with the villain herself. Felicia had filled the entire playground with low-hanging smog, pinning us close to the ground where, according to Milkbar, the "good air" was. The trouble was that The Cloud wanted to fly, and I had his leash. I had to keep dragging him down, and every time I did, Milkbar grabbed my hand and pulled me back into an almost painful crouch.

To make matters worse, Felicia Fire kept throwing illusory fireballs across the sandbox at us, and Fursona had her hands full with Kaiju Kid and Kid Zoomies, who were both trying to *catch* the darned things. The fact that they were illusory was the only reason I hadn't freaked out.

Still, it was time to rain on Mindstorm's parade! "[**Virga**]," I said, waving my blue wand. The Rainy Day outfit was a massive hit with The Cloud, though he still wouldn't call me anything but Understuffy. I'd also learned in "The Root of All 3V1L" that it countered fire pretty well, and against G-rated flames, I wouldn't even have to combo.

[**Medic! +7 Cunning Points**]
[HP 8/12]
[**Doctors Without Borders! -4 Cunning Points**]

The rain cascaded down, punching through the smoke and stifling the flames, but just as it did, Magical Girl Honeycomb screamed theatrically. A fireball had caught her, and her gossamer skirt and wings were engulfed in flames.

"What do I do?!" she shouted, looking back and forth between the kids.

"Stop! Drop! And roll!" the Playpen Patrol shouted back, almost in unison, with Kaiju Kid a beat behind the rest. Honeycomb did it, and the flames went out after just a moment, but in the chaos of five preschoolers swarming toward the superhero to make sure she was okay, Felicia Fire had vanished.

"Ugh, she got away again," Honeycomb said. She looked at her somewhat charred Costume, crestfallen.

Mindstorm had been running circles around us all Episode, making small fires and forcing half a dozen lessons on handling different blazes. Almost all of them ended with "And always get an adult until you're a little-league hero. Then you can handle them yourself." None of us wanted Kid Zoomies or Outlet trying to stop a house fire on their own, although The Cloud had learned a water gun attack where he sprayed it out of his nose. It was super gross but really effective at putting out fires.

The two of us cleaned up the playground, pushing back the illusory fires until they weren't a "threat" to anyone. Then we joined up with Honeycomb, who'd rallied the Playpen Patrol and was giving a lesson about touching hot stuff and why you shouldn't do it. While she taught the kids how to use the back of their hands to feel hot things by holding them *near*, but not *on*, the object, I leaned toward Fursona. "We should scout stuff out."

"Think so? But what about the kids?"

"Well, the kids are all busy, and these lessons usually take two to three minutes, which is long enough for Minds—er, Felicia Fire—to get set up for her next gimmick. And to be honest, I'm not sure how much longer this one has to go. It seems way less engaging than the 'How Bees Work' or 'Why We Share at Christmas' lessons Honeycomb's done in the past." I gestured at the bee-themed Magical Girl, who kept having to stop to redirect Kaiju Kid back to the group, all while wrestling to keep Kid Zoomies pinned down.

Fursona nodded. "Okay, fair. So you think we scout it out and wrap up the Episode?"

"Yeah, exactly."

She stood up from her crouch, bounced on her heels—she was a kangaroo again for this one—and started heading for the door to the building. "Okay, we'll go fast, and we won't engage with Felicia Fire without the kids. I've got a feeling she's holding back."

"Agreed." I followed her to the door, and we slipped inside.

The whole building smelled like smoke; Mindstorm was a top-tier illusionist, in addition to her mind control gimmick, and she'd made it so real I'd thought I was back in the church—or the burning bank back in Riverside. But as I rubbed my finger through the soot, I could feel the intact wooden walls and tile floors. It wasn't real. None of it was real.

"Let's check the offices," I said.

"Sure, why not? Think The Narrator is in there with them?"

"Probably. They're having a quick coffee break or something."

The camera drone bobbed along behind me as we walked down the hallway and opened the door. Sure enough, The Narrator sat at her desk with not one member, or even two, but the entire Anti-Nap League assembled around it. Felicia Fire said, "So yeah, we're all resigning, effective as soon as this Episode's over. We know that's . . . inconvenient for you, and that you could make us finish out our years, but . . . I don't think you . . ."

She trailed off as a half dozen supervillains and The Narrator turned to look at us. The metapowered superhero blinked once, then looked at the assembled villains. "We'll finish this conversation later—after the Episode. It's time for the final fight, correct?"

"Yes," Felicia Fire said, gritting her teeth. "We'll go get ready. You two should get back to the kids. We've got a doozy coming their way for our last show. I got a real fire truck for them to fight me on."

I nodded, gulping as the Anti-Nap League stared me down. "Got it. See you there."

"Wait a moment," The Narrator said. "I'll be seeing you two after the Episode. Please wait out in the hall until I'm done with the League. I'll need a favor."

The Narrator needed a favor? The hands-down most high-potential super in the world, who'd chosen to run a day care instead of fighting, needed something from us other than entertaining her swarm of toddlers? For a moment, I couldn't believe it. Then, I slowly nodded and retreated from the office. Something was happening— something big, if the entire Anti-Nap League had resigned the same day. So, if The Narrator needed something, and she couldn't rely on her power or the half dozen retired villains to do it, the least we could do was hear her out.

The lesson on how to tell if something was hot had just finished up, and I grabbed The Cloud and pointed at the parking lot. "Do you like fire engines?" I asked and immediately regretted it.

"Fire truck! Fire truck!"

"I wanna use the hose!"

"Can we run the sirens really loud?"

The Playpen Patrol went nuts. They rushed the door, with Fursona, Honeycomb, and me all trying to contain the rush. We failed when Milkbar opened a gap in our line big enough for Kid Zoomies to rush through, and by the time we caught up, the entire Patrol was at the front door, staring out the window.

I grinned despite myself. The Anti-Nap League had been busy; The Narrator was going to miss them.

They'd fenced off the whole parking lot in orange construction fencing, with flashing barrels and everything. Then they'd covered *that* with police line tape to complete the fire scene illusion. Two fire hydrants leaked water into the hot afternoon air, and in the center, manned by Felicia Fire and Jungle Jim, was a brand new Tokyexico Fire Department fire truck.

It glowed red in the sun, and its lights flashed. Then, over the loudspeaker, came Felicia Fire's voice. "Attention, Playpen Patrol! It's time to turn up the heat!"

The doors jerked open, and we rushed onto the asphalt—which someone had padded. The Anti-Nap League really thought of everything! Kid Zoomies and Milkbar went straight for the truck, and a moment later, so did Outlet, hitting it with a burst of static that made its siren *WHOOOP!* for a moment.

Then, before The Cloud and I could react, Mister Twi—no, Pranky Jones—leaped from behind the door, throwing a grenade right at us. It exploded, filling the air with reddish-black smoke. "It's time to get pranky!"

[HP 7/12]

"[**Starlance**]!" I shouted. At the exact same time, The Cloud blew water from his nose like a whale spouting. The water cut through the smoke, splashing harmlessly across Pranky Jones's suit, but my bolt of starlight slammed into him a moment later, and that wasn't harmless—not at all. Even a major-league villain couldn't ignore it, and he rocked to the side from the impact.

[**Dramatic Damage! +1 Drama Point**]

We were on the scoreboard, and Pranky Jones was on the run! He threw a few traps, but The Cloud hovered up and down, avoiding them as we chased the villain down. A gust of wind from The Cloud smashed into him, pushing him against the orange construction fencing. A moment later, my [**Bit-Part Barrage**] punched through his supervillain damage, the first beam pinning him down as more and more zipped from my wand to him.

[**Dramatic Damage! +5 Drama Points**]

I landed, half expecting him to surrender, only to catch a fully pressurized burst of water to the face. It shoved me across the battlefield and into the Tottergarten building's walls. I watched as, a moment later, the water beam cut into the air, aiming for a desperately flapping Honeycomb, but before she could finish bringing its firepower—or waterpower?—to bear, Felicia Fire found herself attacked by Milkbar and Kid Zoomies.

The hose started wavering, then thrashing around on the ground as she dropped it. Fursona leaped on it, grappled it under control, and aimed it—but not toward the truck or the villains. Instead, she hosed down The Cloud.

He redirected the water, sending a torrential downpour at Felicia Fire and Jungle Jim.

"And then the Episode was over!" The Narrator's voice echoed from the intercom. "The Playpen Patrol went to take a nap, and the Anti-Nap League, Honeycomb, and guest stars reported to the Tottergarten office."

[Episode Finished!]
[Episode: On Fire - G]
[Penalties: N/A]
[Episode Finished! +3 of each Style Point]
[Call it a Draw! +1 of each Style Point]
[Role Focus: Cunning + Flamboyance - Goal Unmet]
[Alias - Understudy] [Archetype - Magical Girl] [Community Rank - 215/523]
[HP 7/12]
[Styles and Skills]
►Archetype Skill - Transformation Sequence
►Combo Skills - Power-Weaving
►Badass (23)
►Cunning (42)
►Check the Script 1
►Audition Notes 1
►Drama (49)
►Bit-Part Barrage 2
►Flamboyance (30)
►Signature Skill - Adaptive Armoire 3
►Stored Costumes: (Rainy Day, Copy Cat, Lab Assistant Panic)
►Solar Wing 1
►Quick-Time Change 3
►Grit (53) (Skill Roll Available)
►I-Frame Transform 3

As I, following The Narrator's script, walked through Tottergarten's main room and watched the Playpen Patrol fall asleep, I rolled my skill. It was the only thing I could do, and I had mixed feelings about the Episode's ending. On the one hand, it was over, and G-rated Episodes were my least favorite. But on the other hand, I'd wanted to check out the fire truck.

[50 Grit Credits Used. Rolling Skill!]
[New Skill! Stage Presence: Inspire your allies to more incredible heroics through your sacrifice. After taking damage, turn that injury into a temporary group buff]

What a strange skill; it didn't offer any sort of defense or healing; as a Grit power, it worked a lot differently than anything I'd seen before. In fact, the closest power

I'd seen to it was [**Hometown Heroine**], but that buffed me. This seemed reasonably strong for Fursona if I could develop a decent support build.

The Narrator's control broke suddenly about halfway down the hall toward her office. The villains were already inside, so for a moment, I thought that was why. But then my Style System popped up a message that sent a shiver down my spine.

[All Episodes Canceled. New Episodes Initiated]
[Welcome to the Third Power War]

18

Third Power War

I stared at The Narrator's door, hoping I'd misread, but the Style System's words were unmistakable. I regretted casually thinking about Power Wars yesterday; it wasn't rational, but I couldn't help but think my decision to vote for Sara-N-Dipity because "if Power Wars started tomorrow, she'd be a better leader" had made it happen.

I shivered, squeezing my eyes shut as Fursona and I waited in the hall. That wasn't realistic; according to the Ilneats and what I'd seen from old Power War episodes, the System declared a Power War when villainous activity across the world reached certain thresholds. The System created slightly more villains than heroes, in general, so over time, the number of villains got to be too much. When that happened . . .

They started fighting for space.

Not just against heroes, either. The 3V1L vs. Sister Sly conflict, or battles between two supervillains for the best lairs in the richest, least-patrolled districts—Power Wars had always been about that before. And if the villains wanted to fight each other, it'd be easy to let them, except for one problem. Extras . . . no, people . . . lived in the places they wanted to fight over.

So, inevitably, heroes would get involved, and in a Power War, it wouldn't always be a measured, thought-out response. It'd be whichever superhero or team happened to be closest and able to handle it. Then, the villain would start squawking for backup, and one of their allies or bosses would come help. And from there? Escalation on both sides. No one had figured out a way to avoid that, either. If the villains escalated, the heroes lost unless they called in bigger and bigger heroes.

The door to The Narrator's office opened, and the six members of the Anti-Nap League filed by. Jungle Jim nodded as the door shut behind him. "Good luck, kid. You're gonna need it this time around."

I didn't ask him what he meant. The Narrator opened the door a moment later, gesturing at us to come in. The three of us sat at the table while The Narrator read something on her computer. She sighed, clicked a few times, and turned to us, coffee in her hand. "Girls, I've got a problem. *You* have a problem. But you need to under-stand why it's a problem, so background."

The Narrator laughed bitterly. "I've been around for all the Power Wars. All of them. And every time, my day care's the biggest target in Tokyexico. Nothing ever gets within a hundred yards, and the kids are totally safe here—I made arrangements with their parents, and I'll bring them home safely once we know the lay of the land. So, I can offer you three the same protection. You stay here until things calm down from the initial surge, and in return, you keep the kids entertained.

"But that's not the option I need you to take. Honeycomb, I know you need to get home. You've got homework, and your apartment's right between the University and the Poudre districts. Is there anything that'd make your building a target?"

Honeycomb shook her head, but she looked pale. "No? I don't think so? It's just an apartment building. We've never seen a superhero there unless you count me."

"Okay, the safest place for you is at home, in your secret identity, until we figure out where Tokyexico stands. Understudy, Fursona, your debt to Tottergarten's paid in full for the 'On Fire' Episode." The Narrator slid a piece of paper across the table. "Sign here, and we'll call it even. But if you could return Honeycomb to her apart-ment, I'd greatly appreciate it."

"You can't just Narrate her there?" Fursona asked.

The Narrator shook her head. "No. My power only affects what I can see, hear, or otherwise sense."

"Right. Okay. Yeah, we'll get her home," I said. The city wasn't safe, and we'd be less likely to get jumped by McHammer or Lord Destructo as a group of three. Not *much* less likely, but a little. Then I paused, but The Narrator's experience was too much *not* to ask. "Do you know anything about Power Wars that might help us?"

"Yes. The conditions for Episodes change. You'll see more must-participate Episodes, a lot more pickup heroes and villains piling into every possible fight, and multi-Episode layers where you might be in a little-league Episode and a major-league one runs over yours. If that happens, your best bet is to abandon the lower-league Episode, avoid the bigger one, and wait for the top-tier heroes to finish the fight. If they win, they'll clear out the lower-league stuff after."

She smiled sadly. "That'll get you to Honeycomb's apartment, but in the longer term, you'll want to figure out a role you can fill for the Council of Heroes, the Mutual Assistance League, or your TUSSA friends. You'll have the most personal success if you can get in with a team and allow them to help you."

"Hopefully Sara's got a plan," I said. The Council of Heroes probably didn't need a couple of starting minor-leaguers; the battle between 3V1L and the Mutual Assistance League meant they were a spent force, and that left . . . TUSSA or possibly The Triad. Of the two, TUSSA felt like the best option; they'd be local, fighting for places and things I cared about, and it'd be a chance to sway APPEAL's mind—and Su-Bin's as well. But I'd worked well with Tele-Portal before. It'd be a tough choice.

The Narrator cleared her throat. "Tottergarten will owe you one. Now hurry before it gets bad."

As Fursona, Magical Girl Honeycomb, and I stepped out onto the street, though, it didn't seem that bad. In fact, it didn't seem any worse than usual. Fursona couldn't fly as Roo-sona, and Honeycomb couldn't keep up with me on my board or with **[Solar Wing]**, so we walked the eight blocks to her apartment. That left us with a shockingly quiet street, no supers in sight, and no Casting Calls.

And also with a lot of time to talk. Awkwardly.

"So, you're a senior now, right? How's school going?" Fursona asked.

"It's fine. Still on track to be valedictorian, and I'm working on my applications for TU and a few other schools, so I might be your classmate next year!" Honeycomb looked thrilled, and I shot Fursona a look behind the bee-themed girl's back—one that said *don't push it*. The reality was that, with the associate's program, we might not be seeing her on campus at all.

Luckily, she got the hint. "That's exciting! And Jumper?"

"Oh, she's causing problems, but it's not my problem anymore. Ed fired me. Luckily, The Narrator's producer picked me up, so now I'm a part-time employee at Tottergarten instead of a volunteer. It's great! You two have big goals in the minor leagues and even higher, but I think G-rated Episodes are my thing."

"Great," I said, then paused. Was this the right time to ask if she'd gotten any weird texts over the summer? Screw it, it was. "Hey, has a super named Vigilant Vow talked to you about, uh, Magical Girl stuff? I gave him your number because he really needed a role model, and you were perfect for him."

"Vigilant Vow? Doesn't ring a bell," Honeycomb said. She frowned. "What's with him?"

"He needs help. His power's got an amazingly high ceiling, but he can't use it, so he's got a floor that's . . . probably lower than yours, no offense," I said.

"None taken. I accept my power's strengths and drawbacks with grace and serenity!"

"Ha! Glad to hear that. I was hoping he'd learn how to be happy with his powers in low-league situations from you, but if he hasn't texted or called you yet . . ." I trailed off.

"This was the villain in your Heroics 101 season finale last year, huh? He seemed like a real piece of work."

"Yeah, but I don't think it was his fault. I gave him an opportunity for redemption, and I was hoping he'd take it, but maybe he's decided to fall into obscurity instead, or retire." I trailed off. Honestly, retiring like my mom wasn't a bad ending for someone Cartman had gotten a hold of, and maybe it'd be for the best if Vigilant Vow just . . . disappeared. I'd tried, and maybe I'd failed, but I pushed it out of my head. Or at least I tried to.

But it just wouldn't leave me alone. It stuck there, and I stayed quiet as Fursona and Honeycomb chatted about her plans for after she graduated. She wanted to be a surgeon, and the superhero gig was probably getting in the way of that, so her current plan was to stick with Tottergarten until she got into med school, then let Honeycomb retire and focus on her real career. That decision was easier because her powers were so . . . limiting. It felt like the right call for her, though.

I hoped Vigilant Vow would decide to do the right thing. Honeycomb, for all that she was a mess, had really matured in the last year, and she'd be a great rock for the ex-vigilante as he started turning his life around. Hopefully, she'd text me soon with good news about—

[Casting Call]
[Episode: Power War: Summer's End - R]
[Role: A Flame in the Cold! Do you accept the role? (Yes/No)]
[Role Focus: Flamboyance + Drama]

"Shit. You two get that?" I asked, heart pounding. Vigilant Vow's situation fled my thoughts instantly.

"Y-yes," Honeycomb said. "Do I accept?"

"No!" Fursona and I shouted at the same time.

"You don't want anything to do with what's about to happen. How far is your house?" I asked.

"Five more minutes' walk. Are my parents going to be okay? Should I get ready to protect them? What's going on!?" Honeycomb's face was white enough that I could see it between the streetlights. She kept looking from side to side, almost as if Lord Destructo was going to walk out of the shadows any second.

I knew this one wasn't about him, though. And that wasn't good—for me, specifically.

"Fursona, I need you to break off and head for TU. Meet me in the green room as soon as you can. We'll figure out what's happening there." I grabbed Honeycomb, held her, and summoned my sailboard with [Solar Wing]. "I'm taking Honeycomb home the fastest way I can. I'll try to catch up with you once she's safe."

"I can help you, Understudy," Fursona said. She stared at me as I hovered in place, Honeycomb's wings beating in my face.

"Yes, you can. But right now, that help is getting away from here. You can't fly, and we've got to move fast. This is a King Cold Episode, and if I'm right, he'll have Polar Vortex and Black Ice with him. Black Ice might not be a big deal, but Polar Vortex has it out for me. We'll see major-league heroes, too. I'll leave as soon as Honeycomb's safe! Go!"

I took off without waiting to see if my girlfriend would listen to me. She'd forgive me later, or not, but either way, I needed her out of here, and I needed Honeycomb with her parents and in street clothes. Only once she was home could I leave, apologize to Fursona, and start making heads or tails of everything.

We gained altitude, then plunged below the traffic signals. Honeycomb's wings were more of a hindrance than a help, but the poor girl was so nervous I couldn't bring myself to tell her that.

"That's my place," she said, pointing at a glass set of double doors. I slowed the sailboard and landed, and she hopped off. "Thanks!"

The first electric transformer iced over and exploded loudly a moment later, and I took off into the sudden chill.

19

The Sudden Chill

"Oh shit," I muttered to myself as I flew through the snow flurries that had suddenly covered the University district. A moment ago, it felt like summer; now, it felt like New Year's Eve. Polar Vortex and Black Ice couldn't pull this off without help; they were strong, but neither had *this* much power. That meant King Cold for sure. I dove under power lines covered by ice in spite of their insulation, watching as block after block of the University district went dark.

Part of me wanted to turn and fight—if I could take out Polar Vortex again or make Black Ice retreat, that'd make things easier for whoever the first responders were. But more importantly, I needed to find Fursona before she got caught up in everything. She'd take the fastest way back to the green room unless she got the idea that she wanted to headline again.

Dammit. She'd definitely want to headline again.

I turned my board and—finally—accepted the **[Casting Call]** for "Summer's End."

[Casting Call]
[Episode: Power War: Summer's End - R]
[Role: A Flame in the Cold! Do you accept the role? (Yes/No)]
[Role Focus: Flamboyance + Drama]

There wasn't a doubt in my mind that I wouldn't make a difference against King Cold. As my fight against Stella-Lunar had shown me, my powers couldn't dent any major-league villain's defenses. But—and it was a big *but*—I could line up against Polar Vortex or fight a delaying action while I looked for Fursona.

[**Power War: Summer's End: Act One in Progress**]

My phone buzzed in my pocket. After a moment of hesitation, I pulled it out since it was Fursona's pattern.

<Back at base. Whats your eta? - Fursona 4:45>
<Fuck. I got caught in the Episode - Understudy 4:45>
<Thought you got stuck, the ice moved so fast - Understudy 4:46>

She didn't respond right away, and I let [**Solar Wing**] hover me over the iced-over power lines, well out of range of Black Ice and Polar Vortex's attacks. My stomach was in my throat; she'd be so pissed at me for this!

<Okay. Idea. Hold tight, talking w/ someone - Fursona 4:48>
<Got it - Understudy 4:48>

A camera drone zipped toward me, somehow unaffected by the frost. I gulped. Attention meant action was coming my way. Action meant either a minor-leaguer I could handle, two I couldn't, or a major-league villain who'd run me over without a thought.

Then, Polar Vortex appeared on the street below me in his red puffer jacket.

He was surfing the ice, just like he had back in the power plant last year, and he didn't see me. Instead, he iced a power line a little more, then froze a fire hydrant solid, covering it with icicles, humming the whole time.

I followed, thinking up a plan—several plans, in fact.

One: I could get the drop on him, hit him fast and hard, and try to Alpha Strike him out of the Episode. He'd been tough before, but if I could hit him with [**Bit-Part Barrage**] and then roll into a combo, I could pump out a ton of damage. Down a minor-league lieutenant, the other two villains would be in trouble when major-league heroes showed up.

Two: I could follow him, try to figure out his plan, and support whoever was on the way. It could give me an in with a team, but Rocko would be upset if I didn't make this all about me. Then again, it was a major-league Episode. It wasn't all about me. Was it?

Three: I could leave. Right now. Just walk away, abandon the Episode, and be safe. The Narrator would want me to leave. My parents would want me to leave. Hell, even Bee would want me to leave. But I could contribute to a hero win early in Power Wars here, either by going for the glory or by giving a major-league crew information.

The best choice was obvious.

<Give me good news. Engaging Polar Vortex solo - Understudy 4:51>

I dove toward Polar Vortex, the frigid air biting my face, and, as I reached the highest frozen power line, I stopped my downward descent with [**Power-Weaving**] into [**Bit-Part Barrage**]. He never saw it coming—the first beam locked him down, and the rest slammed into him for a good chunk of damage.

[Dramatic Damage! +4 Drama Points]

I didn't have time to celebrate. I was already **[Quick-Time Changing]**, using **[I-Frame Transform]** to take the sidewalk hit instead of trying to fly again. The Itsy Bitsy Spider dance ate some of the speed, and ice shattered around me as I bounced off the concrete in Rainy Day.

[Flashy Fitting-Room! +1 Flamboyance Point]
[Steel Yourself! +1 Grit Point]
[Floating Points: 3 Drama, 1 Flamboyance]

He whirled toward me, lobbing an icicle that slammed into my arm. A moment later, his face contorted in rage. "You again!?"

[HP 10/12]

"Me again. **[Thunderhead]**!" I said, letting the clouds build overhead. More snow fell from them, but I hardly noticed.

[Pause for Effect! +1 Drama Point]
[Power-Weaving! +6 Drama, +3 Flamboyance, and 1 Grit Points]

A barrage of icicles pounded into me as I waited for the **[Thunderhead]** to finish building. They tore into my stomach, shattered against my head, and knocked me sideways but did no damage. Polar Vortex was trying to **[Combo-Break]** me. He remembered the combo I'd used last time, but it was too late—he couldn't stop it because it was already done!

I **[Rode the Lightning]**. Tendrils of pure electricity picked me up and reached across the ice toward the supervillain, then tore through what was left of his superhero damage. More reached down from the empowered thunderstorm overhead, adding to the power surge. And when it was over, Polar Vortex was . . . still standing.

[Electric Lightshow! +1 Flamboyance Point]

Not only that, but he was laughing! Had I overestimated myself that badly? He stomped on the ice-covered ground, and a shockwave rippled through it, throwing me into the air. While I flapped my arms stupidly, he launched a trio of massive ice-balls my way. They hit one after another, catapulting me down the street—and away from TU.

[HP 4/12]

As I flew through the air, I had a moment to think about how badly I'd screwed up. I hadn't Alpha Striked hard enough to take Polar Vortex off the table, and I couldn't return to being a spy now. I might be able to retreat, though. That looked like my best option, unfortunately.

A moment before I hit the asphalt, I used **[Quick-Time Change]** for the last time this Act, switching back to Magical Girl Understudy. Then I hit the pavement and watched my HP seesaw. My phone buzzed again.

[Rejuvenation Activated: HP 8/12]
[HP 6/12]

I picked myself up and checked my messages. I had two.

<Hold tight. Im at the green room. Help is in the way - Fursona 4:51>
<where r u? Address? on our way - Tele-Portal 4:56>
<University and Clifton - Understudy 4:56>

Okay. Okay. I could do this. I breathed deep and threw myself into the air, letting **[Solar Wings]** take me high into the snow-filled sky. The plan had changed; instead of trying to escape, I needed to pin Polar Vortex here. Winning wasn't a necessity, either. If I held him in place, The Triad would finish him off and, most likely, eat Black Ice and King Cold for dessert.

Ha. Ice cream jokes.

The Alpha Strike had failed, but I could still run a delaying fight against Polar Vortex, so I tucked in my magical wings and dove through the street toward him, ripping **[Starlances]** at him as fast as I could. Some hit, others didn't, but they forced him to slow down as he rushed at me, building up a massive icicle.

[Dramatic Damage! +1 Drama Point]

Then the icicle flew toward me, splitting the afternoon air with a whumping sound as it collided with first one, then another of my **[Starlances]**. I pulled up into a fast climb, then dove, but the damn thing was like a guided missile. I couldn't shake it, and with every second, it gained on me. Worse, I'd lost track of Polar Vortex.

Then, as I ducked around a skyscraper with the ice missile closing fast, a portal opened in front of me, and a trio of identical, red-and-gold-clad men soared through.

"Never fear! Lightbeam is here!"

I was saved!

One of the clones took the gigantic icicle on the chest, disappearing along with it. The other two dove toward the street, where Polar Vortex was surfing away as fast as he could, and fired orange energy beams toward the retreating minor-league supervillain.

He desperately dodged back and forth, but another portal opened, and a hulking steel mech stepped through, fired its flamethrower, and melted the supervillain's path.

Then Tele-Portal stepped through a third portal, yawning, and trapped the villain in a portal loop.

The Triad had arrived.

"You good, Understudy?" Tele-Portal asked. Bud Lightbeam zipped overhead, his two bodies moving faster than I could ever imagine while the third started to rematerialize next to him. He'd left as soon as the fight with Polar Vortex ended, and now he crisscrossed the University district, looking for Black Ice and King Cold.

The Underdelver seemed much less interested in scouting. Though the mech's cab was open, he sat in his pilot's seat. Its flamethrower vomited fire into the sky, and its two fans howled, blowing hot air down University Street and melting power lines and asphalt.

"Yeah, I'm good," I said. I stood up, pushing off the curb I'd been sitting on. "Do you need my help for this Episode?"

"Nah. It's one villain and a lieutenant. We're running Bump and Go, so it's all about speed and aggression," Tele-Portal said, naming one of her team's moves. "You want to make yourself useful? Get back to campus, figure out what you want to do in the Power War, and sign up."

I nodded slowly. Then I cleared my throat, stepping away from the blaze Underdelver's flamethrower emitted. "I'd like to keep working with you. What does The Triad need?"

Tele-Portal laughed. "Honestly? We're a complete team in a fight. If you and Fursona showed up, you'd just be in the way, and the heavies couldn't go all-out when they needed to. If you want to sign up as a Triad-auxiliary team, we need eyes to watch our backs, information on where the fight is, and someone to keep the Extras out of the line of fire."

The best support in Tokyexico City needed a support? I suppressed a laugh. "I'd love to do that for you. I'll talk it over with Fursona, but we could probably be scouts for you and might be able to do some Extra rescue, too. I'll be in tou—"

"Hold on," Tele-Portal said, holding up a hand. "Fifteen seconds."

"You're off to battle?" I asked when her hand lowered.

"Yeah. Listen, I'll swing by your apartment Saturday afternoon. We can go over the auxiliary role, figure out how best to use you, and talk things over with you, me, Fursona, and Braningham. But for now, get out of here before someone else engages and things get rough."

I nodded, took to the air, and disappeared from the soon-to-be battlefield. As I went, a new System message filled my vision.

[Episode Canceled! No Longer Cast in Summer's End]
[Alias - Understudy] [Archetype - Magical Girl] [Community Rank - 215/523]
[HP 6/12]
[Styles and Skills]
▶Archetype Skill - Transformation Sequence
▶Combo Skills - Power-Weaving
▶Badass (23)
▶Cunning (42)
▶Check the Script 1
▶Audition Notes 1
▶Drama (61) (Skill Roll Available)
▶Bit-Part Barrage 2
▶Flamboyance (35)
▶Signature Skill - Adaptive Armoire 3
▶Stored Costumes: (Rainy Day, Copy Cat, Lab Assistant Panic)
▶Solar Wing 1
▶Quick-Time Change 3
▶Grit (5)
▶I-Frame Transform 3
[50 Drama Credits Used. Rolling Skill!]
[Rank-Up! Starlance 2: The Starlance tracks targets better, with improved handling]

By the time I landed on Walnut Tower's roof, Fursona knew I was coming, and she was waiting there, helmet barely on. I hit the ground and let the tension melt off as she held me up. She didn't say anything until we were inside, and even then, it wasn't a recrimination about how I'd been stupid or anything—just a long, rambling, "I was so worried about you. Did Tele-Portal get there in time? I couldn't think of anyone else to call! What happened?"

"I . . ." I untransformed, trying to think about how best to explain it. "I got caught up in stuff, and I owe you for bailing me out. But also, I think I got us a job for Power Wars. We're working with The Triad."

20

With the Triad

I bounced on the green room's couch excitedly; Tele-Portal and her lawyer, Braningham, would be here to talk about auxiliary work in less than two minutes. Fursona sat much more calmly, sprawled across the chaise lounge in her Eagle-sona Costume. We'd decided to put our best foot forward, which meant Fursona's more scout-oriented build.

As for me, I hadn't changed my builds around or anything. Tele-Portal already knew what I could do from our patrols last semester, and from all of our training time in The Triad's practice room.

"Anything we missed?" Fursona asked. She was *not* moving from that spot, no matter how tired Tele-Portal looked. None of the other chairs worked with her tail feathers; in fact, it was even worse than Roo-sona's tail had been. But that hadn't stopped her from bossing me around—getting the room ready, moving furniture, and making it look like we'd become a serious team, not some jumped-up little-league heroes.

I shook my head. "No. We're good. We've got this."

The elevator buzzed, and I ok'd it to come up. A moment later, an exhausted-looking Tele-Portal walked into the room. She looked rough, but not as bad as when she'd been on wall duty during the Man vs. Nature. Her lawyer followed, holding his hand out to shake mine; he wasn't as sharklike as the ones Professor Panic kept on retainer, but there was still something off about him.

Once we'd all said hello, Tele-Portal yawned and said, "We're here to discuss the secondary team role for Understudy and Fursona. You two need a team name eventually. You'll work with The Triad, helping us keep Tokyexico safe during the Third Power War, blah blah blah, Braningham, you've got this?"

"Indeed I do, Tele-Portal." The lawyer cleared his throat. "Today, we'll review the job description, figure out a list of responsibilities you can handle, and formally contract you with The Triad."

"Understood." I'd expected Braningham to take over, to be honest. "I talked with Tele-Portal briefly on Thursday. You want us in a support role, right?"

"Move," Tele-Portal said, jerking a thumb over her shoulder and standing beside the chaise lounge. Fursona stood up slowly, and I could practically feel her scowl.

"Yes. You've both got flight powers, which is rare on a single team. That makes you optimal for scout patrols, and in that role, you'd be able to keep out of the fighting, cover lots of ground, and be ready to step into a secondary task as assigned—or as it becomes obvious you need to engage. Those would be easier tasks, like pinning down a lieutenant so they couldn't support a villain or removing Extras from the battlefield."

"Got it. We can definitely do that."

Braningham nodded. "Excellent. Now, legally, there's no restriction on how frequently we work minor-league heroes during a Power War. However, Tele-Portal has said—"

"No more than three times a week," Tele-Portal interrupted. "Preferably less. You've got classes, and your studio will want you fighting your own battles, too."

"Quite right," Braningham said. "Next, Tele-Portal and The Triad have a few questions about how your **[Signature Skill]** works. You can take a part of another super's Costume, correct?"

"No, it has to be given. Otherwise, I'd be a great villain, just ripping apart other supers' Costumes. Once I have a Costume part, I take it to Pataki, and they make me a Costume I can use," I said. "It takes some time, though."

"Great. Braningham, can you go get it from the car?" Tele-Portal asked.

The lawyer nodded. "I'll gather the paperwork as well." He disappeared down the elevator.

"I'm giving you an old model of Portal Cannon. It's not as svelte as this one, and it wore me out more, but it's a solid part of an older Tele-Portal build," Tele-Portal said as soon as the door closed. "I'll be honest, I was about ready to be done with you last January, but you've pulled yourself together, Understudy. You and Fursona will be high-end heroes in no time if you keep it up."

"Thanks. I don't know what to say," I said, stunned. I hadn't expected a gift like *this*. I hadn't expected a gift at *all*. If it gave the right powers, a Tele-Portal Costume could change *everything*. It could make a full-rescue build possible; I had the powers—and the slots—to make it happen. I'd ditch Lab Assistant Panic and never look back if that was the case.

"Say you'll get a proper support build by the end of the week. You do that, and it's yours to keep."

"You've got it, Tele-Portal," I said excitedly. "Let's get that paperwork dealt with. I need to see Rocko and Pataki!"

[Welcome to Rocko's Studio. System Disabled. Now arriving Backstage.]

"What the hell is that?" Rocko asked as I dragged Tele-Portal's portal gun through the door. They dropped their cigar on the floor, wringing their grasping hands and glaring at the chrome-and-white cannon like it'd go off at any second. "That's not . . . no. No. Get it out of here before—"

"DuPont! What'd you bring me?" Pataki rasped. They did *not* drop their cigarette. Instead, they stared raptly at the cannon. "Bring it here!"

"—Before *that* happens. Pataki, you know what this'll do to the bottom line, right? DuPont's no support hero. She'd be wasted in that role!"

"Rocko, I want a support Costume, not to be a support hero," I interrupted.

"Yeah, she wants a support Costume. Besides, I've got an experiment to run, and this is the perfect opportunity to figure out the Ultima hybridization issue."

"Ultima? What's that?" I asked.

"Fine," Rocko snapped, ignoring me. "You want to build Understudy some crappy support Costume as an experiment, be my guest! Just don't involve me in it, and don't blame me when it doesn't work. It'll be coming out of your pay!"

They turned on their heel, picked up their cigar, and climbed into their chair. "I'll be editing last night's Power Wars Episode. Get her into Costuming."

As Pataki escorted me into the Costuming room, where hundreds of supers' Costumes sat on hangers and mannequins, I tried to understand what had just happened. Weren't we meeting Rocko's goals? We'd run the correct Episodes at the right times, and as far as I could tell, the studio was doing fine. I walked toward the table, set the portal gun down, and started climbing into the Costume-design machine, but Pataki waved me off in a cloud of smoke.

"We're not building anything today, DuPont."

"No?" I asked, confused. Wasn't that Pataki's job?

"No. Instead, I'm going to brief you in on something. But it's a secret. Only Rocko and I know about it. We're working on a new suit for you, but it's still in the proto-type stage. I can't tell you what it'll do, but we're hoping for a big power spike if we get it to the point where you can use it."

That got my attention. "Like, extra power slots?"

"No. Like, *all* the power slots. But we're months out, and that's only if you help with the research and development side of things," Pataki said, puffing on their cig-arette. "So, with that in mind, let's talk about your support suit."

"What about it?"

"Right now, I could build the Tele-Portal suit. It'd be a good Costume, with the right powers to play a direct support role. And that'd be the end of it. Or . . ."

"Or . . . ?"

"We could grab another Costume piece from another great support hero and try a hybrid Costume. It's an important step in developing Project Ultima. The other option is to try getting a piece to match with Madame Shockwave's outfit."

"No, that's not an option." My mom had said not until I was a minor-leaguer, and I was one now, so the Shockwave Costume was a possibility, but I wasn't sure

I *wanted* it. It could be super dangerous if it acted like Lab Assistant Panic but with the added power of Mom's voice. It still sat in my closet, and if I ever had it built, it *definitely* wouldn't be spliced with some other super.

"Okay. That's fine," Pataki said. They puffed on their cigarette. "I'll work on breaking down the portal gun into something more . . . Magical Girl. You get a strong support's Costume piece. Come here the second you have it, and we'll get rolling. Oh, and don't tell *anyone* what's going on here. This is supersecret, Cartman and Vigilant Vow-level stuff. But legal, both according to your laws and our regulations."

"Got it," I said, and left, excited about the possibilities. I barely saw Rocko shoot a glare Pataki's way as the door opened, then ignore both me and them until the door to the green room closed behind me. The support possibilities were endless. Warp Tennyson probably had a ton of synergies with Tele-Portal's powers. I could grab Res-Cute, too; the minor-league Magical Girl had made a career not of fighting villains but of saving people from disasters.

The possibilities were endless. I could even grab Lady Lockless's power if I could convince her to give it up, though Tearjerker was probably a no go.

But in the end, most of those heroes and villains were out. I couldn't convince them to help me fast enough, and some villains had real reasons to hate me on top of the whole "don't ask another super for their Costume" thing. There was only one person I could talk to about this.

As soon as I got back to the green room, I started typing.

RE: Personal Thank-You
Sara-N-Dipity,
Can I take you up on that offer? I won't have time to meet since the Power War, classes, and studio obligations are taking up most of my time, but I have a request for that gift.

I'm signed up to work as an auxiliary for The Triad with my partner, Fursona. My power allows me to adopt other heroes' Costumes, as you know. But to do that, I need part of their Costume gifted to me. To fill that role as an auxiliary, I need a solid support Costume, and picking up your power would fill that requirement.

I know it's not usually okay to ask for another super's Costume, but in this case, you want to give me a gift anyway. Could I have something to base my support Costume on?
Thanks,
Magical Girl Understudy

Bee, out of her fursuit, looked over my shoulder. I could see her reflected eyes narrow on my laptop's screen. "Didn't you just get a support Costume?"

"Kind of. It's a supersecret Pataki experiment, just like yours." I pressed Send and stood up. "How about we order dinner in? I'm tired of cooking, and we both need to focus on classwork for a bit."

"Sure. Thai?"

"Thai sounds great." While she ordered, I paced the room, waiting for a response from Sara-N-Dipity.

Instead, my elevator door buzzed. I beckoned it up, but when it opened, it was empty. Instead, a single poker chip sat in the middle, along with a note.

Thought so,
Sara.
PS: We need you on the battlefield tomorrow. 72% chance of Theseus making a move in Mid-Town, and a 54% chance that whatever he does will splash to University. Deal with him before he becomes our problem.

I grinned and picked up the chip, already heading back toward Rocko's Studio. As I went, I looked over my shoulder. "Bianca, it's time for a re-rematch with Theseus!"

"Great! I'm ready to throw hands!"

21

Throw Hands

SUNDAY, SEPTEMBER 28

"Fursona reporting in. Nothing on North Street."

"Copy that. I'm at Colfax—no sign of him. Over," I said into the headphone mic plugged into my cell phone, which we'd figured out how to set to continuous transmission.

"You don't have to say *over*," Fursona's voice—unmodulated, since it was inside her suit—came through, a little staticky. We'd agreed to keep an open line of communication while we scouted for Theseus over Mid-Town. The idea had come from watching The Triad talk to each other, but we hadn't had time to figure out how they'd done it. Underdelver probably had something to do with it, and I wished we had a proper Genius, not just my half-baked, villainous Lab Assistant Panic.

Still, it was better than nothing. We'd found a lot of major-league Episodes and a couple of little-league ones—hopefully those kids were okay out there—but nothing that sounded like Theseus. Luckily, we'd covered most of Mid-Town, which meant there was only one place he could be.

"I don't have to say what? Over," I said, because I knew it'd get a rise as anything else.

"Over!"

"Okay, but seriously, I'm doing a flyover of Fitch Road, then looping back toward the mall. Meet me there, and we'll orbit around Theseus's last known location. Maybe he hasn't gotten started yet."

"Got it," Fursona said. I heard her wings beat. I turned my own flight path to cross over the mall.

The support build wasn't ready. Pataki said they needed a week or so to experiment, so I was on my standard Costumes for now. But other than that, I was ready to rock. I dove down, cutting through the morning air over the busy mall below, and banked toward the corporate towers in Mid-Town's center. Theseus's dot tended to stay near the Alkirk Corporation's tower, so we'd done some digging. They were involved in robotic prosthetics, medical supply chains, and a dozen other business ventures—but the biggest hint that he worked for them was the video footage on their site of him operating the various prosthetic weapon systems they'd developed.

He had to be inside that tower.

Fursona's eagle form circled the building as I got close, and I joined her, flying on my [**Solar Wing**]. We did loop after loop of the building until finally, a [**Casting Call**] we could get behind popped up.

[Casting Call]
[Episode: The Dark Hand of Capitalism - PG-13]
[Role: Heroine! Do you accept the role? (Yes/No)]
[Role Focus: Cunning + Badass]

I accepted the [**Casting Call**], and a moment later, something rocketed from Alkirk Tower's top floor.

[The Dark Hand of Capitalism: Act One in Progress]

I caught a glimpse of a pointed tube as long as my arm just before it turned midair and javelined toward Fursona. She dove, tucking her wings in and aiming straight for it, then stalled just before it reached her, changing directions. The rocket missed, started to turn, then exploded.

I banked, holding my wand at the ready. Theseus *had* to have launched that rocket, and if he had . . .

"Fursona reporting in. Theseus is *armed* and dangerous!"

I rolled my eyes but positioned myself above the tower's pointed pinnacle. Glass shone under us as we searched the building.

And then, there he was, standing on the helicopter landing pad. Theseus.

He waved with a steel arm ending in a huge blade, then aimed his other arm into the sky. Honestly, it barely qualified as an "arm." Everything below the shoulder had been replaced with a massive, multibarrel rocket pod, one of which was still smoking from its launch. He'd swapped out his legs, too, replacing them with what looked like steel spider legs that all split from his waist. But his face still had the same trademark serious smirk.

"Hi, girls. I wondered when you'd show up. I have to *hand* it to you. I didn't think you'd grow this quickly. You might actually be able to give my old self a run for his money. But Alkirk's given me a *leg* up on you all. Or, in this case, six."

I groaned. Theseus only had one kind of joke.

"I'm well on my way to being a whole new supervillain, which begs the question. Once they've replaced my whole body, will I still be Theseus?"

"Only if you keep those terrible puns! [**Starlance**]!" I shouted, waving my wand. The energy bolt ripped from it, arcing as Theseus threw himself over the landing pad's edge. His spider legs grappled the side of the building, and he ran, but my lance arced to hit him. He tumbled down, only for his legs to skitter against the skyscraper's side, finding purchase.

[**Dramatic Damage! +1 Drama Point**]

"Okay, that's how it is, then!" Theseus shouted. He held out his rocket pod arm, and a moment later, white smoke poured from every hole as a few dozen missiles filled the air. I dove, trying to copy Fursona's move. She banked around the skyscraper as a double handful of missiles pursued her.

I faced off against fourteen.

I dodged, spun, and even turned off [**Solar Wing**], trying desperately to escape the explosions behind me, but it was hopeless. As first one, then another, then a third rocket filled the air with shrapnel and flames, I used [**Quick-Time Change**]. The world froze, and I did the only dance that wouldn't get me killed instantly, shifting into Rainy Day.

[**Flashy Fitting-Room! +1 Flamboyance Point**]
[**Steel Yourself! +1 Grit Point**]

An explosion went off the moment I finished my dance, and I started counting. [**I-Frame Transform**] lasted three seconds. More and more missiles poured in, and the heat around me grew and grew with each explosion. Two seconds.

One second. The missiles kept hitting. It wasn't going to be enough.

Zero.

BOOM!

[**HP 5/12**]

One last missile bored in, exploding twenty yards above me and sending a blast of shrapnel that ripped into me. I shuddered, watching my HP plummet almost as fast as I did. Theseus wasn't playing around, and neither was Alkirk.

So it was best to let him think I'd been shot down. I fell and fell, remembering the last time I'd taken a tumble from a skyscraper. Then, two, maybe three, seconds before I hit the ground, I used my second [**Quick-Time Change**] and switched right back to Understudy. "[**Solar Wing**]!" I shouted, and the two wings erupted from my sleeves and stopped my fall.

[**Flashy Fitting-Room! +1 Flamboyance Point**]
[**Rejuvenation Activated: HP 9/12**]

It wasn't a full heal, but it was enough. I banked, then started circling up around Alkirk Tower. If I'd seen it right, Theseus had fired every rocket in his arm. He probably didn't have a reload—that felt like a Genius tech upgrade, not like something a human engineer could design—so now was the time to push the attack!

I had other priorities, though.

Fursona didn't have an **[I-Frame Transform]** to dodge damage, and as far as I could tell, she had no heals. "Fursona, come in," I said into my mic.

Nothing.

"Fursona, are you still up?"

Still nothing. I gritted my teeth and put on speed, searching for Spider-Theseus or a wrecked, smoldering eagle fursuit—whichever I found first.

As I turned around the building, wind whipping at my hair, a shadow fell over me. I looked up to see Fursona's gigantic eagle suit perfectly between me and the sun. Her suit was definitely worse for wear, but she was still up and running. She dove to get on my level, then tapped her head and shook it as she rolled.

I nodded. Theseus's missile barrage must have knocked out her headset, and she couldn't put it back in while wearing the suit. But that was fine; she hadn't been knocked out of the fight, and Theseus had used his ranged attack too early.

We climbed, wings beating pink, blue, and feathery, and arrived at the helicopter pad just as Theseus did. He grinned, popped off his rocket arm, and replaced it with an identical blade to the first. "Well, you can't blame me for trying, can you?"

Before I could retort, he threw himself off the edge, skittering toward the ground below. Fursona dove after him and shrieked, and I fired a **[Starlance]**, but he clattered around the corner and kept descending as glass windows shattered inward. Extras screamed—or maybe they weren't Extras. I couldn't be sure, but if the Alkirk Corporation had built his weapons, were they Extras, henchmen, or villains?

I'd have to ask Rocko later, but right now, I needed to catch up to Theseus. I turned around the building's corner, then braked hard as a sharp, pointed blade sprung toward me. It sliced into my side, and I screamed and back-flapped.

[HP 7/12]

It took a minute—and another Eagle-sona screech—for me to stop falling, turn myself around, and reengage, and when I did, Theseus had almost reached the ground. "**[Bit-Part Barrage]**!" I shouted, spinning as my wings retracted, and fired a half dozen **[Stellar Rays]** his way. A couple hit, but not the all-important first blast. Before I could adjust, he clattered away again.

[Dramatic Damage! +2 Drama Points]

As Theseus touched the ground, one of his arms popped off. A moment later, a pair of drones rocketed past me. The all-too-present camera drone zipped past first, hovering backward to catch the second one, a massive thing with the Alkirk logo plastered on its side. I fired a **[Starlance]** at it, but it threw chaff into the air, and my energy bolt missed.

Then it dropped a new arm, which Theseus immediately installed.

This one looked like a launcher, but not for a bunch of rockets—just one projectile. He aimed it at me.

PFFWUMP!

A hook zoomed right toward me faster than I could bank. It slammed into me, not doing any damage, and then pulled back. I jerked painfully in the air, firing a **[Starlance]** as it yanked me toward Theseus. It zipped toward him just as he swung his blade arm, which sliced into my off-arm. My **[Solar Wing]** retracted a moment later.

[Dramatic Damage! +1 Drama Point]
[HP 5/12]

Fursona shrieked again, buffeting Theseus and forcing him away from me. I rolled the other way, putting distance between the supervillain's grapple and me. He finished retracting it, and this time, he fired at Fursona, who couldn't get out of the way fast enough. I tried to turn **[Solar Wing]** back on, but it wouldn't go! Instead, I received a Style System message.

[Dead Leg Protocol: Mobility Powers Disabled for Understudy. Time remaining: 30 Seconds]

Okay, the hook had some sort of debuff. It had to be the hook because I hadn't lost flight the first time he'd sliced me. Sure enough, Fursona's flight was gone, too—and honestly, that was worse than me losing mine.

"Get a *grip*, ladies. You can't take me, so don't even try! Alkirk is my route up. I'm skipping the lieutenant phase and becoming my own major-leaguer—for myself!" Theseus said. Then he charged, hook firing.

As the cable zoomed toward me, I remembered how we'd almost beaten him in the Roth Arena. We'd attacked his arms, stopping his power. Could we do the same thing here?

I had to find out. The hook reached me just as I fired a **[Starlance]** at the cable. It wrapped around me, jerking me off my feet again, but as I started zooming toward Theseus's blade, the cable snapped. It whipped toward me, crashing into the asphalt next to my feet, and at the same time, snapped back and caught Theseus across the forehead.

"In your *face*, Theseus!" I shouted, then fired another **[Starlance]**, which slammed into one of the villain's legs. It shattered, but before we could press the advantage, a second **[Casting Call]** popped up.

[Casting Call]
[Episode: Power War: Appetite for Destructo - R]
[Role: Collateral! Do you accept the role? (Yes/No)]
[Role Focus: Grit + Drama]

In the moment it took me to decline it, Theseus skittered away, crashed through the glass doors, and disappeared inside the Broadway Mall.

[End of Act One: Act Two in One Minute]

22

Broadway Mall

Fursona and I didn't say anything. We started running toward the mall as our [**Dead Leg Protocol**] debuffs ticked down. We arrived at the caved-in doors just as the first screaming Extras poured out, shattered glass clinking and crunching beneath their shoes.

[**The Dark Hand of Capitalism: Act Two in Progress**]

Extras pushed past us, shoving and battering us back and forth, but Fursona took the lead, and I followed the giant eagle through the crowd. "We need to stop him before he hurts someone!" I shouted.

"Yeah! Think he's still following the code of conduct?" she replied.

"I don't know!" I sure hoped he was, but he'd crashed into a busy mall without any thought toward the Extras' safety. The crowd thinned out as we reached the food court where Tele-Portal and I had done our first patrol, revealing Theseus switching out his hook arm for something new. This arm looked less like a weapon and more like a buckler; as he held it up, a shimmering reddish shield extended from it, covering his side. The center of the metal buckler glowed a dull red.

"Theseus, stop! You're putting Extras in danger!" I said, trying to appeal to his conscience.

"No, I'm not. I haven't held a single one hostage, and I haven't used a single power to keep them here or attack them. They've had every chance to leave," he said calmly. "You can wag your finger at me for a lot of things, but breaking our code's not one of them."

I glanced around. Sure enough, the food court was pretty much empty, except for a few Extras holding up phones and one wearing . . . fuck. An APPEAL shirt.

"Now, hold on, Theseu—"

The supervillain's blade arm zoomed toward me, and I ducked under a table, which crumpled from the impact. Still, it hadn't cut me, and I popped up, already firing a [**Bit-Part Barrage**] just as Fursona shouted, "Wait!"

It was too late, though. I couldn't wait. The first beam caught Theseus dead in the chest—or it would have if not for the shield. As my **[Stellar Rays]** slammed home one after another, the central, glowing light grew brighter and brighter until it was almost white.

[Pause for Effect! +1 Drama Point]

Huh? That message usually only happened when I used **[Thunderhead]**. I'd never checked to see if my opponents got a warning when it was building, but—
BWEEEEW!
The shield exploded, the red transparent barrier fell apart, and the food court's lights flickered. A moment later, a gigantic red beam cut across the room toward me, slicing through garbage cans and fake plants as it leveled the whole room at waist height. It sliced into me, burning through my superhero damage, and then stopped.

[HP 2/12]

I rolled, kicking a leg out to knock a half-melted chair away, and got to my feet. Theseus's shield projection wasn't up, and the buckler's center blinked yellow. "Get him now!" I shouted as another drone—a camera one this time—zipped overhead, taking in the damage.

Fursona didn't wait around. She screeched, pounding away at the shield arm with her sonic attack. Theseus's legs clattered across the food court, closing the gap between her and him in seconds, but not before the shield arm's plating shattered. He reeled back a sword blow, but I charged in, putting myself between the sword and my partner

As the blow bore down on her, I activated **[Hog the Limelight]**, and the sword's angle changed suddenly, rushing toward me. "**[Quick-Time Change]**," I whispered, and a moment before the blow would have sliced into me and knocked me out of the fight, the world froze. I did the Itsy Bitsy Spider, let Theseus's blade pass through me with **[I-Frame Transform]**, and started charging up a **[Thunderhead]**.

[Eye-Catcher! +1 Flamboyance Point]
[Flashy Fitting-Room! +1 Flamboyance Point]
[Steel Yourself! +1 Grit Point]
[Pause for Effect! +1 Drama Point]

The room slowly filled with clouds as Theseus's shield shifted from blinking yellow to pulsing orange. How long did I have? Enough time to get a **[Ride the Lightning]** off? The storm finished building just as his buckler turned red and the shield formed over him.

"We need to change tactics!" Fursona called. "How about Pitchfork?"

"Sure, that works!" I ran left, 6th-grade legs pumping for all they were worth, and Fursona flapped into the air and zoomed right—straight at the APPEAL member, who screamed and ducked behind a planter!

Theseus hesitated for a crucial moment, then turned toward me. The moment he did, Fursona shrieked again, buffeting him to the side and knocking his shield off-balance for just a split second.

But that was enough.

[Ride the Lightning] fired, and I poured electricity into the gap in Theseus's defenses, aiming as best I could for the shield arm's shoulder. Circuits and wires sparked and popped, something exploded with a loud bang, and the red shield flickered off a moment later.

[Electric Lightshow! +1 Flamboyance Point]
[Thunderstruck! +1 Drama Point]
[Good Thinking! +1 Cunning Point]

Another Alkirk drone zoomed in, dropping a new arm for Theseus. He ejected the smoking, destroyed shield arm, but a new message popped up before he could equip it.

[A Powerful Hero is Joining the Fight]
[Name: Bud Lightbeam]
[Powerful Villains are Joining the Fight]
[Names: Lord Destructo, McHammer, Haze-Matt]
[Power War: Appetite for Destructo: Act One in Progress]

I gulped, trying to force down panic. The few Extras still in the food court didn't know what was coming, and while Lord Destructo and McHammer had codes of conduct, Haze-Matt was a whole different animal.

Theseus clearly thought so, too. He'd stopped equipping his arm.

"Fursona, the mission's changed. Think you can take Theseus?" I asked.

She stared at him for a moment. "He's gotta be low, right? At the very least, I can stop him from winning," she said.

"Great. I'm playing rescue and protection. Bud Lightbeam's here. That means The Triad's on its way. We just have to—"

Theseus interrupted. "I'm laying down my arms—one of them literally. I propose an immediate Neutral Field."

"Agreed," Fursona said before I could stop her. "What do you want?"

"I want the three of us to get out of here right now and resume our fight somewhere else. In return, I'll tell you my target for the Episode so you can get there, and we'll pick up right where we left off. The same powers, the same HP totals, and I won't even equip a spare arm," Theseus said. His face was pale, and he narrowed his eyes toward the upstairs, where a greenish fog had started rolling into the food court area.

I nodded slowly. "Agreed, on one condition. You help us get these dumbass Extras out of here first."

Theseus held out his blade, and for a moment, I didn't get it. Then I reached out, gingerly grabbed the tip, and shook it. Then I shifted back to Understudy.

"Hey, everyone, Magical Girl Understudy's selling us out to the—" The guy in the APPEAL shirt didn't get a chance to finish his sentence. Theseus rushed him, tackling him and wrapping the flat of his bladed arm around him. Then he started skittering for the door, putting on speed as he went.

"That's our cue!" I ran to one of the filmers, who backed up as I grabbed him, then summoned my sailboard with **[Solar Wing]**. The board materialized under him, and we rocketed toward the building's exit, Fursona behind us with the other filmer protesting as she was dragged along in my sidekick's talons.

The wrecked doors were twenty feet away, fifteen, ten.

Then, a skate shop's glass facade collapsed outward, and a familiar-looking, gas mask-clad figure crashed into the hall in front of us, filling the air with sickly green smoke. The smell of rotten eggs and almonds filled the hall, and I skidded to a halt inches from the toxic gas. As I backed off, Haze-Matt stood up, gas mask making a click-hiss-rasp as he breathed into it. "You. I remember you," he said.

"No, you don't. I've never seen you in my—"

"The car. You were in the car!" He started laughing maniacally and reached for a grenade at his belt. "I wanted that car, but they wouldn't give it to me! Now I can have it!"

"Hello, Understudy. Greetings, Fursona. Get behind me, and me, and me," a voice said. A moment later, the three red-and-gold triplet-bodies of Bud Lightbeam appeared between us and the villain. "I'll keep you and your rescues safe until the rest of The Triad arrives!"

"You can't deny me the car! I'll have it!" Haze-Matt heaved the grenade toward me, and I used **[Quick-Time Change]** to shift back into Rainy Day. At the same moment, Lightbeam fired a beam that cut the bomb in half. A gray-orange gas started descending on us, and I used **[Wind Front]** to shove it down the hall, back toward Haze-Matt.

[Flashy Fitting-Room! +1 Flamboyance Point]
[Badass Move! +1 Badass Point]

Then, a hammer-wielding, helmet-wearing figure shoved Haze-Matt, pushing through the gas cloud, and swung his hammer in a wide circle. Two Lightbeams vanished, and the third crashed into a wall. But the hammer didn't stop there. It whipped around, slamming into Haze-Matt and knocking him back—

—And giving me an opening. I grabbed the man, who still hadn't stopped filming, and started dragging him down the hall toward the food court. Hopefully, Haze-Matt hadn't shoved enough gas onto the top floor to cover it. Hopefully, I'd be able to find my way to safety.

Hopefully.

[**Powerful Heroes are Joining the Fight**]
[**Names: Tele-Portal, Underdelver**]

I breathed a sigh of relief, looking for the stilt-wearing support hero, but I couldn't find her. The sounds of fighting intensified behind me, though, and when I looked, Underdelver's mech suit had bored a hole through the mall's floor and stood between the villains and us. Hammers clashed against drills, napalm filled the hall with choking—but nonlethal—smoke, and Lightbeam fired lasers into the clogged, opaque cloud.

I turned and kept running, but when I got to the food court, I stopped dead in my tracks and looked at it in horror. Sulfur-smelling yellow smog cascaded from upstairs in waterfalls, and the food court was already filled with the smog. It billowed toward us. We were trapped!

I looked for an option—any option—that'd give us some time or shelter from the incoming gas. It bore down on us, almost like it had a mind of its own. "[**Wind Front**]!" I shouted, blowing it back to buy us some time. Then I saw an open door to a store, and, without stopping to check what it was, I grabbed my Extra and dragged him toward it. Fursona followed a moment later.

[**Badass Move! +1 Badass Point**]
[**Good Thinking! +1 Cunning Point**]

We rolled through the door, which slammed shut behind us, and crashed into a mannequin wearing far too little clothing. "Is this . . ." I started to say.

"Victoria's Secret, yeah," Fursona confirmed. I looked around; lingerie surrounded us, and pictures of airbrushed supermodels in red and black bras covered every wall.

My Extra groaned under me, and I pushed myself to my feet. "Sorry. What's your name?"

"Rob. Thanks, I guess, but we're still stuck here. How do we get out?" the Extra—Rob—asked.

"Simple. We hold position until Tele-Portal gives us an out. If Haze-Matt's gas gets in, we head for the back storage area, and we hope there's a delivery door back there. We should probably check for that now," I said, taking control of the situation.

[**The Dark Hand of Capitalism: End of Act Two! Act Three in Five Minutes**]
[**Power War: Appetite for Destructo: End of Act One! Act Two in One Minute**]

We walked slowly toward the back of Victoria's Secret, passing some cute nighties I wished I could buy, and searched for a way out before this whole mess got worse.

23

This Whole Mess Got Worse

[Power War: Appetite for Destructo: Act Two in Progress]

We hadn't even found the door to the Victoria's Secret storage rooms when a massive boom shook Broadway Mall.

Every pane of glass in the mall shattered. My Extra covered his face, while Fursona's civilian screamed and put her hands over her ears. The building shook a second time, and a familiar voice filled the building, playing from every loudspeaker.

"**[I'm The Star]**. Attention, 'Heroes' of Tokyexico City. This is Golden Goose. Stand down. I'm taking over. Villains on-site at the Broadway Mall, I had to fly down here for this? I'll give you one minute to disengage and surrender. After that, your ass is mine!"

[A Powerful Hero is Joining the Fight]
[Name: Golden Goose]

I flinched; if Golden Goose was here, getting out was even more important! Rocko had said we could bail on any Episode she got involved in, but one look at the increasingly terrified Extras and we knew that wasn't an option. Worse, mustard-colored smog seeped through the Victoria's Secret storefront, past mannequins and shelves, creeping closer to us. We couldn't stay here, either.

A figure appeared, wading through the sickening sulfur smoke. "I said I wanted that car! Golden Goose or not, you took it from me, and I'm going to get it back," Haze-Matt said.

"Plan?" I asked.

"With the Extras? Siegecraft Three, maybe?" Fursona said.

"That works. You two, go in there and try to find a way out." I pointed to the supply room door. I didn't have any illusion we could handle Haze-Matt, but whatever his obsession with me and my mom's car was, he wasn't going to give us a choice. If we could hold him off until The Triad bailed us out, that'd be ideal. If not . . . maybe we could keep the Extras safe, at least.

We took a step back as Haze-Matt advanced. The Siegecraft battle plan involved finding and defending a choke point; Fursona was usually the wall, and I served as the archers and boiling oil. I didn't think it'd work too well against Haze-Matt, but we had a few tricks up our sleeves.

I was up front for Siegecraft Three, and Eagle-sona took a position right behind me, wings spread. Haze-Matt's noxious, foul-smelling cloud rolled toward us, covering lace bras and bodysuits, and I fired a **[Starlance]** at the villain. It hit, knocking the villain back dramatically.

[Dramatic Damage! +1 Drama Point]
[High-HP Hit! +1 Drama Point]

I got bonus damage against high-superhero damage enemies with **[Starlance]**, so I quickly fired another, but Haze-Matt leaned over, ducking the beam at the last moment. He pulled a gun from his tattered suit, pulled the trigger, and sent a cloudy jet of poisonous fumes my way. I pulled back into the storage room's door just as Fursona's wings beat, sending twin tornadoes rippling through the fumes.

Still, I couldn't help but catch a breath of the toxic mixture, and I went down on one knee, coughing.

[HP 4/12]
[Last-Used Power Disabled]

Okay. Standing and fighting wasn't going to work, not without **[Starlance]** to equalize the fighting. I spun and fired a **[Bit-Part Barrage]**, the beams leaving swirls in the puke-colored fog, but only caught Haze-Matt with a single ray. Then we retreated into the storage room, past boxes and plastic bags filled with lingerie.

[Dramatic Damage! +1 Drama Point]

"This guy sucks," Fursona said, flapping her wings again to ward off another blast.

"Yep, sure does. Don't know why he's got it out for me," I coughed out. "I think Siegecraft Three's the wrong call. Improvise?"

"Sure."

I **[Quick-Time Changed]** into Rainy Day, then used **[Wind Front]** to shove Haze-Matt's gas cloud back into the store. "Any luck with a way out?" I shouted.

[Flashy Fitting-Room! +1 Flamboyance Point]
[Heroic Protector! +1 Badass Point]

"No! We're dead. We're so dead," one Extra moaned.

I nodded slowly and started up a [**Thunderhead**]. If we couldn't get out, my only option was to—

CRASH!

The ceiling caved in around us, exposing the whole Victoria's Secret to the bright sun overhead and dispersing my [**Thunderhead**]. The rough circle still glowed molten-hot from where the world's mightiest hero had cut it open, less than a foot from our Extras. Tangled, half-melted steel beams hung overhead, forming a metal net over us; that wouldn't be a way out, either—especially not with what hovered above.

Golden Goose's eyes still glowed a dangerous red as she hovered with one hand on her waist and one pointing at Haze-Matt. Her green-and-gold Costume shimmered in the sun, but her face looked anything but glorious. It looked furious. And . . . bored? "Time's up. You're going down," she said, and dove, crashing through the steel beams.

The villain tried to turn and run, but Golden Goose was too fast. She grabbed him, slammed him into the floor, and fired her laser eyes. The heat rippled outward, the dusty, gas-filled air shimmering, and then, suddenly, the gas ignited.

I watched in slow motion as the Victoria's Secret went from a rubble field to an inferno, and the flames started roaring toward us—and our Extras. I'd probably survive the explosion, and Fursona would definitely be fine, but the Extras wouldn't be. They'd be cooked alive. I remembered my therapist saying that Golden Goose's body count was higher than most villains.

And I couldn't let that happen here.

I only had one line of play, but at least I *had* one. I [**Quick-Time Changed**] back to Understudy, then used [**Hog the Limelight**].

[**Rejuvenation Activated: HP 8/12**]
[**Eye-Catcher! +1 Flamboyance Point**]

As the camera drones all turned from Golden Goose to me, the massive gas fire changed shape. It rushed toward me with a roar, then collapsed onto me. I could feel the flames licking against my skin, my dress and hair bursting into flame, and pain across my whole body.

[**HP 2/12**]

Then, as suddenly as it started, it was over. I panted from the heat, but my suit and hair seemed suddenly intact. I'd successfully eaten a Golden Goose attack, and Golden Goose hadn't even noticed. The Extras screamed behind me, and I felt like joining them; even though the superhero damage had eaten the fire's worst effects, it still *hurt*.

I couldn't move much, or do much of anything, as Golden Goose slammed Haze-Matt into the ground once . . . twice . . . a third time. His hand reached up, tearing at the shining heroine's Costume, and his nails tore into her sleeve. A small piece tore free. Then, a moment later, the heroine's fist slammed into his face, and she tossed him onto the ground.

"Such is the end for all villains in *my* world," Golden Goose said, and I shivered. "I'll see the earth burn before scum like this go unpunished, and put an end to this joke of a Power War."

Before I could say anything, she grabbed her torn sleeve from the floor and stalked off, firing her eye lasers into the Victoria's Secret door with an accompanying gas explosion.

"Holy shit, hoooly shit," the woman Extra said, hyperventilating behind me. "That was . . . that was . . ."

"Golden Goose, yes. We were here, we saw it, now what's next?" Fursona snapped.

"I'm not sure, but I think we need to leave. This place isn't safe," I murmured. I'd been eying that torn sleeve; it wasn't *given*, per se, but it'd still be *something* for Pataki to work with on their supersecret project. I shook my head, dispelling the idea. It didn't matter how brilliant or far-fetched that plan was because I *didn't* have the sleeve. But I *did* have a couple of Extras, a mall that looked more and more on fire with every passing moment, and—

"Shit. Theseus," I said, just as the Style System sent a new message.

[The Dark Hand of Capitalism: Act Three in Progress]

"Do we have time to stop him?" Fursona asked.

I checked my phone.

"No. We can't get there *and* save these two. So, given that, I guess we take the loss with Theseus and focus on the support role for 'Appetite for Destructo'?" I said.

"Got it. Let's get out of here. You two follow me. Understudy, watch our backs. And if you see Golden Goose, say something, *then* run," Fursona said. I pushed a little pang of jealousy down. She'd just . . . *taken* control. And, honestly, her plan was good. It just didn't feel right not calling the shots.

Still, we had a goal, so I shifted back to Understudy and hurried along behind the two Extras as we weaved through burning kiosks and collapsed security gates. Golden Goose clearly didn't care about keeping property damage to a minimum. I stole a look at Haze-Matt, then shook my head. If she'd killed him, she'd killed him, but I didn't have the time to check. Hopefully, a healing Elementalist hero was on the way. If not . . .

No, that wasn't my concern. I'd talk it over with Dr. Ayers later, but right now, we had a job to do.

Smoke choked the air, fighting against the last vestiges of Haze-Matt's toxic gas, and Broadway Mall's halls were choked with rubble. In the distance, Golden Goose's laser eyes lit up a blacked-out department store's entry, and we waited for it to fade, then kept moving toward where there *should* be an exit.

Fursona stopped suddenly, and the Extras ran into her. "Don't tail me that close. We're an easy target that close together."

"You sure are," Lord Destructo said, stepping through the rubble. "You two, I have no beef with, but I need the Extras. Hand them over, and I'll let you leave."

I raised an eyebrow. "How about no?" Fighting Lord Destructo on two super-hero damage wasn't a good idea, but I *couldn't* hand the Extras over.

"Please," Lord Destructo said, an edge of something similar to fear in his voice.

"No." Fursona crossed her wings. "We can't. It'd be a violation of our codes. If you want to take them . . . good luck."

I stared at her, dumbfounded. Our best bet was to negotiate and stall for time, not to flatly state we'd fight a top-tier villain. But she wasn't backing down.

"Fine. I'll—" Lord Destructo started, then stopped as one of the Extras disappeared. A moment later, Fursona tackled the other one into the shimmering portal that'd opened up behind him. They both disappeared even as the supervillain roared and swung his hammer my way.

I ducked the blow—barely—and threw myself into the portal, appearing outside. A tired, worried-looking Tele-Portal stood over me. She offered a hand, and I accepted, letting her pull me to my feet. "Good job, kid. You played it cool and did exactly what a support auxiliary should. Consider yourselves part of The Triad team."

I nodded slowly as another laser—this one tripled thanks to Lightbeam's power—sliced into the mall. It felt like a Pyrrhic victory at best. We'd saved the Extras, yes, but Golden Goose, The Triad, and the villains had combined to wreck the best mall in Tokyexico City. A single camera drone hovered nearby, recording, though it wasn't close enough for a speech. Not that I'd earned one—even for the superhero fans outside.

I pushed myself to my feet and started saying something, but Tele-Portal held up a hand. "Gotta go. We'll talk later, Understudy." Then she dropped a portal at her stilted feet and disappeared.

I turned, shaking my head, and checked on the Extras. "You two okay?"

"Yes. I think so. Maybe," Rob the Extra said.

"Yep, thanks to you. I'm not sure where my keys are, though. Probably inside."

"We'll figure out how to get you home," Fursona said. "I think the Council of Heroes has something for situations like this. If not, Understudy and I will figure it out. It's what we do."

I opened my mouth to agree, but a new message interrupted me.

[Episode Finished!]
[The Dark Hand of Capitalism - PG-13]
[Penalties: N/A]
[Episode Finished! +3 of each Style Point]

[The Agony of Defeat! +1 of each Style Point]
[Role Focus: Cunning + Badass - Goal Unmet]
[Alias - Understudy] [Archetype - Magical Girl] [Community Rank - 215/523]
[HP 2/12]
[Styles and Skills]
▶Archetype Skill - Transformation Sequence
▶Combo Skills - Power-Weaving
▶Badass (30)
▶Cunning (48)
▶Drama (25)
▶Bit-Part Barrage 2
▶Starlance 1
▶Flamboyance (47)
▶Signature Skill - Adaptive Armoire 3
▶Stored Costumes: (Rainy Day, Copy Cat, Lab Assistant Panic)
▶Solar Wing 1
▶Quick-Time Change 3
▶Hog the Limelight 1
▶Grit (11)
▶I-Frame Transform 3

I groaned. Even though I'd expected the loss, it still sucked. We'd run into Theseus so many times, and this time, I'd been convinced we could get the win. It wasn't fair that Power Wars had run over our Episode. And we'd definitely need to figure out how to operate with Golden Goose dropping in. We'd only survived her collateral damage through luck; she was a whole level above Stella-Lunar.

But, on the other hand, we'd nailed the support auxiliary role, with The Triad watching, and that counted for a lot. I couldn't wait to get a proper support hero's Costume, either. I turned toward Fursona. "Let's call in to the Council of Heroes, get these Extras figured out, and get back to base."

24

Back to Base

TUESDAY, SEPTEMBER 30

[Costume - Rescue Girl Lucky Star]
  [HP 12/12]
  [Styles and Skills]
  ▶Archetype Skill - Transformation Sequence
  ▶Archetype Skill - Combat Inhibitor
  ▶Archetype Skill - Rescue Rearm
  ▶Badass
  ▶Cunning
  ▶Card Curio 1
  ▶Audition Notes 2
  ▶Drama
  ▶Noncombatant Teleport 1
  ▶Flamboyance
  ▶Signature Skill - Adaptive Armoire 3
  ▶Stored Costumes: (Understudy)
  ▶Hog the Limelight 1
  ▶Grit
  ▶Jinx-Bearer 0

"Well?" Bianca asked from outside of the bathroom door. "What do you think?"

"It's nothing like I'd imagined," I replied, "but it's also exactly what I needed."

It really was. I'd been looking for a build that would support . . . well, support . . . for a while, and Pataki had really come through with the hybrid Tele-Portal/Sara-N-Dipity Costume. It didn't have many new powers, but they both felt impactful.

[New Skill! Noncombatant Teleport: Instantly move an Extra or unconscious to a random location within 300 yards that's out of danger]

[New Skill! Jinx-Bearer: Some unfortunate souls bear the brunt of the world's bad luck. Take an ongoing status effect from an Extra or super and bear it yourself]

[Jinx-Bearer] seemed highly flexible, though it shoehorned me into pure support. If I'd had it for Theseus, I could have "taken" the movement debuff from Fursona, letting her fly and keeping the pressure on the supervillain instead of allowing him to reach Broadway Mall. That might've been the difference between victory and defeat in "The Dark Hand of Capitalism."

The second, **[Noncombatant Teleport]**, felt like a limited version of Tele-Portal's main power. I couldn't use it to throw Fursona around the battlefield like Tele-Portal had in the "Winter is Coming" Episode, but I *could* use it to save Extras. It had some really powerful synergies with the third Archetype Skill, **[Rescue Rearm]**.

Oh yeah, this build had *three* Archetype Skills, which I'd never seen before. The first was my usual **[Transformation Sequence]**. Nothing new there; I could switch Costumes in-Episode, blah blah blah. And the second one, frankly, kind of sucked. **[Combat Inhibitor]** restricted my powers. I couldn't take anything designed to do damage. It wasn't pacifism; I could still punch and kick. I just couldn't carry **[Starlance]** or **[Spotlight Strike]** or anything like that. But, given the build's purpose, the restriction made sense.

Especially because of the third Archetype Skill.

[Rescue Rearm] reset one random power's per-Act uses on the Rescue Girl Lucky Star Costume whenever I used a power to save someone, whether from superpowered combat, an environmental hazard, or even clearing a nasty status effect. It only targeted powers that weren't at max per-Act uses, too, so with **[Noncombatant Teleport]**, for instance, I could quickly move a whole group of Extras to relative safety, thanks to the reset.

I sat on the toilet lid, fiddling with the remaining powers, and eventually settled on **[Hog the Limelight]**—for the power reset potential—and both **[Card Curio]** and **[Audition Notes]**. I hadn't ever used **[Card Curio]**, and **[Audition Notes]** felt tailor-made for an Extra-focused Costume like this one. **[Audition Notes]** had upgraded after the "Appetite for Destructo" Episode resolved, as had **[Hog the Limelight]**, which now drew fire for longer.

[Card Curio 1: Free-associate more information from your surroundings and a card reading]

[Audition Notes 2: Every Extra brings something to the table. Check their notes to find out what. More detailed information, including name and age, are provided]

Honestly, I hoped **[Card Curio]** played like **[Check the Script]**, but maybe with a little more luck to it. I'd had the power for a year, and it was time to find out what it did.

I made one other adjustment—this one to my Understudy build. [**Hog the Limelight**] could go; it had synergies with [**Quick-Time Change**] and [**I-Frame Transform**], but I wanted to pack more of a punch on my main build. [**Spotlight Strike**] came back, giving me an up-front damage option. I kept my other support-oriented powers on Rainy Day since they did unique things I couldn't replicate with Lucky Star. Then, finally, I replaced Lab Assistant Panic with Rescue Girl Lucky Star.

Satisfied with my Costume's build, I opened the door and posed.

"Cool!" Bianca squealed.

I nodded. I *was* pretty cool, and so was my Costume. It had traded out the overwhelming pastel pink and blue for a dark navy, red, and white color scheme, though the white color dominated the dress—even the tennis skirt with shorts underneath it. Stilts similar to Tele-Portal's gave me three inches of height, making me tower over Bianca and move shockingly quickly, while a stylish red sport coat hugged my chest. A white circle with a blue clover inside it had been embroidered on the right breast pocket, while the left bore a blue swirl reminiscent of Tele-Portal's portals with a red cross superimposed over it. Blinking LED strips ran up my legs and down my arms.

It felt exactly like a hybrid of the two support heroes' outfits should, and I grinned at Bianca. "Bet this build can keep up with you going full speed."

"Maybe. What does it *do*?"

I explained my new powers and couldn't help but see her grin. My own fell just a little. "Yes, it means you're going to be shot-calling more when I'm Lucky Star, but—"

"Annie, we're *partners*. I'm not trying to steal your show or take over. If it makes the most sense for me to call the shots, then I'll call the shots. But when it doesn't, we run off *your* plan. Okay?"

"Okay." I nodded slowly. "I think the right play right now is to do a postmortem on 'Dark Hand.'"

Bianca sighed. "Really? I mean, I agree with you, and it's part of the plan, but I really don't want to."

We sat in front of the TV and turned it on. After the "Gourmet's Glutton Hour" Episode, one thing we'd agreed on was that any losses needed an after-action report, as well as any time we weren't satisfied with how our plans had gone. As our first loss, "Dark Hand" definitely counted. So, for the next half hour, we watched the parts of the Episode we'd been in. And by the end, we'd come up with a lot of room for improvement, including three steps we could take the next time Theseus lined up against us.

The first one involved Theseus directly—or specifically, his weapons. He'd rotated out arms pretty much freely; the only time we'd really disrupted them was after he'd switched them out. Theseus himself was a tough target, but the Alkirk drones bringing arms in and out of the fight? We could destroy those pretty quickly, even with their chaff, and deny the supervillain the very thing that made him hard to fight.

The second was pressure. Against some villains, backing off might be the right call, but with Theseus, we had to push, push, push—especially once we'd damaged one of his limbs. We couldn't let him regroup, or he'd come at us with something new and exciting—and with Theseus, that'd be *handing* him the win. I couldn't help but laugh when Bianca made that joke for the twentieth time.

Our final step was more of a PR error on our part, but I hoped it wouldn't come back to bite us. When we'd ran from the food court with the Extras, Theseus had taken the APPEAL member. We'd *known* he was a TU APPEAL member, and we'd *known* the organization saw Theseus in a better light than me. That'd been a chance to switch their thoughts up, and we'd blown it. In the future, we needed to win all the public relations battles we could.

"Okay, that's not bad learning," I said. "I'll be honest, though. I don't think we could have done a single thing to win that Episode. The 'Appetite for Destructo' Episode landing on top of us, and then Golden Goose, gave Theseus too much of a head start, and even though he waited until Act Three started, we couldn't have gotten to him if we'd tried."

"Agreed." Bianca nodded. She had the whiteboard going. "But we might need to throw more minor-league Episodes, so we need to come up with a plan to disengage gracefully, or to make it harder to straight-up lose them. If we can play for a draw, that'd be huge."

She wrote 'Power Wars Overlaps' on the whiteboard. "Ideas for mitigating losses?"

I paused. Losses stung me, but they positively destroyed Bianca. "Okay, if we can get enough of an early lead, I can switch to a support/survival role to ride out the Power Wars Episode, and you can focus on trying to thwart the minor-leaguer's goals and forcing them to retreat instead of playing for a win. It'd be a lot like that first Episode against Jumper. Aim for a tie?"

"Could work." Bianca wrote it, then wrote 'Call for Backup.' "We know The Triad's out there, and they'll pile in on a major-league sighting, especially if an auxiliary like us calls it in. Maybe we can use them to take the high-powered heat so we can focus on getting our mission done. After all, even if Tele-Portal doesn't consider minor-league Episodes worth jumping in on, we're positioned to win some of those. It'd stop future threats or make them less powerful."

"Yeah. If we'd been able to disengage and go after Theseus, he wouldn't have . . ." *Wouldn't have what?* I thought. The truth was that I didn't know what Theseus even wanted. "Let's watch the other half of 'Dark Hand,' just to see what he might've stolen for Alkirk."

"Agreed." Theseus sat at the base of a skyscraper in Mid-Town, watching the building. His five remaining spider legs skittered below him, punching tiny pockmarks into the cement, and he'd replaced the hook with another rocket launcher and the sword arm with one that looked more like an electric whip. He shook his head. "Late. Can't rely on old partners," he muttered, but the camera drone picked it up.

We'd gotten unedited footage from Rocko, not the cleaned-up, for-Earth-consumption stuff the studios actually ran on TV, so that kind of thing slipped through.

The supervillain started climbing, his head swiveling as he scanned the air—he had to be looking for us. Then, almost thirty floors up, he smashed a window open. The camera drone zipped inside, flipping around to show the villain's face. His chin was set, but a tiny smirk drifted through. He fired a trio of rockets at a steel-reinforced door, blowing it off its hinges, then used the whip to shock a pair of security guards who made the mistake of rushing him with pistols drawn.

Then he smashed a glass box open, grabbed something from inside, and headed back the way he'd entered. And just like that, the Episode was over.

"What do you think that was?" I asked.

Fursona rolled her eyes and grabbed my computer. She typed in 'Tokyexico Daily Report,' waited for the newspaper's page to load, and then searched 'Theseus' as a keyword. Then, she clicked on the most recent link.

Supervillain Raids LeClerk Foundation Building
The minor-league supervillain Theseus took advantage of the Third Power War fighting to shake his heroes, attack a robotics foundation's research facility, and make off with experimental laser technology, officials said on Saturday.

According to Dr. Ferdinand DuBois, the device Theseus stole was "proprietary micromolecular-level technology" being developed to "solve major issues with metal-based construction and demolition, as well as pave the way to near-Ilneat levels of space travel through active particle defense." While the loss of the laser itself is a minor setback, the recent alliance between Theseus and the Alkirk Corporation raises the specter of intercorporation warfare, and the use of supervillains as proxies is also troubling.

"Well, shit," Bianca said. "Next time we fight him, Theseus is gonna have a laser arm."

PART FOUR

25

Remote Learning

"So, we've got options," Bianca said. We sprawled across my apartment's floor, the disembodied voice of Dr. Boulder Vicente telling us about taking pratfalls and how best to hit someone with a sword to get the right look and sound without *actually* hurting them. Our Stage Combat course, like the others, had started recording lessons, and Dr. Vicente was as hilarious on video as in person, but neither of us was really paying attention.

Official school policy on Power Wars—yes, Tokyexico University had a policy for it—matched up pretty well with their policy on full-wall-breach Man vs. Nature situations. The quick version: students didn't have to attend classes except for practical exams. The longer version was a bit more complicated. In order to keep the identities of heroes and villains secret, the university had to make it less obvious when Bee and I had to skip classes. Their solution? Make in-person classes optional.

They even explained why to the whole student body—not that it was much of a secret. And, based on the few classes we *had* attended in person, the student body had decided not to attend pretty much unanimously. Class attendance was down 60%; fortunately, that was well within TU's projections.

"So, option one. We switch to Superpower Legal Issues and dig into the New Gotham Accords. I know you know all about them or whatever, but they're more or less new to me. And option two: Extra Relations and Public Presentation," Bee continued. "I'd rather deal with the New Gotham Accords. What are the odds we'll be managing more Extras when Tele-Portal gets us out there?"

"Pretty high," I replied, turning off Dr. Vicente midway through another tangent on how the Mid-Town Slam move worked. "Let's deal with the New Gotham Accords first, though. We'll do that, then slog through managing whatever hypothetical Extra Relations has for us."

"Got it." Bee didn't take my computer to pull up a lecture. Instead, she grabbed a textbook. *Law in a Time of Superpowers: Third Edition* covered most of the historical legal issues Launch Day had created in passing. It mainly focused on the three Ilneat Compacts that governed how supers, their producers, and humanity interacted. However, the final chapters covered three different visions of the future.

The first came with a disturbing number of problems. In it, a hero or villain grew powerful enough to take over a major world power or rallied enough supers to their cause that they became the de facto world government. A legal framework was in the works to stop the so-called dictator-by-powers from happening, but its final drafts and debate on it were years out—if not decades. Luckily, Golden Goose didn't seem interested in the job.

The second seemed almost as unlikely, based on the book. In it, the Ilneats packed up and left, taking their superpowers with them. The world would need some sort of stability during the transition back to regional governments, militaries, and post-Ilneat economic models, and an attempt at resurrecting the old United Nations model was in the works in case that happened.

Today, though, the professors didn't want us learning about either of those. Neither was super likely, but the New Gotham Accords had a growing groundswell of support.

"In 2038, APPEAL, Antisuper Alliance, and the Society for Yesterday's Tomorrow put together the first draft of what would become the New Gotham Accords," Bianca read. The concept was simple: Supers would be welcome anywhere, but their powers would only be used in a few cities. They initially picked Great Lake City, Yorkston, and Los Francisco—the three biggest cities in North America—to become "New Gothams," as they referred to cities where superpower use would be allowed.

"The basic idea was simple. By putting supers in those few areas, the Ilneats would get all the Episodes they could ask for, the majority of humanity could go back to their pre-Launch lives, and supers could go all-out without worrying about Extras since everyone living in the "New Gothams" would be there of their own free will. The idea had massive support in 2038, but by 2040, it was clear there were some glaring issues."

"Yeah, I bet," I snorted. "Bets on what the issues were?"

"Probably, like, 'I don't want to live with that many supers' and 'as supers, we shouldn't be locked away. We're people, too!'" Bee said.

"Yep. Two of the major complaints right there."

Bee flipped the page to keep reading as my phone buzzed. "The communities of Great Lake City, Yorkston, and Los Francisco, in particular, fought back against—"

"Holy shit!" I interrupted, holding my phone up triumphantly.

"What?"

I showed Bee the text I'd gotten.

<Hey, that guy's here. Mrs. N's giving him the threat talk - Honeycomb 4:15>

"Yes!" Bee shouted, pumping her fist like she'd scored a game-winning goal. "I knew he'd turn! I knew it!"

"Hold on, Bee. We don't know if he's turning. He's taken a single step, but he hasn't texted me, and I doubt he's talked to Dr. Ayers. We need to approach this carefully."

"Screw that. Let's get over there!" Bee dragged me toward the green room, all thoughts of classwork forgotten.

Bee's excitement was infectious.

As we rocketed through the Tokyexico City skies toward Tottergarten, I couldn't help but grin. I still wasn't sure if showing up there would help, but as I saw it, it couldn't hurt things worse than it already had. So we raced across campus, every flap of Bee's wings matched by mine, trying to get to Tottergarten before Vigilant Vow could walk away or change his mind.

A pair of cars sat in the parking lot; Mrs. N's ride wasn't anything special, but Vigilant Vow clearly came from some money—or he'd cashed in on his time working for Cartman. A brand-new Jeep with a lift and everything sat beside her compact car, bright orange paint shining in the afternoon sun. I rolled my eyes; Bee was a professional, minor-league hero, and she drove a beat-up Civic. We'd need to fix that!

As we landed and my wings retracted, the door opened, and a familiar face opened the door.

Vigilant Vow still wore his trademark white hoodie, and the scarf familiar still sat wrapped around his neck. He saw me and shot a glare that would have killed me if he'd still had half of Stella-Lunar's power. A single maroon crystal hovered over his head. The moment he saw us, he reached for it—I raised my wand an inch, and Fursona stiffened.

"What do you two want?" he asked. "Do you just want to follow me around and make my life miserable?"

"No," I said. I fidgeted a little and lowered the wand again. "I've been worried, though. I told you to give me a text if you decided to—"

"Well, I didn't! I didn't decide anything. I *still* haven't decided anything." Vigilant Vow's eyes had teared up, but below the water, they darted wildly back and forth between me, Fursona, his car, and the door. He looked like he wanted to run or fight, but couldn't decide which to do.

"Easy, Vigilant Vow, easy," Fursona said. Something felt off with her voice, and it took me a moment to realize that her voice modulator was off. She'd never shut it off for me! I opened my mouth, but a wing on my shoulder convinced me to shut up. "We're not here to fight you. Understudy and I want to see you make it, whether as a hero who can hold their own in the minors, one who decides Tottergarten work is for them like Honeycomb, or one who retires and lives their best nonsuper life."

"Well, you had a funny way of showing that last spring! I was so close! So close to making it!"

Fursona sighed and sat down on the curb. "And what would that have gotten you? You knew Cartman was using you, right?"

"I had him under control! The Agent and I—"

"The Agent was using you, too!" I said. Fursona shot me a *look* I could feel through her suit; her eagle eyes bore into me, and I clamped my mouth shut.

"Understudy, not now. Vigilant Vow, this is going to sound ridiculous. We set up that final fight so that you'd lose, but we didn't do it because we wanted you to suffer. You were on a bad path, and I think you knew it. You needed to hit rock bottom before you could start fixing it. Now you're there, so now you can."

I eyed the crystal; Vigilant Vow had always used them to summon his stolen familiars, and they'd always been purple. This one, though, was dark red, and it hovered closer to him than any of his purple ones ever had. He noticed me looking and glared. "Fuck you two, you know that? I don't need your help."

"Really? Stella-Lunar would disagree," my mouth moved before my brain could tell it to stop. I clapped a hand over my lips. "Sorry."

"Whatever." He pushed past us, climbed into his driver's seat, and gunned the engine, peeling out of the parking lot and disappearing.

I rolled my eyes. "That went poorly."

"Yeah. Understudy, if we get another chance, let me take the lead. He hates you more than anyone in the universe, and you're not helping with that. I've got those psychology classes, and—"

"Got it. Understood. Vigilant Vow is your show until he calms down," I said, face red and fists balled. If I had my way, I'd be fighting him again. *Why* did I feel that way? It didn't make sense. "Come on, let's go talk to Honeycomb."

But before we could get inside, Honeycomb opened the door, papers in hand. "Did he already leave?"

"Yes," I said shortly.

"Darn. I've got a little more paperwork he needs to fill out to become an employee here. No phone, no address—it's like he's got a secret identity he wants to protect or something!" Honeycomb said, grinning. "You two got to talk to him, though. That's good!"

"Something like that, yeah," I mumbled. "What did he say to you?"

"Just that he'd had some time to think, and he wanted to try to be better. He's studio-less right now, and without his Signature Skill, he's worse off than me! I gave him access to Buzzy on a strict schedule, though."

"You *what*!?" I said, flabbergasted. The last thing Vigilant Vow needed was a temptation to use his powers for evil again. It'd be better if he didn't have any.

Fursona nodded slowly, though. "Understudy, this is literally why you gave him Honeycomb's number, remember?"

"Right." I'd sent him to Honeycomb because she was one of the few Magical Girls he hadn't offended, stolen from, or at least had a contract with. She'd be the most likely to hear him out and sympathize. "I didn't expect her to hand him the keys to her power. You know what his Signature Skill does, right?"

"Yes, of course!" Honeycomb said, exasperated. "He talked me through what'll happen when he uses Buzzer, and we came up with a schedule. He's got two nights a week, both when I have study groups anyway. That's it. If he uses her outside those two nights, he needs to text me right away, and he has to come here and explain to Mrs. N and me what the emergency was."

"And if he doesn't?" Fursona asked.

"Then Mrs. N goes after him. We talked about it together."

I nodded slowly. That seemed reasonable, to be honest, and Vigilant Vow needed *someone* to trust him. "Okay. I trust you and Mrs. N. Just be careful, okay? He's been a villain recently."

"So have all my co-workers," Honeycomb said. "I've got weak powers, but I'm not a dummy. I'll keep in touch with you, let you know how he's doing here, okay?"

"Okay. We might be stuck in some Power War Episodes, but we'd appreciate it," I said. "See you later, Honeycomb."

As we flew back to the green room, I tried to push Vigilant Vow out of my mind and focus on the Power War, my job as an auxiliary, and going full support.

26

Full Support

Bianca and I sat in front of the screens in the green room, staring at our rogue's gallery. The gold circle representing Sister Sly hadn't grown smaller in the weeks following our fight in the Poudre districts. If anything, she seemed to control more territory, not less. 3V1L had to be fighting against her, but it seemed that whatever they were doing, it wasn't working—or at least, not well enough to actually stop her.

Theseus hadn't expanded his territory, but that wasn't surprising. Our fight with him hadn't been about control, but about denying him power. I cringed; he'd no doubt weaponized the laser system we'd failed to keep him away from, and he'd be that much worse the next time we fought, but at least he didn't seem motivated by expansion.

The worst one was Livestream, though.

We hadn't seen him, but his shows were *all* over the internet. He didn't have a studio, just a hacked camera drone that followed him and recorded his every move. That is, his every move *as* a supervillain, but also as a normal person (though he blurred his face). He seemed like the ultimate chaos agent, and sure enough, his electric-blue dot wasn't ever in the same place twice. Worse, he'd piled into a dozen Power War fights, never picking the same side to support.

"Battle plan?" Bee asked. "What do we do here?"

"3V1L is just doing their thing, and if I'm reading this right, they're a little preoccupied with Sister Sly's expansion in North Poudre. We could probably leave them both alone, especially with the Power War going. Then, we have Theseus. We should honestly try to slow him down, but if we can't, that's okay. He's a professional, he's working for a corporation, and he doesn't have any interest in us or what we're doing. He's on the list because of the past, not the future," I said.

"So that leaves Livestream," Bee said. She paced back and forth. "And we have no idea where he's going to strike, when he's going to strike, or what he wants—other than internet fame."

"Right. So, we can't just hunt him down because there's no telling where he'll be, and he's unpredictable. We need more people. How's Tractor-Beam-Girl doing?"

Bee laughed. "Vicegrip? As far as I can tell, fine. She's not exactly rocketing up the leaderboards, though. I get the feeling she needs a teammate to take advantage of her powers—either that or more Skill Rolls so she can do a little more than just—"

"Grab a bad guy, yeah. Should we invite her on a patrol or something? Maybe offer her a minority share of our partnership?"

"Nah, let's wait another week or two. Then we can have it be a school assignment instead of her thinking we need her."

I grinned and stood up. "Smart!"

"I thought so. Let's figure out our recruitment pitch while we wait. Maybe something about possibly beating Flare's ass? That seemed to motivate her last time."

"Har har. Nah, I'm thinking we offer her a partnership, not as a sidekick, but as a heroine. We can bring her in for the six weeks we're studying three-hero teams, then either find someone else as our fourth or cut her loose and pair with another duo for the four-person lessons." I paused, giving Bee a chance to interject. When she didn't, I cleared my throat. "How about a different battle plan? We're meeting up with The Triad later today. What's your plan for support?"

Bianca considered for a moment. Then, after far too much pondering, she started talking rapidly. "Okay, I was going to say I should go Roo-sona and run escort while you take care of any Extras, but that doesn't make sense if The Triad wants us hunting enemies, so I think we could have two plans depending on what they really want us doing. Let's call one plan Serve and Protect and one, I don't know, how about Lieutenant Danger?

"The first one's hunting bad guys, reporting them to The Triad, and doing rescue and support as needed. I'd be Eagle-sona, and we could split up and talk through our phones—"

"Nah, we'll need something better. Hopefully, The Triad will help set us up for success. But I see what you're saying. We'd be better at scouting, we'd both be mobile, and it'd give us the most ability to protect Extras."

"Yeah! And then, for Lieutenant Danger, I'd have to suck it up and go Roo-sona, but you could fly us into range against minor-league lieutenants. That'd give us the most firepower to take them down." Bee sighed. "I wish I could quick-change. That'd be so overpowered."

"It really is. So, for the meeting today, we're going as . . ."

Bianca grinned. "Eagle-sona and Understudy. You can show off your support build if you want, but we'll both fly over ourselves."

FRIDAY, OCTOBER 10

The Triad's secret base wasn't in any way a secret—the massive pyramid loomed over Parker district, taller than all but the tallest Mid-Town skyscrapers. Extras they'd hired bustled here and there, working on computers, cooking, and helping maintain Tele-Portal's gear and Underdelver's mech suit. Almost entirely concrete, tunnels and rooms lay scattered inside the pyramid like an ant nest, with the training room at the very bottom and The Triad's command room near the top, just below an observation deck that gave Tele-Portal instant access to anywhere in south, central, and west Tokyexico City.

We'd been in The Triad's training room before, but never upstairs, so when Tele-Portal called down the elevator and beckoned us inside, I couldn't stop shivering. Nerves and excitement fought a war inside me, and I felt like I'd had three too many cups of coffee this morning. This was the day! The day I'd *finally* get to try out Rescue Girl Lucky Star!

The elevator opened into a high-tech, futuristic-looking command room; Bud Lightbeam waved from one chair while Underdelver grinned near a low workbench. Tele-Portal strode into the center of some device that looked a lot like the Ilneats' Costume designer, and when she raised her hands, a holographic map of Tokyexico City zoomed out to cover the floor. I jumped as the Council of Heroes spire shimmered into reality just below me.

"Okay, Triad and auxiliaries, the reality in Tokyexico is that we're losing this Power War—otherwise, Golden Goose wouldn't be camped out in the CoH building," Tele-Portal said. She snapped a finger, and huge swaths of the city went red. "These are areas currently claimed by Lord Destructo, McHammer, a few recently unretired major-league villains, and King Cold's coalition."

"That's . . . half the city," Fursona said, staring.

"Yep. Hang tight for a second. I'm not done." She snapped again, and more went yellow, this time in islands between the sea of red plus a big continent in the Poudre districts. "These are minor-league villains staking claims on the side, plus 3V1L, which still has enough reputation that the major-league vils aren't going after Poudre. It helps that there's not much there worth claiming, though. Just factories and residential."

More snaps followed: Red-and-black stripes for areas where major-league villains were fighting each other, red-and-yellow for major-on-minor combat, and light blue against red and yellow for places where local heroes fought delaying actions against the encroaching villains. "There's one more color, and that's hero-controlled safe areas," Tele-Portal said. A few navy-blue dots appeared, mostly around the Council of Heroes building, The Triad's Triangle, and Tokyexico University, but with a few other cut-outs around the map—including a huge one far to the north.

"What's that?" I asked.

"Stella-Lunar. The other big one to the east is the In-You-Endos. We don't mess with them, and neither do most villains. Now, since Golden Goose killed Haze-Matt, the villains have actually been doing better. He was such a wild card that they had to manage him almost as much as we did, but they don't have to watch their backs as much with him out of the picture." Tele-Portal clapped, and a series of symbols covered the map.

I stared at them, trying to understand them, but I couldn't keep from shivering. I'd hoped Haze-Matt had survived Golden Goose, and the casual way Tele-Portal mentioned his death felt . . . wrong. Like he hadn't really been a person. One more thing to talk to Dr. Ayers about.

The map symbols were weird—a few made sense, like X and O, but one looked like a pair of Gs, and another was . . . "Is that a . . ."

"Dick, yes. A cartoon dick. These symbols represent patrols. X means it's taken by a *normal* hero. O means it's not taken. The two Gs is Golden Goose. Do *not* go there. The cartoon dick is the In-You-Endos. Do *not* go there!"

"Okay, got it," Fursona said. "We'll stay clear of all that."

"Good. Here's the mission. We're going to assign you three unclaimed patrols into major-league territory. You need to maintain a presence in each of them at least once a week. Just be seen on the streets, let the people know the villains haven't won yet, and *make sure* you carry these," Underdelver said. He handed us each an ear-piece. When I put it on, it locked around the cartilage, sealing itself in place. Then he handed us each a button.

"That one's a personal favorite," Tele-Portal said. "If you push it, it'll open a portal at your location. It's one-way only, but it'll let me know where you are, and I can move The Triad in. Your job is to find the major-league villains so we can fight them."

"We're bait. Got it," I said, wincing.

"No, you're scouts. You figure out where they are, call in The Triad, and we take care of them before Golden Goose or Stella-Lunar gets involved. The second we show up, you switch from finding them to dealing with their lieutenants or evacuating the battlefield. We'll keep the major-leaguers occupied so you can do your job, and you keep the battlefield clear so we can do ours," Bud Lightbeam said.

Tele-Portal nodded. "We want to know three things. First, if Golden Goose, Stella-Lunar, or the In-You-Endos move in, we want to know they're there, and we want you to leave. We don't compete with any of them for . . . various . . . reasons."

"Yeah, things get weird when A Cat Who Can Talk gets involved, not to mention the rest of that pervy team. I have no idea how they keep themselves running," Lightbeam said.

Tele-Portal rolled her eyes. "Right. That. Second, we want to know if a district seems clear. That is, if you show up in Evergreen and there's no sign of villains, we need to know that. We'll update the Council of Heroes, and they can try getting a minor-leaguer established to hold the district down. Even if it's just a neighborhood, let us know.

"And third, we want to know if you find *any* villains minor league and up. If it's a minor-leaguer, feel free to engage, but report in first. Some of our civilian assistants will be on the line for that kind of thing. But if it's a major-leaguer, press your buttons, open a portal, and wait for support."

Underdelver nodded from the machine he was working on. "Kids, she's serious about the 'wait for support' part. Once we land, we'll give you an objective, and from there, you'll be responsible for handling it. But until we show up, do. Not. Engage. A. Major. Leaguer."

"Okay, got it. Call in villains and empty districts, get support for heavy hitters, take out lieutenants, and keep people safe." What they wanted us to do was exactly what we'd prepared to do, so that was nice! "We can do that. Which districts?"

27

Districts

SATURDAY, OCTOBER 11

"I can't believe they assigned us to the Foothills," Fursona complained in my ear as I walked the cracked sidewalk in my Understudy Costume.

"At least they warned us not to hit the East Plains district," I replied. That was where, according to The Triad, a group of recently unretired villains had set up their domain. Together, they were a big enough threat that none of the local heroes could handle them except Stella-Lunar, and they'd made it clear they were just reliving their glory days, so no one wanted to mess with them. Especially me—I had a good idea that it was most of the Anti-Nap League. The Foothills seemed much safer.

The Foothills sat right against the mountains, half in and half outside the wall, and if there was a single district besides Thornton that'd be considered run-down, it was this one. It wasn't a slum—not quite—but compared to University's clean, quiet streets and the shiny towers of Mid-Town, it left a lot to be desired.

It also felt like home, a fact I kept reminding Fursona of. "You might have grown up in Tortuga West, beach-bum, but some of us lived in a trailer park in a small town outside the walls. This is pretty nice compared to a bunch of Riverside."

"Believe me, I am aware," Fursona said. "Who'd they say the villain was out here?"

I shrugged. "We're in contested territory. There's a local hero, but no one's seen him in a week or so. One of Lord Destructo's lieutenants is making a push here, too, and Quickvine's the local villain, but he only just made the majors. He's not really a contender if Lord D or McHammer show up."

Ahead of me, a few people stood on a street corner. One shot a stink eye at me and disappeared into a strip mall. I didn't pay her much attention; we'd been getting rough looks since we arrived.

"I get the feeling most of the locals don't love heroes," I said. "Kind of spooky, to be honest."

"Agreed," Fursona replied. She banked overhead, taking a street a few blocks ahead of me. "Do you think Quickvine's running some sort of PR campaign or mind control?"

"My bet's on PR. If he was a mind control specialist, he'd be as big as Mindstorm, and we'd have heard of him before now." I walked toward the rest of the street-corner-standers. "I'm going to ask around a little. Can you cover me from above?"

"Sure, you got it," Fursona said, turning and drifting on a thermal.

I walked toward the smoking group, putting on my best public relations face. "Hello! I'm Magical Girl Under—"

"You're two weeks late, hero," one woman said around a cigarette butt. "Why don't you just go back to Mid-Town or somewhere you *care* about and leave the Foothills alone?"

"Yeah. Life's not great here with Quickvine, but at least he lets us live our lives as long as we give him tribute," another man said.

"Wait, you're giving a villain tribute? Like medieval peasants? Doesn't that strike you as flawed somehow?" I asked, incredulous.

The woman rolled her eyes, then spat. "Of course, but it's either pay tribute to Quickvine or pay it to the Tokyexico government, and he's a local boy. He knows what's up here, and once he's got control, maybe he'll make life better for us."

"I don't think he will," I said. "I think he's like most villains—in it for himself. If you follow him, you're just another hench."

"Better than unemployed," she shot back. "Look, kid. Your heart's in the right place, but it's been bad out here in the Foothills—almost as bad as Thornton. So how about you take your ass, walk it back to the city, and let us deal with our own problems?"

"Yeah, fuck you, supe!" the guy who'd talked earlier said. The other started heckling and jeering, and I turned on my heel and walked away, then took off to join Fursona.

It was going to be a long patrol out here.

SUNDAY, OCTOBER 12

"Please, stay back! The Triad's dealing with Doctor Danger's lair, and we don't want anyone getting hurt when it ex—er, *if* it explodes," I said to the reporters pressing in around Fursona and me. We stood outside a low warehouse in the shadow of The Triad's Triangle—though, to be fair, half the city was in its shadow this late in the day. Inside, Doctor Danger's factory pumped out bombs, missiles, and explosives by the ton.

We'd found him by accident—sort of. An explosion had ripped apart part of the street and tipped us off to his base's location, and an Episode had started not thirty seconds later. By then, we'd been patrolling the Parker district for hours, and I breathed a sigh of relief as we called in The Triad. Finally, I'd be able to do some support work.

Or not.

Instead of hunting down lieutenants, we stood outside of what Underdelver had confirmed was Doctor Danger's only exit while The Triad stormed the underground lair. Occasionally, an explosion caught the gathered reporters' attention, but for the most part, they only had one thing to watch.

Us.

"Magical Girl Understudy, how did you find Doctor Danger's lair?" a reporter shouted.

"Well, we knew he had to be around here somewhere, and my, uh, partner Fursona and I had been asking around. The warehouses in the Parker district have been abandoned for a while, so we figured we'd poke around, and that's when the explosion went off."

"Do you have any insight on what's going on inside? The Triad's winning, right?"

Fursona cleared her throat. "We can't give out that information, other than that The Triad is definitely winning. Golden Goose does *not* need to get involved in Parker."

"How do you justify your attempts to keep us from reporting on the truth about what's going on in there!? This is an outrage. We're press—we should be able to get footage from inside the lair!"

I groaned. "Ma'am, the lair is a live explosive weapons factory, and we don't know how big it is. Frankly, we're probably all inside of the blast radius if Bud Lightbeam misses a shot, so there's no way I can let you get closer."

"My sources say you're working as support auxiliaries with The Triad. How does that work?"

I rubbed my temples—I was starting to get a headache—and nodded thoughtfully. "How does being an auxiliary work? Well, Tele-Portal, Lightbeam, and Underdelver have the firepower to root out Doctor Danger and his lieutenants, so most of what we do is keep a perimeter so you don't get hurt while they're working, make sure there aren't any E—er, civilians—in the danger zone, and fight any lieutenants that break free. It's pretty simple work, or it's supposed to be."

It wasn't right now, that was for sure. Fursona stood near the door, back facing me in case anyone tried to leave the warehouse. Keeping that perimeter tight was important, but it left me to face the brunt of the reporters myself.

A reporter asked if they were in danger, and I struggled to suppress a groan. "Yes. Everyone here is in danger, and that's why we can't let you inside. You should all back up about two hundred yards, like I said earlier, but you won't listen to me!"

Something exploded under our feet as if to punctuate my words, and the crowd took a few nervous steps back, muttering. Then, before I could press the advantage, they settled back down, pressing in around me.

"Goddammit," I whispered. These reporters were going to get someone killed. Probably themselves.

"You said it," Fursona whispered back. She pointed at the crowd of fans behind the reporters. "I'll be over there, signing autographs. The hyperobsessed ones are better than the press."

MONDAY, OCTOBER 13

"I'm starting to hate support work," I muttered to Fursona as we ate a snack in an empty park in the Evergreen district. Despite being next to the Foothills, Evergreen didn't have the same worn, beaten-down look. Instead, the streets seemed clean, other than signs of supervillain fights. The people were mostly happy, and an actual police presence briefed us on what was happening here.

Acid Burn, an up-and-comer in the majors and an offshoot of 3V1L, had been warring over the district. Everywhere we looked, MIRACLE crews patched holes in the roads, fixed burn marks on buildings' facades, and worked hard to erase the signs of the previous night's battle. The 3V1L subsidiary was slowly but surely losing, and I wondered just how much damage Golden Goose had really done to their organization.

Not that Acid Burn was a slouch. She'd been a Haze-Matt lieutenant before Golden Goose had killed him, but without any of the villain's eccentricities. Instead, she was a Genius, but not the kind who tinkered and perfected a few weapons at a time. Instead, she had one solution—literally—that she handled all her problems with.

Unfortunately for everyone in Evergreen, that solution had a pH of 0.

So, as our final stop of the week, we were in Evergreen, scouting for the big shots. We'd started in the residential areas, where last night's battle had ended. *Maybe*, I thought, *we'd find something there*. But there was nothing. Everywhere we looked, signs of a villain-on-villain power struggle greeted us, but we couldn't find any hints of where they'd actually *gone*. So now we were taking a quick break and pushing toward city hall.

As we sat, I pulled a tarot card from the deck Bee had given me for Christmas. **[Card Curio]** activated as I looked at The Tower. That meant sudden change or disaster. "We're in the right place. Let's try left, but get ready for . . . something. Something bad, most likely. Probably, oh, I don't know? An ambush by an unexpected enemy."

"That sounds great, Understudy. Anything but more walking. There's no way The Triad can say we haven't had a presence in Evergreen."

"Yeah, right?" I said, packing up the remains of our snack and heading down the hill toward the district's center. "Honestly? We've done enough this week. We should take it easy, focus on school, and see if we can catch Livestream out somewhere. Focus on our own stuff for a bit before Rocko gets frustrated."

"Rocko's always frustrated," Bee said. She'd eaten inside her suit—yogurt, pudding, or something equally semiliquid and slurpable. "I'm shocked he hasn't—"

"Shhhh." I held up a hand, cutting my partner off. Someone was chanting in the distance, and I could smell the faint but distinct smell of a burning building. "This way! Hurry!"

I ran toward the shouting chanters, rounded a corner, and stopped. "Oh shit."

"Oh shit is right. Let's go!" Fursona said.

City hall was on fire. The brick-and-marble building wasn't in any danger of a collapse, but its third-story windows belched black smoke out into the afternoon air. A siren went off in the distance, then another, while a fire alarm blared out a relentless screeching beep in the building. But that wasn't the worst part.

There, arrayed in front of the burning city hall, was the Tokyexico University APPEAL chapter. Their signs had changed—now they read Our City, Our Safety, Our Voices and Become Your Own Hero: Reject Superpowers. Su-Bin led them in the same chants and shouts she'd shouted during the Orientation Episode as she stood in front of them, yellow T-shirt brilliant in the sun and a look of fury on her face.

But that wasn't the worst part, either. If it was, I'd have just walked away and let the fire department handle it. APPEAL and I hadn't ever gotten along; just because their arguments made some sense didn't mean they weren't out to get me.

No, the worst part faced the protestors.

The villain looked more and more furious by the second. A scowl plastered her face above the respirator across her mouth and nose, and she wore a gigantic tank of greenish liquid strapped to her back. "Clear the fuck off, or I'll let you have it! First and last warning!"

I didn't have much of a choice; I had to keep the Extras safe, even if they hated me. "Acid Burn? The curtain's closing on your crime spree!" As she turned toward me, face a rictus of anger, I pressed my button.

28

Button

A lot of things happened in the three seconds between my button push and The Triad appearing.

First, I got a **[Casting Call]**.

[Casting Call]
[Episode: Power War: Evergreen Burn - R (Auxiliary, PG-13)]
[Role: Support Sidekick! Do you accept the role? (Yes/No)]
[Role Focus: Drama + Cunning]

Before I could accept, the APPEAL Extras started screaming as Acid Burn lunged into action. Her acid sloshed toward Fursona and me, spraying in a gigantic green wave.

Then a gigantic mech suit squeezed its way through the portal, and the acidic attack sloshed across it, hissing and spitting against the dark steel. "ATTENTION, VILLAIN! SURRENDER! UNDERDELVER IS HERE!"

A trio of identical gold-and-red heroes soared into the air behind him, and Tele-Portal stilt-strode onto the battlefield just before the portal closed. "Good job, kids. Get these crazy Extras out of here. This is gonna be a messy one."

I accepted the **[Casting Call]**. "You got it, Tele-Portal!"

[Power War: Evergreen Burn: Act One in Progress]

As the fighting picked up, I couldn't help but grin. This was my chance to leap into action and finally—after three long days of sitting around, talking to reporters, and putting up with angry civilians—do my full support thing. I slow-shifted into Rescue Girl Lucky Star, the burgundy, navy, and white outfit more subdued and in the background than my Understudy outfit, and Tails's head now covered with a nurse's hat.

"Okay, we're online, Fursona," I said, landing from my spinning transformation and opening my eyes.

"Great! APPEAL Extras are scattering. I'll stay airborne and guide you to them if you can pull them out of the fighting."

"You got it," I said, waving up at her and racing toward the first cluster of scared-looking college students huddled near a storefront on the far side of the street. Acid Burn's goop sizzled in the street as it flew haphazardly everywhere, bouncing off Underdelver's armor and hissing on the asphalt.

"Hi! It's your lucky day!" I said, smiling widely and, I hoped, winningly. When the protesters-turned-victims simply stared at me, dumbfounded, I continued. "Look, I'm Rescue Girl Lucky Star. I'm here to get you out. Who are you?"

They still didn't say anything, though one lifted a sign that said Supers Go Home half-heartedly. I tried—and failed—to avoid the eye-roll. Where did they think home was, anyway? A quick **[Audition Notes]** gave me all the information I needed about him.

[Good Thinking! +1 Cunning Point]

[Audition Notes for John Deer: This Extra is not going to listen to you. He's a member of an antisuper organization, and he's fully committed to the cause—or at least he thinks he is. He doesn't know much about why he's here; he's just supposed to be making a statement about supers.]

"Okay. Great. Listen, I'm going to portal your butt out of here before that acid flows over the curb, okay? Great!" I didn't wait for a response. Instead, I used **[Noncombatant Teleport]**. A pinkish portal—I just couldn't get away from the color—opened below him, and he dropped through, screaming. I didn't know where he went, and I didn't care, as long as it wasn't the middle of the fighting. Hopefully, it'd be somewhere safe.

[Dramatic Rescue! +1 Drama Point]
[Rescue Rearm! +1 Card Curio Uses]

I grinned, quickly dropping more portals under the other three increasingly ter-rified protestors. I got **[Rescue Rearms]** on **[Audition Notes]** once and **[Noncombatant Teleport]** twice, leaving me with most of my charges, but I could already see a possible problem. If I could use **[Noncombatant Teleport]** five times, and I wasn't guaranteed a reset if I used other powers, I could easily run out for the act. I'd have to be careful not to get bad resets.

"Fursona, I've got that cluster. Next? And if you see Su-Bin, can you let me know?" I said into my microphone.

"A block to your left. Might want to move, though. Acid Burn's really going all out there. She might be able to beat Underdelver solo!" Fursona's unmodulated voice said in my ear.

I started running just as the lake of acid on Short Street overtopped the concrete, sending waves of sour-smelling smog into the air overhead. "Got it! On my way!" As I ran, I thanked whoever was looking out for me that Acid Burn didn't have any known lieutenants of her own.

As the fighting raged around the burning city hall, I spent my time dodging rivers of acid, looking for anywhere I could cross the corrosive streams without getting burned, and teleporting Extras away from the fighting. Fursona stayed airborne, though she occasionally gave me a boost when I couldn't get from one side of a street to the other.

The fighting seemed . . . not in hand, exactly, but not our problem. We had a dozen more APPEAL protesters unaccounted for, including Su-Bin, plus locals who needed saving. "Fursona, any sign of President Pak?"

"No. I think she bailed," Fursona said over my earpiece. She banked and turned back toward city hall, then stopped. "Hey, I think the acid's going down. This is gonna be a MIRACLE job for sure. My dad would kill for a contract like this."

"Okay. Let's keep looking around. I'll—"

WHAM!

The breath drove from my lungs as someone in a VR headset and bleached blonde hair slammed into me. "Hello, Livestreamers! We're live and streaming today from Evergreen!"

"That's right, CastorOil736, we've got a very special stream today," Livestream said as he threw me across the street, where I crashed through a plate glass–window. "I've got not only Acid Burn, not *only* The Triad, but Fursona and a hero I can only assume is Magical Girl Understudy!"

[HP 11/12]

I picked myself up, brushing off glass shards and peering out the window. Livestream's signature electric-blue LED lighting rig glowed even in the midday sun, making his silver-gray super-suit positively shine. He pointed at me. "So here's what's going to happen, viewers—thanks for the tip, CaptainS0Obvious, I appreciate them all. You know, working as an independent villain's got its perks, but I rely on you to be able to keep producing this show!"

"Eat talons, Livestream!" Fursona said, crashing down onto the sidewalk, feet-first. She scored a trio of nasty scratches across Livestream's back, but his quick roll dodged the worst of it.

"Hey, now, I haven't finished explaining the rules! They're pretty simple, really. You bid on which power I'll use next, and when I need a new one, the highest value gets used, and half the money bid goes into my account! Ready?" A camera drone painted Livestream's colors took in every bit of the villain's speech.

I started shifting into Magical Girl Understudy, but Fursona said, "No, you've got a job. I'll keep him busy!" in my ear, and I nodded.

"Oh, one more thing! Last night, my bidders said to go after Understudy, not Fursona, so . . . yeah," Livestream said. "No hard feelings, Understudy. It's for the fans! Go!"

I started running as the drone—not Livestream, but the *drone*—surged toward me. Behind me, Fursona and Livestream started fighting, though when I looked back, it didn't seem like the villain really cared about hurting her. Instead, his eyes kept flicking toward me.

I rounded a corner, the painted drone following me, and Livestream's voice came through it. "[**Flash-Intro Punch**]! Good choice!" A moment later, something crashed behind me.

"Okay, now, Magical Girl Understudy doesn't seem interested in the fight. I almost want to take it easy on her just to see what she's up to and why she'd abandon her partner, but—oooh! The viewers have spoken! Let's [**Fast-Forward**] this stream!"

A moment later, something zipped in front of me, solidifying into Livestream. He punched me in the stomach, and I got a brief view of his chat exploding with '*Fs*' and '*Ws*' and all sorts of comments. Then I hit the pavement.

[HP 10/12]

Okay. He really *wasn't* going to leave me alone. I picked myself up as the camera drone blared on about the next move in the lottery, waited for the bird-shaped shadow to hit Livestream again, and slow-transformed back to Understudy. As I spun around, only one thought ran through my head.

If this guy wanted to fight and stop me from saving my friend, I'd give him a quick, explosive fight for the camera. He might not like it, though.

I landed, the music stopping just as Livestream broke free from Fursona again. "There she is! My target for the day!"

"Yep. Here I am, Livestream fans! [**Bit-Part Barrage**]!" I fired ray after ray toward the villain, each piercing the space he'd been in, but I got no hits.

"Good thing you guys picked [**Green Screen**], huh?" Livestream said from behind me. I rolled to dodge an energy pulse that tickled the back of my neck, then fired a [**Starlance**] his way. *That* made contact, staggering him. A Fursona screech knocked him into the road, and he started getting to his feet.

[Dramatic Damage! +1 Drama Point]

Before he could fully recover, a manhole exploded upward in a green, acidic fountain that splashed down over us, then another. It burned through my Costume, singeing my skin even through the superhero damage, and I screamed. So did Livestream, who retreated to the street's far side as a massive surge of acid filled it.

He stood on the far shore, glaring and talking, and his voice blared out of the drone next to me.

[HP 8/12]

"Alright, fans, looks like the Acid Burn fight is heating up! We'll pick up our grudge match with Magical Girl Understudy in just a few minutes, whenever Evergreen's streets aren't green!"

[End of Act One: Act Two in Five Minutes]

The villain—and his camera drone—disappeared around a corner, and a moment later, Fursona landed next to me. "That's a really convenient intermission. What's the plan? We can't fight him if you're in your Rescue Girl form, and we can't save Su-Bin if you're in Understudy. At least, not unless you can convince her to ride your sailboard or something."

"Somehow, I don't think that's happening," I said. "So, here's the plan. We're on Livestream's show. We need to beat him at his own game somehow, but . . . how?"

"It's a little late to stream the fighting ourselves, Understudy. Plus, Rocko would lose their mind."

"They sure would. But can we hijack Livestream's stream somehow? I mean, we're both pretty wealthy—in theory—and maybe Rocko could help out. If we can get him to use the wrong moves, he'll lose a lot of firepower," I said.

Fursona grinned. "Understudy, that's the dumbest idea I've ever—"

My phone buzzed.

<Understudy, thats hilarious. On it - Rocko 1:43>
<Just dont drop the ball here. H101 is counting on you - Rocko 1:43>

"Rocko is in. This is so stupid," I said.

"Okay, so, we just do our thing and don't worry about Livestream, and hope Rocko can take him out of the fight?" Fursona asked. "This feels wildly out of character for Rocko. Didn't he say that he couldn't interfere with Vigilant Vow?"

I started jogging down the sidewalk, past the once-again-receding river of acid. "Maybe it's different since Livestream is independent? They seemed hesitant to go after Cartman directly without unshakeable evidence, but I thought it wasn't because of Vigilant Vow."

Fursona nodded and took to the air. "Either way, we need to be ready. I'll keep an eye on him for as long as I can, but there's another threat—besides the acid lake, I mean. Who knows what else he's done to the drone."

29

The Drone

We found out pretty quickly what else he'd done to the drone.

[Power War: Evergreen Burn: Act Two in Progress]

The drone zipped out from behind a building the moment Act Two kicked off, its camera light flashing in a dizzying array of colors as it sped toward us. My phone buzzed as I fled, trying once again to let Fursona take the bulk of the fighting so I could find Su-Bin and the other goddamned APPEAL members. Screams for help rose from here and there as my phone buzzed, and I checked it quickly.

<Gonna take a few minutes to get control of his stream - Rocko 1:48>
<Bidding cuts off at $2000 - Rocko 1:48>

Something exploded behind me—I couldn't tell if it was another manhole cover or if the drone had crashed—and I put the phone away again. "Rocko's working on it! On my way to the next group!" I half shouted into my mic.

"You got it! Hope they don't pick **[Fast-Forward]** again, or he'll get by me," Fursona replied. I grinned between breaths, knowing that Rocko was listening in on us and that he wouldn't pick something that'd make us lose.

I had more important things to do than find out what Rocko's plan was, though, like finding a way across the acid river swirling between me and a group of APPEAL members standing on a metal bench before their refuge gave way to the rising corrosive tide.

"Okay, we're going to do some shifting," I muttered to myself as Fursona kicked the drone, sending it spinning out over the green stream. I popped into the air with **[Solar Wing]**, then quickly landed on the bench, which groaned ominously under the added weight. Then, before the APPEAL folks could decide whether to push me off, yell at me, or beg for help, I used **[Quick-Time Change]** and switched to Rescue Girl Lucky Star.

[Flashy Fitting-Room! +1 Flamboyance Point]
[Steel Yourself! +1 Grit Point]

"Hi, don't be afraid! I'm here to help!" I said cheerfully. "You want out of here, right?"

"Yes!" One of the Extras started yelling, and then all of them started shouting, screaming, and begging to be flown away first. Their remaining signs splashed into the acid, sending up little droplets that slapped against our legs, adding a few yelps of pain into the mix.

"Okay. One at a time. You're going to fall through a portal and show up . . . uh . . . somewhere safe but still nearby. Don't panic!" I dropped a [**Noncombatant Teleport**] under the first one, then the second, and within ten seconds, I stood on an empty, and very, *very* wobbly bench.

[**Dramatic Rescue! +4 Drama Points**]

Now I just had to get myself moving again. I couldn't justify a [**Quick-Time Change**] for every rescue—not when I'd have to use the regular [**Transformation Sequence**] to change into Understudy after every one. As I slowly did the dance and the bench creaked and started to tip below me, I wished I had another speedy change— or that I'd put the flight power on Lucky Star.

I launched into the sky on [**Solar Wings**] a few seconds before the bench sank into the ever-growing acid sea with a hissing sound and an acrid fume cloud, then spun, looking for the next group.

Instead, I found Livestream.

Rocko had clearly gotten into his stream.

"Okay, we're going to use [**Flash-Intro Punch**], then [**Flash-Intro Punch**], then [**Flash-Intro Punch**], because our anonymous new bidder's dumping all their money into it, even though it's useless against—"

Fursona screeched from twenty feet in the air, drowning out the on-air supervillain.

"—that," he finished, punching in her direction again.

"Don't worry, I've got him under control!" Fursona said.

"Only until the donations stabilize!" Livestream shouted. "I'm ending this game in five minutes!"

Okay, five minutes. I had five minutes to get control over the APPEAL Extras, and then I'd have to convert over to a fight against the supervillain. That was enough time, right?

Right?

I rocketed away from Eagle-sona as she blasted the retreating supervillain again. The camera drone strafed her, trying to keep her attention off Livestream, but she was too focused. I circled up, looking for another group.

Then another.

Then another.

It wasn't until I'd racked up another 7 Drama Points that I found Su-Bin, and when I did, I wished she'd been anywhere else.

A pair of APPEAL Extras stood next to her while she rolled on the ground, her arm covered in burn wounds. I dove quickly, getting a scream from one of the Extras as a reaction, and landed next to her, already shifting into Lucky Star. I used **[Audition Notes]** at the same time as I asked, "What happened?"

[**Good Thinking! +1 Cunning Point**]

[**Audition Notes for Su-Bin Pak: This Extra has been a thorn in your side for an entire semester, but she's also important to you. Doing everything in your power might go a long way toward changing her mind about you, but she might also be so set in her ways that she doesn't change. Su-Bin has some deep-seated hatred of supers—will you be enough to overcome that?**]

"Manhole cover. It flipped acid across her," one of the Extras said. "We can't move her!"

I nodded as Su-Bin writhed in pain, rolling half onto her unburnt side to glare at me. "Screw you, Understudy," she spat through gritted teeth. "I don't need your goddamn help."

I'd never heard her so vehement, and I had to take a deep breath. "President Pak, you need my help badly, and so do your friends. You're stuck on this block, and Acid Burn's filling up the whole neighborhood with acid. Unless you want to stay, you should take my assistance."

"No. You can't help me because I won't let you," Su-Bin said.

I nodded slowly, then knelt beside her. "That's interesting. You think I'm a doctor. I'm not. I'm a superhero, and we help people. It's what we're supposed to do."

Then I reached down, touched her shoulder—she flinched and tried to roll away but couldn't—and activated **[Jinx-Bearer]**.

The pain was unbelievable. It ripped up my arm and the entire side of my body as Su-Bin's burns disappeared, reappearing on my skin. Tears ran down my face, and I bit back a scream but couldn't stop the whimper of pain that came with it. My eyes narrowed as the pain faded slightly but didn't completely disappear.

[**Gritty Sacrifice! +2 Grit Points**]

[**HP 4/8 (Temporarily restricted from 12)**]

Su-Bin gasped, looking at her arm, then glared at me even more. "That doesn't change things. I still don't want your help." She looked relieved and exhausted, and I wondered how long she'd been lying here, letting Acid Burn's biggest power eat at her.

"I don't care if you want it," I said, still gritting my teeth. My superhero damage wasn't holding up against the burn; the max hit point decrease *hurt*! "I'm not here to help people who want it. I'm here to help people who *need* it." I slowly pushed myself to my feet, hoping the movement wouldn't hurt.

It did. But it didn't drop my superhero damage any further, so I kept going, dropping a [**Noncombatant Teleport**] under the first Extra. When she disappeared, I aimed another at the second, who vanished a moment later.

"You ready for yours?" I asked, getting ready to send Su-Bin somewhere safe.

She glared back, but Fursona's voice interrupted me before I could get the [**Noncombatant Teleport**] going. "I lost Livestream. He's heading your way. Ten seconds!"

I paused, head whirling, then started shifting into Understudy. I couldn't get Su-Bin out *and* shift to a combat-ready Costume, but I *could* shift to a fighter, beat Livestream—or at least keep Su-Bin safe—and then turn back to Lucky Star when the fight was finished.

But I didn't know if I'd make it. The villain was closing in; in the moment before I closed my eyes and spun, his camera drone and gaudy electric-blue suit caught my eye. Then the spin kicked in, and I just had to hope I'd be in time.

I was. I opened my eyes as Livestream's fist rocketed toward me, activated [**Power-Weaving**], and [**Quick-Time Changed**] right back out of Understudy and into Rainy Day. The [**I-Frame Transform**] ate his [**Flash-Intro Punch**] and rewarded me with a few Style Points.

[Flashy Fitting-Room! +1 Flamboyance Point]
[Steel Yourself! +1 Grit Point]
[Floating Points: 1 Flamboyance]

It also brought me down to an entire foot and a half shorter than the villain, who swung again as I backed up dangerously close to the acid-covered street. He missed—close enough that I felt the wind in my hair—and I used [**Wind Front**] to force him back. It splashed acid his way, too, and he rolled to avoid it.

[Badass Move! +1 Badass Point]
[Environmental Expert! +1 Cunning Point]
[Floating Points: 3 Flamboyance, 1 Grit]

Then, before he could recover and disrupt me, I [**Rode the Lightning**]. It didn't hit as hard as it could have with [**Thunderhead**], but it drove him backward as the [**Power-Weaving**] combo landed.

[Electric Lightshow! +1 Flamboyance Point]
[Power-Weaving! +6 Flamboyance, +3 Grit, +1 Badass Point]

Fursona hit the ground a moment later, wings catching her fall as she avoided my lightning and tried to slam her talons into the villain but missed.

The earth shook under us, and the acid started to drain—maybe into the sewers, or maybe Underdelver had found somewhere to put it all. With the threat of instant, painful death receding, I pressed the attack, **[Quick-Time Changing]** back into Understudy.

[Flashy Fitting-Room! +1 Flamboyance Point]
[Rejuvenation Activated: HP 8/8 (Temporarily restricted from 12)]

It wasn't full superhero damage, but it'd do for now. I fired a **[Starlance]** at Livestream, whose drone caught it on camera—and then right in its lens. It didn't crack—the Ilneats built them strong—but it wobbled and had to recover a few yards out of the way, facing the wrong way.

[Dramatic Damage! +1 Drama Point]

He punched out, this time catching me twice in rapid succession and driving the air from my lungs. As I spun with the second blow, I saw Su-Bin running toward a street corner. She shot a glare our way, and I realized that, more importantly than beating Livestream, I needed to catch up to her, make sure she was okay, and try to—somehow—explain my version of what had happened to her.

[HP 6/8 (Temporarily restricted from 12)]

Otherwise, APPEAL would only go after Understudy even more, and I was already on their enemy list.

The ground shook again, and Underdelver's massive mech arm reached through the sidewalk and grabbed Livestream's leg. It pinned the villain in place, the camera hovering overhead. Livestream looked into it and said, "Looks like this stream's done, Livestreamers. I'll catch you next time! Keep your feeds pointed my way!"

[End of Act Two: Act Three in Five Minutes]

I didn't listen to the rest of it. I was already airborne, riding my sailboard as I searched the streets below for Su-Bin.

By the time I found her, the intermission between acts was almost over. She'd run for a park nearby, away from Acid Burn's rivers and Livestream's shenanigans. I dipped my windsurfer's bow toward a nearby park bench and landed beside her. "Let's chat."

30

Let's Chat

But we didn't get a chance to talk. At least not right away.

[Power War: Evergreen Burn: Act Three in Progress]

Someone stepped out from behind a tree—a familiar villain in a devil helmet and red cloak. Instead of a sword, though, this woman carried nothing but her fists and her bare feet. She grinned at me, poison in her expression. "Hello, Magical Girl Understudy. The One *L* told me you'd be around here. You're in our territory."

"Let me guess," I said, squaring up as a dozen henchmen stepped out in similar helmets. "You're one of the Three *Vs*."

"For the moment, yes," she said, grinning. "The second one."

"And you're here to propose a Neutral Field and tell me something important that'll change how I view your organization?" I asked, hoping she'd say yes.

"No." She leaped toward me, foot lashing out, and changed it into a knee-thrust as I went to block her kick. Then she followed it up with a blow to my shoulder that sent me flying.

[HP 4/8 (Temporarily restricted from 12)]

I caught myself midair with **[Solar Wing]**, hovering over the villain. Then I fired a **[Starlance]** her way, but she backflipped over it, and it slammed into a henchman. "Fursona, if you're here, I could use your help!" I said into the mic, trying to keep my cool as I weaved past the trees, sending freshly fallen leaves whirling behind me.

[Dramatic Damage! +1 Drama Point]

The first gun went off a moment later, and Su-Bin's scream followed almost immediately. I heard the bullet whistle past my head and breathed a sigh of relief that it wasn't aimed at her. A moment later, my vision went red. These assholes were *shooting* with my friend *right there*!

I shot back, spraying a [**Bit-Part Barrage**] into the crowded henches after making sure Su-Bin was clear. The beams crashed into henches, sending them flying; they sprawled across the dying grass and crunched into leaves.

[**Dramatic Damage! +4 Drama Points**]

I didn't care that I'd knocked four henches out of the fighting. As far as I was concerned, the fight wasn't over until Su-Bin was safe. So, spinning in midair and braking in the air, I fired a single [**Starlance**] straight up to signal to Fursona where I was—the Broken Comms plan—and then called in again. "Park west of city hall. Hurry. 3V1L's here!"

I flew backward, gaining some distance and trying to draw the Second *V*'s attention away from her, but to my horror, the other henches turned at her shouted command and chased after APPEAL's president while she squared up on the ground and balled her fists. "Not sure why you're protecting her, but we'll take whatever advantages we can get," the Second *V* said.

I fired another [**Starlance**] her way, but she ducked under it easily, the pinkish spear fizzling out harmlessly against a massive old oak. "Nice try, Understudy. What's your cooldown? Two seconds? That's a second too long, and you used your barrage already."

"Dammit! It's a power? Of course it's a power," I complained. "Why are you here?"

"Two reasons, and the One *L* gave me permission to share them both," the Second *V* said. She punched toward me, the air splitting around her fist, and I dove wildly for the ground as a shockwave blew through the air I'd been hovering in a moment before. "First, you're in future 3V1L territory. We weren't here for you originally. We were here for Acid Burn."

I fired one more [**Starlance**], this time at the swarm of henches, but even though it knocked one across the park, the others kept up their pursuit, gaining on Su-Bin, who was running for all she was worth. "And the other reason?" I asked, shifting to try to keep the henches in range.

[**Dramatic Damage! +1 Drama Point**]

"Once we realized you were here, taking over Evergreen became secondary," she said, grinning. "So now we're here for you."

"Well, here I am!" I dove toward her, activating [**Power-Weaving**] and [**Quick-Time Change**] to become Copy Cat. Tails and I merged seamlessly in midair, our minds becoming one and her plushie claws stiffening into real ones on my hands and feet.

[**Flashy Fitting-Room! +1 Flamboyance Point**]
[**Steel Yourself! +1 Grit Point**]
[**Floating Points: 1 Flamboyance**]

Then my fall turned into a graceful pounce as I used [**Leaping Leopards**] to launch myself right at the Second *V*, who blocked my outstretched paws with her crossed arms.

[**Badass Damage! +1 Badass Point**]
[**Floating Points: 3 Flamboyance, 1 Grit**]

Then, as I started activating [**Hometown Heroine**] to complete my combo and get a massive speed buff, the Second *V* ducked in close and punched me in the nose.

[**Combo Broken! Floating Points Lost. Power Lost.**]

She laughed and pressed her attack as we exchanged blows back and forth, with her blocking my scratches and me taking her brutal punches with [**Fursonal Furcefield**]. Fists, paws, and feet flew briefly before we both backed away, panting.

[**Badass Damage! +1 Badass Point**]
[**Tough Kitty! +1 Grit Point**]
[**HP 3/8 (Temporarily restricted from 12)**]
[**Badass Damage! +1 Badass Point**]
[**Badass Damage! +1 Badass Point**]
[**HP 2/8 (Temporarily restricted from 12)**]

I'd done more damage to her than she had to me; scratches covered her red outfit, and I'd nicked one of her horns badly enough to spin it so it faced backward. But I also couldn't take as much. With my superhero damage low, even a positive trade could be trouble.

Then she activated [**Power-Chaining**] and ducked right back into the fighting.

[**Fursonal Furcefield**] took the first blow as I tried to find a way to disrupt her—but without [**Combo-Breaker**], I didn't have anything for this situation. Fursona had always taken care of me! I'd never *had* to worry about combos, to the point where I hadn't even noticed other supers using them.

[**Tough Kitty! +1 Grit Point**]

She pressed her attack even as I [**Doom Balled**], scratching into her cloak and leaving thin, bloody lines across her back and right arm.

[**Badass Damage! +4 Badass Points**]
[**HP 1/8 (Temporarily restricted from 12)**]

I needed Fursona here, and I needed her here *now*. Otherwise, the Second *V* was going to combo off, and I doubted [**Fursonal Furcefield**] would hold. Her next punch bounced off Tails, who, as always, was my protection in the Bruiser Copy Cat Costume.

[**Tough Kitty! +1 Grit Point**]

Then, grinning in triumph, the Second *V* reeled back a fist that seemed to grow bigger with each moment. It swung forward—

—and slammed into a wall of feathers that exploded in a puff of plumage. Fursona rolled across the leaves, then grinned up at me, her beak shattered so I could see her goofy smile. "Hi. Made it!"

"You sure did," I said, and used [**Cat-Scratch Fever**] to slap the stunned-looking Second *V*.

[**Dramatic Damage! +1 Drama Point**]

She blinked, then blinked again, looking confused, almost as if she couldn't figure out what had happened. I stared at her, ready to dodge, but she whirled and started fleeing, one hand in front of her to find the trees as her eyes swelled up. I watched her go for a moment, then turned to Fursona. "Hey, thanks. You really bailed meow't there." I flushed as I said it, hoping the fur would catch most of it.

"What?"

"I, uh, said you really bailed me out there."

"Sure." She grabbed my wrist and pulled herself to her feet, looking at a lopsided wing mournfully. "I don't think I'm flying like this, though."

"Okay. We'll go on foot. The 3V1L henches went that way," I pointed and started walking. "You good?"

"Yeah, I'm good. They got Su-Bin?"

"Yep." I took the time to shift into Rainy Day—the perfect Costume to go into a firefight with 3V1L's henchmen with—and then kept jogging toward the last place I'd seen them.

We didn't have to search for long.

Honestly, we barely had to search at all.

Su-Bin's screaming and shouting guided us toward her before we'd crossed half the park. She was howling up a storm, saying, "You're all traitors, you know that? You're repressing other regular people in the name of some aliens and the supers who work for them! You're symptoms of the crime that's grabbed all of Tokyex—"

Someone cut her off before she could yell too much more, thankfully. I needed to have my chat with her, but not as a screaming conversation with half of Evergreen listening. We approached the public restroom, half expecting the 3V1L henchmen to be hunkered down inside. After some quiet planning, I went left, and Fursona went around the right side.

We ran right into the henches.

They'd made a perimeter, staying spread out far enough that I couldn't catch them all in a single power; clearly, they'd learned something from our earlier encounters. There were eight in all, and two had a kicking, flailing Su-Bin. She might have been short, but she packed a punch. They started yelling as I ducked behind a tree, and the first pistol shot went off. "Hey! Come out, hands up! Otherwise—oof!"

I spun around the corner as Fursona slammed into the henches, already using my first power—[**Wind Front**]—to break up their perimeter. It slammed into several goons, bowling them over before losing steam and ruffling Su-Bin's hair.

[**Badass Move! +1 Badass Point**]

I dashed into the gap as pistols popped and bullets ricocheted off trees and concrete. I didn't have much time; one or two bullets would take me out of the fight. So, instead of setting up a combo, I just [**Rode the Lightning**] and sent electricity surging toward the nearest henchman. The tendrils tossed him aside and onto the ground.

[**Electric Lightshow! +1 Flamboyance Point**]

Fursona was slamming henches around, and as I watched, she reached Su-Bin's guards. She screeched one off the president-in-distress, then clawed at the other as Su-Bin punched him in the face. He let go, surprised, and threw his hands up.

And that was all the opportunity Su-Bin needed.

She was up and running a moment later, and I used [**Wind Front**] one more time to knock over a pursuing hench. Then I nodded at Fursona. "You've got this?"

[**Badass Move! +1 Badass Point**]

"Yeah, I've got this!"

She looked like she had it, so I [**Quick-Time Changed**] into Understudy for the heal, fired a [**Starlance**] at a hench with a pistol just before she could fire it, and leaped into the air with [**Solar Wing**]. The lance hit the hench, toppling her to the ground and knocking the pistol away.

[**Flashy Fitting-Room! +1 Flamboyance Point**]
[**Dramatic Damage! +1 Drama Point**]
[**Rejuvenation Activated: HP 5/8 (Temporarily restricted from 12)**]

Then I was in pursuit of Su-Bin. Fursona could handle the few remaining henches herself.

I landed at the park's edge and sat down on a bench, waiting. She'd seen me fly over, and she had to know I was at the only exit to the park on this side, so it was only a matter of time before she showed up. I'd just sit, wait, and think about what I'd say to her.

What *was* the best thing to say to her?

I had no idea. I *wanted* to mention something about her family and what they'd been through—their forced move out of Seoul, the house in Thornton and The Bear Lord, and then the apartment they lived in now. I *wanted* to tell her that it wasn't *my* fault that'd happened. I *needed* to shake her silly and explain how stupid all this was— that we were all just trying to make it through the day with whatever cards fate, the Style System, or whatever had dealt us.

But the reality on the ground was that President Pak wouldn't listen to any of those arguments—and one of them would probably out me as Anika DuPont to some- one who absolutely *couldn't* be allowed to know. So, as Su-Bin rounded the corner, saw me sitting there, and froze, I stood up and waved. "Hello!"

She glared and started stalking toward the entrance, clearly ready to ignore me completely. I wasn't about to let that happen, though, so I took two steps and blocked her path. Her eyes narrowed even more, and I realized that any conversation I could have with her wouldn't matter.

But the camera drone hovering overhead reminded me that maybe, just maybe, I wasn't actually talking to the president of the TU APPEAL chapter. Instead, I was talking to everyone watching, and she happened to be a surrogate for them. So I cleared my throat. "President Pak, we need to talk."

31

President Pak,
We Need to Talk

[Episode Finished!]
  [Power Wars: Evergreen Burn - R (Auxiliary PG-13)]
  [Penalties: N/A]
  [Episode Finished! +3 of each Style Point]
  [Winner Winner! +3 of each Style Point]
  [Role Focus: Drama + Cunning - Goal Partially Met! +10 Drama Points]
  [Alias - Understudy] [Archetype - Magical Girl] [Community Rank - 201/523]
  [HP 5/12]
  [Styles and Skills]
  ►Archetype Skill - Transformation Sequence
  ►Combo Skills - Power-Weaving
  ►Badass (48)
  ►Cunning (57) (Skill Roll Available)
  ►Drama (78) (Skill Roll Available)
  ►Bit-Part Barrage 2
  ►Starlance 1
  ►Flamboyance (65) (Skill Roll Available)
  ►Signature Skill - Adaptive Armoire 3
  ►Stored Costumes: (Rainy Day, Copy Cat, Rescue Girl Lucky Star)
  ►Solar Wing 1
  ►Quick-Time Change 3
  ►Spotlight Strike 1
  ►Grit (28)
  ►I-Frame Transform 3

We'd finished the Episode, so by all rights, I should be rolling my skills, freed from the camera drones overhead. I didn't know how The Triad had wrapped things up with Acid Burn, but they'd gotten the win, and so had we, so it must've gone well.

I should have been checking out my new Cunning, Drama, and Flamboyance skills, making adjustments to my builds, and meeting up with Fursona.

Instead, I stood in front of Su-Bin with my arms out, blocking her path.

"President Pak, have a seat," I said, gesturing to the bench. She glared but followed my direction, and I relaxed slightly. Maybe she was here to listen. Could we actually have a reasonable conversation? I sat next to her. "What do you think happened here? No, that's a bad first question. Why were you here? Aren't you in school?"

"Yes, but thanks to this Power War bullshit, I've got the days off as long as I can keep up with my classes. We've been hitting up town halls across all the districts, trying to get our faces on camera so people will wake up and see what's happening!" Su-Bin practically spat those last words.

"I see. And what do you think is happening?"

She paused, noticing the camera drone for the first time. "This is still an Episode, huh? And let me guess? I'm the bad guy, right? Well, I'm not gonna be your propaganda. What's happening is there's a system in place that benefits from the deaths of 'Extras,' the destruction of their homes, and the breaking of their societies. There's a whole world out there beyond what you're doing, but you're too stupid and self-absorbed to see it."

"I . . ." I paused, breathing deeply. This was a much more aggressive President Pak than I'd experienced last semester. "I'm just as opposed to the bad things happening to people as you are, President Pak. Why do you think I put myself between your people and the acid? Why do you think I ignored the good, easy fight against Livestream to find you? It's a flawed world, sure. There shouldn't *be* villains to fight, but there *are*, and if heroes don't fight them, they won't back down and retire or anything."

"So you're doing me a favor by fighting? You know, Man vs. Nature didn't destroy my life—not really. It was the supers. They showed up, fought the 'good fight,' and then left without really seeing the consequences of their heat rays and superstrength. They always leave without seeing the consequences, and unpowered people have to bear them."

Something about those words stung, and I couldn't figure out why for a minute. Then I nodded slowly. "So that's why you hate me? Because I didn't have to help fix the Grant Building?"

"No. I hate you because you're a stupid college student who's got delusions that you're something special."

"Okay, let's step back. What do you think would have happened here today if Fursona and I hadn't been here?" I said, standing up.

Su-Bin stood, too, sighing. "If you and Fursona hadn't shown up, we would have shouted slogans at Acid Burn while on her cameras. She would have made some threatening gestures at us, maybe sprayed the road with a little acid, and then gotten away, and we would have had another peaceful protest on the news. Or, *maybe*, The Triad would have rolled in a few minutes later, and we could have had some footage with us protesting them, too.

"Instead, we got this. I'll have to rally the troops and see who's still with us. You know, we've protested half a dozen supervillains and superheroes in the last week, and nothing's gone this badly."

"I don't see how it's my fault," I said. I really didn't. I'd been patrolling, and I'd done my job perfectly, bringing in the major-leaguers to deal with Acid Burn, then running rescue while Fursona fought Livestream. So far, APPEAL members had complicated two of our Episodes since the Power War started, plus the Orientation Episode, and who knew how many more times we'd run into Su-Bin and her friends?

"Let me guess? 'I'm just doing my job, citizen.' Give me a break," Su-Bin said. "If you really wanted to help people, you'd—"

"Enough," I said. "This isn't helpful for either of us. I'm trying to help protect people from villains because, like it or not, the world we live in *has* them. They're here, and they're not going anywhere. I did a lot of thinking after our last conversation. If I don't help people with my powers, what's the point of having them? So I'm trying, and it seems like no matter what I do, you APPEAL people won't be happy until I'm in some superpower-dedicated city under the New Gotham Accords."

"No, I won't be happy until there aren't superpowers anymore," Su-Bin said.

"Okay, there's no reasoning with you, President Pak. Do you want a lift back to campus? I can drop you off at the Student Union Building."

"Yes. That's the least you can do since Carl's car is melted."

As I used [**Solar Wing**] to summon my windsurfer, I called Fursona. Her fursuit had gotten wrecked, but she'd still be effective as a fighter. Still, I wanted to check in with her before I left. "Hey. I'm heading back to campus. Are you okay to get back on your own? If not, Su-Bin and I can figure out how to get you back."

"Yeah, I'll be okay," Fursona said into my ear. "Did you talk some sense into her?"

"No. See you at the green room."

The whole flight home, I waited for Su-Bin to say something—anything—but she stayed silent. The moment the camera drone left, she lost all interest in talking.

Honestly, though, that was a mercy for both of us, because I was furious, and so was she. I couldn't figure out how to make her listen to my side of things, and even though I understood *why* she thought what she did, she wanted me to stop existing— at least how I was. Sometimes superhero work was frustrating, but I *liked* doing what I did, especially now that I had a Costume I could dedicate to rescue work and help-ing people.

She didn't *get* that, though. Was she right that people—innocent people, mostly— got screwed over by the fighting? Yes. But the MIRACLE program and Ilneat money fixed those issues most of the time, and Thornton was a rare, early failure. From every-thing I'd read in school, MIRACLE had succeeded at rebuilding 94% of the time, and usually came in under budget and ahead of schedule; that was rare enough in government projects that it'd stuck in my head.

And when MIRACLE rebuilding wasn't enough, some teams of supers, like The Triad, stepped in. When they couldn't, the Council of Heroes seemed willing to help. Thornton aside—and Tele-Portal had said their problems were mundane, not super— the city seemed to be doing alright. At least, it would be if we could get this Power War under control.

I landed fifteen minutes later, at the parking garage, and Su-Bin stepped off my sailboard and disappeared into the rows of cars. Presumably, she didn't want to be seen with me; I understood, since hitching a ride from the superhero she hated the most probably wasn't a good look. I took off, not bothering to say goodbye since she hadn't either. Maybe a long flight would clear my head.

I banked over the University district, then dove low to get a good look at Tottergarten. Inside, The Narrator and Honeycomb were probably managing the Playpen Patrol, although I couldn't figure out how they'd do *that* without their retired villains. Nearby, a little-league Episode popped up, but I ignored it. Some other hero could take that one.

I'd saved a lot of lives today. I'd done good work, and we'd proven that an Eagle-sona and Lucky Star combo could play the auxiliary role The Triad wanted from us. We'd even won the Episode despite not one, but two drop-in villains showing up to spite us.

So why did I feel off about the whole thing?

I pulled up on the border between University and the Poudre districts and sat staring into the 3V1L-controlled neighborhoods on my sailboard. The villainous group hadn't gone after Fursona and me since "The Root of All 3V1L," so why did they suddenly have it out for me now? They'd dropped their goal of beating Acid Burn and sacrificed their entire mission for a chance at taking Fursona and me off the board.

That begged the question of why. We'd left them alone, and with their organization's model, they'd be able to grow faster than we could. The reality was that if we didn't start dealing with 3V1L soon, they'd have the Poudre districts completely locked down again, and we'd need a Top Ten hero to dislodge them. And we'd been playing right into their hands.

All they would have had to do was leave us alone, and we'd have done the same thing. Instead, they'd dropped everything to attack us.

I watched the border for another ten minutes until a text pulled me from my vigil.

<At the green room. You okay? - Fursona 2:55>
<Yeah, just thinking - Understudy 2:56>

Whether I'd figured out anything or not, it was time to go home. Fursona was waiting, and we needed to talk this Episode over, because things didn't sit right with me.

While I flew, I finally rolled my new powers.

[Rank-Up! Card Curio 2 Temporary buffs based on the draw to help with the future]

[New Skill! Spatial Warp 1: Move an enemy or ally ten feet in any direction. Must end in a safe location, but the location doesn't have to stay safe]

[Rank-Up! Cat-Scratch Fever 1: Initial impact fully blinds opponent for five seconds]

The new power seemed useful, but I couldn't figure out if I wanted it in Lucky Star. It might take the place of [**Hog the Limelight**], but I couldn't be sure. Was it offensive? Would [**Combat Inhibitor**] stop it from being useful? If not, maybe I could bend the rules with other powers, at least to protect myself.

The rank-ups were just rank-ups, although the [**Card Curio**] one had the potential to boost me a ton if I could line up those buffs with [**Hometown Heroine**]. [**Cat-Scratch Fever**] had a lot more utility as a combo piece now, since it could lock down villains for a few seconds, letting me combo off more easily. Still, they weren't anything to be excited for—not really.

I landed on the roof and hurried inside the green room, where Bianca lounged on the chaise. She'd unsuited, and I hurried to join her. Once I'd finally untransformed, I rolled my eyes. "I don't think Su-Bin's going to come around, Bee."

"No. But that's not what kept you out, is it?"

"Nope. We've got other problems." I sat down. "We've been playing this wrong."

"About what?" Bianca asked.

"3V1L. We've got to be more proactive in dealing with them, or they'll get back up to their major-league power. I propose we shift our focus. We'll still do some work with The Triad, but from here out, our main goal is figuring out how to manage the rise of 3V1L. We'll start by learning 3V1L's history."

32

3V1L's History

TUESDAY, OCTOBER 21

Our appointment in the Council of Heroes archives started at 9:15, so Fursona and I blew off our classes to get there early. We'd watch the video lectures later, but I was excited to dive into the old newspapers and recordings of news shows for anything we could find out about 3V1L.

Between patrols and classes, we'd been busy over the last week, and today was our first real "day off." Sort of. The homework piled up any day we weren't in classes, and the video lectures *worked*, but they didn't feel the same, and the lack of a schedule was rough. We'd also dropped The Triad on a pair of major-league villains in the Parker and Evergreen districts, although why anyone wanted to fight over the acid-pocked, MIRACLE-clogged streets of Evergreen was beyond me.

We'd at least be able to disengage for three or four hours, hit up the archive, and see if we could start building an idea of how 3V1L operated. This felt different than Professor Panic, who was someone I'd been familiar with and underestimated, or Vigilant Vow, who'd descended into villainy while Fursona and I did other things.

This was an organization with a history, and Fursona and I needed to understand that history if we wanted to stop them.

So, as we rode the elevator to the CoH building's fourth floor, got off, and signed in with the tired-looking old super at the desk, I reviewed the plan we'd made on the whiteboard.

Step One: Find out about the pre-Goose 3V1L. How did they operate? What were their leaders like? How did they hold their own against major-league heroes? What strategies were used against them, and how could we copy them?

Step Two: Compare the pre-Goose 3V1L with the current one. Figure out if anything had changed. If so, try to explain *why* it was changing.

Step Three: Build a plan to defeat 3V1L, test run it in the Poudre districts, and go from there.

We walked through the shelves into the section labeled Villain Records (Deceased and Retired). I figured we'd find information on the Three *V*s there, if nothing else, and I wasn't disappointed. Articles, Episode clips, and TV reports— the CoH archive had everything we needed. I sat down with a newspaper article and began to read.

The organization known as 3V1L took over the South Poudre city hall today, result- ing in seven injuries as they held hostages and demanded the literal keys to the district. When informed that the keys were a metaphor, not a real thing, they began threatening to hurt hostages, at which point Liege Lord was forced to engage.

The hero was able to save all the hostages, although in his fight against the Three Vs, *the city hall building was destroyed. MIRACLE crews are hard at work in the Poudre district, working on repairs and rebuilding. Of particular note was an interaction between Liege Lord's "Imminent Domain" power and the* V *known as Landcrawler's "Ground Pound," which resulted in most of the destruction.*

"Hey, did either of the *V*s we've fought have names?" I asked Fursona quietly.

She shook her eagle head. "No. I've got Ghost Ronin here with a similar weapon choice to the *V* we fought in 'The Root of All 3V1L,' but the descriptions of her powers are totally different. Also, that *V* was a guy, right?"

"Yeah. That's strange. See if we can track down any of the other letters. That's a definite weird situation, no doubt about it."

I kept reading, switching to a new article.

Yesterday, an incident between the Three Vs *and Stella-Lunar resulted in all three being arrested. While Landcrawler and Ghost Ronin got out quickly, Crystal Cannon is still in custody as of this morning.*

The fighting took place around Tokyexico General Hospital, which was both far out- side of 3V1L's territory and much different from their usual targets. Stella-Lunar responded first and quickly defeated the three villains while nearby lower-league heroes fought the lieutenants and henchmen who'd accompanied the Three Vs.

Gradually, article by article, a picture started to form of who 3V1L was. But at the same time, every article had a similar theme; the Three *V*s moved together, usu- ally along with a swarm of lieutenants and henches, and the One *L* never showed their face. I didn't even have info on who they were, and as far as either Fursona or I could find out, they'd never been identified, much less arrested.

"This is so weird," Fursona said. I looked her way and nodded for her to con- tinue. "Okay, their MO doesn't match what we're seeing in the field. We see a solo *V* with a few mooks. The old 3V1L never went anywhere alone—they always had henches. So, something changed in their leadership or strategy. They're playing a wider game than they used to."

"They are," I said slowly. The whole thing made me a bit uncomfortable. No, not uncomfortable. Curious. "They had a big leadership shake-up when Golden Goose killed the Three *V*s. Let's watch that. Maybe we'll see something there. We need a viewing room and the Golden Goose vs. 3V1L Episode. Maybe there's a tell there."

"Due to unforeseen circumstances relating to her personal life, Magical Girl Stella-Lunar is canceled. Golden Goose has graciously agreed to shoot the Episode, excluding point-of-view filming and with a five-minute delay. Stella-Lunar thanks you for your understanding," the TV said.

The last time we'd watched this Episode, Bee and I were drunk. We'd been plastered and cuddly by the time Golden Goose really went on the offensive, and I couldn't even remember the ending.

This time would be different.

We sat in the small, dark room, staring at a TV less than half the size of mine, pens ready to take notes as Golden Goose hovered over the 3V1L base. She shouted out her typical time limit ultimatum, then started her attack by lasering open the roof. Then she peeled it open like a can of cat food, not quite ignoring the Three *V*s and the swarm of lieutenants that came out to fight her. "I'm here for the One *L*!" she shouted, sparring with Landcrawler and Ghost Ronin with an expression between boredom and annoyance on her face.

"He's not around! Die!" Landcrawler launched massive stone pillars from the ground, surrounding Golden Goose, and for the first time, I really paid attention to the Three *V*s and how they fought.

It was like a dance. As Golden Goose broke through the stone barriers, Crystal Cannon opened up from three blocks away, spraying shards of glass so sharp they actually left scratches on the overpowered heroine's perfect skin. Not cuts, but scratches. When the superhero tried to fly that way, Ghost Ronin slid into the space between, sword somehow managing to deflect a mid-powered eye beam.

Against anyone but the Top Ten, they'd have had a chance.

But Golden Goose was number one for a reason, and one by one, the Three *V*s and their lieutenants fell to her punches, laser, and raw power. Then Golden Goose went inside, and the fighting was in close quarters—and more intense. Hand-to-hand with unpowered henchmen and little-league villains, a back-and-forth with a minor-league Tank vil who lasted a shockingly long time, and then a burst of flames and fumes that left Golden Goose coughing.

Then she turned to the camera. "This is a warning to villains everywhere. If you get too big, too uppity, you *will* draw my eye. And if I have to fly halfway across North America to deal with you, I *will* be pissed—and you *will* regret it for the rest of your lives." She pointed at a hench who'd wisely surrendered instantly. "Call an ambulance."

Fursona lunged for the remote and paused it. Then she rewound and pointed at the screen. "There! What's that?"

I stared at the dark, grainy screen, trying to piece out what she was seeing. Then she ran her finger around it, and I saw the strange shape for what it was—a shadow. "There's someone else in the room with her, and they're not dead or beaten."

"Exactly. But who?" Fursona said. She nodded her eagle head slowly. "Let's take another look and see if we can figure it out."

We'd watched that clip a dozen more times, but the most we'd seen was a single arm and half a torso in the shadows. It just wasn't enough to go on, and we couldn't exactly ask Snowball or Golden Goose who'd been there. For starters, they wouldn't tell us; the studios didn't talk much about the behind-the-scenes, or at least not as much as you'd expect.

Golden Goose had also been in nearly seventy Episodes since then, so she probably didn't even remember mopping up 3V1L. It wasn't like a single Episode could stick in your head when you did five years' worth of my career in eight months.

The point was that we couldn't just fly to Yorkston or go upstairs to her temporary base and talk to her—not about a minor-league problem.

"Should we keep digging?" I asked.

"Nah. We know enough to make a plan for 3V1L. That'll have to do for now." Fursona flicked on the lights. "Let's get to work."

As we compared our notes, though, it was clear that nothing we'd learned about the old 3V1L could help us handle the new one. Nothing flowed; the organization had no before-and-after continuity. "The One *L* wouldn't change plans so completely. There's no benefit to running wide right after taking a Goose-sized punch to their organization, and whoever they are, they'd try to rebuild a similar dynamic. Three main villains, a bunch of lieutenants, and as many henches as they could recruit. Remember the recruiting booth at the job fair last year?" I asked.

"Yeah. They're really hurting on the lieutenant front," Fursona said.

I thought for a minute. "Are they? They keep introducing themselves as 'for the moment, the Second *V*' or whatever. That doesn't sound like a small organization. It sounds like one playing at being small and working toward being bigger. Temporary jobs while they find bigger villains to take those positions. Whoever we're fighting this month as a *V* won't be one in two or three. Ha, that rhymes."

"Sure does. So, can we build a plan to handle Sword *V* and Punch *V*?"

"Yeah. We can. Of the two, Sword *V* is the tougher opponent. He's aggressive, confident, and competent with his weapon. I think we can beat him with a good ranged game. That means Eagle-sona and Understudy for the flight, the distance, and the ranged damage. We can try the opposite with Punch *V*, but that's risky. We can't range her down, though—at least, not unless I save **[Bit-Part Barrage]**, and I tend to use it as soon as I see an opportunity."

I paused, then thought for a moment. "I think the bigger concern is fighting them with a group of henches, or fighting them with each other, *or* fighting them with another villain. We need to be ready for anything."

But the plan wouldn't come together—we knew a ton about 3V1L's old operations but nothing about what they were up to *now*. They wanted Evergreen. They wanted Sister Sly gone. They wanted University. None of it made *sense*. After a frustrating hour and a ton of paper heading to the tower's incinerator, I finally stood up. "I think we're done here. There's only so much we can learn from the past when we don't know what the present looks like. Let's go back to TU."

"Agreed," Fursona said. "We need a plan to push against 3V1L."

PART FIVE

33

Board Games

SATURDAY, OCTOBER 25

The dice clattered across my coffee table as Su-Bin rolled to move. She cursed under her breath, and I laughed as she tapped her piece across the board onto her boyfriend Cam's square, then forked over a few hundreds and a fifty. "I'll get you for this. You'll see."

Su-Bin and Cam hadn't been together long—they were still in their relationship's lovey-dovey, touchy-feely phase, but I'd reached out to her after the Evergreen Episode. I'd hoped that we could still be friends, and so far, it was working—as long as we kept our other identities out of it. We'd set some ground rules; since neither Bee nor I wanted to talk about APPEAL, and she didn't want to talk about superhero shows, we banned both topics.

Instead, I'd made dinner. I'd planned and proportioned it all out as Ramsey Fieri earlier in the day, and then when the time came to cook it, I'd done it as Anika. And that brought up an interesting point—and one I'd need to talk to Dr. Ayers about.

With the Power War going, all my classes superpower-related, and most of my free time being spent researching 3V1L and planning our first patrol, not to mention recruiting our third member for Team Composition, Anika DuPont felt more and more like another Costume for Understudy to wear. I wasn't sure how I felt about that. Actually, that wasn't true. I knew how I felt about it. Uncomfortable.

Really, really uncomfortable.

So, while I waited for my next appointment with Dr. Ayers, I'd decided I wouldn't spend any more time in-Costume than I needed to, and that I'd do normal stuff with normal people. It was a foolproof plan to keep my superhero identity and my secret one separate and make sure the superhero knew who was in control.

Foolproof except for the fact that I didn't *know* many normal, unpowered people. Avan wasn't an option for . . . a variety of reasons. I had a few friends from prop-making, but the play started soon, and they'd all be busy. And that left . . . Su-Bin and Cam.

"Nice roll, Su-Bin," I snarked as I grabbed the dice and rolled double threes. I dutifully moved my token across the board and put the piece down on a thankfully empty square. Then I grinned. "Safe!"

"For now, but you just wait. You're coming up on my blockade," Bianca said, grinning. "I'll knock you out of the game for sure."

"Like hell you will!" I rolled again. "How did you two meet? Not your club, right?"

"Right. Cam's in my Advanced Calculus course," Su-Bin said. She squeezed his hand.

I moved my character four spaces, landing on the first of Bianca's squares and handing over more money than I could really afford. "And are you solo-rooming this year?"

"For now," Su-Bin said. She frowned as I handed the dice to Bianca. "Mom and Dad aren't very thrilled about the Power War. They wanted me to go home, but I told them I couldn't. Even the commute takes time—time I could be spending putting together the next protest, or writing letters, or trying to get people to sign petitions."

"Shop talk!" Bee said, rolling the dice.

Su-Bin drank from her Coke cup. She wasn't a booze drinker, so we'd agreed to let her bypass the rules. Cam *was* a drinker, though, and he took a shot in her place. "Su-Bin's just really dedicated to her club, that's all," he rumbled. He was a big guy— the kind who looked like he'd give Punch and Grapple a run for their money in the weight room if he ever actually worked out, but who had a farmer's physique. I felt a moment of envy as Su-Bin grabbed his arm.

Then Bianca poked me in the side, and I remembered I had it pretty damn good, too. She handed me a single fifty—she'd landed on my space. "Here you go, babe."

"Thanks, Bee!" I rolled my eyes and tucked the cash under my side of the board as she handed the dice to Cam.

"Yeah. Speaking of my club, how are you two holding up with the Power War?" Su-Bin asked. "I'd be happy to get you into another meeting if recent events have changed your mind about us."

"I appreciate the offer, but I'm booked with classes," I said. The plan to keep shop talk out of our conversation had failed, so I buttoned up as Cam rolled, then paid back every dollar he'd gotten from Su-Bin as she held her hand out smugly.

It *was* nice to be just another college kid, playing games and drinking the night away in my dorm room—even if it was a little fancier than the average one, or if we'd had pita, falafel, and lemon chicken that no other student on campus could have prepared. But as the conversation turned toward the "environmental, economic, and personal disaster in Evergreen last week," I stood up and slipped into the bathroom. I needed to think.

Su-Bin wouldn't ever get it, that superheroes had to be here now. And she certainly wouldn't get it from talking to Understudy while we both had adrenaline and anger in our veins, like on the park bench. Plus, in the aftermath of the Evergreen Episode, APPEAL had come out aggressively against Magical Girl Understudy. It seemed like I was their favorite punching bag.

I'd been dealing with it by separating Su-Bin and President Pak. But it was getting harder to do it. I spent too long sitting on the toilet lid, reminding myself that they, just like Understudy and Anika DuPont, were separate people. I just had to pretend I didn't care about APPEAL, superheroes, or the Power War. I was a normal college girl, and I was *going* to have a normal college Saturday night, dammit!

Then, once I'd reassured myself about that, I rejoined the game.

"Okay, my turn? Great!" I rolled the dice and . . . landed straight on another Bee-controlled space. "Shit."

Bee and I staggered to the door. "Bye, Su-Bin! Bye, Cam! See you next weekend?"

"Hopefully, if I can find the time," Su-Bin said. She grabbed Cam's arm, and the two of them disappeared down the hall for the elevator.

The moment we shut our door, Bee grinned at me. "I saw how you looked at him. What? Am I not good enough for you?" she teased, poking my side again.

"You're plenty good enough, but did you see him? He's built like Brick House. Even you had to be impressed," I replied.

"Impressed, not into," Bee clarified. Then she cleared her throat. "Now that that's done with, let's go over tomorrow's plan . . . and the new addition."

"Oh right. Damn, I wanted to finish the bottle," I complained.

The new addition to our team was Vicegrip, and I wasn't sure how I felt about her yet. On the one hand, it meant we'd be able to write our essays for Team Compositions, and since the Trios unit was running, working with an Elementalist like her would give us a solid theoretical group. With Fursona on the front line, Vicegrip running ranged, and me filling the gaps, we shouldn't have weaknesses.

On the other hand, though, the Yorkston superheroine was woefully inexperienced for what we wanted to do.

We took our places in the green room—me on the couch and Bee at the whiteboard—and she started writing and talking. "Poudre Patrol: Investigative Episode/Patrol. Goals: We're there to try pinning down one of the Three *V*s, or at least to figure out where they like to operate. We're also putting on a public face so the district knows they're not abandoned like . . . uh . . ." She trailed off.

"The Foothills?"

"Yeah, the Foothills." She wrote three columns, one titled 'Pin Down *V*s' and one labeled 'Public Face.' The third stayed blank for a moment, then she wrote 'Vicegrip Team Comp.' "Our third goal is to work with Tractor-Beam-Girl and see how that goes. So, first objective. Ideas on how to complete it?"

"I think we set a patrol route that hits the west and north Poudre borders, gets dangerously close to Sister Sly's little pocket around the church, and hits up places they've both been. We'll do a little digging at each conflict hot spot and see if we can't find out where the villains are going. Then, once we've done that, we can visit their mayor's office or try to get in touch with the local police. Think Rathburn will give us an in?" I asked.

'Rathburn,' 'Hot Spots,' and 'Mayor' went under the 'Pin Down *Vs*' column as Bee nodded. "I don't know, but he's worth a shot. Want to call him tomorrow?"

"Yeah," I nodded. "As for the public-facing stuff, how about we focus on street-level, casual interactions? We've been slacking in the Poudre district, so we need to be casual but serious. I think we can pull that off."

"Yeah, me too. We'll just answer questions, see what people need help with, and try to make that happen. I'm not worried about us at all," Bee said.

"Yeah. The two of us are fine."

"Tractor-Beam-Girl," Bee said.

At the exact same second, I said, "Vicegrip. I'd be more comfortable doing this without her. She's an unknown. All I really know about her is what her [**Signature Skill**] does, and that she's got enough of a temper to go *right* after Flare. That feels like a recipe for disaster."

"I did some digging on her Yorkston career," Bee said. I breathed a sigh of relief; I could always count on Bianca to be well researched. "She's got a shockingly high win rate. Essentially no Investigatives or patrols, though. From the Episodes I watched, she always seemed to know exactly where to be, and that tells me she had someone feeding her Episodes like a baby bird with a worm."

She wrote 'Baby Bird' under 'Vicegrip Team Comp.' I laughed. "That's kind of suspicious. Do you think she's got a patience problem? I know all about those, and unfortunately, the best way to deal with them is to be patient."

"No idea. But if she's been getting spoon-fed Episodes, we'll need to keep an eye on her. She might go chasing leads and getting in trouble," Bee said.

"Got it."

We spent the next hour checking out hot spots on the Poudre district's borders before we settled on five possible places the Second and Third *Vs* had been, and where they'd fought Sister Sly. The first was a park next to Sister Sly's church, the second a bar that'd been robbed by 3V1L twice in the last few months, and the third a safe house that'd been firebombed three days ago. The other two were alternates in case we couldn't make it into the first three or we got sidetracked by a lead and had to change our patrol route.

The route itself felt weird. Instead of a single destination, we planned to move through over half of the Poudre districts in a long, sweeping arc. We wouldn't be staying at a park or mall; instead, we'd try to be everywhere. It made sense for the goal we had in mind, but it didn't seem like any of my patrols with Tele-Portal.

I still wasn't comfortable with Vicegrip, though. The whole time we got ready for bed, I couldn't shake the feeling that she wasn't ready for a fight like 3V1L. Even when Bee wrapped her arms around my waist and dragged me into the little spoon position for some mandatory cuddling time, my mind couldn't unstick from Tractor-Beam-Girl and the Poudre patrol.

34

Poudre Patrol

The next morning, I wasn't any more confident that the white-armored freshman superhero was really our best choice. If anything, my apprehension had kept both Bee and me awake way past our bedtimes.

Still, we'd told Tractor-Beam-Girl—honestly, the name was one hundred times better than Vicegrip—to meet us at the Mister Felsic statue at 8:30, so we both crawled out of bed, changed into our superhero outfits, and headed over. The hulking stone figure of Tokyexico's greatest former hero loomed over TU's quad, and I landed on the dying grass nearby, let Roo-sona off my sailboard, and strolled over.

"Took you two long enough," Vicegrip's cutting, sarcastic voice said, and the tiny heroine stepped out from behind a pillar. She stood shorter than Bianca—shorter than Su-Bin, too, I realized—and her dark eyes glared out from under her helmet, which covered her hair completely. Each of her two gauntlets included flared metal, almost looking like loudspeakers, with her hands shoved through the middles.

"It's 8:24, kid," Fursona said through her modulator; I'd spent enough time with the kangaroo to know she was annoyed. "We're right on time."

Then, in my ear, Bianca's voice said, "Nod if you think she should go home."

I shook my head slowly. Whether we liked it or not, we'd committed to the patrol, and to mentoring Tractor-Beam-Girl for at least the next couple of weeks. We needed her to pass Team Compositions, and she needed to see what superhero life was really like without whoever had been helping her out. "Okay, Vicegrip, we're going on a patrol in the Poudre districts today. There's an organization called 3V1L that's been growing in power there, so we have a few goals."

Tractor-Beam-Girl seemed to be listening as I explained what we wanted to accomplish. Then I got to the stinger. "So, it's a long shot, but if you can fly, we can get to our start point in just a few minutes. Otherwise, we'll take a bus."

"I can definitely fly," Tractor-Beam-Girl said. She glowered at me as if daring me to ask her to prove it.

I wasn't in the mood to play games, especially with Fursona complaining in my ear. "Great. We're heading to Poudre North. Let's go."

Fursona stood in front of me, and I summoned my sailboard with **[Solar Wing]**. We took off, hovering nearby—both of us wanted to see Tractor-Beam-Girl fly.

She put her arms to her sides, seeming to press her elbows into her waist until the armor practically merged, and then fired two gravity beams from her hands. They pushed her up into the air, where she wobbled, staring defiantly at us. "Show me where we're going."

As soon as we landed at the park, I could tell it was a bust.

The fight between 3V1L and Sister Sly's weird religious cult or whatever had been drawn out, and a bunch of the playground and skate park were still wrecked. It made sense; MIRACLE contracts were awarded in a priority, and with all the fighting over the last few weeks, no one had the time to fix up a city park—especially not when it was in contested territory.

But just because construction crews weren't here working didn't mean we'd find any evidence of 3V1L. Someone had been over the park with a fine-toothed comb—and a bunch of garbage bags. Honestly, I'd never seen a city park so spotless. Riverside didn't have the resources to hire this kind of maintenance, and Confluence Park in Tokyexico was never this clean. Even the beach near Tortuga West, where Bianca and I had spent a couple of lovely weeks this summer, didn't hold a candle to it.

That meant someone had cleaned it up with serious intention, and I could tell immediately that they'd intended to throw anyone following them off their tracks.

"So, who won?" Tractor-Beam-Girl asked, staring at a swing set's scorched, mangled remains. The rest of the park wasn't much better—clean, but destroyed. 3V1L had attacked in force, and Sister Sly hadn't spared any expense in fighting back.

"No one," I said, shifting into Lucky Star. As I did, I fired up an **[Investigative Casting Call]**.

[Investigative Casting Call]
[Investigative Episode: North Poudre Patrol - PG]
[Role: Amateur Sleuth! Do you accept the role? (Yes/No)]
[Role Focus: Cunning + Flamboyance]
[North Poudre Patrol: Act One in Progress]

"So, what am I supposed to do with this?" Tractor-Beam-Girl asked defiantly.

"Accept it," Fursona said. I could tell her patience wasn't high—probably from the lack of sleep last night, but also from Tractor-Beam-Girl's attitude problem. "Then start looking around. They have to have missed *some* sort of clue. If you find it, I'll give you a gold star."

"Wow, Fursona, that was rude," I said once Tractor-Beam-Girl had disappeared into the nearby trees to look for a retreat path.

The kangaroo heroine nodded. "Yep. Tractor-Beam-Girl doesn't have a clue how these work. I almost want to ask her if her mother helped her find Episodes, but I'm afraid it might be true. Someone definitely did, because her Episode backlog's too extensive to have *never* done an Investigative."

"Uh-huh." I used [**Card Curio**], looking for a clue—any clue—that might've been missed. I stared at the old, bearded man. "The Hermit. We're looking for accomplishment and success, and someone who needs to be alone to accomplish those? So, let's try poking around near Sister Sly's side of the park."

[Good Thinking! +1 Cunning Point]

"You've got it, Understudy," Fursona said. Then she shouted over her shoulder at Tractor-Beam-Girl. "Let's go! Over here! Bet we'll find something."

"But . . . no, this doesn't seem right. This doesn't seem right at all. If we needed to track down Sister Sly, we'd know right where she was. We wouldn't need to hunt for evidence. She's in her church, ten to one odds," I said, still walking toward where the Hermit was sending me.

I hadn't taken fifteen steps when I saw something half buried in the mud. This was it! What the tarot card wanted me to find! It had to be! I reached down and dug through the mud until I'd uncovered it. Then I wiped it clean enough to read. "Fred Callahan, 25679 Madrid Street? A driver's license. There's *no way* someone would be dumb enough to leave this behind, is there?" I asked.

"Nope," Tractor-Beam-Girl said. "They'd have to be a real idiot. This is someone else's."

Fursona didn't say anything for a long moment. Then, slowly, she started talking. "It . . . *could* be what we're after. Henches act pretty stupid sometimes. I think part of it is the Style System rewarding them for it somehow. But the point is that a hench could easily have left their ID here and not found it again."

"So, if that's true, let's go bust Fred Callahan!" Tractor-Beam-Girl said.

I held up a hand to keep her from running off. Then, before she could get too bored, I used [**Audition Notes**].

[Audition Notes for Fred Callahan: This Extra is . . .]

"That's weird." I waited a moment as the rest of the text appeared.

[Audition Notes for Fred Callahan: This Extra is not currently home. In fact, he hasn't been home in nearly a week. He may still be in the Poudre districts, but if he's not, he definitely hasn't flown anywhere.]
[**Good Thinking! +1 Cunning Point**]

"Ooookay, we'll check out 25679 Madrid," I said, summoning the sailboard.

"This has to be your guy," Tractor-Beam-Girl said.

Fred's house—and it was an actual house, though not anything like the one Vigilant Vow had used as a hideout—was full of evidence to support her claim. From the devil mask and red cape left on a chair to the stacks of hundred-dollar bills in the corner, everything about it screamed "supervillain." And that was a problem.

"I'm not convinced . . ." I mumbled. Something felt *off*. Almost like . . . like . . . "Remember the setup by Sister Sly?"

Fursona nodded. She hopped up from where she'd been checking out the basement. "Yeah, the helmet planted to get us fighting 3V1L. You think this is another trap?"

"I don't know. It all feels too convenient." I reached for another tarot card, but something between the mattress and box spring in Fred's bed caught my eye before I could pull it. "Hold on a second."

I lifted the mattress, and there, lying mostly covered by the mattress, was a sword. A vicious-looking sword—one I'd seen before. The Third *V* had used it in "The Root of All 3V1L." If it was here . . .

"Fursona, this isn't a hench. This isn't a hench at all. Fred Callahan is the Third *V*," I said.

[**Good Thinking! +1 Cunning Point**]

"Oh [**Beep!**]," Fursona said, looking at the sword. I put it down and sat on the bed while she talked. "This is way bigger than we thought. Fred is the Third *V*. That's almost unbelievable."

"Yeah, it is." I couldn't believe it, even after the Style System confirmed it. The Third *V* had been wildly competent; he'd outplayed us at every turn, the whole Episode, right up until I'd been kidnapped, when he and his henches had just melted away. For him to screw up this badly—and not once, but twice—didn't make sense. Fred barely seemed like the kind of guy you'd want henching for you, much less as leadership in a villain's organization.

But as I looked around the house more and more, I started to change my mind. "It's too much evidence to be a setup. If Sister Sly were trying to point us at 3V1L, she'd have laid out a better first bait and made this one harder to figure out. We've got swords, guns, a pile of cash, and a *V*'s uniform, all just sitting here. This Fred guy's not the brightest."

The doorbell rang, and I jumped. "Vicegrip, can you get that?" I asked.

"Look! It's a whole god **[Beep!]** map of the district," Fursona said, racking up her second censorship warning. I followed her pointing paw, and sure enough, a map of the Poudre district sat half folded in a corner. Someone had colored chunks red with a marker and then drawn black lines across it.

"Hold on, I'll get a picture." I snapped photo after photo of it, then started taking pictures all around the house. This would be a massive setback for 3V1L; I just knew it! We'd struck a massive blow against 3V1L today, and we'd done it without raising a fist in violen—

The doorbell rang again.

"Fine, I'll get it." I huffed to the front door and opened it.

A uniformed police officer stood there, her braided black hair tucked into a hat. She took her hand off her hip when she saw me, then nodded. "Magical Girl. We got word someone had broken into this address, and my partner and I were available, so we swung by to take a look." A second cop waved from their patrol car's driver's seat.

"Yeah, that'd be Fursona, Vicegrip, and me. I'm Magical Girl Understudy. We're starting a series against 3V1L, and the three of us were getting the lay of the land and patrolling a bit. We stumbled across a clue that this guy might be a big deal in 3V1L, and when we followed it up . . . well, want to come inside and have a look?"

"No thanks. We don't have a warrant, and if it's an 3V1L matter, it's past our pay grade," the officer said. She stuck out a hand. "Sergeant Conner."

"Nice to meet you." We shook, and I kept going as Fursona appeared behind me. "Is there anything else we can do for you officers, either now or in the future? We've worked with Detective Rathburn on the TUPD before."

"Actually, if you'll be in the Poudre districts, could we put you on our call list? We try to keep a roster of superheroes on call for quick reactions since 3V1L's so active. The new 3V1L's tougher to manage, so having a few more options to handle them would be great."

"Sure," Fursona said. We exchanged numbers—I made sure they had the Understudy number, *not* the Anika one—and they said their goodbyes. Fursona shut the door and turned to me. "Where's Tractor-Beam-Girl?"

35

Where's Tractor-Beam-Girl?

As Fursona and I searched Fred's house for our missing sidekick, I had to choke down a combination of fury and panic. It grew with every room full of supervillain outfits, henchman helmets, and weapons until we'd checked the entire house. The only hint was the wide-open sliding glass porch door and the smashed-in circles on the house's cement porch.

"Did we give her comms?" I asked Fursona, already knowing the answer. We didn't have spares for the Triad-built communicators, and neither of us had imagined that Vicegrip—no, she'd *earned* the name Tractor-Beam-Girl—would run off without us. She couldn't be this stupid . . . could she?

Apparently, it was more common in superheroes than I'd thought. I knew *I'd* have done the same thing, but . . .

"No," Fursona said, confirming what I already knew. "But we've got a lead. We know where she's flying, thanks to her beams. They crater the ground if she gets too low or tightens the beams too much—like for takeoff."

"So, we hunt down Tractor-Beam-Girl, then?" I asked, summoning my sailboard.

"Yes. I'll stick to the ground in case there's evidence here, and you patrol from the air? We'll run a reverse Eagle Eye in the Sky," Fursona said.

I felt a familiar pang as she made her suggestion, but we were partners, dammit, and right now, she had the best idea of the two of us. Besides, she didn't have Eagle-sona, so the reverse made the most sense. "You got it!" I said, abandoning the sailboard for a solo [**Solar Wing**].

It took three and a half blocks to find our first piece of evidence.

Outside an abandoned video store—I couldn't tell why an artifact from that long ago hadn't been repurposed—Fursona found two massive cracks in the asphalt. They rippled outward from a pair of depressions, and she called me in to check them out because they weren't alone. Broken glass, an abandoned 3V1L helmet, and a pair of dazed-looking henchmen littered the ground.

"What happened to you two?" I asked.

The woman clammed up while the man muttered something about "My rights as a forced hench. I never asked for this."

I rolled my eyes. "You know, I think I saw you two last year at the job fair at TU. Remember that? I don't think you were forced."

"Sure we were," the first one—a woman—said. "The financials are too good to turn down. 3V1L made me an offer I couldn't refuse—money!"

"Okay. So where'd she go?" Fursona asked, ignoring the joke.

"If we tell you, you'll let us go?"

We didn't have time for this. I **[Quick-Time Changed]** into Lucky Star and activated **[Audition Notes]**.

[Flashy Fitting-Room! +1 Flamboyance Point]
[Audition Notes for John Deer #1: This Extra isn't from around here. He's part of a hench-sharing system that allows henches whose villainous bosses aren't using them to loan them out to a select network of villains. However, after running into his second set of superheroes today, he's starting to regret his life choices.]
[Good Thinking! +1 Cunning Point]

"Yep. We'll let you go. We'll turn around and count to thirty. When we turn back around, your helmets will be on the ground, and you'll be done with henching. But *only* if you tell us where Vicegrip went." It was a gamble, but I figured that, given the information in the **[Audition Notes]**, it had a chance of working. If not, we'd probably still be able to track our prodigal sidekick down.

Sure enough, the two henches looked at each other, almost debating with each other. Then the man nodded. "Counteroffer. Let 'Bob' go as she is, and I'll tell you what you need to know. Deathblood's gonna hear about this. The union will be pissed."

I filed *that* tidbit away; I'd never heard of Deathblood, a henches' union, or hench-sharing before, and I wanted to check in on all three when this patrol was finished. But for now, I needed to make a choice. I glanced at Fursona, who nodded slowly. Then I stuck a gloved hand out. "You have a deal, 'Bill.' 'Bob,' get out of here. Go home and stay out of Poudre for a while, okay? It's going to be messy."

She nodded and started jogging away while Fursona's plastic eyes glared at her retreating back. I turned my full attention to 'Bill,' who'd also stood up. He grinned beneath his 3V1L mask. "Alright, what do you know?" I asked.

"Simple story, really. Your girl jumped 'Bob' and me out here. She must've followed us over from the safe house, but we didn't see her until she'd clobbered us. Thing is, we weren't here to sell Girl Scout cookies, you know?"

"Yeah, I figured," Fursona said. "Get this story moving. We might be on a time crunch."

"So, we were meeting up with some bigwig in 3V1L for a job, and after we'd surrendered, she showed up with a whole truck full of henches, whooping and hollering up a storm. Big old 3V1L flag sailing behind it and glowing lights all along its sides. 'Bob' and I thought they'd come to pick us up, but they parked, jumped your superhero, and started fighting. She hopped into the air on her hands and took off down Lime Street. The truck burned rubber after them."

"So they just left you here?" Fursona asked.

I sensed an opportunity. "Yeah, that doesn't seem like something the union would like, does it, Fursona? Abandoning henches to a superhero? That'd probably get 3V1L in hot water."

"Yeah. So, can I go now?" the hench asked.

"I'd say so. That's plenty of intel. Don't forget to leave the helmet," Fursona said.

What followed was a nerve-wracking thirty seconds as the hench unbuckled his devil-horned helmet with clunking, clattering sounds, then started running. As his footsteps faded into the distance, I turned toward Fursona, sniffing the air. "Follow the diesel fumes?"

The diesel fumes led us into the industrial heart of South Poudre. The Suntech refinery vomited foul-colored smoke into the air, and a chemical stench hung heavily around us as we followed the occasional crater and more frequent tire brake tracks through the streets. The visibility dropped more and more from the smog, and I dropped out of the sky to land next to Fursona, who coughed into her modulator. "What the hell? Who makes a base in this mess?"

"I bet it fits 3V1L perfectly," I said. It had to. No one would willingly build a base in an industrial hellscape like this, so it was the perfect camouflage.

"Yeah, I guess, but the health impacts. People live like this? Outrageous," Fursona said. She pointed at a warehouse. "Let's poke around a bit. I bet there's something in there; it's too convenient."

Part of me wanted to argue. There was no way 3V1L was stupid enough to have a lair in an industrial warehouse; it'd check every stereotype in the book! But another part of me knew, without even looking, that it was the right place. It had to be, *because* it was dumb. So I walked to the door, looking for cameras the whole time, and grabbed the handle. I held up three fingers, and Fursona readied herself for a [**Springtail Kick**]. Two. One.

I pulled the door open. "Surprise!"

[**Explosive Entry! +1 Badass Point**]

As I yelled it, Fursona flew through the open door feetfirst and slammed right into—
"Hey, what the [**Beep!**]" Tractor-Beam-Girl said.

[**Episode Finished!**]
[**Investigative Episode: North Poudre Patrol - PG**]

[Penalties: N/A]
[Episode Finished! +3 of each Style Point]
[Winner Winner! +1 of each Style Point]
[Role Focus: Cunning + Flamboyance - Goal Met! +5 to Focused Styles]
[Alias - Understudy] [Archetype - Magical Girl] [Community Rank - 200/523]
[HP 12/12]
[Styles and Skills]
▶Archetype Skill - Transformation Sequence
▶Combo Skills - Power-Weaving
▶Badass (51) (Skill Roll Available)
▶Cunning (18)
▶Drama (17)
▶Bit-Part Barrage 2
▶Starlance 1
▶Flamboyance (23)
▶Signature Skill - Adaptive Armoire 3
▶Stored Costumes: (Rainy Day, Copy Cat, Lab Assistant Panic)
▶Solar Wing 1
▶Quick-Time Change 3
▶Spotlight Strike 1
▶Grit (30)
▶I-Frame Transform 3
[50 Badass Credits Used. Rolling Skill!]
[Rank-Up! Jinx-Bearer 1: Allows up to two status effects to be transferred to the user]

I rolled my skill. Fursona and Vicegrip untangled themselves as an alarm went off, filling the air with its shrill claxon. Another one started shrieking into the air, and I made a rotating motion with my arm that Fursona recognized. She hurried to her feet. "What do we have?"

I was busy looking at my new skill. Status Effect still felt like such a vague term; I'd been able to transfer acid burns, reducing my total superhero damage. What else could I take for an ally? I'd have to find out soon because it could be an incredibly powerful ability or a waste of a slot, and I didn't have enough information to be sure yet.

"Well, while you two were staring at clothes back there, *I* tracked the villains to some abandoned parking lot, then chased them out here," Tractor-Beam-Girl said. She sneered under her white helmet. "I'm not wasting time with the outliers. If we're after leadership, let's go find their leadership."

I bit my tongue—literally, but not very hard—to keep a sarcastic comment down. Instead, I took a deep breath. Either she was lying, or the hench had been. Either way, we were here, in a totally empty warehouse; the only things I could see were bare shelves and a door on the far side. "So, where'd the truck go?"

"Garage. It's under one of the buildings. Can we please hurry up?"

A new voice echoed over a speaker. "You won't have to. We're coming after you!"

[Casting Call]
[Episode: Power War: Beyond Good and 3V1L - PG-13]
[Role: Interloping Investigator! Do you accept the role? (Yes/No)]
[Role Focus: Cunning + Grit]
[Power War: Beyond Good and 3V1L: Act One in Progress]

"Shit," I said.

BANG!

The doors at the building's far side burst open, and a whole swarm of henches piled in.

Fursona kicked the first and second with a **[Double-Kick]** while I fired a **[Starlance]** into the third. A moment later, the first gun went off with a bang, and Tractor-Beam-Girl screamed. I looked over, but she didn't look hit, and a moment later, she held out her hands and started ripping weapons away from the swarming henches.

[Dramatic Damage! +1 Drama Point]

For a few moments, the empty warehouse was nothing but chaos—henches flying every which way as Tractor-Beam-Girl tossed them around, Fursona a whirlwind of kicks and punches and even an occasional air-shattering tail-slam, and beams whipping into the crowd as I got my rhythm going. We had this covered. Henches weren't a problem at all!

[Dramatic Damage! +1 Drama Point]
[Dramatic Damage! +1 Drama Point]

Then the door burst open again, and not one but *two* red-cloaked villains stalked in. I tried to get a read on which ones they were—if we had the Second or Third *V*, Fursona and I had a plan to handle them—but before I could, one of them hopped into the air over the battlefield and started sliding overhead on a board shockingly similar to mine, while the other began fiddling with a case she'd set on the ground.

"Who are these guys?" Tractor-Beam-Girl asked.

I burst out laughing. I shouldn't have—if these were both *V*s, it had some disturbing implications for 3V1L, because neither matched the *V*s we knew about. The villainous organization was evolving, and it was happening way faster than I'd expected it to. But Tractor-Beam-Girl hadn't been paying *any* attention, and she certainly hadn't done any research on what the three of us were up against in the Poudre districts.

Then, still laughing, I pointed at the one with the case. "That's a Genius. Stop her!"

Fursona lunged toward the villainous *V,* but Tractor-Beam-Girl had to deal with the rest of the henches, and I had my hands full as the surfboard-riding *V* descended on us. And if we failed, we were up a creek with no paddle!

36

With No Paddle!

The case turned out to be, of all things, a small remote control, which the villainess pushed. The moment she did, a rover appeared, shimmering bright neon colors and swinging a turret around to face Fursona. She dodged as it opened fire, filling the room with popping, cracking sounds and the smell of gunpowder.

I wanted to help her out, but one look at the flying villain, and I knew the moment I did, he'd slide over to take out Tractor-Beam-Girl. She tossed another henchman back at his friends, using him like a bowling ball, but her focus was fully on them. If the surfboarding supervillain got a clean shot at her, she'd never see it coming.

I used [**Solar Wing**] and leaped into the air, hovering between my teammates and the villain. "What are you doing here?"

"I should ask you the same thing! You're in our territory. As the Second *V*, I hereby declare war on you, Magical Girl Understudy!" The Second *V* shot forward, not giving me time to think about how I'd already *fought* the Second *V*, and she was a melee-focused ground fighter.

I dodged left, avoiding his ramming attack, but he turned on a dime as I lowered my wand to fire a [**Starlance**] at him. The board sliced across the gap between us like a knife, and as it did, I saw the sharp-looking edge parting the air with a hiss.

I thought quickly as the board seemed to move around in slow motion. My [**Starlance**] fired, but it wouldn't be enough to stop the board, and if I shifted to a different Costume, the team would lose air support. I had only one play.

I took the hit right in the chest, letting my superhero damage eat it.

[HP 8/12]
[**True Grit! +1 Grit Point**]
[**Dramatic Damage! +1 Drama Point**]

The board slammed me into a shelf, which wobbled and collapsed sideways into another, but I managed to keep my wings under me. I shook my head and raced to get back between him and Tractor-Beam-Girl. If he wanted to play a ramming game, my best play was to give him no space to ram in.

So I dove, tucking my wings in, and slammed down onto the board feetfirst.

The Second *V* looked at me, eyes wide, and I pressed my advantage with **[Spotlight Strike]**. It highlighted his nose. A moment later, my fist crashed into it.

[Stylish Strike! +1 Flamboyance Point]

He blinked and recoiled, destabilizing his surfboard, then kicked out at me. It went high as I ducked, and the board rocked above the still-collapsing shelves. Somewhere in the rubble, Fursona and Tractor-Beam-Girl were locked in combat—had I helped them or messed up their plans? None of this was going the way we needed it to!

Then the Second *V*'s boot slammed into my stomach, and I tumbled off the surfboard.

This time, I used **[Bit-Part Barrage]** even as I fell. I'd been saving it for the Second *V* I *thought* we'd see, but if she wasn't going to show up, I'd give this guy everything I had. The half dozen **[Stellar Rays]** punched upward toward him, puncturing his stupid surfboard. A moment later, my temporary hovering stopped, and we both fell toward the ground.

[Dramatic Damage! +4 Drama Points]

I used **[Quick-Time Change]** to activate **[I-Frame Transform]**, merged brains and bodies with Tails, and fell harmlessly through the twisted, mangled shelving to hit the ground. The Second *V* wasn't so lucky; as I watched, he hit seemingly every single shattered strut he could find. He skidded across the concrete floor and crumpled into a pile in the corner, then started pushing himself slowly to his feet.

I had to press. Pressing might knock him out of the fight. If I could take him down, Tractor-Beam-Girl and I could crush the rest of the henches, then help Fursona. So I rushed him, activating **[Hometown Heroine]** for the speed boost and **[Leaping Leopards]** to close the gap.

In response, he lifted his surfboard and slid it onto his arm. It clicked into place. "The Second *V* knows no fear!"

THUMP!

I hit the surfboard shield, bounced off it, and lost my **[Leaping Leopards]** damage, but the impact knocked the Second *V* off-balance, and he wasn't ready for my **[Doom Ball]** follow-up. My scratching claws and kicking paws ripped across his armor and skin, and his yelps of pain competed with Tails in my head. *<Yes! Yes! Give him the cat scratch!>*

I tried to, but the surfboard's blade crashed into me as the Second *V* swung wildly.

[HP 7/12]

The blow didn't do much, but it was enough. In the moment it took me to recover, he sprinted toward Tractor-Beam-Girl. I whirled to help, but I'd used my best movement power, and he tossed the board back under his feet for extra speed. At the same moment, the other *V*—and she had to be a *V*—abandoned her rover. "Go! Go!" I shouted, as much at Fursona as myself, but it was too late.

Both villains hit Tractor-Beam-Girl from behind, driving her to the ground. The Second *V* grabbed his shield, holding it up to block their retreat as the henches piled in, pinning Tractor-Beam-Girl and dragging her down the hall. "Guess you lose this round, Magical Girl Underloser!"

"That's a super dumb insult!" I shouted back, rushing to the door, but he slipped through it and slammed it shut. I kicked it. It shuddered in its frame but refused to budge.

[**End of Act One: Act Two in Three Minutes**]

"Well, shit," Fursona said. The sounds of a struggling superhero faded into the distance as I kicked the door a second time. [**Hometown Heroine**] faded away, and my next kick barely budged it. I sat there dumbly while Fursona tried the handle. "No dice. We need to get outside before the next Act starts. They won't stay here!"

Fursona was right. It didn't matter that Tractor-Beam-Girl had been caught or that our patrol was a disaster. What mattered was that we figured out where they were taking her so we could bust her out and turn this around. I'd traded well with the Second *V*, and if we could get a mismatch, whichever *V* Fursona had fought would go down. We just needed Tractor-Beam-Girl to create that mismatch.

We picked our way across the wreckage and stepped outside just as Act Two started.

[**Power War: Beyond Good and 3V1L: Act Two in Progress**]

"It's weird that it's a Power War Episode, huh?" Fursona asked. I paused halfway through summoning my sailboard under us. She was right. Our other 3V1L Episodes hadn't been—or at least hadn't started as a Power War. Whatever that meant, I doubted it'd be good.

"Hang on, Fursona. They took a truck to get here. They'll be on the move again. Keep your eyes open." [**Solar Wing**] finished, the sailboard popped into existence, and we took off, Fursona as stiff as the neon board beneath our feet. Vicegrip was our sidekick. We'd brought her into this patrol, and I'd look as hard as I had to to get her out.

We didn't have to search for long, though.

We caught the tail end of 3V1L's convoy surging up from an underground garage. The black SUVs stood out like a sore thumb in the rundown, industrial Poudre district, but their identical looks and blacked-out windows made it impossible to tell which one Tractor-Beam-Girl was in—if she was even in one.

I got overhead and pointed. "Okay, we're going to tail the convoy from as high up as we can. Think you can change into Eagle-sona on the board? It'd give us some flexibility."

She tried—I'll give her credit for that—but halfway through shouldering off her bag, Fursona froze up completely, shivering. She couldn't even pull the bag back up; it hung there, dangerously close to the steering bar. "I'm sorry," she chattered through her shaking.

"It's okay. We'll come up with a different plan, that's all. Maybe we just tail them and hope they all go to the same place." I wrapped an arm around her kangaroo waist. In truth, I didn't see any way they *wouldn't* split up. It was the best tactical choice they had. Split up, put both *V*s and Tractor-Beam-Girl in one convoy, and try to get us to split, too. That way, they could overwhelm whoever went after the right convoy and sacrifice the wrong convoy to keep the other hero distracted.

"Sorry," Fursona sniffled again.

"Don't be sorry. I knew that was a big ask." Even though I was trying to play it cool, I gulped as we gained altitude. I had a backup plan, but honestly, it was an even bigger ask than my first plan. I decided to put it on the back burner for now. Maybe we'd get lucky and they wouldn't split up. "It'll probably be a short drive. South Poudre isn't that big, right?"

"Uh-huh. You're right. We'll only be up here for a minute—maybe two—and then you can put me down," Fursona said. Even through the modulator, I could hear her almost crying *and* gritting her teeth at the same time, and my heart broke a little bit.

"I'm sorry I freaked you out, Bee," I whispered, ensuring the camera drone wasn't close enough to pick it up. "I won't drop you."

"I know, but it's a long way down. What if—"

One of the SUVs' skylights opened, and a surfboard-riding Second *V* erupted into the air.

"—that happens!?" Fursona wailed.

"Shit," I muttered. Then I dove, racing down to meet the villain. "I'm not going to drop you, Fursona, but you've gotta trust me. Grab the steering bar!"

She did, and I let go. "Good, now keep us in the air. I don't care where we go, but keep us in the air. If I say left, pull left. Right, go right!" The Second *V* came closer and closer, and I fired off my first **[Starlance]**. It ripped across the sky, leaving a pink-and-blue trail behind it, and fizzled out of existence somewhere behind him as he rolled.

"Okay. Got it. I've got it." Fursona turned the sailboard slowly, bringing it around and speeding away from the Second *V.* I turned, hanging on to her shoulder, and readied my wand. With her piloting, we couldn't outrun the Second *V.*

"**[Starlance]**!" I shouted, firing another lance through the air. This one hit, but not hard enough to knock the Second *V* off his surfboard. "Fursona, turn us all the way around! We can't lose the convoy!"

[Dramatic Damage! +1 Drama Point]

She listened, and the sailboard slowly spun around. "Good job, babe. Now, no matter what happens, keep us over them. If they split before I beat this guy—"

He dove from above, and I used **[Bit-Part Barrage]**, hoping it wouldn't cancel **[Solar Wing]**. If it did, I had no idea how I'd keep my promise to Bianca, and I couldn't let her fall, but I couldn't let his bladed surfboard crash through my sailboard, either. The world froze as I spun, struggling to find him and aim. Then, beam after beam surged toward him, lighting up the bright noon street even more.

[Dramatic Damage! +3 Drama Points]

I breathed a sigh of relief as the surfboard broke off just twenty feet away; I'd missed my first stunning shot, which might've been enough to knock him out of the fight. Still, we'd bought a moment. I took a deep breath. "You're doing great, babe. You're doing great. Now, how's the convoy doing?"

"They're splitting up!" Fursona said. "Two groups! What do I do?"

I grimaced. This was it—the nightmare scenario. We had an airborne enemy, and the SUVs below were about to scatter. "Dive. Pick one of the groups and dive!"

She stiffened again but pushed the sailboard's steering bar forward, and we started descending. The stinking industrial air whipped past my face as we raced for the right-side group. Then, suddenly, we were right on them. Behind us, the Second *V* bore down, gaining by the second. I gulped again and made my next big ask. "Fursona, I need you to jump into the last car!"

37

The Last Car

To her credit, Fursona didn't *completely* freeze this time.

And to my credit, I tried to explain why I wanted her to jump off my perfectly good sailboard. "You can drive! If you can take over that car, you can follow the right convoy, and I can tail the left! I can't do it without you!"

She stared at me for a moment. "Not a Dive Bomb?"

"No. Split Ends. We keep in touch, and as soon as we know which convoy to follow, we break off."

"Okay," she said quietly. She gathered herself as I dipped low, trying to stay in the last SUV's blind spot. I couldn't tell if I'd succeeded, but I tapped her on the shoulder as we got to within a few feet of the skylight. She flinched, then hopped off my sailboard and through the sunroof with a crash.

The car swerved and skidded, but I had other things on my mind. The Second *V*'s surfboard sliced through the air, blade humming, and I barely pulled up in time to avoid it. The very tip of the blade caught my sailboard's tail, and I had to deactivate and reactivate [**Solar Wing**].

[**Gutsy Drop! +1 Badass Point**]

Worse, the left-hand convoy was pulling farther and farther away, and the Second *V* was already looping around. I had three jobs to Fursona's one.

First, I had to keep tabs on the left convoy. Easy peasy, except they kept accelerating to put distance between us.

I also had to handle the Second *V*'s attacks against me. He surged toward me, then broke off as I whipped a [**Starlance**] at him. It pursued, chasing him into an alley before fizzling out. As I waited for him to show up again, I thought about the third job—and the hardest.

I had to keep him away from Fursona.

In her Roo-sona fursuit, she didn't have a single ranged power. He hadn't shown any, either, but that didn't mean he didn't have any, and if he did, he'd take out her car without ever being in danger. I couldn't let that happen!

So, instead of zipping off for the far convoy, I waited to see what the Second *V* would do. As I did, I whispered into my mic. "Fursona, how's it going?"

"Great. Just great. I've got the car, and I'm back in line, but I'm not sure if they know I'm here." A gunshot cracked in my ear through the headset, and Fursona yelped. "Scratch that! They know I'm here!"

"Do you need help?" I asked, just as the Second *V* appeared in hot pursuit of her car. "Cancel that. You do need help! Incoming!"

I tore off after her, firing **[Starlances]** the whole way. One. Two. Three. The first hit as I cast my fourth, and the Second *V* started trying to evade in midair. The second caught him, too, but the third and fourth missed.

[Dramatic Damage! +1 Drama Point]
[Dramatic Damage! +1 Drama Point]

Then, suddenly, I was over the convoy, and the antiair fire intensified. The whole world seemed like muzzle-flashes as guns went off below me. First one, then another, then a *third* bullet hit me, knocking me off course, spinning me around, and most importantly, *hurting*—a lot. I screamed in pain; I'd have bruises tomorrow from this!

[HP 2/12]

Then *I* crashed into a car—luckily bouncing off the hood and landing on the SUV's front window. As I caught my breath, I glanced through the cracked windshield and saw Fursona's plastic eyes staring back at me. "Uh, hi."

[HP 1/12]

"Hi," her voice said in my ear. "Get in here!"

I fell through the shattered sunroof, crunching shards of glass under me. "Okay, so, Split Ends didn't work. He headed straight for you; she's gotta be in this group."

"Yep. Can you do something about that?" Fursona glanced back and gestured at my face. I looked in the mirror and realized I was bleeding—and not just a little. My nose looked like a fountain.

"Through the superhero damage? Really?" I said, **[Quick-Time Changing]** into Rainy Day. As I used **[Virga]** and glared at the unconscious henchman I'd just noticed—who'd woken up when the heal hit him—something thumped against the car.

[Flashy Fitting-Room! +1 Flamboyance Point]
[Medic! +2 Cunning Points]
[HP 3/12]
[Doctors Without Borders! -1 Cunning Point]

It wasn't enough, but I didn't have time to heal the rest. I poked my head through the ruined skylight, then pulled back as the Second *V*'s surfboard screeched across the SUV's roof, showering me in sparks. "Plan?"

"Okay, uh, we haven't tried this before, obviously, because how could we have possibly practiced this, but," Fursona said. She was rambling, and I waved her on as the SUV rocked and the back windshield shattered. "You can be a turret in the sunroof, and I'll try to catch us up to the other cars. We'll stop them, and if the convoy turns to fight us, that's the one with Tractor-Beam-Girl!"

"Got it!" I poked my head out again, and when the Second *V* once again tried to decapitate me, I hit him with a **[Wind Front]** that popped him into the air and off to the side. I grinned; the extra control from Rank Two was already paying off!

[Badass Move! +1 Badass Point]

But knocking him around wouldn't stop him. He couldn't have much superhero damage left; I needed to *hit* him, not keep him from hitting us. The villain dove, and I charged up a **[Thunderhead]** as he did. Then I ducked back into the SUV.

[Pause for Effect! +1 Drama Point]

This time, his blade caught a gap in the roof and peeled it like a potato instead of scraping against the metal. The thin metal body curled into a perfect spiral, then flew off to bounce along like a spring in front of us. Fursona grabbed the wheel and spun, putting us into a spiral as bullets slammed all along the car's side—we'd pulled up next to another SUV, and its passengers kept right on shooting.

"Oh shit!" Fursona said as our car slammed into the other, jolting me across the back seat. "Buckle up, buttercup!"

"Har har!" I popped back out. The **[Thunderhead]** had almost finished, And the moment it did, I held my breath, hoping . . . hoping . . .

Yes! The Second *V* dove toward us, a manic smile on his surfboard as he aimed low enough to peel another layer off our car. The moment he got in range, I used **[Ride the Lightning]** and sent a tendril of lightning rippling toward him. He couldn't dodge—his blade was already in our back hatch—and it caught him straight in the face.

[Electric Lightshow! +1 Flamboyance Point]

A second later, his surfboard tipped, spilling him onto the asphalt. He tried to get up, then collapsed. His lips moved, but I couldn't hear any words. It almost looked like the word *made*, but I couldn't be sure.

"One down, one to go!" I cheered. Fursona whooped from the front seat, and we sped off toward the rest of the convoy. With the Second *V* out of the picture, we had a window to start finding Tractor-Beam-Girl, and Fursona pushed our busted, smoking SUV to the limit to catch up with the next car.

Shockingly, after our fight against the Second *V*, it felt massively under-protected. A single hench stuck his head out of the sunroof, leveling a gun and firing a burst that slammed right into our windshield. It held, though Fursona could barely see the road. But when I tried to pop out and use **[Wind Front]**, the minion opened fire, his gun sending bullets flying wildly at us.

"We need a plan!" I shouted.

"I've got one! Switch to Understudy!" As Fursona pulled our car closer and closer to the henches, I started a slow transformation. It took too long—valuable seconds we didn't have—to switch, but eventually, I returned to my pink-and-purple dress and familiar tourmaline wand.

[HP 8/12]

"Okay, now what?"

"Bulletproof power windows. Lower, fire, raise. Try to knock out a tire." Fursona spun the wheel, and we rocketed around a corner, wheeling on the cracked sidewalk. The SUV shook, and when we bounced off the curb, a rattle in the engine wouldn't stop. "Hurry. This thing's gonna come apart!"

"Got it!" I readied the power window button, then waited until we'd pulled up next to the other SUV. The window dropped, I fired a **[Starlance]**, and bullets sprayed against the car's side, leaving dents and ringing my ears. But the henches' ride wobbled for a moment before the driver recovered.

"Again! Fast!" Fursona's whole suit shook as she wrestled with the wheel. Even armored against bullets, 3V1L's SUVs had never been built to take this kind of abuse, and her entire concentration—and all her strength—was taken up in the fight against the broken power steering and trashed alignment. Or something like that; cars weren't my thing.

My thing was fighting villains.

The window dropped again, and this time, I fired two more **[Starlances]** at the front wheel. The moment I did, the SUV jumped in place, then swerved. Fursona cranked our wheel again, but too slowly—we slammed into the henches and skidded across the asphalt, engines both smoking and steaming from a dozen leaks. Then we hit the side of a building and stopped with a jerk.

[Dramatic Damage! +1 Drama Point]
[Dramatic Damage! +1 Drama Point]
[HP 5/12]

I pulled myself together and limped clear as Fursona thrashed to free herself from our driver's seat. One of the henches had gotten out by the time we did, and he sat there, mouth agape beneath his helmet. I pointed. "I know, I know, they forced you. Get these guys out of the cars. There's one in ours, plus however many you had."

Then I started helping Fursona out. It took a second—and a few [**Spotlight Strikes**]—to free her, and the moment she came loose, she pointed at me. "We need to fly. We can still catch them!"

[**Stylish Strike! +1 Flamboyance Point**]

"Seriously?" Fursona accepting a ride on the sailboard was one thing; Fursona demanding one was totally different.

"Yes! Hurry!"

I used [**Solar Wing**], and she hopped on. A moment later, we zipped through the air after the retreating headlights. As we tore past smokestacks and the kind of stores that had barred windows and cages over the doors, ducking street signs and the highway overpass, I held my wand ready. Only two cars remained. Just two. Tractor-Beam-Girl had to be inside one.

The camera drone caught our pursuit as we lanced across Adams Street and into North Poudre. The buildings slowly shifted from industrial factories and plants to towering apartments and sprawling stores. I readied my wand for a shot from maximum range, but before I could, both SUVs whipped left, right, and tucked into a parking lot. A quartet of henches exited the first, surrounding the right side of the second with guns drawn. I pulled up. "Think we can Dive Bomb?"

"No. Get us out of sight. Third *V*'s still there somewhere," Fursona said.

I pulled up, gaining a few hundred feet of elevation. Then, the door opened, and the Third *V* appeared. She turned, reached in, and grabbed something. A familiar something. Even from this high up, I could hear the [**Beeps**] as Tractor-Beam-Girl used the kinds of obscenities that Fursona had already poached for the Episode. The henches grabbed her and hustled her toward an abandoned big box store. As they disappeared inside, the Third *V* looked along the horizon. She paused, then shook her head and disappeared inside.

"Whew," Fursona said. "Get us back on solid ground, and let's crack this egg."

[**End of Act Two: Act Three in Three Minutes**]

38

Cracking the Egg

We had three minutes to come up with a plan that beat the Third *V*, an unknown number of henchmen, and whatever else 3V1L's lair had inside. Our resources were reset: I had Understudy, Rainy Day, Copy Cat, and Lucky Star, while Fursona was sticking with the Roo-sona fursuit.

We had options. But they weren't great ones.

"Through the front door? I go first; you cover in Understudy? That might work," Fursona suggested from our perch on the roof.

"Maybe. But I don't want to get into a messy firefight when they've got a hostage. Remember my team's battle plan during Combat Styles?" I asked. We'd tried splitting up as villains to pin down the heroes and beat them before they reached the hostage. It hadn't worked. "I don't think we'd get that lucky. This is a professional supervillain organization with experience in its own base. They won't separate."

"No, you're right. That'd be too much luck to hope for. We could call for help?"

"Two minutes. Not enough time for help to get here, and Rocko would kill us. We're all we've got." I grinned. "How about we try stealth? We sneak in, take out the henches between us and Tractor-Beam-Girl, and sneak out."

"It might work. Think Tractor-Beam-Girl would ever be stealthy?" Fursona asked. "I bet she starts complaining the moment we find her."

"Maybe. Good with that plan?"

"Hell yes. Let's find a back door." Fursona hopped to the building's edge, then slid down a ladder like it was nothing. I followed a little more sedately. The whole block didn't have power—or at least, none of the buildings had working fans on their roofs, so they probably didn't have cameras. We wouldn't have to worry about that.

[Power War: Beyond Good and 3V1L: Act Three in Progress]

Fursona cracked a door open, peeked inside, and waved me forward. Together, we crept into 3V1L's lair. Her fursuit's footfalls were silent, but my boots clicked just slightly. "I almost want you in Copy Cat," she murmured through our headset.

I shrugged. We'd never tried stealth before, and she was right; Copy Cat had the best setup for quick, sneaky movement. But I didn't think this would stay a stealth mission for long—not in Act Three. We crept through the store's back rooms, avoiding the floppy plastic doors separating the stock rooms from the selling floor, and pushed through a transparent, hanging barrier between two sections.

Suddenly, Fursona sprang forward and slammed into something with a thump!

I held out my wand and hurried forward, but Fursona had already taken out the hench. He lay on the ground, unmoving except for a slight rise and fall in his chest. "Good job," I murmured.

"Thanks!" Fursona didn't need to be as quiet. Her modulator blocked out her regular voice when she used The Triad comm system, so I could feel her excitement. "One down, a bunch to go."

"Yep." We stepped over the unconscious henchman, and I took point for a moment. My wand glowed in the dark passageways, and the moment I saw something move ahead of me, I activated [**Spotlight Strike**]. The highlight marked a spot between the henchman's shoulder blades, and a moment later, my fist connected. She dropped like a sack of potatoes.

[**Stylish Strike! +1 Flamboyance Point**]

We kept pushing into the building, knocking out henches and trying to stay out of sight in the stacked cardboard boxes that had once held bottles of ketchup and mayonnaise but now probably hid something more nefarious. Past a trash compactor filled with recyclables, up a flight of stairs, and into a break room where an old, boxy TV had once played crappy daytime TV for the baggers and checkers on their breaks. I was starting to believe this whole place wasn't a lair at all.

Then I opened the door to the manager's old office, expecting more of the same.

Instead, I saw a circular steel door ajar on its massive hinges. It led into a space that *wasn't* dark, and I hesitated, fidgeting. Had they seen us coming? If they had power inside, they could have a security system running.

Then Fursona pulled the door open, and all hell broke loose.

Bullets started flying, and Fursona tanked them on her [**Fursonal Fursuit**]. I pushed her forward to clear a shot for myself and fired a [**Bit-Part Barrage**] into the waiting henches, which took out three. Then, without needing to tell me, Fursona rushed into the gap I'd just cleared, bounding across the room and slamming a hench onto the floor hard enough that I felt it in my boots.

[**Dramatic Damage! +3 Drama Points**]

"This isn't a stealth mission anymore, Understudy!" Fursona yelled. I nodded and rushed one of the remaining henches, ducking under his pistol's barrel before he could fire it and using [**Spotlight Strike**] to punch him in the kidney.

[Stylish Strike! +1 Flamboyance Point]

Another pair of henches rushed in with batons. One swung at Fursona, but she leveled him with a [**Double-Kick**] to the chest. The other shouted into a headset. "Boss, it's the Magical Girl! The Magical Girl and the—"

WHAM!

My [**Spotlight Strike**] marked the side of his head, and a moment later, my kick followed it, crushing the headset and dropping him.

[Stylish Strike! +1 Flamboyance Point]

"Okay, stealth's done! Fast and hard!" I said. I rushed down the wide hall before more henches could fill it, then took a left. Fursona followed half a step behind me. We bowled over another henchman, not bothering to use a power and just shoving past. Wherever they were keeping Tractor-Beam-Girl, it couldn't be too far—the building wasn't *that* big.

A right, one more left, and I heard a familiar voice from inside a locked room. "What the hell? I *told* you I was following them, and you didn't listen! Who are these guys, anyway? 3V1L? What kind of name is that?" Something slammed against the door from inside just as a pair of voices rang out on the store's intercom.

"Third *V*, First *V*! We need a cleanup on Aisle Three!" The voice sounded synthesized but definitely male, and even through the static-fuzzed PA system, it oozed authority. I ran through my list of villains with that kind of power in their words before landing on the only suspect I felt confident in. Monologue. It had to be Monologue.

"Fursona, Monologue's the One *L*," I said. It explained everything—the leadership changes, the low-powered operation compared to before, and especially how he managed to avoid being pinned down. He didn't *have* to be here. He didn't *have* to attend Episodes to have an impact.

Fursona kicked the door, then kicked it again. It popped off its hinges, and she cracked her fursuit's knuckles as Tractor-Beam-Girl's pissed-off face popped into view. "That's a great theory, babe, but maybe we put it on the back burner for now. Two *Vs* incoming!"

After seeing all the different *Vs* so far, I expected the First *V* to have some gimmick. We'd had a swordsman, a melee-only martial artist with ranged protection, a flier, and a vehicle Genius with a remote control and rover. I guessed the most recent *V*—and the third this Episode—would be a ranged specialist.

And I wasn't disappointed.

Fursona, Tractor-Beam-Girl, and I ran for the exit with everything we had, but as we reached the wide hall, we ran into the Third *V* setting up a new, neon-glowing rover. It wheeled toward us, a riot shield in one mechanical hand and an electric baton in the other. It'd be a menace wherever it went, and the Third *V* had hunkered down behind a plastic-and-steel barrier; she'd be a tough target to get to.

"Howdy," the First *V* said, stepping through the round steel door and shutting it behind him. I cringed at the greeting, but it fit him; he was long and lanky and wearing a cowboy's duster—red, of course. He held a pair of wide-barreled revolvers, one in each hand. His lips pressed into a smirk. "You're kidnapping what we've right-fully stolen, rustlers."

I didn't waste any time, firing a **[Starlance]** at him; it slammed into his duster as he whirled, vanishing without seeming to hurt him, but I still got a Style System notification.

[**Dramatic Damage! +1 Drama Point**]

"So it's a shootout, then? Alright, partner." The pistols went up, both muzzles flashed, and a moment later, the whole world started spinning as he threw himself into the air. Fursona, Tractor-Beam-Girl, and I tilted in a full circle along with the world as he jogged through the air in seeming slow motion, and bullets ripped through the air, leaving ripples behind.

Every shot hit home. Every. Single. One. They slammed into Fursona and me, leaving Tractor-Beam-Girl untouched for now. I rocked backward, falling dramati-cally to the floor as the cowboy-themed *V*'s power ended.

[**HP 1/12**]
[**Debuff Acquired: Gun-Fu Fuzz: Speed reduced by 1%, stacking**]

"Okay, new plan," I muttered into my mic. "We need to get out of here!"

Fursona nodded. "I agree."

But before we could escape, Tractor-Beam-Girl dove toward the cowboy, reach-ing out with her two gravity grips to disarm him. His guns flashed, she flew back-ward, and he dropped them—only to pull two more from nowhere as the first two vanished. "[**Never Reload**], ladies and gents. Now [**Dance**]!"

As bullets cracked from his barrels and ricocheted around the room, I ducked and leaped over them. Then I realized, in horror, that he was herding the three of us toward the robot. "We're about to be caught between a rock and a bullet-filled place!" I said.

"Plan!?" Fursona shouted.

"Nope!" I didn't have anything. None of my powers could get us all out of this.

Wait. None of my powers could get us *all* out of this. I **[Quick-Time Changed]**, letting **[I-Frame Transform]** eat some shots until I was on the other side of the shooting and shifting into Lucky Star.

[Flashy Fitting-Room! +1 Flamboyance Point]
[Steel Yourself! +1 Grit Point]

"Get Tractor-Beam-Girl hit! Use her as cover!" I said through my mic, following the wave of bullets as the First *V* grabbed *another* gun, this one a handheld submachine gun, and kept firing. Fursona looked at me, and even though she wore her helmet, I could see her thoughts; I'd clearly lost my mind.

But she did it. She ducked behind our sidekick.

A moment later, bullets started hitting her, and she dropped to the floor. I immediately activated **[Noncombatant Teleport]** before she could do something stupid like try to get back up. A portal opened under her, and she disappeared—safe and away from the fighting. A moment later, the bullets stopped.

[Dramatic Rescue! +1 Drama Point]
[Dangerous Idea! +1 Cunning Point, +1 Badass Point]
[Rescue Rearm! +1 Noncombatant Teleport Use]

"What in tarnation?" the First *V* asked.

A moment later, the electro-baton-wielding rover slapped Fursona with it, and she screamed. I caught it through the modulator and my mic simultaneously, the two voices mixing as electricity coursed through her fursuit. Plushie fur singed and curled as it blackened, but after a moment, my partner disengaged and flopped onto the ground, panting.

I saw an opportunity and dashed forward, but a storm of lead cut me off as the First *V* opened fire. "No, little lady, can't let you do that," he said, dropping the submachine gun and pulling out a battle rifle. I'd seen those before, in history books about pre-Launch Day militaries, and as he pulled the trigger, its thunderous retort drowned out whatever else he'd been saying.

I threw myself into the air, trying to **[Gun-Fu]** my way across the battlefield to reach Fursona, but the bullets caught me and shoved me into a wall.

[HP 0/12]

Still, I was close. Close enough that I could get her out of here. I opened a **[Noncombatant Teleport]** under her. As the portal opened, she stared at me. Then she threw herself at me, *away* from safety. I had just enough time to swear under my breath. My girlfriend wasn't taking our best way out. She was going to throw the whole Episode right here!

Then the kangaroo fursuit crashed into me, pushing me up against the wall again. As we tried to untangle ourselves, the baton-wielding robot rolled forward, and the First *V* pulled out a rocket launcher.

I didn't have anything left. Lucky Star was the right Costume to save Fursona and Tractor-Beam-Girl, but not to fight against two *V*s. So I did the only thing I could. I pushed the emergency Triad button and asked for help.

39

Help

The seconds ticked by. The First *V*'s rocket launcher rose as he pulled it toward his shoulder. The Third *V*'s electro-baton robot clattered toward Fursona and me. Would The Triad accept our call for help? Would they show up in time?

My heart pounded as I squeezed Fursona and activated **[Emergency Teleport]** again. The kangaroo heroine broke my embrace and rolled out of it. "No! I'm sticking it out with you!" She held up her own Triad button, which blinked a dull green.

Green. Green had to be good, right? Green was good everywhere else. My **[Emergency Teleport]** fizzled out, and the First *V* pulled the rocket launcher's trigger. The cone-shaped explosive zoomed toward me just as a portal opened, and three identical figures stepped through.

They'd responded. Bud Lightbeam was here to help.

One clone tanked the rocket, which vanished just like Polar Vortex's ice-missile had. The other leaped toward the baton-bot and grappled with it, firing an energy beam into it even as the baton crashed into his side repeatedly. And the third—the real Lightbeam—stood over us heroically. "Understudy, we have *got* to stop meeting like this!"

I could have hugged him. Instead, I pointed and shouted, "Behind you!"

He whirled as the First *V* activated his **[Gun-Fu]** power and opened up. Lightbeam took the shots on his back and chest, and I winced as the debuff stacked up and he slowed down. I only had seconds—maybe not even that long—before Tele-Portal grabbed me and yanked me out to The Triad's base, so I lunged at the hero, grabbed his wrist, and activated **[Jinx-Bearer]**.

[Debuff Acquired: Gun-Fu Fuzz x12: Speed reduced by 1%, stacking]
[Gritty Sacrifice! +1 Grit Point]

He nodded at me. "Get out of here. I'll take care of this." Then he turned and zipped into the air, ignoring the First *V* and rocketing straight for the Third. As he attacked the suddenly panicking *V*s, a portal opened, and Tele-Portal pulled the two of us out.

We didn't land at The Triad's base, though.

Instead, we arrived on a battlefield—one The Triad had won. Smoke poured from Underdelver's mech as he loomed over a villain being escorted away by the police. The field they'd fought in was scorched and pocked with craters from explosions and holes from where his mech had dug in and out of the earth. A few buildings nearby burned as fire crews struggled with the blazes, and somewhere between me and the mountains, The Triad's base loomed over us.

"Kid, you're lucky we finished this when we did," Tele-Portal said. She leaned against the remnants of a wall, breathing heavily and half closing her eyes. "What'd you run into?"

I told her everything in a long breathless sentence, and when I finished, she nodded slowly. "Do you have anything left in the tank? You're not done with that Episode yet."

I nodded slowly; I had Rainy Day, and I could get us both into . . . not exactly fighting shape, but *something*. "What else do we need to do?"

"You've left a teammate back there. You need to go get her," Tele-Portal said slowly. She yawned. "I'll give you a minute, then port you back in. Once you land, you're on your own, though. I'll put you at your sidekick's last known location."

Fursona stretched and popped her neck. "Okay, okay, we've got this. It's just a rescue and extraction, not a full-on fight."

But Tele-Portal held up a hand. "No, you're out of it. If you go in, you'll just be putting pressure on Understudy. All she has to do is get the little-league heroine— Vicegrip, right?—out."

I shifted into Rainy Day and used **[Virga]**, then immediately shifted again, this time into Understudy. Then I hugged Fursona; even inside her suit, she looked dejected—or maybe furious. I couldn't tell if she wanted to cry or fight Tele-Portal. Maybe both. "Hey, babe, it's going to be okay. I'll meet you back at the green room in half an hour. You'll know I'm safe when you get the victory message."

[Medic! +3 Cunning Points]
[HP 2/12]
[Rejuvenation Activated: HP 6/12]

She nodded slowly. I could see her arm through the fursuit. "If you get in trouble, say something. I'll see if Tele-Portal can get me into the fight again."

I smiled back. "You've got it." But even as I said it, I knew Tele-Portal was right. Having a nearly depleted Fursona on the battlefield took away my options, and I'd need them all if Lightbeam couldn't stop both *V*s or if 3V1L had more henchmen nearby.

And 3V1L always had more henches nearby.

I landed on a street corner near the North Poudre box store—far enough from the fighting inside that Lightbeam's weapons couldn't hit me, but close enough to hear the sounds of gunfire and energy beams going off. The moment my feet were under me, I threw myself into the air, a camera drone following me. I already knew exactly where I needed to go; over the constant fire of the First *V*'s guns, I could hear a second set of pops and an occasional shout. I flew that way as fast as I could, using **[Solar Wing]** to duck between buildings and under streetlights.

I turned a corner to see a terrified-looking Tractor-Beam-Girl holding a car door over herself as a half dozen henches fired at her and three more ran forward with baseball bats and crowbars. She looked terrible; she'd run out of superhero damage back in the grocery store and had been fighting since then. A handful of other henches lay on the street, slumped over the curbs or tossed aside.

She'd been doing well, but she was outgunned, and if nothing changed, she'd be overwhelmed soon. One of her gauntlets had shattered, and she held the car door one-handed.

I used **[Starlance]** and took out one gunman, then another. As I went for a third, someone shouted, and a trio of shooters switched toward me.

[Dramatic Damage! +1 Drama Point]
[Dramatic Damage! +1 Drama Point]

I ducked as they opened fire, but I was a beat too slow. A bullet caught me, then another, and I dove behind a bus stop for shelter. The impacts stung, but I had superhero damage to spare—unlike Tractor-Beam-Girl.

[HP 2/12]

Not *much* superhero damage, but *some*.

I ducked out, blasting away and trying to close the gap. As I did, the car door flew by, smashing a henchman into a nearby building's wall. I waved at Tractor-Beam-Girl, who . . . flipped me off.

Whatever. The drones and Rocko would edit it out later.

As I got in close, I used **[Quick-Time Change]** to dodge a pair of bullets with **[I-Frame Transform]**, became Copy Cat, and activated **[Hometown Heroine]** to close the gap even faster. I'd committed myself, but the Copy Cat Costume had the speed, toughness, and firepower to clear the henches, and nothing else did right now.

[Flashy Fitting-Room! +1 Flamboyance Point]
[Steel Yourself! +1 Grit Point]

Bullets bounced off my **[Fursonal Furcefield]**. I dashed through them, trusting Tails to keep me safe and the blue halo around me to speed me along. A hench flew out of my way as Tractor-Beam-Girl grabbed him and tossed him aside. Then I was in the middle of the group.

I [**Doom Balled**] the first hench, claws ripping razor-thin gashes in his outfit, then used [**Leaping Leopards**] to gap-close the remaining gunman. A moment later, he went down screaming as I pulled back and hissed.

[Badass Damage! +3 Badass Points]
[Badass Damage! +1 Badass Point]

A few henches remained, most with melee weapons, but as I whirled to face them, Tractor-Beam-Girl pulled one off her feet and slammed her into a building. The remaining ones broke and ran, fleeing down the street. Tractor-Beam-Girl took three steps toward them. "Get your asses back here! I wasn't done! I wasn't done!"

I grabbed her before she could keep going. "Vicegrip, you're done. We're done. The Triad's Lightbeam is mopping up the *V*s, and I'm only here to get you out. Can you fly?"

"No," Tractor-Beam-Girl said, deflating. "They knocked the stabilizers around."

"Great." I shifted back to Understudy—every second felt too long, like the henches would be back with friends or the One *L*—and grabbed her. "Hang on."

"Wha—"

I didn't let her finish. Instead, I summoned my sailboard and tossed us both into the air. "We're getting out of here."

"But we haven't won yet," she protested.

I grabbed her arm with one steely grip and the steering bar with the other, then squeezed both. I doubted she felt it through her armor. "Listen. Right now, the win is that we get out. We're going to walk away from this one, and if the System gives us a draw or even a loss, we're going to take it. We underestimated 3V1L, and that won't happen again."

She sniffled, then started sobbing. I glared at her. "What?"

"I've never lost an Episode before. I've never even *tied* an Episode before."

I struggled against the groan building inside of me with every ounce of my will and, somehow, grappled it down. Then I took a deep breath. I didn't care if this counted as a loss. I didn't care if I won. Right now, I just wanted to get back to TU and finish the Episode. We whipped through the streets silently, leaving pink and blue streaks in the air behind us.

I cleared my throat as we crossed the border between South Poudre and University. "I'll drop you off at the SUB. We'll debrief this Episode some other time." I didn't want to deal with her anymore. Vicegrip's decisions had ruined our patrol, set up the Episode after it, and forced us to ask The Triad for help with something we could have handled.

[Episode Finished!]
[Episode: Power War: Beyond Good and 3V1L - PG-13]

[Penalties: N/A]
[Episode Finished! +3 of each Style Point]
[Winner Winner! +3 of each Style Point]
[Role Focus: Cunning + Grit - Goal Unmet]
[Alias - Understudy] [Archetype - Magical Girl] [Community Rank - 196/523]
[HP 2/12]
[Styles and Skills]
▶Archetype Skill - Transformation Sequence
▶Combo Skills - Power-Weaving
▶Badass (14)
▶Cunning (29)
▶Drama (47)
▶Bit-Part Barrage 2
▶Starlance 1
▶Flamboyance (40)
▶Signature Skill - Adaptive Armoire 3
▶Stored Costumes: (Rainy Day, Copy Cat, Lucky Star)
▶Solar Wing 1
▶Quick-Time Change 3
▶Spotlight Strike 1
▶Grit (38)
▶I-Frame Transform 3

Overall, it didn't feel like a win. But the System disagreed, which meant we'd done something right. So, what had we learned about 3V1L? I pondered it as I zipped back to Walnut Tower and landed on the roof.

By the time I landed and stomped down the stairs into the green room, I was in a foul mood. I couldn't figure out why we'd gotten the win. Had we shut down The Triad? No. If we were lucky, Lightbeam had gotten one of the *V*s arrested, but that setback was the best we could hope for. Had we struck a blow to their operation? Maybe, but not a permanent one. At best, we should have gotten a draw. Not a full-on win.

So, when I saw the whiteboard, I groaned. Bianca grinned, half out of the kangaroo suit, and waved. "Hey, about time you got here! I know something you don't know!"

"What?" I untransformed slowly, ignoring her teasing face, and slumped into the couch's warm embrace. I needed a snuggle. I needed a *nap*. What I didn't need was a lecture from my girlfriend, *or* her holding out information on me.

She spun the whiteboard around. It was covered in lines, crossed-out words, and scribbles. She couldn't have been working on this for more than five minutes—maybe ten—but it looked like she'd been at it for hours. "I have a theory about how 3V1L is structured. If I'm right, it means that no amount of Golden Goose pruning could stop it. I think that as long as the One *L* is in charge, they'll have three *V*s, even if they're not the originals."

"How so?" I asked.

"I haven't figured that out yet, but all my theories point to the One *L* as the root of all 3V1L!"

I laughed, then groaned. My bruises hurt *way* too much for this. "Okay. Let's call it a day and start working out who he is later."

PART SIX

40

Priorities

SATURDAY, NOVEMBER 22

<So yeah, he's been here every week - Honeycomb 4:13>
<idk. Theres nothing weird about him other than he's mad - Honeycomb 4:13>
<You probably shouldn't come here though - Honeycomb 4:13>

I looked at my phone, frowning. According to Honeycomb, Vigilant Vow had actually followed through on following her schedule—or at least, she hadn't noticed any power disruptions. Even more encouraging, he'd signed up to replace the villains Tottergarten had lost when the Anti-Nap League resigned. It wasn't enough for me to tell if his redemption was working. But it was *something*.

<Got it. I'll play it cool - Understudy 4:14>
<Thanks - Understudy 4:14>
<No, thank you - Honeycomb 4:15>

Well, that meant something, but I couldn't be bothered to puzzle it out. I had far too much on my mind.

The debriefing with Tractor-Beam-Girl had gone . . . interestingly. We'd agreed to go our separate ways, but with the condition that we'd work together on TUSSA-approved missions only. Sara had sent a fortuitously-timed text that convinced us both that *that* was necessary. I still didn't understand how she could know so *little* about superheroing as an undefeated little-leaguer, but that wasn't my priority, either.

In the last few weeks, we'd raided 3V1L lairs all across South Poudre, but we hadn't caught so much as a whiff of a *V*, much less the One *L* we were hunting for. Bianca firmly believed we could find him, but our Episodes never amounted to much more than another stormed lair, usually with minimal drama except for the clues that we'd missed leadership by a week, a day, or even an hour—but always too late.

It'd be frustrating if it weren't for The Triad auxiliary Episodes, which almost always ended in wins. Between The Triad, Stella-Lunar, Golden Goose, and the dozens of other heroes in Tokyexico City, the Third Power War's Tokyexico campaign looked like it was just about over. Sure, 3V1L still controlled most of the Poudre districts, and McHammer and Lord Destructo had an enclave north of Thornton, but Acid Burn had fallen off as a threat, and several other villains had been sighted in different towns. Even the Anti-Nap League had backed off a little.

The situation was so good, in fact, that Golden Goose had left—and Lord Destructo *still* refused to leave his lair. She'd said her goodbyes publicly last week, along with a threat: if things got worse, she'd be back. And she'd be *pissed*.

The Third Power War was well in hand.

Which made Sara-N-Dipity's all-member TUSSA meeting the main priority for the evening. Not only did she claim to have an important strategic shift to tell the club about, one that she claimed would secure the campus from disruption over the ever-nearing finals week, but she'd sweetened the deal with carry-out pizza.

So, while Fursona filled her drink bladder with something Hephaestus had poured her and I munched on a pizza, we listened to Sara lay out her plan.

"Okay, agenda first. We're covering club priorities for the long stretch to finals," she said, signing. This time, Springlock watched her fingers, not Milo's, though they sat next to each other in the front row. She nodded along as Sara kept going. "We've been working hard across the board, all of us, and we need to celebrate our wins, too. We'll do that before the main topic. And, as usual, we'll open up the floor for concerns, because I may be a master of probability, but I can't see the future!"

That got polite laughter, and she waited for it to fall off before continuing. "Celebrations first. This has been the third-lowest year for super-related crime on campus so far—and the lowest for a Power War year. We're down almost 60% from last fall, which is huge. I think a lot of that can be attributed to our decisive win in the Orientation Episode. However, I want to specifically thank Punch, Grapple, and the Springlock team for pushing hard against any SSS pop-ups."

She waited until the smattering of applause stopped, and I saw Punch look at me smugly. I shrugged back at him; we'd never gotten along, and his twin brother was by far the cooler of the two. Once things calmed down, Sara kept going. "Now, I have a feeling that something's going to change soon, and we'll be seeing the SSS again—probably over finals week when they can maximize chaos on campus. So, I have a few ideas to keep them in check.

"First, I'm calling an all-hands for the week before finals. Cancel your plans if you can. Springlock will explain more."

As the blue-clad superheroine and Milo stood up, I winced. She seemed happy enough in her role as vice president, but my vote had propelled Sara to the seat of power, and I couldn't help but feel guilty. Her fingers started flying, and a moment later, Milo started interpreting. "Alright, after some discussion, Sara and I have decided on a modified version of my original plan. She saw a lot of problems with it in its original form, but this new one helps solve some of those.

"First, we're going to launch a major offensive against the SSS starting on December 2. We'll try to knock their operations out completely, and not give them enough time to rebuild or make an alliance elsewhere. From what Sara says, Iron Fist is pretty much in control, with a small Tearjerker alliance acting as a check against him. If we can split them, we can beat both factions without too much risk. Of course, ideally, we win right there."

I nodded slowly, but already I could see problems. Aside from the risk of an all-out Episode—I still remembered the "Grant Building Dogpile" from last year—Fursona and I *needed* to deal with 3V1L. Rocko had put all his advertising budget into our war with them, and he'd be furious if I got pulled off onto something else.

But I bit my tongue for now. The nice thing about Sara-N-Dipity meetings—other than the pizza and beer—was that she gave everyone an opportunity to pitch in with her ideas. Just because she was 93.5% right about something didn't mean she couldn't be *more* right, and despite her ego, she knew it.

So I waited while Springlock finished telling us about the battle plan, then while Sara took the podium back. "So, what do we think about this plan? Open floor."

"Hey, we're in the middle of a war," Fursona said before I could open my mouth. "We can't just bail on 3V1L."

"Yeah, The Triad doesn't need us at this point, with the Power Wars being so close to resolving," I pitched in. "But our studio's really pushing the 3V1L problem. How will this all-hands offensive against the SSS play into that?"

Sara nodded slowly. "I understand the question. You're worried about your show's future, right?"

"Yeah," someone said from the audience. I thought I recognized the voice, but I couldn't be sure.

"We've got a chance to wrap up 3V1L. Our Investigative Episodes and raids on their lairs are going really well," I lied. I didn't care that she'd probably see through them. I needed to make my case as best I could. "We need a few more weeks, and we'll have 3V1L rooted out."

"Against that, I've got a pair of probabilities. If we have your help, we've got an 87% chance of a quiet finals week. If we don't? 63%. That's math," Sara said. Then she sighed. "If we delay our offensive until the seventh, we can have a 79% chance instead. That's the best I can do, and you *have* to be with me. Can I count on you and Fursona to be there?"

I hesitated, gulped, and nodded. "Yes. You can count on us."

Bianca and I had *never* planned this hard, but we needed a fast win. Sara was right. She needed us. But we were right, too, and if we didn't have the time for a solid intel-gathering series, we'd have to be perfect. So, as the evening grew later and later, our planning got more and more frenzied.

We stood at the whiteboard together, uncapped markers in hand. On one wall, we'd printed a map of the Poudre districts and University, and we'd used old-fashioned push pins to mark not only 3V1L's territory, but every lair's location—every one we knew about. On the whiteboard, we'd written and erased a dozen theories about where the One *L* was, his plans, and how we could catch him off guard. Bee didn't buy that he was Monologue, and she even had me questioning myself. We had new battle tactics for the two of us; we'd calculated that we could BS a four-person team essay for Team Composition and still pass the class easily, and neither of us wanted to bring in more people after Tractor-Beam-Girl.

So, instead of making a plan with the idea that The Triad would be right there if we needed them, we'd drawn up a plan of attack that let us isolate a single *V*—based on where we'd been seeing them pop up—and quickly beat them before rotating to another. The plan was to mop up all three, then wait for a fourth to show up. Wherever that one did, we'd find the One *L* nearby. It wasn't a perfect plan, but it *was* ambitious, and if it worked, we'd be free to deal with the SSS.

And, on one screen and in defiance of all our plans, half of North Poudre blinked gold and red.

Sister Sly had begun her next gambit to take control, and it was a big one. The other screen played news from North Poudre as her invention-wielding monks rolled across the district, taking over lairs we hadn't even known existed while talking heads made a big deal out of it. "Why did Golden Goose leave?" one asked. "If she only knew what was happening, she'd surely have stayed to put an end to 3V1L."

I laughed and put a cap on my marker; Golden Goose wouldn't have stayed for a minor-league problem. No way. Then I sat on the couch, stretching until my shoulder popped. "Let's just watch this for a bit, okay? Our best plans don't take a distracted 3V1L into account, and since we're not committed, maybe we should just let Sister Sly's henches weaken 3V1L."

Bianca nodded but grabbed her backpack. "Agreed. This is our chance, though. We'll get a good picture of what's happening, then commit to an Episode."

We watched the news for almost half an hour before coverage looped, and in that time, we started to get a good idea of the evening's chaos. Cameras always made it look worse than it was, but the 3V1L and Sister Sly spat had definitely turned into something more.

A dozen street fights had broken out around Sister Sly's church—it looked like 3V1L had been making a move, and Sister Sly had caught them out. A few minutes later, firebombs started going off across the district, and habit-clad henchmen attacked the 3V1L minions fleeing the fires. Now, both sides seemed completely committed; in the half hour we watched, I caught sight of Sister Sly and two possible *V*s leading 3V1L teams.

According to the news, emergency services were overwhelmed, and resources from nearby districts were flooding in. A few little-league heroes had carved out sections of the district and kept the henches back, but wherever the *V*s and Sister Sly fought, the heroes melted away.

After watching another pointless fight resolve with a *V*'s appearance, I'd had enough. Regular people who lived in the Poudre districts—people who hadn't asked for this—needed help, and Fursona and I were ready to go. We might not find the One *L* if we attacked now, but we'd definitely give both Sister Sly and 3V1L a black eye, and that had to count for something.

"Come on. We're going up there and landing a real blow against 3V1L." I transformed into Understudy, helped Fursona into her Eagle-sona Costume, and headed for the roof. A camera drone met us up there, and we took off into a **[Casting Call]**.

[Casting Call]
[Episode: Power War: Prayers for the 3V1L - PG-13]
[Role: Avenging Angel! Do you accept the role? (Yes/No)]
[Role Focus: Flamboyance + Badass]

On the horizon, the Poudre districts glowed orange.

41

The Poudre Districts

[Power War: Prayers for the 3V1L: Act One in Progress]

Okay, so the news exaggerated a bit. And so did I.

The Poudre districts *were* a war zone, and fires *were* popping up, but to say the whole skyline was orange would be a lie. As usual, the cameras—both drones and news crews—were focused on the worst of the district, and as Fursona and I flew down Fritch Boulevard toward the factories, I passed a few isolated fires with crews already working to halt them. Even more encouraging, 3V1L's henchmen avoided the fires as best they could.

But they couldn't always.

Fursona and I landed near Fritch and Border, where a group of 3V1L mooks and a handful of men in yellow-red robes fought. "Who are *we* supposed to fight?" Fursona asked, pointing.

I took a moment to think, then fired a [**Starlance**] into the crowd. "Everyone!" The bolt caught an 3V1L mook and launched him across the battlefield.

[**Dramatic Damage! +1 Drama Point**]

I got two more blasts off as we charged headlong toward the fighting. One hit, the other missed as its target got flattened by one of Sister Sly's henches, fizzling harmlessly into the air.

[**Dramatic Damage! +1 Drama Point**]

Then, suddenly, we were in melee range, and I [**Quick-Time Changed**] into Copy Cat. "I'll cover you!" I said and pounced on the nearest 3V1L mook with [**Leaping Leopards**]. The force of my jump slammed him into the ground, and I whirled to catch another with my claws.

[**Flashy Fitting-Room! +1 Flamboyance Point**]
[**Badass Damage! +1 Badass Point**]

Fursona shrieked, the sonic waves picking up henches and tossing them aside. I grinned stupidly—she'd upgraded that power recently—and then backhanded one of Sister Sly's monks before leaping on him with **[Doom Ball]**.

[Badass Damage! +3 Badass Points]

And that's when the 3V1L henches broke and ran.

I didn't expect it, and looked around for the trap, but there wasn't one—at least, not one I could see. The devil-helmeted henches just turned and started retreating, occasionally firing a shot over their shoulders that either ricocheted off the concrete or bounced harmlessly off my Tails-enhanced fur. Weirdly, Sister Sly's goons didn't stick around to fight us, either. They chased the 3V1L henches instead.

"After them!" Fursona shouted. I raced around the corner, a little confused but also excited. They're retreating to a *V.* They had to retreat to a *V,* and that'd give us a chance to take out some 3V1L leadership, so if there was a chance this was a trap? That was fine! We could strike the blow we needed to.

Around the corner, I lashed out and caught one of Sister Sly's armored henches with a **[Cat-Scratch Fever]**, but instead of getting the usual Style System message, I got a different one.

[Armored Adversary! +1 Drama Point]
[The target has resisted your status effect]

I blinked, then smacked the minion until he hit the ground with his hands up. He tried to say something, probably along the lines of how Sister Sly had made him do it, but I didn't bother to listen. It was always the same with henches.

Instead, we took off, pursuing the 3V1L henches. We chased them through a stoplight and into a convenience store parking lot—the gas station *was* on fire—where they turned and formed a ragged-looking line of battle. I smirked. This wouldn't take long.

But as I barreled toward them, still in my Copy Cat outfit, a car door opened, and a woman in a red cape and open-chinned helmet stepped out. She snapped her fingers, and the sound lanced toward me like a spear, tossing me into the street. Then she clapped just as Fursona shrieked. The two sounds slammed into each other in visible waves and detonated over the henches' heads. They scattered like pinballs.

[HP 11/12]

I pushed myself back to my feet. "Let me guess? You're the First *V*?"

"For now." Her voice shoved me back like getting hit by Jumper's white van. I tried to roll with it, but I still hadn't gotten a grasp on her powers, and it knocked me right back into a nearby alley.

[HP 9/12]

Okay. That hurt. I needed a tactical switch. So, as Fursona engaged, I laboriously switched back to Magical Girl Understudy. If her sound attacks fell off over distance, I could outrange her. And if not? I could switch to something better. As I spun and choral music swelled, Fursona shrieked again. Another sound-bomb detonated, and as my ears rang, I finished the transformation and ran out into the street—

Just in time to catch another speedy lance of sound that spun me in a circle.

[HP 8/12]

The First *V* was fighting to get back to her car, where a pair of henches sat in the front seat, honking and revving the engine. Fursona had dropped in between them. Now, she dove and spun in the air, trying her best to avoid supersonic bullets from the car, and claps and shouts from the First *V*.

I got myself oriented again, then fired a **[Starlance]** at the supervillain, expecting her to dodge. She didn't even move—I couldn't tell if she hadn't seen me or didn't think I was a threat, but the **[Starlance]** knocked her onto the pavement.

[Dramatic Damage! +1 Drama Point]

Unfortunately, as she fell, she screamed, and the whole gas station erupted in smoke and shook under her voice's assault. I kept my feet somehow, and Fursona was fine in the air, but before the smoke cleared, the car's engine revved, and the First *V* disappeared, leaving behind a pair of burned-out tire streaks in the parking lot.

"I'm getting so sick of car chases!" I said. "**[Solar Wing]**!"

"Agreed," Fursona said. She looked a little worse for wear. "At nine superhero damage."

"Eight here." I hopped onto the board and took off, Fursona gliding above me as we weaved through streetlights and traffic signals, chasing the only car on the road.

We were gaining on her; the compact car couldn't keep up with our powers on the winding streets of South Poudre. In just a few more seconds, we'd be in range to start taking out its tires. It wouldn't keep moving for long after that since it wasn't a Road Rage special. Five seconds . . . two . . .

WHAM!

Something hit me from the side, and I spiraled out of control toward the street below as it exploded into a net that bound my magical wings to my body. I had a weird sense of déjà vu as I plunged toward the asphalt. Two seconds. One.

CRUNCH!

[HP 4/12]

I bounced, the sharp stones in the street ripping at the net. It shredded as I skidded to a stop, and I thrashed and struggled my way out, already looking for the next *V.*

Instead, I watched as a rocket zoomed toward Fursona, exploded twenty feet away, and threw a similar net her way. She rolled with it, then dove for the street. My heart sank as another rocket streaked toward her, and I tried to follow the missile's trail back up into the apartment buildings.

That's when I saw her.

Sister Sly stood atop a building's flat roof, her reddish fur contrasting with her black-and-white habit and a spent rocket launcher in her hands. She saw me staring, waved, and threw herself off the roof. Her grapple caught her fall. A moment later, she swung through the air and tossed a red-tinted grenade as she landed.

I had just enough time to see its gold-embossed cross pattern before it exploded.

BOOM!

The street filled with smoke and fire—again—but the explosion missed Fursona and me. I shouted, "Split!" Fursona launched herself up and right, and I started running left toward the shattered, weathered sidewalk. Dealing with the First *V* would have to wait.

I fired **[Starlances]** at the supervillain, who produced a shimmering shield that dissipated them around her in a fading drizzle of energy. Fursona shrieked, pushing air toward Sister Sly and knocking her back a step before her habit tightened around her head, blocking her human ears but leaving her too-large fox ears exposed.

Sister Sly laughed as she grabbed the next item from her bag of tricks. "You two haven't changed at all! I recorded our entire fight, then built counters for your favorite attacks!" She tossed something into the air, and a grid of lasers leaped into the sky overhead, cutting the space between the apartments into two: on one side, Fursona and Sister Sly, and on the other, me.

"Ahahaha!" Sister Sly went for her next grenade as Fursona dipped to avoid the laser wall and wheeled around toward the supervillain. I couldn't reach them, but I *could* still help my partner. I fired a **[Bit-Part Barrage]** at the villain, who'd just dashed out of a shriek.

Instead of hitting the villain, the laser grid seemed to redirect the attack, and beams filled the air inside their half of the road. I cut off the attack. "Shit! Fursona, I'm working on a way around. Hold your own till I get there!"

I dashed off down the street, using **[Solar Wing]** to get a little extra speed. Her laser grid couldn't take up the whole city, so eventually, I'd find a way through. I only hoped it wouldn't be too late.

As I pushed myself faster and faster, trying to find a gap or the end of the beams, they started wavering, then faded away into nothing. Of course! The laser grid had a limited battery, and producing that many beams had to burn through it like crazy. Kicking myself, I turned to rejoin the fight—only for a pair of her henches to jump me.

I blasted the first with a **[Starlance]** as I soared past them, but the second threw a sphere at me—one that exploded into a wall of goo. A moment later, I spun toward the ground again. She really *had* figured out counters for our tactics!

This time, the goo cushioned my landing, though I received a debuff message similar to the one we'd gotten from fighting Theseus.

[Goop: Mobility Powers Disabled for Understudy. Time remaining: 30 Seconds]

"Goop? Really?" I squared my shoulders, then dashed toward the last hench even as he reached for another bomb. I used **[Spotlight Strike]** and punched him in the face the second it got highlighted. He hit the ground, blinking and tearing up.

[Stylish Strike! +1 Flamboyance Point]

Then, without waiting for his admission of surrender, I sprinted back toward the two fursuited superheroes.

Shrieks and explosions filled the air—and so did another laser grid, but one that lay across the battlefield horizontally and kept Fursona from getting any space as the fox hounded her mercilessly with bombs and gizmos. But the supervillain wasn't watching for me, and I threw myself into a tackle as I used **[Spotlight Strike]** again. My arms slipped through her shield, or maybe her shield didn't handle melee attacks well, and I drove her to the ground.

[Stylish Strike! +1 Flamboyance Point]

A moment later, a gizmo activated, electrifying her whole fursuit and launching me into the air. I hit the ground with a thud, still twitching, and rolled awkwardly to avoid a grenade that went off next to me in a burst of smoke, fire, and asphalt chunks.

[HP 2/12]

Still, while I coughed from the acrid smoke, Fursona got through and hit the villain with a pair of talons. Sister Sly fired her grapple into the sky, pulling herself up and landing on a roof just as the laser grid popped off. She ducked down and came back up with another rocket launcher. I pushed myself to my feet, readying **[Quick-Time Change]** for the damage dodge. "Plan?"

"Get up there, dodge her missiles, and finish her off!" Fursona said. "She's gotta be close to done."

"Sounds good," I started to say, but as I readied myself to fly again, a black SUV pulled onto the street, and a handful of goons in red masks piled out—along with a hulking figure in power armor, a red cloak, and a spiked helmet.

42

Spiked Helmet

As two more SUVs pulled up and disgorged another pair of caped, helmeted villains and a half dozen more henches, I realized that the villain in the power armor *probably* wasn't a *V*. For one thing, the *V* we'd chased earlier, with the sound powers, wasn't here. For another, the two supervillains stood in front of the power armor wearer, almost as if protecting him. One wielded a familiar-looking hammer, though I couldn't quite place it, and the other sparked yellow lightning between his fingers. Both men were dwarfed by the power armor, though.

In a way, it reminded me of the FEAR armor Professor Panic had used.

His voice was heavily modulated when he spoke, to the point where it almost sounded mechanical. "Hello, Magical Girl Understudy. I've been waiting for this for a long time. I propose an immediate Neutral Field so I can explain how I'm going to kill—"

BOOM!

A bomb went off, and as the explosion echoed in the street, Sister Sly's voice boomed out almost as loudly. "No! I came here to do two things: beat all the *V*s and you, and take out Fursona! And I'm not going to stand here and listen to the five of you talk! That's all you ever do!"

This wasn't a *V*, then. And if he wasn't a *V*, he had to be the One *L*, in which case, we had the chance to deal not only a blow to 3V1L but to take out its head. Before I could move, though, the street burst into flames as the second stage of the bomb activated.

I used [**Quick-Time Change**] to switch into Rainy Day and avoid the worst of the damage while Fursona flew straight at the supposed One *L*, but the *V* with the yellow lightning *moved* and stepped in between the eagle and his boss. "Speedster," Fursona said over her mic. "I've got this."

[**Flashy Fitting-Room! +1 Flamboyance Point**]
[**Steel Yourself! +1 Grit Point**]

She started trading blows with the Speedster, keeping the fight away from the power armor and the hammer-wielding man, who swung awkwardly and missed my eagle-formed partner. I had other problems, though.

Sister Sly leaped from the roof, grapple snaking out, and hooked onto a telephone pole. Then, slingshotting around, she led with both feet, and I realized she'd built metal boots that oscillated back and forth like Iron Fist's . . . fists. I ducked her attack, but her follow-up smoke bomb choked the street and blinded me with acrid yellow fumes. I used [**Virga**] to quell the smog.

[**Medic! +2 Cunning Points**]
[**HP 4/12**]
[**Doctors Without Borders! -13 Cunning Points**]
[**Adjustment: Not Enough Cunning Points. -2 Cunning Points**]

I winced at the lost points, glad I hadn't built up more this Episode. [**Virga**] had the potential to be really dangerous, but in this situation, it—

Wait. *Thirteen?*

I disengaged from Sister Sly and dashed toward Fursona, who'd managed to keep airborne against the combined efforts of two *V*s, the One *L*, and nine henches, but couldn't accomplish much besides an occasional screech.

I used [**Ride the Lightning**] to blast a minion, then squared off against one of the *V*s, trying to take the pressure off. [**Power-Weaving**] into [**Wind Front**] shoved him back but locked me into a less-than-great shift to finish the combo.

[**Electric Lightshow! +1 Flamboyance Point**]
[**Badass Move! +1 Badass Point**]

Then Sister Sly hit from behind. Her bombs arced over my head, glittering crosses shining in the streetlights just before they detonated. 3V1L minions scattered like bowling pins, and I took advantage of the interruption to [**Quick-Time Change**] to Understudy. The combo wasn't worth saving compared to that form's versatility.

[**Flashy Fitting-Room! +1 Flamboyance Point**]
[**Rejuvenation Activated! HP 9/12**]
[**Combo Lost!**]

Then, almost as one, the battlefield ground to a halt as our phones went off, one after another. At first, we ignored them, but when even *minions* started ringing with text messages, I grabbed mine.

<All Heroes' Message - Maximum Importance: Withdraw to secret bases. Abandon Episodes. Await Further Instructions - Crossbow 7:43>
<This is not a drill - Crossbow 7:43>
<Disengage as quickly as possible - Crossbow 7:43>

All three messages came in within five seconds of each other; they had to be preprogrammed. I glanced at Fursona. "How about Running Retreat?" I asked over our comms.

"Sounds great," Fursona said. Her unmodulated voice sounded uncertain, and I couldn't blame her. I'd never gotten a message like this. Not ever. My stomach, which had been roiling at the fight we had in front of us, practically tied itself in knots as I glanced at each of the four villains.

They all looked hungry, like they'd just been handed the keys to an all-you-can-eat buffet after-hours. "Fursona? Let's do it now!"

Thirty seconds ago, our goal had been to decapitate 3V1L and maybe take Sister Sly down with them.

Now, we were fleeing for our lives, flying through the air as the Speedster *V* dashed below us, Sister Sly swung from stoplight to stoplight, and the hammer *V* and One *L* stomped behind.

Worse, my phone wouldn't stop going off. The push notifications were out of control, and I couldn't stop to check any of them. What was going on? Why the hell had the Council of Heroes told us to retreat? And why did it have to happen *now*?

I didn't have time to find a single answer. All I could do was fire a [**Starlance**] back toward the pursuing *V*s while Fursona shrieked at Sister Sly, then dodged a net missile. The brilliant pink energy bolt slammed into the hammer *V*, who took it and kept coming.

[**Dramatic Damage! +1 Drama Point**]

I wished I had access to some heavier-hitting moves, but this Act One had gone on way too long, and Fursona and I were running on fumes. I ducked under a telephone line just as the Speedster *V* got ahead of us, activated [**Spotlight Strike**], and kicked him as we sped toward each other. He bounced off onto the sidewalk, and I stopped for a half second to wonder why he hadn't dodged.

[**Stylish Strike! +1 Flamboyance Point**]

That was enough for a henchman's bullet to find my back, and I rolled onto the asphalt with the 3V1L supers closing in. I leaped into the air and back into my [**Solar Wings**] as Fursona shrieked at them, forcing them back, but we couldn't shake the villains—not with Sister Sly and the Speedster around. "We need to knock out their chasers!" I shouted.

[HP 6/12]

"Yep!" Fursona flipped around in the air, stalling herself out, and slashed at Sister Sly as one of her swings got too close. She missed—or at least I thought she did—but the grappling hook's cord snapped, and the villain plummeted toward the street below. She hit with a crunch, took one look at the hammer *V* and One *L*, and reached into her bag. A moment later, she vanished.

"Did you get her? Is she out?" I wasn't sure, but maybe we'd shaken one of the worst hounds. At the same time, I fired a **[Starlance]** at the Speedster *V*. This time, he got out of the way, but only *just barely*. The beam singed his helmet as he ducked.

"I think so!"

"Good! Idea! Up!" With Sister Sly—hopefully—out of the picture, I catapulted myself straight up into the air, Fursona flapping for all she was worth to follow. We zoomed past windows—some lit up, others darkened for the night, and quickly passed the tops of the skyscrapers. "North!"

"North?" Fursona asked.

I nodded and surged toward the industrial maze we'd fought in a few weeks ago. The moment we hit the yellow-brown smog, I dove into it, coughing; my pink-and-blue trail would mark our passage, but the smog would do a great job of hiding it. Then we turned into a nearby street, keeping low so 3V1L couldn't see us dash away, and headed south toward Tokyexico University's safety.

[Good Thinking! +1 Cunning Point]

It took nearly thirty minutes to escape 3V1L.

They kept chasing us, and their henches were everywhere. Fursona and I ended up over in Evergreen before they finally broke off their pursuit, and the moment they did, I got a new message.

[Episode Canceled! No Longer Cast in Prayers for the 3V1L]
[Alias - Understudy] [Archetype - Magical Girl] [Community Rank - 196/523]
[HP 6/12]
[Styles and Skills]
►**Archetype Skill - Transformation Sequence**
►**Combo Skills - Power-Weaving**
►**Badass (19)**
►**Cunning (30)**
►**Drama (52) (Skill Roll Available)**

▶Bit-Part Barrage 2
▶Starlance 1
▶Flamboyance (45)
▶Signature Skill - Adaptive Armoire 3
▶Stored Costumes: (Rainy Day, Copy Cat, Lab Assistant Panic)
▶Solar Wing 1
▶Quick-Time Change 3
▶Spotlight Strike 1
▶Grit (41)
▶I-Frame Transform 3
[50 Drama Credits Used. Rolling Skill!]
[Rank-Up! Thunderhead 2: A thunderburst after the empowered power adds a shockwave and crowd control]

Walnut Tower's roof was clear, and Fursona and I landed and quickly went inside. Her helmet lay in the corner, eagle eyes staring at me almost as intensely as Bianca's did at the green room's info screens. Where the map had once shown the positions of our four rogues, now it simply showed a red-tinged blob shaped like Tokyexico City, with the words "Danger: Approach Episodes with Caution" across it.

There was no mention of 3V1L, Theseus, or any of our rogues. They'd seemingly disappeared as far as our information screens showed.

Before I could check my notifications, my phone rang. I looked down at it and sighed. Then I picked it up. "Hello, Rocko. Sorry about the Ep—"

"Screw that Episode, DuPont. Is Marino there? Put me on speaker. We've got problems. Big ones."

I dutifully pressed the speaker button, sighing. "Okay, you're on speaker with Bianca and me."

"Great. Listen up. You're gonna be on your own for a bit. The studio's going dark. *All* the studios are going dark. So here's the plan. I'm sending a couple of camera drones to the green room and one to the Outback Stakeout Zone. You keep them running—find a Genius if you have to—and shoot your own Episodes for a couple weeks. Got it?"

"Rocko, what's going o—"

The Ilneat interrupted me before I could finish the sentence. "No time. Drones and charging systems are heading over. Keep them running, keep the Episodes flowing, and we'll all be happy, okay?"

"Okay," I mumbled.

"Rocko, it's not okay. What's going on?" Bianca asked, an edge of panic in her voice. "You need to tell us what's happening."

"You don't know? You really don't know?" Rocko said, voice incredulous. "The whole balance of power just shifted. Check the news."

They hung up before we could keep questioning them, leaving Bianca and me in total silence. I had a bad feeling about this in my gut; whatever had Rocko *and* the Council of Heroes spooked, it couldn't be a good thing. Not. At. All.

Bianca headed for the door to my dorm room. "I'll check the news. You get the drones in order."

I nodded slowly, waited until a pair of chrome camera drones hovered into the room, then accepted the charging systems from a panicked-looking—though it was hard to tell with Ilneats sometimes—Pataki. As I plugged in the drones, I couldn't help but remember how much of a stink Rocko had made when Peter had gotten a hold of an old, half-destroyed camera drone. And now, the Ilneats had just handed three of them to Fursona and me, fully operational.

I finished fiddling with them and joined Bianca in the living room. I expected her to be out of her eagle suit, but instead, she sat perched on the sofa's back, Costume half-off, glued to the TV. Her face was ashen, and her mouth hung half-open as she watched, unmoving. A talking head kept going on and on about something that'd happened in Yorkston, but it took almost a minute before he looped back to the story's headline. On the screen, police tape and officers—along with a few of the highest-powered Yorkston heroes—surrounded a building.

The voice kept talking. "And for those just joining us, we're following the most important breaking story across the globe—and perhaps in all of Ilneat space: the death of Golden Goose."

43

The Death of Golden Goose

"Just forty minutes ago, Jasmine Saxton, also known as the superhero Golden Goose, was found dead in her Yorkston penthouse suite. She was twenty-nine years old. Police and local superheroes suspect murder.

"Preliminary statements from both the Yorkston police and the League of Order, Yorkston's superhero organization, say that both organizations are working on a few leads but that there are currently no suspects. According to the joint statement from the chief of police and Cannonball, Golden Goose's death was reported by a concerned member of the Ilneat Network, who'd tried several times to contact her about a possible supervillain to fight. When they found her body, they attempted to resuscitate her but were unable to. At that point, they called the police and League of Order.

"Tokyexico, North America, and the world will all be mourning the death of Earth's greatest heroine, and looking toward new sources of hope amid the Third Power—"

I stole the remote from the unmoving Bianca, who continued to stare at the screen after I pressed Mute. I couldn't help but shiver, and she reached down mechanically to put an arm around my shoulder. I shivered again, then laughed, even though nothing about this was funny. "Feathers, Bee."

"Right. Sorry."

As she changed, I let a third shiver build until I couldn't stop it. I hadn't *liked* Golden Goose. Very few superhero fans on Earth had, as far as I knew. But she'd been a force for order—as long as you didn't get in her way. I remembered her careless destruction of the Broadway Mall when we were in it, and how she'd demolished 3V1L almost without lifting a finger.

For better or worse—and it *was* worse a lot of the time—the world had been better with her in it. Or at least, it had been more understandable. A great power was on top, as she should be, and below her were the rest of the heroes and villains. She kept the villains in line; her presence in Tokyexico had probably shifted the balance of power enough for us to get control.

And now? The only reason I didn't shiver a fourth time was that Bee *finally* struggled free from the Eagle-sona suit and got her arms around me. "What does this mean?"

I took a deep breath, then another. My head wouldn't stop spinning, but I stood up and found my laptop before flopping back down. "I'm not sure. We need more information. As much information as we can find."

I typed in 'Golden Goose Death,' 'Yorkston Superhero Deaths,' and even 'Was Golden Goose Assassinated?' But no matter what I searched, I couldn't find more information than what was displayed on the ticker tape at the bottom of the TV screen. Sometimes, back in Riverside, the police would say they had no leads even though they knew everything—and even when I'd already solved the crime—so that it'd look like they could say they'd cracked it when it suited them best.

It didn't look like that here.

The TV kept saying that no one knew what had happened, but they also kept giving more and more information. She'd been stabbed—and not once, but a half dozen times. That ruled out a revenge attack by any of the Tokyexico City villains. None of them carried knives—or at least, none of the major-leaguers did. It also ruled out a bunch of villains around the world. According to the police spokesman and the internet, the most powerful knife-using villains were being brought in for questioning—with their lawyers present, of course.

"They'll find him," Fursona said. "Whoever killed her, they'll find him. There are only so many supervillains who could do it—sneak into a building, bypass security, and do enough to punch through her superhero damage, even as an ambush. They'll have this whole thing resolved soon."

"I'm not so sure. I think . . ." I paused. What *did* I think? I wasn't sure yet, but I knew that losing the most powerful hero in an area resulted in chaos. I knew it from *experience*. When I'd left Riverside last year, Professor Panic had pushed Collidus hard—and why shouldn't he? I'd been a cap on the amount of shenanigans he could pull. If he wanted to rob a bank, he'd have to go through me. When I was gone, he could do anything.

Golden Goose represented a similar cap, but on the dastardly deeds any villain in the *world* could pull off. And now she was gone.

"I think the whodunit is more interesting for Extras—unpowered people—but there's something the media isn't saying. I think the Power War is about to get worse without Golden Goose as a threat."

"You think so?"

"Yeah." I set the laptop on the coffee table. "I do. Who can replace her? Stella-Lunar? In her Eclipse Form, she can fight anyone, but a smart villain can wait until she rotates back to Moon and beat her. Liege Lord? He's old and washed-up—almost forty. He's starting to lose steps."

"Jackson and Mays?" Bianca asked, grinning a totally fake smile at me.

"Sure. Sure, Jackson and Mays. They beat everyone, but look, the reality is that they're not Golden Goose. They don't win fights. They end them, and there's a big difference between being the biggest on the playground and having the whistle to end recess."

Bianca grabbed the computer. As I watched, she clicked on my email and shoved the machine at me. "Password."

I typed it in as she squeezed her eyes closed. "You know, you could just ask for it. I don't have anything to hide."

"Sure, whatever you say, babe." Bianca pecked my cheek and stole the laptop back, and we both delved into my new emails.

And oh boy, did I have a lot of new emails.

Bianca and I read through them, ignoring almost every message sent to Anika DuPont. The only one we read was from Helen Barber, and only because it wasn't for me specifically. Instead, it was an e-blast for every student on campus, and it had information we could use to figure out what the school was thinking.

Subject: Power War Change and Finals Week Updates
To All Students
Due to an unexpected change in the Third Power War's trajectory, all students are strongly advised to stay on campus until security in Tokyexico City can be updated. The death of a major superhero will have far-reaching consequences, and until we understand those consequences, the Tokyexico University administration has student safety as its highest priority. Therefore, similar protocols to Man vs. Nature Seven are in place as of midnight tonight.

We understand that this is incredibly inconvenient, but we want to clarify that our number one concern is the safety of students on campus. Therefore, we're asking all students in the minor and major leagues to volunteer for campus protection duty, regardless of hero or villain status. As with Man vs. Nature, little-leaguers and unpowered students are to avoid Power War Episodes at all costs, but may defend themselves as necessary.

Thank you for your cooperation,
Helen Barber
Vice-President of Student Services
Tokyexico University

A second email popped into my inbox not even a minute after that one arrived. This one was from Sara-N-Dipity, and it did not inspire confidence that she knew what she was doing.

Subject: TUSSA BATTLE PLAN 11/21

Understudy,
95% chance we'll have to launch our offensive against the SSS early. Be ready, stand by, and do your part!
Sara-N-Dipity

"She's going to get us in over our heads," I complained. It was true. I still wanted to finish the fight against 3V1L. We could have ended them tonight. It could have been over—the biggest threat in our rogues' gallery defeated. Instead, we were checking our emails.

"Nah. I trust her. She hasn't messed up yet," Bee said. "I'm more worried about the next email. Power War changes from Crossbow? That's not good news."

Subject: Power War Changes
Magical Girl Understudy,
I am Crossbow, current Speaker for the Tokyexico Council of Heroes. The city needs your help, and you've been called to assist.

As you know, Power Wars threaten the balance between heroes and villains. The Council of Heroes is concerned about recent events in Yorkston and how they'll spill over into our territory. Therefore, we've developed a comprehensive plan that should allow us to counter most of the incoming villainous threats over the next several weeks.

For your part in our plans, we need an immediate (within twenty-four hours) victory against the villain Theseus. By removing him as a threat temporarily, we'll be able to secure the Mid-Town district with minimal major-league heroes and focus our efforts on other districts as hot spots arise.

Following that victory against Theseus, you and Fursona are most valuable keeping 3V1L in check. Focus your efforts on the South Poudre district, and do not get involved in Power War struggles between 3V1L and Sister Sly unless you can deliver a blow to 3V1L.

We cannot demand your help, but it would be greatly appreciated.
Please let us know if this arrangement works for you and your sidekick,
Crossbow
Speaker, Tokyexico Council of Heroes

I shut my eyes. "Bee, they all want something from us. All these emails are pulling us in different directions, and Rocko too."

Bianca set the laptop aside and wrapped an arm around me again. "Hey, babe, they're all panicking just like us. They all think they need a plan to get on top of things, and none of them are talking yet because it's nighttime on a Saturday. It's going to be okay; we need to wait for the chain of command to solidify, and then we can decide whether to follow it."

"Yeah? How do we plug Rocko into that chain?" I said bitterly.

"Don't snap at me, Annie," Bianca said, frowning. "I'm doing my best here."

I reached out to touch her shoulder and realized she was shaking, too. I patted her for a moment, then grabbed the laptop with my free hand. "Sorry. It's all just a mess. A real bad mess."

"Yep. Let's read everything, see if we can come up with a plan, then get some sleep. We can't change anything right now anyway."

"That's not true." There was one thing we *had* to do if we wanted to fit into both the Council of Heroes' and TU's plans. We had to fight Theseus, and we had to do it soon. But I gave in when Bee raised an eyebrow at me and clicked on Tele-Portal's email next.

Subject: Power War Triad Stuff
Understudy,
Crossbow's going to get in touch with you. Do what he says. I'll have Braningham look at his orders for legality later.
Good luck out there.
Tele-Portal

We looked at each other, but that didn't give me much information to go on. It certainly didn't change any of our nonexistent plans; I still wanted to get out there and fight Theseus, and Bee still wanted to go to bed. That left one last email—it actually came in while we read the one from Tele-Portal.

Subject: We didn't do it
Magical Girl Understudy,
This wasn't us—the national wing, I mean. We aren't responsible for this. Email me back so we can make a statement together.
Su-Bin Pak
President, TU APPEAL Chapter

Bianca rolled her eyes. "*Now* she wants to talk? Unbelievable."

"Bee, she's a friend. We should respond, pick a date—something."

"She's not a friend, not when you're Understudy and she's President Pak, remember?" Bee sighed and leaned into me, snuggling her head against my shoulder. "Annie, you want her to be happy, and maybe we can have Su-Bin over next week, and her boyfriend too, but right now? Right now, you need to be in Understudy space. Your best play is to go to bed, ignore all these emails, and deal with the consequences tomorrow morning when you're thinking better."

"No, our best play is to head to Alkirk Tower and hunt down Theseus before he—"

"Annie! No!" Bianca glared at me. "We're not hunting Theseus!"

44

Theseus

"I can't believe we're hunting Theseus," Bee grumbled as we rolled the whiteboard into the middle of the green room.

I wasn't thrilled about it either. One of my least favorite things about working for Rocko had always been high-pressure "do this now" Episodes, and now I had that same pressure from the Council of Heroes. On the other hand, every instinct said to withdraw, dig in, and try to play defense as the villains took advantage of the chaos Golden Goose's death had caused. That wouldn't work, but it felt like the right thing to do.

"I know, I know. Let's run this assault through our usual planning so we know it'll work."

"Got it." Bianca grabbed the marker and started writing in three columns: 'Known Problems,' 'Likely Problems,' and 'Solutions.' "Okay, we're going to start with what we know. Alkirk is a robotics, medical prosthetics, and experimental weapons corporation, so I'd expect 'henchmen' with power armor, lasers, missile launchers, and guns. We know Theseus has rocket launchers, spider legs, grapples, sword arms, and now he's got a laser cannon arm, too. Anything else?"

"Yeah. He's still following the code of conduct, so we don't need to worry about him intentionally endangering Extras or anything like that. We also know that the balance of power outside the tower's going to be a mess, so we'll want to move fast in case McHammer and Lord Destructo make a play somewhere nearby and we get sucked into it." I pointed at the screen, where the whole of Tokyexico City glowed an angry red. "So, under solutions, we can put speed and stealth."

"Ha. I don't think either of us can do the stealth thing."

"TA-1LZ can, and honestly? We did okay getting into the 3V1L base. I'll ditch Lucky Star for Lab Assistant Panic on this one. If they're working for Alkirk, they know Theseus is working with them, and they're okay with villainy. We won't need to save any Extras on Saturday night, anyway. Besides, we'll be quick. In, fight Theseus, and out . . ." I wasn't thinking right. Did I have a stealth power I'd never used? I couldn't remember, and I couldn't deal with builds right now. I could barely deal with *this*.

"Okay, okay. We'll try stealth until it doesn't work. What about our 'Likely Problems'?"

"Move Theseus's laser weapon over there. It could be something defensive like Sister Sly's laser grid grenade, or it could be a full-on weapon system. My money's on weapon system, to be honest. If we can counter that, it's possible that Alkirk won't be able to replace it."

Bee grinned. "Remember, we're going after any offensive arms first, then running Safety Pin while I break up Theseus's mobility. That'll leave him pretty powerless if you can keep the rearm drones out of the fight. Can you do that?"

"I think so. Yes." We'd come up with the plan after our last encounter, and if it worked, we'd keep Theseus from hitting full power and get a quick win. "As long as Alkirk feels like they're well protected enough. I think our best bet is that they won't want to overengineer the drones themselves, so they'll have the minimum protections in place."

"What if he doesn't use drones?" Bee asked.

I paused. "Like, if he's got a different rearming system in his base? Then we break that up or shut it down. The plan is the same every time, just the specifics change."

"Okay. Alright." Bianca finished scribbling on the whiteboard. I nodded slowly. "So, break in, find Theseus, pin him down without his best arms, and Chokehold until we win. Then get him to the police and . . . what? Let them take it from there?"

"Yep. That's the best we can do. It'll relieve pressure around Mid-Town for a bit, and that's what the Council of Heroes asked for." I grabbed Tails and my wand. "Okay, transforming. Let's get to it."

[Casting Call]
[Episode: Power War Short: Armed and Dangerous - PG-13]
[Role: Assault Hero! Do you accept the role? (Yes/No)]
[Role Focus: Cunning + Flamboyance]

We flew through the night toward Alkirk Tower, heading for the helicopter pad where Theseus had started the "Dark Hand of Capitalism" Episode. There'd be a door there, and since they wouldn't want Theseus wandering through the entire building every time he wanted to leave, his quarters would be close to it. He probably had a penthouse and everything.

[Power War Short: Armed and Dangerous: Act One in Progress]

The moment we landed, I blasted a pair of security cameras with [Starlances], and Fursona hopped off my sailboard with a breath of relief. I felt for her; we were every bit as high up as we'd been for "Gourmet's Glutton Hour," and the only way she'd get off this tower was through the air with me. But we'd both agreed that Roosona would be better for handling Theseus than Eagle-sona.

She kicked in the glass double doors, which shattered into a white-and-chrome atrium filled with fake plants as I shifted into Lab Assistant Panic and **[Speed-Hacked]** the security system so it wouldn't go off. TA-1LZ activated her active camo—I'd dropped **[Check the Script]** for it—and crept forward on two perfectly silent metal paws, her **[New Head-Cannon]** not spooling up to keep her movements even quieter.

[**Good Thinking! +1 Cunning Point**]

We were in, just like that.

Fursona sneaked down the hall a dozen steps behind TA-1LZ, who kept pausing mid-stride to look around. I didn't know what senses she had, but she quietly motioned us forward with a paw, and we stepped around a corner and into a white-padded corridor. I stopped and emptied a small bag, then started fiddling with it as TA-1LZ said, "74% probability of a trap here. Probably laser grids or something similar. Recommend a counter-play, or just rushing it and hoping it activates too slowly."

"Has anyone ever told you that you sound like Sara?" I asked my robo-cat.

"Not anyone who's lived."

"Great. You sound nothing like her, then. Okay, **[Science has Rules?]** not on my watch—this watch, specifically, which jams passive sensor signals using theta waves and ion pulses so that defenses can't trigger." I held up the bulky bracelet I'd created. It looked vaguely like a watch if you squinted right.

[**Pseudoscientific Mumbo-Jumbo! +1 Drama Point**]

We sprinted down the hall as the watch hummed and hissed, then broke apart around us. Sure enough, lasers filled the hall, but the chunks of watch reflected them away from us, almost like a pocket without any danger at all. Then, suddenly, we were at the far door, without any laser grids, tear gas bombs, or other nefarious traps going off.

"Nice," Fursona said.

"Thanks. Breach in three. Two. One." I kicked the door as hard as I could, and TA-1LZ and Fursona dashed into the room beyond. It was round—almost perfectly circular—and a dozen machines whirred and buzzed around a figure standing on a white-and-chrome platform in the center. Theseus raised one arm, this one with a sword attached, in greeting. More fake plants lined the walls, and I stared for a bit; this wasn't what I'd imagined Theseus's lair would be like, but Alkirk had its fingerprints all over it.

"Hi, girls. I applaud your efforts—or I would if I had hands!" Theseus said. A robotic arm holding *another* robotic arm descended from the ceiling. "You got in a lot faster than I expected, but that's okay. You're in my lair now, Golden Goose isn't around this time, and Alkirk's given me a leg up while I'm in here."

Rubber bullets bounced off the unattached arm harmlessly, and I told TA-1LZ to switch to taser rounds. Fursona dashed forward, trying to get in between what was obviously a laser cannon arm and its intended recipient, Theseus's empty shoulder socket. I stuck with the plan—the Chokehold plan, the one that required me to take out Theseus's rearming machine while Fursona and TA-1LZ defeated him.

I tried a **[Speed-Hack]** on the arm-mounting arm. Green ones and zeroes filled my vision, and it started moving more jerkily before stopping in place a foot away from the supervillain. He groaned in frustration, parried Fursona's tail slam, and threw his body into the arm. "I have to do everything myself!"

[Good Thinking! +1 Cunning Point]

I'd hacked the machine, for now, but Theseus had successfully rearmed, which meant it was time for Phase Two. I ducked behind a computer console and started transforming into Rainy Day. I'd go for an overload on the whole damn system, forcing him to *really* reequip everything manually.

Bweeeeeeem!

A red beam cut through the computer and slammed into me, burning through superhero damage at a disgusting rate. Since I was stuck mid-Itsy Bitsy Spider, I couldn't dodge, so I ate the burning feeling in my stomach and chest until Fursona landed a blow that knocked his beam off course. Its whining, high-pitched scream stopped a moment later, and a beeping filled the air.

[HP 7/12]

"He's recharging! Hurry!" Fursona shouted.

I finished with an "Up the spout again!" The machines above me had started to move, looking disturbingly spiderlike. The illusion was only made worse by the literally hundreds of taser wires crisscrossing the room like webbing; rearming arms had tangled in them, and they snapped, sending sparks showering down on us.

That smelled like an opportunity—and electrical wires burning. I used **[Thunderhead]** and filled the air with even more charge. A shockwave crashed out from my outstretched arms, knocking machines off-center for a moment but not doing any permanent damage. I could feel my hair standing on end as the power built and built, and I regretted not being able to set up a proper combo.

[Pause for Effect! +1 Drama Point]

Theseus and Fursona traded blows, and even with only one melee arm and no spider legs, it was clear that he still outgunned her. His sword flashed out, and she blocked it with her arm, letting her **[Fursonal Furcefield]** take the hit. Her counterkick landed to basically no effect. It looked like a clean trade, but he'd probably overpower her on a long enough timeline.

I couldn't give him the time. The clouds built, the tasers sparked, and as the charge in the air reached a crescendo and my hair stood perfectly straight up, I used **[Ride the Lightning]**.

[Electric Lightshow! +1 Flamboyance Point]
[Environmental Combo! +1 Cunning Point]
[Thunderstruck! +1 Drama Point]
[Feedback 1]
[HP 6/12]
[Confirm Combo Continuation?]

The room sparked and crackled as I overloaded the combo, trying to maintain it. The longer I could keep hold of the power surging out of me—out of the tasers and the cloud, too—the more damage I'd cause to Theseus's rearming machine. I kept going.

[Electric Lightshow! +1 Flamboyance Point]
[Environmental Combo! +1 Cunning Point]
[Thunderstruck! +1 Drama Point]
[Feedback 2]
[HP 5/12]
[Confirm Combo Continuation?]

The storm crackled out of me, filling the whole room with lightning that jumped from surface to surface. Fursona screamed and threw herself away from Theseus, who leaped in the other direction, landing on his sword arm with a sickening crunch. I tried to keep the combo going even longer, but as I went to confirm, one more beep filled the air, and Theseus's laser fired again—straight for my chest!

Bweeeeeeem!

[HP 4/12]

I rolled onto my back to get out of the worst of it, waited until the whining scream of the cannon stopped, and hurried to my feet to press our advantage. The whole room smelled like electricity and smoke, and I could barely see two feet in front of me. "Fursona! You good?"

"Yeah, I'm good. I think Theseus bailed, though."

I took a deep breath. "Okay. He's going somewhere to get more arms, and maybe his spider legs. Let's keep up the pressure!"

45

Pressure

This was it. Theseus wasn't getting away this time, and together, Fursona and I out-gunned him. Nothing he'd pulled so far was a surprise; it had been a misplay to slow-transform in front of him, but it wasn't surprising to eat a laser for it. It wasn't even a shock that he'd chosen to run. Theseus was always pragmatic in classes, and if he had a backup plan for being attacked in his lair, it wasn't inside his arming room.

Besides, moving him away from the sparking, shorting rearming machine only benefited us because we'd be able to return to our original plan.

Fursona slipped through the half-ajar door first as I switched back to Understudy.

[Rejuvenation Activated: HP 8/12]

I hadn't used any critical resources yet besides my **[Ride the Lightning]**, and I could still combo off in all sorts of fun ways, but Understudy worked best as a back-liner to Fursona's Bruiser. By the time the music faded, she was waving me forward into another hall. Something at the far side hummed slightly, and a rhythmic thud-ding sound pulsed down it. "Trap?"

"No, maybe not. Remember Professor Panic's factory? What if this is Theseus's?" I glanced at the far door but couldn't see any security other than cameras we'd already—in theory—hacked.

Fursona nodded and hurried down the corridor. I followed, wand at the ready for a **[Starlance]**, but nothing jumped out at us, and no alarms or traps triggered. I punched the door's opening button, and it slid open. Fursona rushed in, with me a step behind.

The room was nothing like Professor Panic's factory under the Grant Building.

If anything, it outclassed it by miles. Instead of a slapped-together assembly line made of corrugated tin and rickety scaffolding, this one had the financial weight of one of Tokyexico City's most powerful corporations behind it. Everything looked clean, efficient, and high-tech, from the smooth rubber conveyors to the perfectly calibrated lasers fusing arms together.

Not that most of those arms looked built for fighting with. Almost every line in the factory room was filled with arms and legs that looked more suited for an unpowered person than for Theseus. In fact, the villain was ignoring everything on the belts. Instead, he made a beeline for a drone that cut through the air toward him.

"Not so fast! [**Starlance**]!" I fired the pinkish-blue bolt toward the drone, and to my surprise, it hit. A moment later, it detonated, throwing Theseus back to land on a conveyor belt that carried him away from the wreckage as Fursona sprinted to get between him and it.

[**Dramatic Damage! +1 Drama Point**]

Theseus fired his laser back my way, filling the air with its whine, but I dodged onto my own conveyor and fired back with [**Bit-Part Barrage**]. If we could knock him out quickly, maybe he wouldn't be able to—

[**Dramatic Damage! +3 Drama Points**]

"Understudy!" Fursona shouted. She cut in, kicking at Theseus and knocking his laser off course and into the ceiling. "Deal with the drones!"

"You got it!" I yelled back. Another drone was coming in, this one with legs that looked suspiciously spiderlike. I fired a [**Starlance**] at it, but this one vomited chaff like the one during "Dark Hand," and the lance hit a piece of junk instead of the drone. A moment later, it dropped the legs right next to Fursona, and Theseus quickly leaped out of his own limbs and into the spidery ones.

"Alright, now we're in business! When I'm finished with you, you won't have—"

"A leg to stand on, I know," I interrupted before Theseus could finish.

Bweeeeeeeem!

His laser cut across a conveyor, which snapped from the sudden heat. Metal prosthetics flew everywhere, and in the chaos, Theseus leaped from the room's floor and spider-gripped onto the ceiling. "I do whatever a spider does!"

His sword arm stabbed down at Fursona, who ducked under another belt; the torque from its movement almost ripped Theseus from the ceiling, but he wrenched his blade free. Then, scuttling like an upside-down crab with a laser cannon, Theseus charged me.

I fired a [**Starlance**], hoping to knock him off his feet and onto the floor. Instead, I blasted the ceiling tile as he moved *ridiculously* fast. His sword arm flashed out, catching me across the chest, and even though superhero damage took the worst of it, it still *hurt.*

[**HP 6/12**]

I rolled with the blow as best I could, ending up under my own conveyor. Before I could recover, the blade thrust through the rubber and steel overhead, stopping on the floor three inches from my nose. I bit back the second half of my scream and tumbled away from it, only for him to stab down on my other side.

I was stuck, bracketed in with nowhere to go, and a sparking, screeching conveyor overhead. The next stab was going to be on me, so I braced myself. The moment I thought it was coming, I used **[Quick-Time Change]** and went to Lab Assistant Panic. I sat there as the seconds ticked by, waiting to eat Theseus's slice with **[I-Frame Transform]**. One second. Two. Three.

[Flashy Fitting-Room! +1 Flamboyance Point]
[Steel Yourself! +1 Grit Point]

My power faded.

The second it did, Theseus's arm punched into my stomach, and this time, I didn't hold back a scream.

[HP 3/12]

The bastard had waited. He'd *known* what I was going to do. TA-1LZ leaped from under the conveyor and opened up on the supervillain with her Gatling tasers. Theseus pulled his sword free from my stomach and didn't stab again. I sighed in relief, gasping. I'd have a bruise across my entire stomach, but superhero damage had definitely saved me there, and I crawled out, coughing.

"You good?" Fursona asked. She hopped back into battle, kicking out at the supervillain.

I nodded. "Yeah."

"Great. Then stop the rest of those from getting to him!"

I looked over my shoulder. Three drones cut across the room toward the fighting, bringing weapons closer to Theseus. The first looked like the energy shield. The second might've been the debuff-grapple, and the third? I couldn't identify the third, but it didn't look *good*. There were at least five arms all attached to a central shoulder joint; how many limbs could Theseus *control*?

I didn't want to find out, so I dove toward the first drone's rubble, dodging another whining laser that nicked the back of my lab coat. Then I used **[Science Has Rules?]** and started assembling . . . something. "We're going to use microphysical energy and tension-release valves, plus Higgs-Bolton particles—"

"Higgs-*Boson*," Theseus interrupted.

"—Yeah, those, to build a catapult! TA-1LZ, get over here!" I slapped the device together, and my power activated. My familiar leaped across the room, servo-powered legs propelling her through the air in just a few bounds. She landed on a flat surface that, almost uniquely to the whole device, *wasn't* crackling with energy. I pulled the trigger, and she shot through the air with a yowl.

[**Pseudoscientific Mumbo-Jumbo! +1 Drama Point**]

She hit the first drone as my cat-apult fell apart around me. I activated [**Speed-Hacker**] to knock out a second one, and it fell out of the air and onto a conveyor belt, which dragged it into a quartet of cutting lasers.

[**Good Thinking! +1 Cunning Point**]

TA-1LZ opened up on the third drone, sending a web of cables across the battlefield and, a moment later, shorting it out. It plummeted onto the battlefield, its wreckage sliding between Theseus and Fursona, and I spared a glance their way. She'd managed to break the focusing lens on his laser, and without his ranged weapon, she was more or less holding her own.

That left the last drone with the shield arm. As it drew closer, TA-1LZ fired into it point-blank, but it managed to drop its rearm package right next to Theseus, who swiftly popped the ruined laser arm off and installed the shield.

I cursed and shifted from Lab Assistant Panic to Copy Cat, hating every second of the slow transformation. By the time I'd finished, Theseus was pushing Fursona back toward the door, looking worse for wear but not out of the fight yet. She'd clearly started getting the worse end of the trades now that he had two arms again, and I used [**Power-Weaving**] and [**Leaping Leopards'd**] my way into battle.

[**Badass Damage! +1 Badass Point**]

I landed on Theseus's back before he could skitter out of the way, and the impact knocked him aside. Then, Fursona kicked his legs as he whirled to face me, and he buckled for a moment. A drone entered the room, but I ignored it. We'd entered the damage race part of the fight.

Theseus's sword slashed at me, and I took it with [**Fursonal Furcefield**]. Then, before he could raise his shield, I swung in with a [**Cat-Scratch Fever**]. The attack hit, and Theseus flailed in panic as the blind effect set in.

[**True Grit! +1 Grit Point**]
[**Dramatic Damage! +1 Drama Point**]
[**Floating Points: 1 Badass**]

I cursed, realizing too late that I didn't have a combo setup in Copy Cat, and then slashed out with my claws as Fursona kicked out another leg. "Surrender, or I'll finish my combo!" I yelled, bluffing as hard as I could.

And, shockingly, it worked. Theseus glared at me as his vision returned, then slowly disconnected both of his arms. "Get me back to my lair, let me pick up my regular arms and legs, and you can march me off to the police. This is getting too expensive."

I nodded slowly as one of our camera drones ducked down next to the three of us. "Alright, Theseus. Since you're disarmed, I guess we can give you a hand on this one thing. But be careful. I've got my eye on you, and if you try anything funny, I'll have to put my foot down!"

"Stop, please," Fursona laughed through my earpiece as Theseus scowled at me. "I'm gonna piss myself, and that'll look *great* on camera."

[Episode Finished!]
[Episode: Power War, Short: Armed and Dangerous - PG-13]
[Penalties: N/A]
[Episode Finished! +3 of each Style Point]
[Winner Winner! +3 of each Style Point]
[Role Focus: Cunning + Flamboyance - Goal Partially Met: +5 Cunning Points]
[Alias - Understudy] [Archetype - Magical Girl] [Community Rank - 192/523]
[HP 3/12]
[Styles and Skills]
►Archetype Skill - Transformation Sequence
►Combo Skills - Power-Weaving
►Badass (26)
►Cunning (46)
►Drama (34)
►Bit-Part Barrage 2
►Starlance 1
►Flamboyance (54)
►Signature Skill - Adaptive Armoire 3
►Stored Costumes: (Rainy Day, Copy Cat, Lab Assistant Panic)
►Solar Wing 1
►Quick-Time Change 3
►Spotlight Strike 1
►Grit (52) (New Skill Roll Available)
►I-Frame Transform 3
[50 Grit Credits Used. Rolling Skill!]
[Skill Upgrade! I-Frame Transform 3 to Freeze-Frame 1: Freeze time for up to one second at a time after a transformation. No powers may be used while time is frozen, but you may move as normal]

I put a hand on Theseus's back and pushed him—not roughly—toward the door back to his lair. "So, how's the new gig?" Behind me, Fursona gathered up Theseus's legs.

"It's fine," he said, glare fading. Then, a grin broke out on his face. "I'm giving Alkirk a hand with their Research and Development. Turns out, I'm an ideal test subject for their prosthetics division, because they can install anything on me, run their diagnostics, and then reinstall my regular limbs. It's going to give them a leg up on the competition."

"Stop," Fursona snorted from inside her suit.

"Okay, but why run as a villain in that case?" I asked.

"Well, Alkirk's working on a bunch of different projects, and sometimes, they need a little corporate espionage to solve a problem. I provide that service, and in return, I get this awesome penthouse that you two half destroyed." He led us to a door, waited for me to open it, and stepped inside on his remaining spider legs. "A little privacy? There's no way out, and I've already surrendered."

I glanced at Fursona, who nodded. "Just follow the code, Theseus."

"More than you, Fursona," he shot back, then dipped inside. "Legs, please."

PART SEVEN

46

So Call Me Maybe

The news wouldn't stop talking about supervillain aggression; all across the Evergreen, Foothills, and even Parker districts, the major-league vils had come out of the woodworks. In theory, The Triad, Stella-Lunar, and even the In-You-Endos were busy fighting.

In practice, Fursona and I had been on two patrols and were just finishing up our third, and we hadn't so much as pushed our Tele-Portal call buttons. And, I crossed my fingers, we wouldn't have to.

We had other plans tonight.

Eagle-sona flapped her way toward Mid-Town ahead of me, and I blazed a pink-and-blue trail across the sky on my sailboard. Neither of us *wanted* to find a supervillain tonight. We'd staked out our real target earlier in the week, and it was perfect for what we needed. Fursona landed quietly on the roof, and I joined her a moment later. "Phase One complete. Beginning Phase Two."

"Shut up, Understudy," Fursona said. She pulled up the vent, and we dropped the ten feet into the closed women's restroom. Outside, the park was silent; no one was out and about, and no one had heard us enter.

We quickly untransformed and changed, the whole Eagle-sona suit somehow fitting inside Bianca's backpack, and slipped out the door. "Phase Two complete," I whispered in her ear. I had a longish, dark yellow wool dress on, plus flats.

"I said shut up, Annie," Bee said, smiling and grabbing my hand. She'd opted for heels and was almost as tall as me—almost. Her blue dress brought out her eyes beautifully, though. "Come on. Reservation's in fifteen minutes."

Official TU policy was that all students needed to stay on campus, where it was safe. They didn't want any super-related incidents like during Man vs. Nature, so the administration kept an eye on all the super-students—but Fursona and I had an ace in the hole. We'd told Tele-Portal we couldn't do patrols for her anymore, and thirty minutes later, Braningham had worked his magic, and we had a license to leave campus.

Tonight, we planned on abusing that license for some *good* Italian food.

Bee practically skipped down the almost abandoned sidewalk, dragging me along. "Remember, no shop, no school, and especially no shop. Yes, I said *shop* twice. No, I'm not kidding about it."

"Agreed. I need a break from it." We stepped into Antonio's Kitchen, got directed to a booth, and grabbed menus. "You know, I could have cooked most of this stuff."

"Yes, but this way, you don't have to. You need a break, like you just said," Bee said, sticking her tongue out at me. "Now, tell me your deepest, darkest secret!"

"Oh god, *that*?" I asked, laughing and thinking hard. "Okay. How about this? When I was eight, in third grade, I told everyone in my class I was going to marry Locust."

"*Locust*? Really? Wasn't he an Italian villain?"

"Yep," I said, flushing redder by the minute. When the waters came, I gratefully grabbed my cup and drained it. "He was, but he also had style, and he seemed like a really funny guy."

"Yeah, glad you didn't follow through on that. From what I hear, he got busted attacking the Colosseum. That was a bridge too far for the Italians, and—"

"Twenty in their super-prison. Yeah, it was a bad move, but I think a bunch of vils learned a lot about not attacking culturally important—this is drifting toward shop. Sorry." I reached over the table and grabbed Bee's hand. "What about yours?"

"One time, I ran away from home, got out of Tortuga West, and built a raft. I was two hundred feet off the beach when I decided I wanted to go home, so I spent the next hour fighting the tide, then had to walk home for two more hours because the waves had pushed me so far up the coast. I told my parents I'd been out playing. I told the police who found me the same thing, but I don't think either of them believed me," Bianca said.

"And you're afraid of falling, not the ocean?" I asked, grinning.

"Yeah, but that's not a deep, dark secret. That's from my dad's work truck. When I was a toddler, I toddled right off the tailgate and busted both my knees open. Ever since, heights aren't great, and the skyscraper fall didn't help. Sorry, it's old news, but you brought it up."

"Okay, yeah, that makes sense. Sorry again, by the way." I waited for her to say something about the Gourmet Episode.

"It's okay. I'm working on it with an online therapist."

"Not with Dr. Ayers?" I asked.

"Nope. It's not a Dr. Ayers problem. It's a normal therapist's problem." Bee grinned sheepishly. "*That's* too close to shop, though. I'm getting spaghetti. You?"

"Lasagna. It's the one thing I don't have the patience to deal with most of the time, and I've heard good things about it here."

A few minutes later, the waiter came by to take our orders. Bee made a half-hearted attempt to get a glass of wine, then settled for more water when he raised an eyebrow. I laughed at her as he left. "You better tip him well for putting up with you, Bee."

We'd worked through breadsticks, a salad, and several glasses of water, and the candles at the table had burned down to almost nothing by the time the food arrived. It felt silly being out on a date with Bee when we spent so much time together, but it was also really nice to set college and Heroics 101 aside for a bit. *Not* being followed by camera drones and just being Annie and Bee for a while was something we'd been doing less and less.

Was this what life would be like without powers? Or was it the constant pressure to get out there and be a super that did it? I thought back to our time on the beach near Tortuga West. Blowing off that Episode had felt great, and at the time, I'd just thought we'd been burned out from pushing hard to get to the minors, but what if that wasn't it?

"Hey, Bee, I know we're not talking shop, but—"

My phone beeped the email pattern. "Shit. Hold that thought for a sec?"

"Sure, Annie. But I'm pretty iffy on shop talk." Bianca slurped a noddle into her mouth. "This better be good."

I glanced at my phone, said "Shit" again, and passed it to Bee. She read it, then shook her head. "She's persistent. Su-Bin's playing with fire if she wants you to get back on the radio with her. What's her angle?"

"I'm not sure. I'm going to table all the shop talk, though. As team leader, I hereby declare tonight a shop-free time until we get back to campus." Bee opened her mouth, and I held up a finger. "As the team leader, I'm empowered to make this decision, and no others, without talking to the rest of the team."

"Fine," she said, snorting. "We'll put off the talk about Su-Bin until later. Let's enjoy this date, dammit."

By the time we landed at Walnut Tower, a few flakes of snow had begun to fall, and I felt bloated and overstuffed. I hurried into the green room and raced to get to the bathroom before Bee; I'd already stashed *normal* clothes there, and when I emerged, it was in PJ bottoms and a plain gray T-shirt.

Bee, of course, was halfway undressed in the bedroom with a robe on the floor. She looked over her shoulder, then kept undressing. "Takes longer for me," she said, wrapping the robe around her body.

"Uh-huh. Sure, babe." I smirked. I flopped onto the couch, and she joined me, sprawled out with the back of her head on my leg. I let a hand drift onto her stomach, and she smiled up at me.

"Okay, so what are you going to do about President Pak?"

"Su-Bin? I don't know," I said.

"No, we're going to have Su-Bin over for game night next week. That's already planned. Her and her boyfriend. It'll be great; I'll make sure there's plenty to drink, you'll cook again, and it'll be a good time for all four of us. I'm talking about President Pak." She reached under the coffee table and came up with a bottle. "Drinkie-drink?"

"Sure." I waited while she fished up a pair of shot glasses, and we downed our first after clinking them together. "To us, powered or not. I think I'm going to do it."

"You're really going to get on the radio with her tomorrow? Holy shit, Annie, that's walking into the lion's den. There's brave, and then there's stupid, and that's probably stupid."

"Maybe so, but it's a chance to move the needle a little with APPEAL. If you want, you can come with me, and Su-Bin's already proposed scripting the whole conversation—and keeping it to five minutes this time. She's got a possible script, and she's willing to accept any changes except to her core message." I was talking too fast, but I had to convince Bee that this was serious—and possible.

"And what's that again? We hate supers?"

"No. Here's the email again."

Subject: Possible Collaboration with APPEAL

Magical Girl Understudy,

We've got some bad blood between us, but I think it's important that we're on the same page here. So, here's the situation.

APPEAL chapters across North America are getting blamed for Golden Goose's death. There aren't any leads; they've even brought in supers with all sorts of crazy powers to try to look back, and all they see is a man in a mask, but no actual evidence. It could be a super, or it could be an unpowered person. Either way, APPEAL has denied any connections with it.

But you know as well as I do how fast rumors spread on campus. Better, even, because you've been on the receiving end. Sorry about that. I propose a truce. APPEAL has other goals besides getting in your way. If you join me on DJ Smooth's radio show tomorrow and say you believe the larger APPEAL group wasn't involved, I'll stop having any APPEAL protests anywhere near you, and I'll even let the Grant Building fiasco go.

If you're interested, I'll send you a script a couple of APPEAL members worked on. You can make any changes you want, and we'll roll with them as long as they don't make us look bad.

Thanks,

Su-Bin Pak

President, TU APPEAL Chapter

"Gimme your laptop," Bianca said. She sat up, let me log in, and started typing while I watched and poured us another drink. She stopped after almost ten minutes of writing, deleting, and furrowing her brow. "Here. Send this."

Subject: RE: Possible Collaboration with APPEAL

President Pak,

At the moment, Fursona and I are both very busy studying for finals, pushing back minor-league supervillains across the city, and doing our best to help with the major-league ones. Unfortunately, we won't have time to work with you on this until after finals week.

In the meantime, if you want to prove you're serious about not going after us with your protests, you can stop making me your enemy. Stop protesting my old Episodes, and stop using me as an example of everything that's wrong with superheroes. That'd help me trust you.

Send me your script. I'll take a look for later.

Magical Girl Understudy

I nodded slowly and pressed Send. Then I pushed Bee back down so her head was on my lap. I played with her curly black hair for a minute, then reached over to close the laptop. "Hey, Bee? No more shop talk tonight, okay?"

She winked up at me and propped herself up on one elbow. "What do you mean by that?"

I leaned forward to kiss her, but the motion accidentally dumped her on the floor between the couch and the coffee table. The bottle of vodka went flying, and I cursed before helping her up.

She scowled dramatically, then broke into laughter. "Bedtime?"

"Yeah, bedtime. The script should come in tomorrow." I grabbed her hand, and, this time, I dragged her along. "Until then, let's not think about it."

47

Think About It

MONDAY, DECEMBER 8

A lot can change in ten days.

Ten days ago, Bianca and I had been on our date. We'd rejected Su-Bin's request to talk; surprisingly, she was playing ball so far. So that was good. The rest of the news out of Tokyexico was . . . less so.

We hadn't won our campaign against 3V1L like I'd thought we could. Every time we took out a *V*, someone else rose up to take their place, and in the last ten days, the organization had all but disappeared. The One *L* seemed to have no interest in fighting us. Worse, our auxiliary work with The Triad had gotten a lot more dangerous. With Stella-Lunar in Yorkston trying to get a handle on all the villains Golden Goose had been keeping down, The Triad was up against the best Tokyexico had to offer—and usually in greater numbers. We'd been doing a lot of crowd control and not much Episode work, which meant not many style points. Some, but not many.

It'd gotten to the point where I wanted to ask Sara to delay her assault on the SSS by just a couple more days, on the off chance that we could get a meaningful win against 3V1L. But no. Sara's plan required a big strike a week before finals, and this was as close as we could cut it.

So, instead of sneaking off-campus to fight 3V1L or patrolling for The Triad, Fursona and I were in our assigned positions, ready to clear out the Student Union Building. And we weren't alone—which was good news, in a way. Our team of four was optimized for Team Composition class.

With Fursona as a Bruiser and me filling . . . every other role . . . we didn't really *need* an entire team, but Sara thought groups of four made the most sense, so we'd deployed with Waterspout—the Elementalist/Tank hybrid Candi Crush and I couldn't beat last year—and Vicegrip. Neither had made the minor leagues yet, so officially, I was supposed to be giving the orders.

In reality, all I had to do was stick to my part of the script.

"Why didn't we do this earlier?" Tractor-Beam-Girl asked. She pointed at the building. "We should have attacked right away, not twiddled our thumbs outside and waited for their lair to be defended."

"Shhh," Fursona said.

"Sara-N-Dipity has a plan, and it's calculated out. We're probably trying to get the villains all in one place and surrounded so we can shut them all down at once," I added.

"Actually, I agree with Tiny here—" Waterspout said.

"Hey!" Tractor-Beam-Girl whirled on him, but he held up a massive, watery hand.

"—but I think the opposite. We should have waited until Sunday. If we win here, we're just giving the SSS time to regroup."

[Casting Call]
[Episode: Power War: Sayonara, Student Supervillains! - PG-13]
[Role: Heroine Herald! Do you accept the role? (Yes/No)]
[Role Focus: Drama + Flamboyance]

I accepted the [Casting Call]. "That's our cue. Move in!"

[Power War: Sayonara, Student Supervillains!: Act One in Progress]

Fursona's voice came in over my headset as we pushed through the double doors into the Student Union Building's main hall. "Hey, it's weird that this is a Power War Episode. I wouldn't have expected it since there shouldn't be any major-leaguers on campus."

"Yeah. Just keep it cool. No need to panic, anyone," I muttered, jerking my head at Tractor-Beam-Girl. "We'll just do our part and hope there's no interference."

We hadn't made it two steps in when Tearjerker's battle cry echoed through the atrium. "Waterspout, [Cry for Me]! You had a pet cat once, right? What was her name?"

"Wrong move, Tearjerker," Waterspout said, already blubbering. "Her name was Cindy, and she was great!"

I ducked around him as Fursona dashed toward the villain, but a massive jet of water slammed into her before she could get there. Waterspout's eyes streamed tears with the pressure of a firehose, and I couldn't believe the recoil wasn't hurting him, but not as much as it hurt Tearjerker, who slid across the SUB's floor into a wall.

I followed up his attack with a [Starlance] that hit the villain, but as the attack punched into her, two more SSS members and a handful of henches appeared. Fursona shouted, "Flare!" and raced off to fight the Speedster, while Waterspout whirled to face his attacker, only to eat a cane to the face. A moment later, he vanished, trapped inside Lady Lockless's [Escape Room].

[Dramatic Damage! +1 Drama Point]

I had tricks of my own, though, and instead of fighting the ballroom-dressed supervillain, I used **[Spotlight Strike]** and a spotlight highlighted Lady Lockless. A moment later, I tapped Lady Lockless's head and she fell to the floor.

[Stylish Strike! +1 Flamboyance Point]

If she wanted to use her power to get out, she'd have to free Waterspout, too. And having both of them out of the fight suited TUSSA's plans more than the SSS's defense. As for Flare, he kept up a game of keep-away with Fursona's Roo-sona suit, but it couldn't last forever. He couldn't counterattack her without trading poorly, so all he could do was—

"Stop!" Tractor-Beam-Girl yelled, grabbing him out of his sprint and pinning him to the wall with her power. A moment later, Fursona hit him feetfirst and knocked him off the stairs to the second floor, then leaped into the air to hit him again.

I whirled to find Tearjerker, but she'd disappeared. A moment later, a red-hot blur zipped past me toward the club offices—where the unpowered students could rent club space from the campus. "They're on the retreat! Stick to the script!" I shouted and stared at Lady Lockless's glass-headed cane. Sure enough, moving inside at a crazy speed were Lady Lockless and Waterspout. Every time he solved a puzzle, she built a new one to slow him down; it remained to be seen who'd win the race.

Either way, they wouldn't be around for the next step in the plan. That was fine. Everything had happened pretty much like Sara had said it would, and her team had almost certainly hit the SSS's base from the service door outside. We just had to keep the bigs from running now, and that'd be easy enough to do.

So, of course, the moment I thought that, something went wrong.

Three villains appeared in the center of the room. The first looked familiar, but he vanished into the offices before I could get a good look. "Was that Monologue? What's he doing back here?" I asked Fursona.

"No idea." She balled her fists and watched as the other two villains turned toward us. They clasped hands, and then the first one disappeared again while the other turned to face us.

He wore black robes, and an SSS henchman's helmet covered the top half of his face. The bottom half was painted pale white, and his lips were curled in a sneer. A bo staff hung loosely from one hand, and he bounced on the balls of his feet. "It seems I had perfect timing," he muttered. "Again."

I didn't wait for more. "**[Bit-Part Barrage]**!" I shouted, spinning and aiming my wand at him. The **[Stellar Rays]** surged toward him, but he held out a hand and caught the first one, which fizzled out, then flipped over the rest of the volley. The last one caught him in the shoulder, but he landed smoothly.

[Dramatic Damage! +1 Drama Point]

"Okay. Is that it? Yes? Great. Then let's begin." The villain lunged toward Fursona, who ducked back, but he *kept lunging* even after he should have stopped, his feet moving flawlessly under him. The tip of his staff caught her in the pouch, and she slammed into a wall, cracking the drywall.

I hit him and sent him flying, but he seemed to run midair and got his feet under him—all without touching the ground! He wasn't flying; instead, he appeared to be hovering on the strength of his pumping legs.

Then, suddenly, he was running right at me!

I used [**Quick-Time Change**] to change to Rainy Day and dodge his attack with [**Freeze-Frame**], and when I turned, his staff was lashing out against Tractor-Beam-Girl's grip as she tried to wrest the weapon from his grip. "He's a Bruiser!" she shouted.

[Flashy Fitting-Room! +1 Flamboyance Point]
[Steel Yourself! +1 Grit Point]

"Agreed," I said. "Keep your distance if you can. He'll take you apart up close!"

"I know that!"

"Great!"

"It *is* great!" Tractor-Beam-Girl hadn't gotten less snarky, that was for sure. She flipped the villain around in the air, but he landed on his feet, jerked the staff away from her beams, and whipped it right at my head.

"Two minutes till Phase Three," I said, starting up a [**Thunderhead**] and shockwaving the robed villain away from me before his blow could land. That was when Sara and her team had to be past all the defenses and only have supervillains to deal with. The villain was fast, but could he dodge—lightning? I was going to find out!

[Pause for Effect! +1 Drama Point]

Then, before I could finish the [**Thunderhead**] charge, he was on me. The staff lashed out like a snake—the big megafauna kind, not a little yard snake—and crashed into my ribs on either side of my body, then down. I barely got my head out of the way, and the blow drove into my shoulder and forced me to the ground.

[HP 10/13]

But for all that he'd driven the air from my lungs and knocked me around, he hadn't done much actual damage—and he'd gotten into the perfect position. I used [**Ride the Lightning**].

[Electric Lightshow! +1 Flamboyance Point]
[Thunderstruck! +1 Drama Point]

The electricity surged toward him, and the lights in the SUB flickered wildly for a moment as a shockwave ripped out ahead of the blast. He tried to dodge, but the tremor knocked him off-balance, and the lightning punched into him, dancing across his black robes and arcing off the metal tips of his staff.

Fursona lunged toward him and kicked him hard enough to send him catapulting back into the club office hall, but he rolled with the landing and somersaulted over his staff. I slow-shifted to Understudy while Fursona and Tractor-Beam-Girl kept up the pressure; I wasn't the frontliner in this team, even with Waterspout out.

And speaking of Waterspout . . . there was fighting behind us, too. If you could call it a fight.

I turned to see Waterspout grappling with Lady Lockless, who kept trying to reach her cane. She screamed as he bent her arm backward, then went limp in his watery arms. "Alright, fuck! I surrender! Jesus [**Beep!**]. Shit!"

Part of me worried as Waterspout lowered her to the ground, but another part was happy for the win—and for our Tank to be back in the fight. I pointed down the hall. "I've got her. You get him."

"Got it." Waterspout surged down the hall just as Fursona flew backward, propelled by the bo staff.

She rolled, tail and legs flailing, then got back to her feet and rushed the supervillain. "Who is this guy?"

"No idea. Maybe the new kid Mindstorm mentioned at the beginning of the year?"

"He's a freshman? Holy crap, he's strong!" Fursona took off toward the fighting again, and I [**Quick-Time Changed**] again, this time into Rescue Girl Lucky Star.

[**Flashy Fitting-Room! +1 Flamboyance Point**]
[**Steel Yourself! +1 Grit Point**]

I hurried over to Lady Lockless, whose arm looked jarred horribly. I frowned; Waterspout shouldn't have been able to do that to her, not through superhero damage. Something seemed wrong, and I looked for her cane, but it wasn't anywhere near her. Her face looked contorted in pain—the kind of grimace someone used to pain made.

"Do you need help?" I asked, standing back far enough that she couldn't use a power on me. She'd surrendered, but that didn't mean she *couldn't* try something.

"Shit yeah, I need help." Lady Lockless's Roaring Twenties persona had disintegrated entirely. "I promise not to betray you, blah blah blah."

"Okay. Stay still." I walked over to her and used **[Jinx-Bearer]**. Immediately, my right shoulder started to ache, and when I moved it, it popped and ground painfully. "What did you do?"

[Tough Cookie! +1 Grit Point]
[HP 7/11 (temporarily reduced from 13)]

"Nothing I haven't done before. Thanks, though. I'm done here," Lady Lockless said. "I'm not participating in Monologue's plan for postgraduate glory."

48

Postgraduate Glory

I [**Noncombatant Teleported**] Lady Lockless away; wherever she landed, she'd be out of the fight. Even though I'd taken her debuff, she still looked shaky and miserable, and I'd handed her cane back to her just before sending her away. A few moments later, the first act ended.

[End of Act One: Act Two in Three Minutes]

The team had assembled outside the somewhat beaten-up glass doors to the club offices, and they kept looking back and forth as if unsure what to do. I cleared my throat. "What happened?"

"He just started *running* along the ceiling," Tractor-Beam-Girl said. "We couldn't keep up, especially when the tiles started falling behind him."

Sure enough, the entire hallway was covered in messy ceiling tiles and hanging wires, and half the lights were out. "Who was he?" I asked.

"Quickstrike. He's in my Superpower Ethics class," Tractor-Beam-Girl said. "He's a pain in the ass, thinks he knows everything, but at least he's not on my team. I'm stuck with the teleporting kid who brought him in. *He* thinks he's cool because he's got Dr. Tennyson's power, but he's going to be a lieutenant, and he'll never be anything more than—"

"Okay, focus up," I said. "So, we've got a pair of little-league vils who stalled us out after our initial attack. They weren't in Sara's calculations, so she must not have known about them. She might not know other stuff if she didn't predict they'd be here. So, I think we need to . . ."

I trailed off. What did I think we needed to do? The two little-league heroes kept looking at me, Waterspout expectantly and Tractor-Beam-Girl with a look of defiance and disbelief on her face. We had a lot of firepower here, and we *could* just force the issue with an attack on the SSS's main base. But, according to our briefing with Sara, the SSS wasn't looking for a fight. They were working on something to attack finals week with, and maybe to take over the campus, but they didn't want a fight— at least not yet.

So keeping them from moving whatever their plan was elsewhere was more important than rushing off to battle. Which meant it was time to stick to the script—the one Sara had given us.

"Alright, here's the deal. We're finding the SSS's entryway, getting inside, and making sure nothing gets out," I said, giving my orders with confidence I 100% didn't have. "We're supposed to be security and a backstop for the assault teams, not an assault team ourselves. That's why we're tanky and full of crowd control."

"Okay, got it. I'll get in there and block the doors," Waterspout said. I nodded appreciatively. He'd kept two heroes occupied completely last year, all by himself. With a team around him, he'd be the perfect blockade hero against anything who couldn't shut him down. Unfortunately, at least one villain could.

"What do we do about Monologue?" Fursona asked.

"We kick his ass," Tractor-Beam-Girl said.

I opened my mouth to argue, but the next act began.

[Power War: Sayonara, Student Supervillains!: Act Two in Progress]

"Okay, we'll kick his ass," I said, knowing that *that* wouldn't be easy. I could only hope that Springlock and Milo ran into him first. And *why* was he here, anyway? There were so many unanswered questions.

And I didn't have time to find out any of them. I started slow-shifting back to Understudy, cursing myself for not doing it during the intermission, as the rest of the team pushed down the hall toward the door they'd seen villains retreating through.

"Okay, we're running Blockade. Fursona, you're on protection duty for Waterspout. Keep him upright. I'll bounce between Understudy and Rainy Day and try to do ranged coverage. Waterspout, keep the doors shut, no matter what happens, and Vicegrip? Try to keep people away from Waterspout. Toss them around or whatever." I put a hand on the door, then turned the handle. "Go!"

Fursona rushed in, right into a handful of villains. Gourmet, in full dragon form, grinned at us from the impossibly high ceiling. Quickstrike and Tearjerker stood near a door on the far side. And, in the center, already squaring off against Fursona, was Iron Fist. I grimaced; this would be a tough one.

Then Fursona kicked out at Iron Fist, and Waterspout sealed all the doors except the one leading farther into the SSS lair. I rolled to the left, and Tractor-Beam-Girl went right. We almost felt like a proper team—either that or the opposition didn't have a good plan for fighting together, either.

I started out with **[Power-Weaving]**, hoping to get a combo off before Gourmet found me, but she pinned me to the wall with a breath of fire that left the carpet smoldering and me rotating into Rainy Day for the fire control and protection.

[Flashy Fitting-Room! +1 Flamboyance Point]
[Steel Yourself! +1 Grit Point]
[Floating Points: 1 Flamboyance]

She landed next to me, already snapping into her jerky. The wings disappeared, replaced with horns, and I cursed quietly—Lady Lockless had already taken the best word. Gourmet had played it perfectly, switching from ranged flying to melee the moment I rotated. I couldn't use any powers because she'd break my combo, and the team *needed* the big hit to win this fight.

"Cover!" I shouted, and Fursona bounced across the battlefield to catch Gourmet in the side, knocking her away from me. I rotated onto Iron Fist, hoping he hadn't seen me starting my combo up.

"You again! I'll pound you into dust," he grumbled.

"No, you won't." I used [**Thunderhead**] to knock him back and started running away. The clouds built up overhead as Fursona lost ground to a very determined Gourmet. She held the line for another second . . . two . . . three . . . four, then broke as Gourmet's bull horns stampeded past her. Iron Fist swung his fist my way, and I ducked it.

My [**Thunderhead**] finished, and I fired up [**Ride the Lightning**] just before the two heavies hit me.

[Electric Lightshow! +1 Flamboyance Point]
[Thunderstruck! +1 Drama Point]
[Power-Weaving! +6 Flamboyance, +3 Grit, +1 Drama Point]

The crowd control shockwave went off at precisely the right moment, throwing both villains away from me—and toward Waterspout. A moment later, the lightning surged out, catching Iron Fist in the chest and coursing over his body like a cartoon. I grinned but didn't have time to say anything. Gourmet rolled to her feet and headed straight for me while Iron Fist attacked Waterspout.

Tractor-Beam-Girl had her hands full with Quickstrike, and Fursona was moving toward Tearjerker to keep her out of the fight, but that left both heavies for me, and I could just about take on Gourmet on a good day.

Or . . . maybe that wasn't true anymore.

I'd grown a lot since the last time we'd fought, and she'd found her calling in her cooking show. She wouldn't be getting stronger, so maybe I could handle her quickly enough to stop Iron Fist from rolling over Waterspout.

I had to give it a go, so I started up another [**Power-Weaving**], switched to Understudy, and tried for a backward combo. Gourmet knew all my old combos, but I had something new in mind for this one.

[Flashy Fitting-Room! +1 Flamboyance Point]

[Steel Yourself! +1 Grit Point]
[Floating Points: 1 Flamboyance]

Waterspout flailed around, knocking tendrils of cold water into Iron Fist as he tried to close the gap for a big hit, but the defensive-minded Tank/Elementalist wasn't so easy to move. That left me with Gourmet, who hadn't seen me start my combo, but *had* seen me switch to Understudy.

She went for the hot sauce and started going dragon—just like I'd hoped. I grinned at her and fired a single **[Starlance]** her way, as much to bait a retaliation as for anything else. It hit, shimmering against her wing momentarily before she shrugged it off. She had *so much* superhero damage!

[Dramatic Damage! +1 Drama Point]
[Floating Points: 3 Flamboyance, 1 Grit]

She breathed a blast of fire at me; this time, I couldn't dodge it. Dodging it would have meant a wasted combo, even though it would have finished successfully—no damage, no point in combo-ing. So I ate the flames, feeling the heat increase as my superhero damage melted away.

[HP 6/11 (temporarily reduced from 13)]

Then I spun, using **[Spotlight Strike]** in close, where she couldn't use her fire breath, and she crashed toward the ground.

[Stylish Strike! +1 Flamboyance Point]
[Power-Weaving! +6 Flamboyance, +3 Grit, +1 Drama Point]

Before she could recover—while she was still reaching for a beef stick, in fact—I spun in midair and blasted her near-point-blank with **[Bit-Part Barrage]**. All five shots hit her, one after another, and she held up a hand. "No more, Snack. You got me."

[Dramatic Damage! +5 Drama Points]

I wanted to sit down and talk with my friend; we hadn't seen each other much this semester, and I needed to know how her mom was, but Waterspout called for help before I could decide to take it easy, and he was right; Iron Fist was out of his league, and it'd only be a matter of time before he lost.

My first thought was to Copy Cat and get in the way, but then I got an idea . . . a terrible, stupid idea. Instead, I started attacking Quickstrike, forcing him onto defense with a volley of **[Starlances]**. He dodged them, backing up, and I pointed at Iron Fist as he did. "Hold him."

"You got it," Tractor-Beam-Girl said and fired a gravity beam his way. It grabbed him and stopped his attack just out of range from the battered-looking hero, who visibly relaxed.

Unfortunately, that left me going one-on-one with Quickstrike, who seemed more than capable of closing the gap with Understudy or Rainy Day. I backed off, using **[Solar Wing]** to get a little more distance, but I couldn't stop to fight him, and I only had one **[Quick-Time Change]** left. If I went Copy Cat and it was the wrong call, I'd be stuck.

Fursona couldn't leave Tearjerker alone, or she'd shut down Waterspout. Tractor-Beam-Girl was stuck, barely holding Iron Fist back, and I had Quickstrike occupied, but we couldn't *win* this way.

And worse, the sounds of fighting from the only unsealed door were getting closer. Did that mean the villains were about to break out? Or were we about to get much needed reinforcements?

Then, a familiar voice echoed throughout the building.

"Good morning, Tokyexico University! Nobody move—not that you can! I, Monologue, the Sultan of Speeches, Lord of Loquaciousness, have returned to stake my claim over this district. That's right, ladies, gentlemen, and heroes, I'm officially throwing my hat into the ring for the Third Power War, and you're my chosen peasants!"

On and on he went, spouting off about how great the campus would be under his rule, and I wished for intervention from the Superpower Studies professors. Where were they, anyway? Wasn't this part of why they were here? The thoughts of reinforcements disappeared from my head as Monologue's power echoed across campus, and all I could do was hope that the one counter we had got to him soon.

But hey! At least none of the villains could make a move, either!

49

Make a Move

When we—finally—snapped back to reality, everyone in the room took a couple of seconds to figure out the new situation, except for Gourmet. She leaned back against the wall and started snacking with one arm tucked behind her head. "Well? Who's going first?"

I realized right away that it'd either be me or that the villains would get away. Monologue's power had stopped Waterspout from pinning the door closed, and judging by how he was moving to cover it with his body, he couldn't do it again.

The other six of us moved at the same time.

Fursona crashed into Quickstrike before he could get moving again, stopping him from pressing his attack on Waterspout with a well-placed pair of kicks. He wasn't going anywhere anytime soon—her pressure was too high for him to ignore.

But both Tractor-Beam-Girl and I went after Iron Fist—her with the grapple beams and me with a **[Starlance]** that singed his mechanical fist just before he punched into Waterspout. Three vs. one, we should have been able to take him easily, but a voice shouted, "**[Cry for Me]**," and suddenly, Tractor-Beam-Girl was sobbing about an elementary school friend who she hadn't talked to in years.

[Dramatic Damage! +1 Drama Point]

Iron Fist slammed into the watery hero, who absorbed the blow seemingly without a problem. But then his fists started oscillating faster and faster until they were nothing but blurs, and one final, heaving blow splashed the hero across the room. That meant it was up to me, and I only had one Costume that had much in the way of juice.

I'd use it if things got more dire. Right now, I had an advantage I hadn't been using. I flew into the air with **[Solar Wing]** and started firing **[Starlances]** down at the villains, trying to split them between Iron Fist and Quickstrike as much as I could. If I could stall Iron Fist for just a couple of seconds . . .

[Dramatic Damage! +1 Drama Point]
[Dramatic Damage! +1 Drama Point]

Yes! Out of the corner of my eye, I watched as Quickstrike's staff blurred and split into four: red, blue, green, and a normal wooden one. Each of them hit Fursona from a different angle, and she spun; her [**Fursonal Furcefield**] had clearly taken some of it, but not all. I didn't have time to worry about her, though; instead, I used [**Spotlight Strike**] and pressed the attack.

I landed a solid hit to his back, and he flew away from the door. I landed in front of it a moment later.

[Stylish Strike! +1 Flamboyance Point]

"If you want to escape, you'll have to go through me," I said with more confidence than I felt. I'd avoided the worst of the damage so far, but what I was about to try? That wouldn't be an option. Waterspout was still shaking off the massive blow he'd taken; he was out. And Fursona hadn't finished off Quickstrike yet, either.

I used [**Quick-Time Change**] to pop into Copy Cat, merging with Tails. Then, before my [**Freeze-Frame**] could fade, I rushed Iron Fist.

He looked woozy and out of it, and I glanced over toward Fursona to see her in the same state. I'd help her when I could, but first, I had a villain to deal with, and I'd take any advantage I could get. I hit him with [**Cat-Scratch Fever**], leaving a thin scratch across his cheek, then spun away as the blindness set in for a few seconds. His flailing fist parted the air where I'd just been.

[Dramatic Damage! +1 Drama Point]

I had five seconds to drive in as much damage as I could. I used [**Leaping Leopards**] to close the narrow gap, then activated [**Hometown Heroine**] and [**Doom Ball**] as close to the same time as I could. My claws lashed out at Iron Fist's chest faster than they ever had, and I zipped away from him as the damage piled up.

[Badass Damage! +1 Badass Point]
[Badass Damage! +3 Badass Points]
[Dramatic Damage! +1 Drama Point]

Then, as he recovered, I ducked back behind him and clawed at his back. It didn't knock him out of the fight, but between the wooziness and the double vision debuff from [**Cat-Scratch Fever**], I'd have a moment or two to focus on other problems.

Which was good, because Fursona was losing.

Quickstrike's staff was a blur. He was either using a similar power to [**Hometown Heroine**] or was just too fast for Fursona. Either way, she needed me over there, so I used [**Leaping Leopards**] and landed on his back as a battered-looking Waterspout took up a position near the door.

[Badass Damage! +1 Badass Point]

I scratched and clawed at the freshman villain's back as Fursona recovered enough to kick him in the face. Then he started dodging and playing defense, and we chased after him, ducking under staff strikes and trying to get hits of our own in when we could. We'd pushed him almost to the door farther into the lair when Tearjerker shouted, "**[Cry for Me!]**" and I realized we'd messed up—bad.

As Tearjerker stepped over Waterspout's sobbing body, Fursona and I surged toward the door, but the villainess slipped out, and a moment later, so did Iron Fist, leaving us with Quickstrike and a laughing Gourmet. He surrendered quickly, outnumbered and outgunned, and scowled at the room's floor. "Dammit! They said they'd take me with them if I helped."

[End of Act Two: Act Three in Three Minutes]

I ran to the door and checked it, but even though I could open it just fine, there was no sign of either of the SSS's leaders. As I transformed back to Rainy Day, I shook my head in defeat. "They got away. So now what?"

The script was supposed to be the four of us as a backstop, but we'd leaked the two villains we had to stop the most. Granted, Iron Fist was probably out as a serious threat for this Episode. He might be able to ride out my **[Cat-Scratch Fever]** damage-over-time effect, but either way, he wouldn't have the superhero damage to take the fight to anyone.

But that left an uncontained Tearjerker, and with a teleporting villain about, that meant she could drop into the fight at any moment. Worse, who knew where they'd end up or how long it'd take them to rebuild?

"I don't know," Tractor-Beam-Girl snarked. "Maybe we go find them before they cause trouble across campus. Every hero in TUSSA is involved in this attack somehow, and that leaves no one to stop either of them."

"I *know* that. But we're not going after them. We've got to keep pushing into the lair. If Iron Fist and Tearjerker—and Lady Lockless, I guess—are the only villains at large after today, Sara's plan will probably still work."

"What *is* Sara's plan, anyway?" Fursona asked.

"I'm not actually sure. I think she's going with a tweaked version of Springlock's—"

"Uh, are we pushing into the lair?" Tractor-Beam-Girl interrupted.

"Yes. One second. We need to wait for Waterspout." I didn't want to push in. I'd just suggested it, but this wasn't a throwaway SSS lair. This was their main base, under the Student Union Building, and if TUSSA hadn't had the power to attack it even after my *Small-Town Super* series finale, it'd be wild in there for sure.

So, as the minutes ticked by until Act Three started, I hoped he'd snap out of it before we had to deal with any other vils. The fact was that even though I hadn't taken much damage, Fursona was on the ropes, and I'd be frontlining unless our tank got back into it. I wanted to save my healing for once he was up so I could hit everyone—before we pushed in, not after.

"Why is this Episode a Power War Episode, anyway?" I asked. "Just because of Monologue? It doesn't seem like that'd be enough, and he *had* to have known that he couldn't *really* take over the school. The moment he got close to a win, the professors would show up."

"So where are they?" Tractor-Beam-Girl asked.

Before I could answer, Waterspout pulled himself together with a shake that splashed droplets across the room. "Okay. Okay, you can do this. Don't think about her. Just focus," he mumbled to himself.

"Easy there, big guy," Fursona said, clapping him on the shoulder. "Power through, let's get this job done, then you can mourn your . . . fish?"

"Gerbil."

"Your gerbil, then."

[Power War: Sayonara, Student Supervillains!: Act Three in Progress]

With everyone up, I used **[Virga]** to give the team a bit of superhero damage back. Lady Lockless's superhero damage debuff that I'd taken for her had faded, and I smiled as Fursona and Waterspout stood a bit straighter.

[Medic! +4 Cunning Points]
[HP 8/13]

Then, without more hesitation, we pushed into the lair.

The room we'd been in had been a pretty typical club office, except that the computers weren't plugged into anything and everything had a fine layer of dust from before we'd even wrecked the room. But the hallway behind it felt absolutely spartan. Tile walls, a concrete floor, fluorescent lights, the smell of stale air, and a slight hum as an overworked air system pushed lukewarm air through the long, narrow space—but no matter how hard we looked, we couldn't find a single sign of supervillains.

It almost felt like the SSS had vanished, and I was halfway through checking my fourth maintenance closet when Waterspout cleared his throat. "Team, over here."

Closing the door, I hurried over to him, with Fursona and Vicegrip—I *had* to stop calling her Tractor-Beam-Girl—right behind me. He had a door open, and a reddish glow silhouetted him as he stared down at . . . something.

I pulled up next to him and joined him, gaze transfixed.

Whatever it was, it clearly should have been more at home in the Grant Building—or maybe the biology program, I wasn't sure. It *looked* like a metal; its surface was reflective and shined red in the room's light. But it didn't *act* like one. The tank it occupied in the middle of the room seemed built to handle water, and indeed, it sloshed back and forth, seemingly trying to escape.

"Hello, Understudy," a voice said, and I looked up to see a woman a year or two older than me, in fishnets and a black-and-red outfit—Dark Girl Anima.

"Anima, what are you working on here?" Fursona asked, pushing past me and raising her fists.

"I'm not working on anything anymore, thanks to you and the rest of TUSSA! This is a nanometal cluster, and I was working on it for our takeover attempt, but since you've interfered, I'll have to let it loose now instead!" Dark Girl Anima looked over her shoulder, and as I watched the motion, I realized that we weren't the only hero squad going after her. A pair of her giant cat-bots fought against two heroes while a third stood farther back, directing them.

"Is that . . . Punch and Grapple?" Fursona asked.

"Yep," I muttered. "They'll get the glory, and we'll get . . ."

Dark Girl Anima pressed a button, and the tank opened. Metal poured out of it, and I expected the floor to hiss and bubble from the no-doubt hot steel. Instead, it slid across it, gathering itself up into a blob, then started oozing toward my team. As it went, it ate chunks out of the building's big metal beams, leaving behind just enough to avoid a collapse and growing bigger with every bit it dissolved.

"I guess the glory's not important," I said. I touched The Triad button in my pocket but didn't press it. "Team, be careful, but we have to win this!" If we didn't, it'd keep growing, and the whole campus would be nothing but gray goo!

50

Gray Goo

I had just enough time to curse under my breath as the nanometal slime surged toward us like a wave of red-gray mercury, eating away at whatever metal it could find. I [**Quick-Time Changed**] into Understudy and fired a [**Bit-Part Barrage**] into the oozing steel, stunning it and getting a new message from the Style System.

[Dramatic Damage! +1 Drama Point]
[Resisted!]
[Rejuvenation Activated: HP 12/13]

Resisted? What did that even mean? Was I not *doing damage*? I took a few steps back as Fursona's feet flashed out and slammed into the metal with a crunch. Then she pulled back suddenly, hissing in breath through her modulator. "I can't get in close," she said. "It's munching my superhero damage."

"Okay, battle plan. We can't let it eat the building, and we can't get in melee. Fursona, watch our backs. Vicegrip, slow it down. Waterspout, can you keep water between it and whatever it's trying to eat?" I whipped [**Starlances**] at it the whole time I talked, but almost all of them just read [**Resisted!**] in the System.

"Sure, I'll try. Maybe it'll slip and get stuck," Waterspout said. He formed another watery barrier and projected it in front of the gray goo traversing the room and oozing out into the hallway. "I can't cover all the sides, though."

"Just herd it away from the building's supports!" I shouted. What the hell had Anima created? I fired another [**Starlance**], this time at the Dark Girl, and got a hit that knocked her off-balance just as Grapple got a hold of her. Then, the ooze pushed up against the wall of water in front of it, and we had to step back into the hallway.

[Dramatic Damage! +1 Drama Point]

The ooze pressed against its watery confines, trying to reach Tractor-Beam-Girl, who pushed back with all her might. Her emitters hummed and whined, but the nanometal mass gained against both her and Waterspout's best efforts, gaining ground and leaving the walls pitted and scoured as it consumed electric wire. It shuddered and jerked to a halt periodically as tiny shocks rippled through it, but didn't seem to be falling apart. If anything, its growth from the metal outpaced its damage from the sparks.

I fired another **[Starlance]**, not expecting anything, but this time, instead of the **[Resisted!]** message, I got an actual, physical result: a small piece of the metal mass peeled off and slopped into a dull gray puddle. The rest of the nanometal oozed around it, carefully not touching it, and found a couch, which it consumed, leaving behind a trail of faux leather and plastics.

[Dramatic Damage! +1 Drama Point]

Buoyed with a tiny victory, I kept unloading, firing off **[Starlance]** after **[Starlance]** as I backpedaled. But even though I occasionally knocked a chunk off the thing, and the sparking electricity surging through it left behind thin trails of dull metal, I had a sinking feeling in my stomach.

We weren't winning this.

Not with the current plan.

So we needed to change it up.

Fursona had disappeared, and I heard the sounds of fighting coming from behind us. I had no idea how to beat this thing, but whoever she'd picked a fight with, she'd probably need help. "Waterspout, go!" I said.

Then I had an idea. It wasn't a good idea, but it was the best one I had. "Actually, Tractor-Beam-Girl, you go! Waterspout, fall back but keep your barriers up. Slow it down."

While Vicegrip scowled and ran off to help Fursona with whatever she was up to, I filled Waterspout in on the new plan. He started out unsure, but by the end, he'd cracked a smile and looked like he was trying not to laugh. "That's really stupid, Understudy."

"Yeah, but it's what we've got. Now, let's give it a go."

I waited as Waterspout reinforced the liquid barriers holding the nanometal ooze back. He gave it everything he had, and after a moment, the thing stopped pushing forward. We'd successfully frozen it in place!

But that wasn't my goal—not really. I wanted to win, and I had an idea of how to do it. I slow-transformed into Lucky Star. I wouldn't have any offensive powers, but I needed access to something only she could do. As soon as I finished the slow transformation, I reached out with **[Jinx-Bearer]** and touched the slime.

[HP 10/13]

[True Grit! +1 Grit Point]

[Debuff Acquired: Shocked: Complex movement is much harder, and overall **speed is reduced**]

The sparks that'd been dancing across the nanometal slime's body hopped over to me, and I gritted my teeth as they coursed through my nerves and tears welled in my eyes. My water walls collapsed, and the slime started pushing Waterspout's back.

I took three pained steps back and used [**Power-Weaving**] and [**Hog the Limelight**] to draw the slime's attention, then started *another* slow transformation. I was still halfway through when its mass oozed up my foot, tearing at my boot and chewing into my superhero damage. Had I miscalculated?

[HP 8/13]

No. I finished my transformation, sparks still dancing, and hurried as fast as my shocked sixth-grade legs would carry me. As I ran, I used [**Virga**] and rained down even more water—and healing—into the hall.

[Medic! +2 Cunning Points]
[HP 7/13]
[Doctors Without Borders! -1 Cunning Point]
[Floating Points: 1 Flamboyance]

The plan was coming together; I could feel Waterspout working on his own [**Power-Weaving**] next to me, though his probably focused on Badass or Grit. Either way, I didn't have time to waste. I used [**Thunderhead**], sending sparks rippling up my arm, into my wand, and toward the cloud with a sigh of relief as the shocked feeling in my limbs stopped. I hadn't been sure that'd work, but the storm overhead looked way bigger than usual.

[Pause for Effect! +1 Drama Point]
[Floating Points: 3 Flamboyance, 1 Cunning]

Waterspout's control broke, and the slime surged forward into a lake of water, leaving a wake as it sank deeper and deeper into it. I backpedaled, and Waterspout ran alongside me. Then, when the storm overhead peaked, I [**Rode the Lightning**].

[Electric Lightshow! +1 Flamboyance Point]
[Environmental Combo! +1 Cunning Point]
[Thunderstruck! +1 Drama Point]
[Power-Weaving! +6 Flamboyance, +3 Cunning, +1 Drama Point]
[Feedback 1]
[HP 5/13]
[Continue Combo?]

Chunks of nanometals flew off the ooze as the massive tendril of lightning arced up into the [**Thunderhead**] and then hammered down onto it. The boom was deafening; it threw Waterspout and me back toward the room where Fursona and Tractor-Beam-Girl fought. But I had the option to keep the combo rolling, and I was determined to do everything I could to the slime right here, right now.

[**Electric Lightshow! +1 Flamboyance Point**]
[**Environmental Combo! +1 Cunning Point**]
[**Thunderstruck! +1 Drama Point**]
[**Feedback 2**]
[**HP 3/13**]
[**Combo Collapse**]

I'd given what I could, and as I watched the nanometal ooze disintegrate faster and faster, I crossed my fingers that it'd be enough because if it wasn't, I didn't know what else I could do. It fell apart in huge slabs that melted away into the puddle until the water was a filthy gray color, and I watched as Waterspout's power swirled it around, keeping what was left of the ooze from fighting its way free.

It stopped moving, and even its core went the dull gray of broken nanometals. And a few moments later, I got a welcome message from the Style System.

[**Episode Finished!**]
[**Episode: Power War: Sayonara, Student Supervillains! - PG-13**]
[**Penalties: N/A**]
[**Episode Finished! +3 of each Style Point**]
[**Winner Winner! +3 of each Style Point**]
[**Role Focus: Drama + Flamboyance - Goal Met: +10 to Focused Skills**]
[**Alias - Understudy**] [**Archetype - Magical Girl**] [**Community Rank - 180/523**]
[**HP 3/13**]
[**Styles and Skills**]
▶**Archetype Skill - Transformation Sequence**
▶**Combo Skills - Power-Weaving**
▶**Badass (39)**
▶**Cunning (64) (New Skill Roll Available)**
▶**Drama (75) (New Skill Roll Available)**
▶**Bit-Part Barrage 2**
▶**Starlance 2**
▶**Flamboyance (92) (New Skill Roll Available)**
▶**Signature Skill - Adaptive Armoire 3**
▶**Stored Costumes: (Rainy Day, Copy Cat, Rescue Girl Lucky Star)**
▶**Solar Wing 1**

▶Quick-Time Change 3
▶Spotlight Strike 2
▶Grit (29)
▶Freeze Frame 1

Sara had her work cut out for her.

As Punch and Grapple escorted the furious, cursing Dark Girl Anima out of the lair and into the waiting arms of the TU Campus Police, she was already striding toward me, looking remorseful. "Sorry about that. I only calculated a 32% probability of a new Anima trick, and a 78% chance we'd get there in time to stop it, so I figured you'd be a solid enough backstop—and I was right, wasn't I?"

"Yeah, that was pretty lucky," Waterspout said. Sara glared at him, and he smirked. "Oops."

"Anyway," Sara said, trying to recover. "I have a meeting with the TU president to explain all this. I'm pretty sure I can talk my way out of it, but Springlock's in charge of the cleanup while I'm at Beaumont. Don't touch anything that looks like it could give us an idea of the SSS's plans."

"Did we win?" Fursona asked. She'd been fighting two of Anima's cat-bots when the Episode ended. "I mean, we won, but did we meet your goal?"

Sara paused, unsure. She reached for a coin and flipped it absent-mindedly; it landed on its edge in her palm, and she glared at it for a moment before putting it back in her breast pocket. "I don't know. I don't think they'll be a threat, but we'll have to see how this week plays out. Anyone with SSS members in their classes, let me know if they show up or if they're online only. I'll get enough information to make a good prediction based on that."

I nodded, and Sara disappeared, jogging toward the Beaumont Administrative Building. For a moment, I thought about going back into the SSS's lair, but my part in it was done. Springlock and her team had the investigation, and Sara would take it over; whatever help they needed, it wasn't from me. Instead, I rolled my skills.

[50 Cunning Credits Used. Rolling Skill!]

[50 Drama Credits Used. Rolling Skill!]

[50 Grit Credits Used. Rolling Skill!]

[Rank-Up! Speed-Hacker 2: Defeat complex systems and shut down major-league heroes' inventions if unprotected]

[Skill Upgrade! Bit-Part Barrage to Limelight Barrage: An upgraded version of Bit-Part Barrage; this one fires a half dozen Starlances]

[New Skill! Improvised Ovation 1: Replicate a power another hero or villain has used in the last minute, gaining Flamboyance points instead of its original point type]

The campus police had finished arresting most of the villains, and I didn't feel like signing autographs, so I walked over to Gourmet's car. She grinned up at me. "Hey, Snack!"

"Hi, Gourmet. I hope you learned something here," I said.

"About justice and morality? Nah. But I do have some good news for you. Charlene and I are the best-rated cooking show in North America. And even better, Mom's getting out of the hospital next week. I've gotta get permission from my professors to take finals early, but it's a huge step for her, and I'm so excited I went and bought an apartment for her so she can be close by."

Gourmet's excitement, and earnest happiness were contagious, and I spent a good five minutes talking with her as the officer whose car I was holding up grew more and more frustrated. Eventually, after the eighth or so throat-clear, I took the hint. "Alright, Gorgonzola, I've gotta get going, but I'm sure I'll see you around."

"Yep, the lawyers are already working on it. See you later, Snack." Her window went up, and the police car gunned it out of the SUB's parking lot.

I turned and started walking toward Roth Arena. Fursona caught up to me after a moment, and I slipped my hand into her paw almost without thinking about it. My mind was thinking about the implications of [**Freeze-Frame**]. It had felt almost like a cheat code; I could dodge *anything*? There had to be a catch somewhere; had I lost anything by switching?

As we walked through the tunnels, Fursona popped my thought-bubble. "I have a bad feeling about all this, Understudy. Something tells me we haven't seen the last of the SSS."

"I think you're right. But there's not much we can do about it right now. We'll just have to wait for Sara to give us new targets after she pores through their base. In the meantime, finals week is coming, and we've got to hit the books."

51

Hit the Books

WEDNESDAY, DECEMBER 10

The investigation into the SSS's plan was, according to Sara-N-Dipity, "Proceeding as expected."

At least, that was her public statement. Privately, in the TUSSA group text and our emails, she kept sounding more and more frustrated. She *knew,* with 80% certainty, how to beat the SSS's security, but without cooperation from Dark Girl Anima, it wasn't a matter of luck. TUSSA simply didn't have access to her unique powers, and no amount of probability manipulation could change that.

So, instead of a quick investigation and a wrap-up that'd force the SSS's hand and let TUSSA chase down the few who'd escaped, we had a mess. At least we hadn't seen any villains in classes since, with the exception of Gourmet. Her lawyers had gotten her off almost instantly, and she was shooting another Episode of *Gourmet's Glutton Hour* later that night.

Still, curiosity was killing the cat—and it wasn't just Tails who couldn't wait to know all the SSS's secrets. Bianca and I had spent two long days wishing we could figure out the mystery ourselves; it had messed with every bit of studying we'd tried to do. Worse, I'd suggested that we cancel our plans tonight to deal with it.

"Fuck no, Annie," Bianca said, leaning against the maintenance room door that led to our green room. "Su-Bin and Cam are coming over in twenty. They're even doing the cooking, or getting take-out, or something. All we have to do is make sure the decks are shuffled. Now, sit down and relax."

"Okay, babe. I'll do my best." I flopped down on the couch as Bee's hands worked across my too-stiff shoulders, shuffling the decks of black and white cards until they'd been well randomized. But the tension wouldn't bleed out of my back no matter what I did. After my third shuffle-through, I put the cards back in their long, skinny box. "I thought for sure that Sara's power would break in, no problem."

"Yes, yes, I know. Now, no shop talk. Only fun." Bee kept working my shoulders and upper back until, finally, I relaxed a tiny bit.

That lasted until the doorbell rang, and Bianca let Su-Bin and Cam in. Cam looked like part of a mountain had decided to take a walk, then put on a few pounds of muscle. He filled the door, lugging a pair of slow cookers under his arms, with a thin layer of snow on his simple haircut and jacket shoulders. "Kitchen? Gotta get these plugged in again."

Bee pointed him toward the kitchen as Su-Bin pulled off her knee-length coat and tossed it onto a rack near the door. "The weather outside is frightful—and no, I'm not starting a sing-along. It's gonna be a long walk home later."

"I bet," I said, glancing at the melting flakes in her hair. Was Polar Vortex or Black Ice out there? Would I have to figure out a way to change into Understudy, protect Walnut Tower, and keep my identity safe from President Pak? Bee's hand clamped on my shoulder, and she raised an eyebrow. I nodded slowly. "How about a couple of hands while we wait for that to heat back up? I've got them all shuffled up and ready to play."

Su-Bin snorted into her Coke. "Annie, you're great, but I'll give them one more shuffle, just to be sure?"

"What's the matter? Don't you trust me?" I managed to give it enough snark to disguise it and pushed the card box across the table toward her.

"Thanks." She shuffled, dealt a handful of white cards to each of us, and flipped the first black one over. "The card is 'During sex, I like to think about . . .'"

"I've got this one." I flipped my card onto the pile, followed by two others, and Su-Bin snorted into her Coke again as she read them off.

"And the winner is . . . 'All the single ladies,'" she declared. "Really, Cam?"

"Wasn't me," the big guy said. "Funny, though."

"I'll take that," Bee said. She reached for the card as I glared dramatically at her, but even though it was hilarious, my mind wouldn't stop turning to Polar Vortex and Black Ice, or about President Pak being here—right *here*—in my apartment, and how much APPEAL needed that radio pitch. Bee drank a shot and flipped the next black card. "'Before blank, all we had was blank and blank.' A triple! So exciting!"

We played another eight or nine hands—I couldn't keep count—before Su-Bin finally checked on the chili smell from the slow cookers. "Alright, let's eat it," she said, opening my cabinets to hunt down some bowls.

It was pretty good, to be honest; my taste buds were a bit spoiled by Ramsey Fieri—every time I cooked, I thanked whoever was out there that Gourmet had never taken the Costume back—but it had the right spices in the right places, and Su-Bin or Cam had done a good job with it. Bee had three bowls, and then right back to the game we went.

But something had changed. Su-Bin looked increasingly anxious about something, and she kept checking her phone. After the fourth time, Cam put a gigantic hand over it. "No more checking unless you tell us what's up."

"But it's shop talk," Su-Bin said. Before I could stop her, she continued, "Look, you know Magical Girl Understudy's been a *problem* for APPEAL. I'm trying to make some sort of peace with her, but she's been reluctant to let that happen. She keeps saying she's too busy or pushing us off. It's really frustrating, and the club's starting to lose patience with it as a strategy."

"Well, maybe—" I started to say, but Bee kicked me in the shin. "Never mind."

"Never mind what?" Su-Bin asked.

I could practically hear Bianca's groan, but I'd kind of committed myself, and there wasn't another option except to BS an answer. "What responsibility does APPEAL have for making amends? I get that you think she's been a problem for the campus and you guys, but don't you have some sort of responsibility, too?"

"Of course we do, but that's why we're trying to make peace here. If you just—"

"Hang on," Cam said.

"Wait a minute," Bee interrupted at the same time. "Annie, are you okay?"

"I'm not sure." My head was spinning, and my throat felt tight. I stood up. "I need to take a few minutes. I'll be back."

"Okay, babe. See you in five?"

"Ten."

I slipped into my bedroom—I *wanted* the green room, but with Su-Bin right there, it'd be like admitting I was a hero—and opened the closet door. Mom's suit hung in the back, and I grabbed a sleeve. It wasn't like her actually being here, but it was close, and I needed someone to talk to.

For a moment—just for a moment, but for long enough—I hadn't been Annie. I'd been Understudy, if not in powers, at least in my attitude toward my friend. My clothes pressed around me as I pulled out my cell phone and texted a familiar number.

<Understudy here. Does Dr Ayers have appointments soon? - Understudy 7:13>

This whole mess seemed like the exact kind of thing super-counseling was for. I'd spent so much time in my Understudy Costume that Annie was starting to become her, too, and I didn't like it one bit. I held my mom's Madame Shockwave outfit until a message came back in.

<Dr Ayers. Can we call? - Angie A 7:15>
<Sure - Understudy 7:15>

My phone buzzed a moment later, and I picked it up instantly. "Understudy here."

"Hey, Annie. My schedule is packed, but I wanted to make sure you're not having a crisis. If not, I can get you in on Friday afternoon, if that works." Dr. Ayers's voice was chipper as usual, if a little staticky from my speaker.

"No, I'm okay. I'm just . . . I'm looking for ways to balance what I'm doing here with my personal life. They've started to feel . . . kind of the same? It's hard to explain."

"Okay. How about I pencil you in for Friday at 3:30, and we take it from there?" Dr. Ayers said. "What you're dealing with is surprisingly normal for heroes on the edge of going full-time, and we've got some plans for helping you navigate that process. I'll get some resources together, and maybe I can set you up with a mentor hero, too."

"That all sounds great. I'm already working with—"

"Annie, you good?" Bee's voice cut in from the bedroom door.

"Yeah, I'm fine. Just need a couple more minutes."

"Ooookay. I'll let Su-Bin and Cam know, alright?" Her voice dropped. "You might want to keep it down, though."

"Thanks, Bee." I turned to my phone. "Yeah, Friday sounds great. I appreciate it. I've gotta go, though."

"No problem. I'm happy to help," Dr. Ayers said.

I hung up, took another minute to pull myself together, and opened the closet door. Then, after checking to make sure I seemed okay, I wandered back into the living room and sat down. "Thanks for being patient."

I was dreading the moment Bianca turned on me.

She'd been every bit the perfect hostess the whole game, even after she lost hand after hand. She grumbled good-naturedly about her bad cards and, after the game ended with Su-Bin winning, showed that she'd somehow managed to draw almost ten extras. We all yelled at her, and she defended herself by consulting the rules. Sure enough, they stated that cheating was acceptable, but being caught cheating was against the rules.

"What kind of game is this, anyway?" Cam complained.

"A good one." Bianca smiled widely and held the door as he trooped by with the much-lighter slow cookers.

Then the door clicked shut.

"I posit you were pondering your personality problems," she said, leading me back toward the couch. "You haven't been acting like yourself the last couple of weeks."

"It's that noticeable?" I grinned sheepishly and sat down. She went right back to rubbing my shoulders, this time getting her hands under my sweater, and I jumped at how cold they were. "Yeah. I've got an appointment with super-counseling on Friday."

"Alright. But in the meantime, why don't we talk it over?" Her hands kept pushing, and I melted into the back of the couch. "You seem okay on our dates, right? How's that different than when we play games with Su-Bin?"

"Uh, you know my secret already, so I don't feel like I'm pretending to be someone I'm not. With Su-Bin, it's all about managing two different relationships, between

Annie and her, but also between Understudy and President Pak. And that was working for a while, but it's harder to keep the shop talk out of game night."

"So what do you want?"

"I hate that question so much, Bee," I complained, leaning forward out of her back rub. She walked around the couch and sat down next to me as I kept talking. "I don't know. That's why I'm seeing Dr. Ayers."

"Okay. Look. I'm here for you. I know some of the tricks, and I've got your back. You want to step back from superhero stuff for a bit? We can do that. The campus should be safe, and we're not going to end the Third Power War ourselves or anything, right?"

I tried to keep a straight face, but before I knew it, a giggle forced its way out of my mouth. Then it was a laugh I couldn't stop, even though I wanted nothing more than to take it seriously. "Fursona and Understudy save all the days," I gasped between almost painful breaths.

"Yeah, it's a little hard to even think about with so many ridiculously powerful heroes out there," Bee said. "And look, we're in the minor leagues, but that doesn't mean we have to be heroes all the time. We really *should* take some time just to be us."

I took another deep breath, let one last giggle go, and then waited to see if more were coming. When they didn't, I grabbed Bee's hand and held it. "We should. But the superheroes are part of us, too."

"I think—"

Before she could keep talking, I interrupted her. "Bee, I'm going to see Dr. Ayers on Friday. Until then, let's just keep on doing what we're doing. She'll have some new ideas."

52

New Ideas

THURSDAY, DECEMBER 11

The TV in the Student Union Building silently blared out the news, its red-and-blue screen covered in captions and ticker tape urgent warnings about the most recent drama in Europe, India, and all the other places where things were happening. The Power War was worldwide, but I didn't really care how the East Asian superheroes were handling their villains. I ate my SUB burrito quietly, eyes glued to the screen, with Bee watching an identical TV over my shoulder.

The picture on the screen changed to Yorkston's skyline, specifically, to a familiar skyscraper's penthouse. I read the headline. 'Police Investigation Reveals Thefts.' Then I swallowed and took a sip of water. "Wonder what that's all about."

'Yorkston Police Department representatives today revealed a list of items taken from Golden Goose's penthouse at the top of the Independence Building. Included were several items Jasmine Saxton considered personal and private, including jewelry, identification cards, a notebook, and other odds and ends. A complete list is available on our website. The Saxton family and the Ilneat studio Snowball Productions are asking for items to be returned promptly, promising not to investigate further.'

'"We just want our daughter's locket back," Alyssa Saxton said on the screen. "We don't care about the rest of it, but that family heirloom's important to us. Please."'

I glanced at Bianca, then back at the TV. She was glued to it, her burrito forgotten as the subtitles kept going. 'In Golden Goose's absence, chaos has engulfed Yorkston. Magical Girl Stella-Lunar has rotated her coverage to help, leaving Tokyexico City in the hands of less powerful heroes. To those heroes fighting now-overwhelming numbers of villains and henchmen across North America, we ask you to keep holding the line.'

"Yeah, with what?" Bianca asked.

It was a good question. Things across southeast Tokyexico were looking bad. The Triad had told us not to patrol down there anymore and that they were splitting coverage with the In-You-Endos. Worse, they'd lost control of their own district—with the exception of their pyramid, the whole place belonged to Lord Destructo and McHammer.

There just weren't more heroes to hold the line with. Tokyexico needed Stella-Lunar, and it needed her yesterday. Either that, or it needed Mays and Jackson to shut down the villains one at a time. The problem was that the moment they ended their neutrality, the campus was a target for more than an ill-advised attempt at glory from Monologue.

"Come on." I stood up and bundled the remains of my bacon-and-egg burrito up. My stomach was rolling, and I couldn't have finished it if I tried. "Let's go back to my place and try to get some studying in. We're both behind."

The truth was, neither of us cared. We'd been in Episodes, patrols, or trying to investigate the SSS's lair for so long that signing up for the associates' program felt like a lifetime ago. But Bianca wanted us to do normal college things, and there wasn't anything more normal than cramming before finals, so we walked through the freezing wind and took the elevator up to 1301 Walnut Tower.

Bianca took her place with her head on my stomach. I cracked the book on Extra Relations and started reading out loud, and she scribbled notes in a light blue notebook. "The reality is that most Extras interacting with superheroes don't need a hero to solve their problems. Understanding your role in an Extra/super dynamic is critical to producing the desired result; to convince the Extra that you're *listening* to their problems and maneuvering support their way."

Bianca shifted, her pencil stabbing at the paper, and I paused to let her catch up. Then I continued, on and on, through example after example. After reading through a story about a man whose neighborhood had been flooded during a fight and who just wanted to know someone was going to help, I yawned. "We shouldn't have procrastinated this bad. If I get another chance, I'm staying on top of my homework."

Bianca shook her head; it rolled back and forth across my stomach. "I doubt it."

"What? You don't believe me? It's true! I'm going to grab my classes by the horns next semester and not let go. I want to finish my career at TU strong, get my degree, and move on."

"To major-league work?"

"Why not?" I gently pushed her off of me and rolled off the bed. "Studying isn't working right now, though. I need some air."

I stood on Walnut Tower's roof in my street clothes, shivering as the wind blew the storm's first flakes at me sideways. The mountains were already whited out, but the sky to the east was perfectly clear; it was a slow-mover, which meant Tokyexico was in for a big one. And it had happened so fast after last night's snowstorm that I'd actually checked for any of the winter-themed villains just to see if they'd been active.

They hadn't. As far as I could tell, it was a normal weather pattern.

So, instead of watching it with the anxiety I'd felt last night, I got to enjoy the snow melting in my hair. It felt nice, not worrying about which villains were out there or about my overdue homework and just having a moment in the snow. Below, in the snow from last night's storm, a few freshmen had started building a snowman. They didn't look up at me, but I watched them for a while. I didn't feel like Power Wars was rolling. It felt normal . . . comfortable.

So, of course, my phone rang.

"Hello?" I asked.

"Aaaaayyy! DuPont, it's Rocko!"

I sighed. It had been a nice fifteen minutes or so as Anika. Then I took a deep breath and let Understudy take over again. "Hello, Rocko. What's going on?"

"Oh, just checking in with my number one superhero! How's the superheroing going?" The Ilneat's voice echoed out of my phone's speaker, and I turned and headed back down the stairs into the green room. It'd be easier to hear them without the wind, anyway.

"It's going well. We just wrapped up the Student Supervillain Society, but . . . you know that already, huh?"

"You got it in one, DuPont. Listen, I'm still gone for a while until things stabilize down there. For some reason, the Network doesn't want us in the Hot Zones while you people figure out the Golden Goose situation. Something about 'too risky' and 'what if they blame us'? A load of ridiculousness, but it means you're on your own for the season finale."

"The . . . season finale?" I mumbled. "Let me go get Bianca."

"What, she's not with you right now? Thought you two were peas in a pod, DuPont. Alright, but make it fast. I'm burning money every second this connection's open, and that's all money that could make *Heroics 101* better!"

I muted my phone, opened the door, and yelled for Bianca. She showed up on the third yell, and I said, "It's Rocko. We've got a season finale coming up, and I guess they want to plan it out with us or something."

"Can you tell them to shove it?" Bianca asked jokingly. "We're trying to do more normal stuff, and finals are coming up."

"No." I unmuted the phone. "Okay, Rocko, what do you have for us?"

"So far, you've got definitive wins against two of your four rogues, right? You beat Theseus pretty handily, and Livestream turned out to be a pushover, thanks to me. Last I heard, he hasn't run that promotion again since, which is smart. All the studios are ready to pay him to lose if it comes to that. But your fox-furred rival is still out there, Marino, and she hasn't lost yet." Rocko sucked in a breath and exhaled, and even though I couldn't actually smell the cigarette smoke, my imagination supplied the scent perfectly.

"Yeah, we've been focusing on 3V1L this season. They're the biggest problem, and if we can beat them, we'll clear the Poudre district so some little-league heroes can keep it under control. Then we can focus on Sister Sly," Bianca said. "Besides, this rivalry's clearly artificial. She doesn't care about me, and I *really* don't care about her."

"Yeah," Rocko said, sighing dramatically, "I guess I'll explain that one. DeeDee is a new producer, with just enough leverage to get a single minor-leaguer, but not a hero. They're making a play, and I agreed to add their villain to your rogues. Sister Sly doesn't care about the Poudre district. She's not even from Tokyexico. It's just interstudio politics, but I need you to deliver another Sister Sly Episode either way."

"Seriously, Rocko?" I asked.

"Yes, seriously, DuPont. You do the superpowers part of our show, and I'll take care of all the money and politicking. We'll both do what we're best at, alright? Great. Now, tell me about your plan for handling 3V1L."

I hesitated, and Rocko kept talking. "No plan, huh?"

"We're in between Episodes with them, and finals week's here. Cut us some slack, okay?" Bianca snapped. "We've got the beginnings of a plan, but it won't happen overnight."

"Alright, Marino. Alright. I'm just trying to keep *your* show on track so that *you* can climb the ranks. That's what you want, right? So how about this? I've got meetings up to my gripping hands, and you're both busy with finals. How about by the twenty-fifth? That gives us two weeks to get it together, find a way to make a finale, and get it filmed, and one week for me to get it edited and out there. Easy peasy."

"Easy peasy," I said. "Bye, Rocko."

When the cell phone beeped to let me know they couldn't hear anymore, I groaned. But before I could start complaining, Bee held up a hand. "Annie, we're not going to deal with this tonight. Rocko's going to have to wait until after your super-counseling meeting, at the very least. Ideally, we can make them wait until after finals."

"Really? They're our boss, so we kind of have to listen to them," I said, clenching my fists.

"Yeah, but they also said two weeks. That's a long time to get something together, and Rocko's used to us jumping whenever they say jump." Bianca grabbed my hand and dragged me back to the couch inside. "Let's watch something. Not a superhero show, though. Anything but that."

"*Gourmet's Glutton Hour?*"

"No." She shook her head and pushed me down onto the couch. Then she flopped down beside me and fiddled with the remote until she found an ancient cartoon about a talking lion. "We're going to take it easy, not worry about Rocko, and be college kids procrastinating our homework."

"Fuck. The homework." I tried to get up and grab the Extra Relations book, but Bianca pulled me down, using her superstrength to do it. I struggled until she pinned me to the couch and pressed play, then gave up. I couldn't fight a Bruiser like her, and it was pointless to try.

Instead, I cuddled against her and let her play with my hair while all the animals sang a song about the circle of life, and I tried not to think about 3V1L.

53

Think about 3V1L

Dr. Ayers stood up, closing her notebook, and I heaved myself off the couch and grabbed my stuff from the coffee table in her office.

"So, in conclusion, I think you're on the right track," Dr. Ayers said. She handed me a few pamphlets with titles like 'Maintaining a Healthy Superhero/Life Balance' and 'How to Manage Identity Issues.' I tucked them under an arm as she kept talking. "Many supers embrace the mask full-time and let it become who they are. The hero becomes their main persona for others, with their secret identities taking a back seat. It doesn't sound like that's what you want, though."

"Definitely not," I said, laughing. The counseling session had been helpful. We'd talked about my worries, and Dr. Ayers had assured me that it was surprisingly normal and nothing to be worried about.

Still, a voice in my head kept telling me that maybe it *was* something to worry about in the longer term. Tele-Portal's real identity was probably fine. She treated superhero work like a job. But even for her, the job had changed how she viewed other people, especially Extras, and I didn't want *that* either. "Can we meet in early January to follow up?"

"Sure, Anika," Dr. Ayers said. She opened the door. "I'll call you about it later, alright?"

"Alright."

Fursona was waiting in the, well, waiting room. I handed her the pamphlets, which she tucked into her pouch for safekeeping. "Ready for Phase Two?"

"You don't want to know how it went?" I asked as we headed for the elevator.

"Nah, you'll tell me on the way home or back at base. Right now, it's time to focus up." She pressed the button, and the elevator whisked us off to the archive. "Last time, we looked at 3V1L's past, but we need to know everything they've been up to now. We've got two weeks for a season finale and to wrap up Sister Sly, so let's figure out what that's going to require."

"Yep. We'll figure this out."

The elevator opened, and a familiar face dropped into a glare as he recognized us.

"The Agent. They're still letting you into this place?" I asked, returning his angry look.

"Now, now, you know I was cleared of all wrongdoing, and your attempt at blackmail wasn't enough to discredit me, either," The Agent said, adjusting his suit and smoothing out his face with sheer force of will. "I'm actually just leaving. I contracted a new power for **[Hire a Temp]**, which means new research on how it works, and I can't just . . . hire a temp to do that, sadly."

I blinked, shocked at how quickly the anger had seemed to fade and been replaced by The Agent's snake-oil salesman persona. "Well, make sure you keep it all above-board this time, yeah? Wouldn't want another embarrassment on your business record, would we?"

"I was found innocent, as I said, and I'm still one of the most trustworthy heroes in North America when it comes to stopping crime. Now, how about you two run along and let the real heroes do their jobs instead of lurking around here? I'm sure there's a middle-school villain somewhere with your names on them."

"I don't think I've seen you outside the Council building except that one time at the job fair. Do you live here?" Fursona sounded calm through her modulator.

"I have a lot of business to take care of. Some of it has to be done here." The Agent nodded, picked up his briefcase, and slid past Fursona and me. "And some of it elsewhere. You two stay busy, okay?"

"Always." I kept my glare on the door until it slipped shut with a ding, then turned toward the Council of Heroes' archives. My fists unclenched slowly, and I breathed deep, slow breaths to calm myself. "What a jerk."

"Yeah, right? Come on, let's focus on the goal. New 3V1L, right?" Fursona said.

"Right."

An hour later, with the archive close to shutting down for the day, I had to admit defeat. The shelves seemed to press in on us in the near silence, and even though the smell of old newspapers and books should have been comforting, it only reminded me of failure.

It wasn't that there wasn't anything about 3V1L. It was that anything from the last three months or so was checked out for study. We'd gotten a few duplicate articles, but all they told us was that there were at least two *V*s out there that Fursona and I hadn't fought. And if there were two, there had to be more. But we couldn't find anything definitive on their power sets, tactics, or even how many of them 3V1L had.

"Shit," Fursona muttered, poring over an article for the third time. I'd already read that one, too, but with most of the material checked out, we didn't have many other options. We'd even asked the attendant about it, and he'd confirmed that a few different heroes had been in over the last couple of weeks but that things should start returning just before Christmas. That wasn't quick enough for us.

"Yeah. Who else would have an interest in 3V1L? They're our rogues, not someone else's."

I have a theory, but it's one with no evidence," Fursona said. "There's gotta be another hero working on 3V1L. Maybe a local in the Poudre districts who's trying to keep their home safe or something."

"Makes sense, but wouldn't we have heard about them? We've been pretty active there recently." I turned a newspaper page, only to find that the article ended after one more paragraph on B13. "Ugh."

"Yeah, this isn't working. We're going to have to go in blind or something. There's no time to wait for the articles to come back. I checked Super Watch"—Fursona was talking about the secret fan site for superheroes and villains—"and there's practically nothing but home videos of us fighting them. There's no way they're this invisible. No way."

I pushed my chair out and stood up.

"Excuse me," a superhero said, pointing with a gloved finger at the chair. He wore an off-white hood and a full-face mask that looked like a grinning spirit or something, and his armor almost seemed like it was glowing. More importantly, he carried a pile of books and newspapers as he headed for the archive desk.

I pushed my chair in to let him by, and he nodded politely and continued on his way. As he worked his way past me, I caught one of the books' titles: *A Legacy of 3V1L: Corruption, Villainy, and the Fall of the Poudre Districts.*

An alarm bell went off in my head, and I watched as the hero walked toward the desk and parked his pile, then went back for more. I pointed and whispered to Fursona through our comm system the second he was out of earshot. "Something's off here. That hero's clearing out our rogue's section. I'm going to check it out. Make sure he doesn't leave."

It took a minute or so to slip off to the bathroom, transform into Lucky Star, and get back to the archive, but I made it okay. I didn't want to be *too* obviously Understudy while I spied on another hero, and being Lab Assistant Panic or something similar would be too uncontrollable, so Lucky Star it was. Then, creeping through the rows of shelves, I took up a position near the 3V1L shelves.

"Pre-Launch crime . . . 3V1L's foundations . . . the first Three *Vs* . . ." On and on the guy muttered as he labored through the shelves. "Fuck, there's not much here. Already been cleaned out . . ."

Another alarm bell went off. He'd been so polite when he knew I was there, and now he seemed annoyed at his whole search. I got that, believe me. Fursona and I had been here for an hour, and we hadn't found anything. But something about the hero's whole demeanor had caught my attention, and now all those little things kept adding up.

"Fursona, something's really off. If he heads for the front, stall him," I whispered into my mic. "I'm going to try talking to him."

"Got it. I've got a plan for that."

I took a deep breath and rounded the corner.

". . . Articles . . . so many articles . . . how long were these assholes act—uh, hello," the hero said. He jumped back from the shelf, almost like he'd been caught doing something wrong. "How are you today?"

"I'm great," I said, smiling as brightly as possible. "I was doing a school project on villain groups, but there's not much here on 3V1L. Do you know why?"

It felt like an obvious ploy, but the hero nodded slowly. "I've noticed that, too—a lot of historical information, but anything recent's cleared out. I've got a project for school, too. I won't ask where you go—secret identities and all that."

"Oh, if we're not at the same school, we could work on it together, though. That way, we're not stepping on each other's feet." I didn't expect him to say yes.

The hero didn't disappoint. "I . . . don't think that'd be a good idea. My, uh, teacher is pretty strict about stuff like that. Honestly, I'm not even supposed to be here. I'm supposed to use public library resources, but this is *kinda* a public library. But if she finds out I've been here or copying other people, I'll fail, and I don't want that. Sorry."

I blinked, taking a breath that I turned into a yawn to hide my shock. His personality had switched again! Instead of pressing, I smiled sadly. "Alright. I'll keep searching. Maybe I'll still find enough to get a B in my class."

"Good luck," he said and turned back to the shelf.

The rest of the walk down the shelf felt like it'd never end, but at the same time, I hadn't gone four steps when I heard him grab something and start walking quickly toward the archive desk. I spun around and crept to the end of the shelf. His off-white cloak was still in view, so I used [**Audition Notes**], not expecting a response, but not having anything else to do and knowing it wouldn't warn him.

[**Audition Notes for John Doe: This Extra is . . .**]

I blinked at that. The readout looked identical to another one I'd seen: Fred Callahan, the onetime 3V1L *V* whose house we'd broken into. He kept walking, squeezing past the table where Fursona sat—but as he tried to get past her chair, her tail flicked out and tripped him, and he hit the ground, sending books everywhere.

"Sorry, it's got a mind of its own!" Fursona said, hurrying to help the hero recover his books and newspapers. When he wasn't looking, she surreptitiously kicked one farther under the table, and I nodded.

"It's . . . fine," he muttered. The politeness he'd shown earlier was gone; instead, he sounded like he was barely holding it together. He gathered his books, choked out a "Sorry about that," and hurried toward the desk, where the attendant waited to check out his teetering tower of books.

"You forgot one!" Fursona shouted. The attendant glared, and she put her paws over her mouth, then reached for the book. The rest of my [**Audition Notes**] finally came in as she did.

[Audition Notes for John Doe: This Extra is in over his head and nervous. He's playing a dangerous game with powers that are beyond him, and it's starting to get to him. He just wants to go home and take off the mask for the day, but he has so much to do. If someone could help him out, he'd be thankful, but he also doesn't want help for some reason.]

[Good Thinking! +1 Cunning Point]

"What the hell does that mean?" I muttered. This whole thing kept getting more and more suspicious.

54

Suspicious

[Investigative Casting Call]
  [Investigative Episode: Archive Anxiety - PG]
  [Role: Amateur Sleuth! Do you accept the role? (Yes/No)]
  [Role Focus: Cunning + Drama]
  [Archive Anxiety: Act One in Progress]

It was *too* suspicious, and as the hooded hero ducked into an elevator, I fired up a **[Casting Call]** for an Investigative Episode. "Come on, we've got a lead here."

"You're sure?" Fursona looked back at the newspaper-covered desk, and I winced. It looked like someone had gotten halfway through a paper-mache party and decided not to clean up.

But the facts were the facts, and they told me that we hadn't seen *any* heroes interested in 3V1L in the last three or four months except us. Sure, The Triad had bailed us out once, but after that? They'd gone right back to pretending the Poudre districts didn't exist. Heck, even villains didn't mess with 3V1L. And that meant this hero was up to something.

"No time. We'll make it up to the attendant later . . . somehow. Let's go!" I grabbed Fursona's paw and pulled her toward the stairs. She followed reluctantly— we had a long sprint if we wanted to beat the hero to the exit on the first floor.

Our feet pounded the steps as we ran down, sliding on the handrails where we could to get some extra speed. The staircase was packed with Extras—employees working in the Council of Heroes building or people asking for help from supers— and we had to look our most serious the whole way down. By the time we'd descended twenty-plus flights of stairs, I wished we'd just taken the elevator, even if we'd lost the guy.

But we *did* catch a glimpse of his white cloak flapping as he pushed through the revolving doors at the skyscraper's base and out into the street.

I pulled a **[Card Curio]** card. "The Sun. That's got to be a good omen. We're on the right track, and the sun's setting. I bet he'll go west; let's get a move on."

[**Good Thinking! +1 Cunning Point**]

As we hurried to keep up, the hero lugged a backpack filled with books and newspapers along the street. He was moving shockingly fast, and I paused for breath—and to wonder if he was a Speedster or a Bruiser. Either way, I wouldn't be running him down as Lucky Star. "Keep on him. I'll switch to Understudy and get some air."

"Okay. Hurry up," Fursona said, a tinge of nerves in her voice. "You're right. This all feels off."

"Will do." I started transforming back to Understudy, letting the slow transformation play out and drawing eyes as Fursona dashed ahead. The choral music and light show drew eyes from the nearby Extras in a way that, somehow, my Lucky Star Costume and Roo-sona hadn't, but as a few closed in—maybe to ask for autographs, or maybe to ask for help—I used [**Solar Wing**] and jumped into the air. "Sorry, I'm on a mission. I'll be back to patrol later, though!"

The air whipped through my hair, threatening to pull my tiara off my head as I gained altitude. "Where are you?" I asked.

"Slinky bus, heading west. He's up front. I'm in the back," Fursona said. "We just passed the Westfield train station, if that helps."

"Yeah, it does. Be there in a minute."

I rocketed through the urban canyons, past skyscrapers that got shorter and older as we reached the edge of Mid-Town. The bus came into view just on the edge of South Poudre's industrial smog cloud, and I dipped lower to try to get under it. Last night's snow already had a hint of yellow-brown to it from the factories and refineries.

The bus stopped, and the white-cloaked hero stepped out. "I've got eyes on him, Fursona," I said. "He's still heading west, further into the district."

"Got it. I'm out of the chase. I'll head toward University and try to avoid any 3V1L patrols."

"Understood. Be safe."

The smog cloud forced me lower and lower until my stomach all but grazed the tops of smokestacks, and I had to loop through the haze to keep an eye on the hero as he jogged down the street. I kept silent, thinking owllike thoughts; if he heard me and looked up, he'd realize he'd been followed, and that'd be the end of this Investigative Episode.

Truth be told, I didn't expect a lot of points here. But it *felt* like a big lead, and I was determined to—

A black SUV pulled up in front of the white-cloaked hero. A door opened, and he stepped inside. As the SUV sped away, I circled over the spot where my quarry had just been.

"Fursona, he's not a hero. He's with 3V1L!"

[Good Thinking! +1 Cunning Point]

I tried to follow the SUV, but it ducked into a tunnel, and I couldn't get low enough to keep up the chase before it vanished. Still, I'd been *right*. The white-cloaked villain *had* been up to something, and I raced south into the University district to meet up with Fursona and tell her everything I'd found.

That meant, of course, that I beat her back to the green room by almost twenty excruciating minutes. Worse, the Investigative Episode hadn't ended yet; I didn't want to get back out there and comb South Poudre for a villain when I knew he'd already vanished, so I spent the time trying to wrap my head around what I'd tell Fursona when she eventually arrived. Maybe a good conclusion would end the Episode with a win.

If not? That'd be fine, too. We'd learned *something*. The ideas crystallized in my head—it all made sense, and I'd definitely been wrong about who the One *L* was. This Investigative hadn't revealed their identity, but I knew, for sure, that Monologue wasn't in action right now. He'd crossed a line with his assault on TU during the Power War, and his lawyers were struggling to get him out of jail.

So if 3V1L was acting this boldly, he couldn't be in charge of it.

But even more interesting was how unbelievably bold the plan *was*.

3V1L, formerly one of the most notorious villain groups in Tokyexico, had walked into the Council of Heroes building through the front door, strolled into the archives, and checked out as much material about themselves as possible. Then, they'd loaded it into a backpack and walked right back out, and no one at the Council building had suspected a thing. How many times had they done this? This wasn't their first, but had they done it twice? Or two dozen times?

It didn't matter. What mattered was that whoever the One *L* was, they were a planner. They knew that the longer information on their minions was outdated, the better it'd be for them, and instead of going after *just* money and territory, they were waging an information war.

And, honestly, that information war was why Fursona and I hadn't had a big win against 3V1L yet—why we couldn't push into the Poudre districts without all hell breaking loose. It felt a lot like we'd been targeted by it. I just couldn't understand *why*.

Not why we were the targets, but why the One *L* would go through so much risk to beat a couple of early minor heroes when they could put that effort into rebuilding into something like their glory days. I stared at the whiteboard in the corner, then shook my head. Some problems didn't need organization; they needed a spark of inspiration instead. And I didn't have that, either.

When Fursona finally emerged from our secret elevator and pulled her helmet off, I had my speech ready. "So, here's what I think. 3V1L is making plays to get rid of information about them. They've got a hench pretending to be a little-league hero or something, and they're raiding the archive for everything they can find."

"Yeah, that tracks. It explains why we couldn't get anywhere in our investigations. The first time, all we had was old material; this time, what new stuff we had was too hole-filled to piece together a clear picture." Bianca sighed. "Help me out of this thing."

As I undid the straps holding her fursuit together, Bianca kept talking. "So, if we can't form a good picture of 3V1L, we need a battle plan that reduces variables."

I groaned. "Not math. Anything but math!"

"Not math." Bianca laughed. "Although Su-Bin could probably help with this if we could enlist her. If we hinted that a certain villain's lair was in a certain location, she'd probably gather up her club and protest there. But . . . actually, probably a bad idea. Has she been emailing you?"

"Yes, she's still emailing me constantly. I'm almost tempted to get on the radio with her just so she'll stop."

"Don't. She can wait. So, we have variables." Bianca went for the whiteboard, and I reached out and grabbed her hand. "What?"

"I don't want a plan on this one. Not yet. Let's work through it and wait for inspiration to hit," I said.

"Okay. Sure. Variables, though. We don't know where 3V1L's bases are, we don't know which Three *V*s we're going to fight on any given day, and we don't know who the One *L* is. That's a lot to work through, and with them blocking out research, we can't Investigative Episode our way through this. We can't patrol in the Poudre districts because they attack us every time we show our faces publicly. So, we have a lot of things we can't control and not much of a way to counter them."

"Yep. We do have some options, though." I took a deep breath and laid out the only plan I had. "This is a stupid plan, but I think if we tried to map all of this out on the whiteboard, it'd be a rat's nest of lines and dots. 3V1L is too big to attack in the Poudre district, and right now, they're stuck there because they're sandwiched between us, Mid-Town, the wall, and Sister Sly. I *know* they haven't beaten her yet because if they had, she wouldn't be our problem anymore."

"Okay. How does that help us?" Fursona asked.

"This next part's going to sound dumb, but hear me out. We need to take pieces off the table. I don't think targeting henches or *V*s is the way to go, though. The fact is that we've had at least two Episodes against 3V1L that have had outside interference. Three if you count the Foothills fight against Livestream, but I think that's a little different."

"So you're suggesting . . ." Bianca trailed off, grinning suddenly. "You're suggesting that Rocko was right to push an Episode with Sister Sly."

"No. I'm suggesting that your so-called archrival is an annoyance, but also that she's forcing 3V1L into a defensive position while they try to deal with her. That's not helpful to us right now. She's dug into that old church, and they can't root her out of it. If we get her out and take away her lair, that'll relieve some pressure on 3V1L, and we can get them to overextend to the north—or, if we're lucky, Mid-Town. They go there, they'll draw some serious major-leaguers' attention, and that'll break them up enough for us to finish them off."

[Good Thinking! +1 Cunning Point]

Bee sat on the chaise lounge; she'd taken to using it even when she wasn't in her fursuits. She shook her head slowly, her grin widening. Then she stood up. "Okay, you're right. This is a stupid plan. But it's the kind of thing that 3V1L might actually fall for because there's no way we'd be so stupid as to ignore them and go after Sister Sly *intentionally*."

"So, you're in, then?" I asked, crossing my fingers.

"Yeah, I'm in," Bianca said as she headed for my apartment door. "Today, we're taking it easy. Tomorrow's the weekend before finals, so let's make the most of it and beat Sister Sly."

[Episode Finished!]
[Investigative Episode: Archive Anxiety - PG]
[Penalties: N/A]
[Episode Finished! +3 of each Style Point]
[Winner Winner! +3 of each Style Point]
[Role Focus: Cunning + Drama - Goal Partially Met: +5 Cunning Points]
[Alias - Understudy] [Archetype - Magical Girl] [Community Rank - 179/523]
[HP 13/13]
[Styles and Skills]
►Archetype Skill - Transformation Sequence
►Combo Skills - Power-Weaving
►Badass (45)
►Cunning (29)
►Drama (31)
►Limelight Barrage 1
►Starlance 2
►Flamboyance (48)
►Signature Skill - Adaptive Armoire 3
►Stored Costumes: (Rainy Day, Copy Cat, Rescue Girl Lucky Star)
►Solar Wing 1
►Quick-Time Change 3
►Improvised Ovation 1
►Grit (35)
►Freeze Frame 1

PART EIGHT

55

Faith, Hope, and Charity

SATURDAY, DECEMBER 13

[Casting Call]
    [Episode: Faith, Hope, and Charity - PG-13]
    [Role: Super Sidekick! Do you accept the role? (Yes/No)]
    [Role Focus: Flamboyance + Badass]
    [Faith, Hope, and Charity: Act One in Progress]

I wasn't surprised when the **[Casting Call]** appeared halfway through North Poudre. A little disappointed that it wasn't *my* Episode? Sure. But not surprised. After all, we weren't striking against 3V1L; this one was all about Sister Sly. And if it was all about Sister Sly, it was also all about Fursona.

She rode on the sailboard, clinging to the steering rail as I navigated through the North Poudre apartments with one hand—the other was on the kangaroo suit's waist to keep her steady and reassure her.

The plan was simple, and as we rocketed toward the old abandoned church's stained glass bell tower, I set the first part in motion. "Ready?"

"Uh, sure. Yeah. Yeah, I'm ready," Fursona whispered. "You can do this, Bee. You can do this."

"If you want to back out, we can try a different strategy. It's really okay," I said, even though having her in the tower would give us a huge advantage. "You can hit the front door with me instead."

"No. I can do it." Fursona gathered her legs under her, let go of the sailboard's handle, and jumped as we zoomed past the bell tower. I watched her fall feetfirst as she screamed into my comms.

CRASSSSH!

[Badass Bomber! +1 Badass Point]

The circular stained glass window just below the bell tower came apart, shattering inward in a hail of sharp shards. I pulled back on the steering bar, leaning against it with all my weight, and did a quick circle of the building. "You good, Fursona?"

"Whew, okay." Fursona laughed, the nervous tension bleeding off through my earbud. "Yeah, haha, I'm good. I'm good. I'm in. Let's do this thing. I'll see you by the pews."

"You got it." I circled one more time and headed for the front door.

For this one, I'd brought every ounce of firepower I could. Understudy, Rainy Day, and Copy Cat, of course, but also Lab Assistant Panic. I wasn't carrying a single Investigation-oriented power, and I didn't have anything to save Extras with. We were hard committed here: win, beat Sister Sly badly enough that she couldn't recover, and let 3V1L off the chain, so to speak. And I had a couple of new tricks up my sleeve, things I'd gotten from that Investigative Episode. They'd help make this quick—at least, I hoped they would.

I landed and pushed the front door open; it squeaked on its hinges as I peered inside.

Sister Sly's henchmen had cleared the room. Every pew was stacked neatly against the walls, forming a long, dark hallway with an arched roof overhead. Across the room, near the podium where the preacher should have been, a few more pews had been stacked to make a wall. I stopped with my head in the door. How had they known we were coming?

"Boss, boss, it's not 3V1L! It's a Magical Girl! We've got a Magical Girl!" a hench shouted, throwing a metal orb my way. It bounced along the floor, skittered to a stop by my feet, and exploded as I threw myself to the side. Chunks of metal bounced off my back and side, gouging holes in my superhero damage that would have been a *problem* if I didn't have any.

[HP 10/13]

I took aim at the handful of henchmen as I came around the corner, then spun and used [**Limelight Barrage**]. Five [**Starlances**] raced off toward their targets, each veering toward a different one, though one unfortunate hench took a pair to the chest. Within a second, the henches—who'd been on the attack a moment before—were down, clutching wounds and moaning about how their boss had made them do it.

[**Dramatic Damage! +5 Drama Points**]

So, that was my first new trick, and frankly, it'd worked great! I stepped into the now cleared room, glancing back and forth in case I'd missed a hench or two. I had, and a gunshot cracked out but whizzed over my head as I ducked. Then I fired a [**Starlance**] toward the gunman, who crumpled in a pile of brown monk's robes a moment later.

[Dramatic Damage! +1 Drama Point]

The attack was going great so far; I'd secured the church's nave, and Fursona should be clearing from the top down. We'd pin her down, one way or another, and then Sister Sly would be out of the picture.

A camera drone—one from Rocko's collection I'd been storing in the green room—hovered overhead, filming me as I headed for one of the unblocked side doors. The next part of the plan would be room-to-room fighting, where a hench could easily ambush me and knock off a few points of superhero damage. So, as I pushed forward, I used **[Quick-Time Change]** and transformed into Lab Assistant Panic.

[**Flashy Fitting-Room! +1 Flamboyance Point**]
[**Steel Yourself! +1 Grit Point**]

"THE PANIC IS BACK, SHE'S READY TO GO!
SO YOU'D BEST WATCH OUT, CAUSE SHE'S READY TO THROW!'"
"Reading your villainous breakdown levels at 34%. Take it easy, okay?" TA-1LZ advised.

"Yeah, whatever, just go stealth and start clearing rooms." I reached toward a device on my wrist that hadn't been there before, then activated **[Set Dressing]**. I'd gotten the power last *year*, but it was niche enough that I hadn't bothered carrying it before. Invisibility was powerful, yes, but working with others weakened it a lot. Fursona and I rarely went stealth, anyway, so it wasn't worth the slot. Usually.

But TA-1LZ and her active camo? That was a match made in hell—at least for our opponents. I shimmered and faded away, and so did my cat.

[**Dastardly Plan! +1 Cunning Point**]

As I crept through the church's offices and storage rooms, I'd occasionally point out a target for TA-1LZ to mow down with rubber bullets and tasers, and every once in a while, I hacked a device when a hench noticed our near-invisible advance. The war cat's Gatling gun whirred on her head, giving away our position in quiet rooms, and I started wondering if I should make a weapon with **[Science has Rules?]**. I'd accumulated a half dozen Cunning Points and a handful of Badass ones by the time we finished the loop around the burned-out courtyard.

But I hadn't found Sister Sly.

I returned to the church's nave in time for Fursona to come down the tower stairs. "How'd it go?"

"Uh, Understudy? Where you at?" Fursona asked, looking around.

I deactivated [**Set Dressing**] quickly, shimmering back into existence. "Yeah, sorry."

[**Good Thinking! +1 Cunning Point**]

"New power?" Fursona asked, glancing at me as I slow-transformed back to Understudy. It took a moment, but all signs of villainy had faded when I'd finished. A good thing, too; I'd been planning on taking over the building once Sister Sly was out of the way. It'd be a perfect lair for Lab Assistant Panic to start her reign of terror, and honestly? She wanted to make her mark on Tokyexico, just like every other vil—

Fursona cleared her throat, and I flushed. "Sorry. No, not new. I've had it since the Episode with Professor Bagges. I didn't find Sister Sly anywhere. I checked every room down here."

"Same for the tower. There were a few monk mooks up there, but mostly just electric gizmos and wiring. I think she's been using the bell tower to gather electricity, though, and storing it below. Maybe she's doing Frankenstein shit or something."

"Okay, then. If she's up to something below, we'll need to stop it *and* beat her. Let's get to it." I headed for the stairs into the church's undercroft. Some churches were more modern, but by the fourth step down, I knew for sure this one was a classic, and that whoever had built it had spared no expense in making it as authentic as possible. As my feet hit the flagstone floor below ancient arched ceilings, I wondered briefly if the whole church had been imported.

"Careful," Fursona said. "We're in a Genius's lair now."

"How do you kno—" A laser wall shimmered into the space in front of me, its grid similar to the grid grenades Sister Sly had used before, and I stopped a few inches from it. Then a turret popped from the ceiling and filled the hall with fire before sliding toward us!

I leaped back as the flamethrower pushed through a gap in the laser grid and then rolled along the ceiling. My wand came up, and I fired a [**Starlance**] at it. It exploded, filling the room with even more fire for a few seconds; I could feel the air being pulled from my lungs as it ate up every ounce of oxygen and then burned out.

[**Dramatic Damage! +1 Drama Point**]
[**HP 8/13**]

I gasped for breath as air rushed back into the hall from the stairwell. Then I shivered once and pointed at the now cleared hall. "Let's keep it moving, yeah? Don't want to get trapped in here before we find her."

"I don't want to get trapped in here *after* we find her, either," Fursona quipped.

I laughed and kept pushing forward, down the hall. As I went, the flagstones under my feet all felt like land mines, but shockingly, none clicked underfoot to reveal a massive killbot or horde of henches. In fact, the whole lair felt quiet.

Too quiet.

I rounded a corner toward a glowing, blue-green light, wand at the ready. This had to be something bad . . . something dangerous. But as I pressed forward, all I could see was a cavernous room filled with different computers. Lab equipment covered every wall, from robotic arms that'd make precorporation Theseus jealous—and postcorporation Theseus laugh at how pathetic it all was—to simple beakers and welding equipment.

And in the center back wall sat a gigantic aquarium. Its round wall loomed over the rest of the room, and a shadow swam back and forth inside. "Is that . . . ?" Fursona asked.

"Yeah. Baby maneater. I can't believe she still has those things." I shivered. The last time I'd seen the thick green-gray scales, sharp teeth, and powerful tail of a maneater, I'd been strapped into a chair—no doubt it was still there, behind the pews in the church's main room. I stopped another shiver with sheer force of will as the small Florida maneater looped around its tank repeatedly, floating serenely on the surface. It'd only be serene until it found prey.

But we weren't prey right now because we weren't in the tank, and the glass had to be thick enough to let Sister Sly work in the lab. So, forcing myself to relax, I started looking around.

[End of Act One: Act Two in Three Minutes]

Fursona held up an empty orb; when she tossed it my way, I could see the holes where a laser grid emitter was supposed to be. I dropped it on the floor and wandered across the lab to a collection of arms and a person-shaped indent in the wall. "What does this look like to you?"

As Fursona hopped over, I checked out the sparking conduits, wires hanging from the ceiling, and the open steel restraints. The whole thing looked way bigger than a person should be. When Fursona finally arrived, she took one look. "Didn't your ex use power armor?"

"Yeah, that's what I thought. He usually worked on workbenches for something this custom, but maybe Sister Sly prefers building while it's standing? Either way, it's not here, so we've missed our shot at Sister Sly. Let's get going. Maybe she's further in, but I doubt it."

I turned toward the wooden door on the room's far side, but a yellow light started flashing before I could get there. A moment later, Sister Sly's voice echoed over a loudspeaker. "Don't get cold feet, Fursona. Or, actually, maybe do!"

The aquarium's walls parted, sending a wall of water crashing toward us—along with the Florida maneater!

56

Maneater!

[Faith, Hope, and Charity: Act Two in Progress]

At least it wasn't full-grown.

As the salty water and smell of rotten meat hit me like twin tidal waves, knocking Fursona and me against the far wall, and the Florida maneater surfed the tide toward us, I got my first good look at its head and realized that its size was the only good news. "That's a fucking laser cannon! Where'd she get that?" I screamed, throwing myself into the murky water.

Bweeeeeeem!

I surfaced, spluttering, a moment later. The undercroft had filled up to our knees in water, and though the lab tables were still above the surface, getting there would be a chore—especially with the maneater thrashing through the water toward us. Fursona tossed herself toward a workbench that was only partially underwater, and I used **[Solar Wing]** to fly toward the vaulted ceiling overhead.

Once I'd broken free from the disgusting water, I whirled to face the—

"Oh shit!"

Bweeeeeeeem!

As I circled, I saw the maneater's head whip around to face me, and the laser sliced toward my face. It only touched my head for a moment, but the beam ate superhero damage like Gourmet going through a beef stick, and I dove for the water to avoid it as it whipped back and forth through the air.

[HP 6/13]

"No air support on this one," I muttered. The speed that its laser beam had flipped to me told me it'd just target anything in the air. Would it do the same for a workbench?

Sure enough, it flipped around, sending its beam slicing through robotic arms and carefully organized tool racks as it whirled to face Fursona, who dove into the water just before the beam made contact. She splashed back to the surface as the red light stopped, then waded toward the maneater. "We've gotta take it out!"

"But how?" I remembered the beating a full-grown one had given Brick House; he'd only survived it because of his ludicrous, Tank-based Grit and sheer guts. Worse, it'd taken him a full Episode to wear down the real Florida Maneater, and he'd been a major-league villain. Did we have that kind of firepower?

"Get it on you!" Fursona shouted, and I fired a **[Starlance]** its way. The scales almost seemed to absorb the blow, and a moment later, I dunked myself into the water as the laser spun toward me.

[Dramatic Damage! +1 Drama Point]

"You two in over your heads?" Sister Sly's voice asked over the laser and the sloshing water. "How about I give you a hand?"

The remaining, undamaged robot arms activated, moving mechanically toward tubes, which dispensed various grenades and devices. A laser grid sprung across the room as one grenade hit the water, cutting me off from Fursona and the maneater. Another flew through the air and hit the water near me, filling the room with fire for a moment before it went out.

"Only Theseus gets to make dumb arm puns!"

I whirled toward the arms, dodging another set of fire grenades that pushed me through the water as the maneater's lasers whipped back and forth across the room, and used **[Improvised Ovation]**.

[Faker with Flair! +1 Flamboyance Point]

As my beam shut down, though, I realized we had another problem. "You didn't think that'd stop me, did you?" Sister Sly said.

"I was kind of hoping, honestly." I jumped toward the laser grid, **[Quick-Time Changing]** into Lab Assistant Panic.

"EVERYONE STOP! THE LAB ASSISTANT'S BACK!
TIME FOR THE GENIUS TO START HER ATTACK!"

[Flashy Fitting-Room! +1 Flamboyance Point]
[Steel Yourself! +1 Grit Point]

I crashed through the beams, the **[Freeze-Frame]** eating the damage and popping back up as TA-1LZ swam for the nearest workbench. Her rubber bullets were already firing at the baby maneater, whose scales bounced them effortlessly, but the distraction gave a window, and Fursona's **[Double-Kick]** slammed home, knocking the gator down into the water.

It surfaced quickly, thrashing water across the room as I lunged for an unlasered workbench. The grenade dispensers were still pushing bombs into the room, and what was left of the robotic arms reached down and failed to grab them. Instead, they floated across the churning water, riding the waves and gradually covering the surface as Sister Sly laughed through the intercom.

I grabbed some tools and an inactivated bomb, pulled myself onto the workbench, and got to work. "Okay, we're, uh, building a Phalanx-Breaker. It's an armor-piercing weapon using resistor-loop physics and quantum-proton generators to break down steel and carbon-fiber ceramics. **[Science has Rules?]**, but I don't have to follow them!"

[Pseudoscientific Mumbo-Jumbo! +1 Drama Point]

The maneater's laser swept overhead twice, and the water looked more like the West Coast reservoirs that used floating balls to keep the sun off the water than a flooded workspace when I finished building my improvised device. Worse, the Phalanx-Breaker wasn't a weapon; it was a bomb! It sat in my hand, ticking down faster and faster.

I had to get rid of it!

As the ticking reached a fever pitch, I lunged off my workbench into the bomb-covered water. The maneater spun to face me, its tail knocking TA-1LZ from her perch and into the pool. The lasers cut across the water, and I threw the Phalanx-Breaker at the same time my head went under.

Bweeeeem!

WHUMP!

As the explosion detonated, the shock wave pushed me to the bottom. A moment later, the maneater's massive claws tore into my lab coat, ripping it to shreds and leaving scratches that would have been lethal across my back and shoulders.

[HP 4/13]

I pushed myself to the surface amid roaring and screaming. The smell of burning wire and flesh filled the room, and as I got my bearings, I saw that the maneater's laser cannon was little more than a twisted hunk of sparking scrap.

"You **[Beep!]** assholes! That cost me a fortune to get! I'll make you pay!" Sister Sly shouted.

The maneater thrashed toward Fursona, who hopped from one platform to another but couldn't outrun the gator's churning legs and tail. Still, she had its attention, and I clambered onto my own platform. I was soaking wet, shredded, and ready to try something new.

I *could* try Rainy Day; I'd almost certainly be able to get a combo off, and with the disgusting water filling the room and sparking wires overhead, it'd probably take out the maneater. But the whole room was soaked, and I couldn't do it without also hitting Fursona and myself. So, cursing, I watched as my partner fled from the maneater, dodging this way and—

WHUMP!

—that.

Something detonated under the gator, sending a spray of water across the whole room, and just like that, I had a plan. "Lead it toward the bombs!" I shouted and started transforming into Copy Cat.

Fursona gasped for breath as she hopped to another workbench, this one next to me. "It's not that easy! The damn thing really wants us dead!"

"I know, I know. Transform!" I said, starting to merge with Tails.

<Transform!>

Another explosion rocked Sister Sly's lab as my familiar and I became one; I couldn't see where it was, but it shook the table I was on, and I fell into the water. The maneater stopped thrashing after Fursona and cut through the water toward me.

Which, unfortunately, was exactly what I wanted it to do.

My transformation finished, and I used **[Leaping Leopards]** to close the gap, splashing down onto its back. My claws barely cut into its thick, scaly hide, and it hissed—the sound gripped my stomach like Iron Fist's fist. But I pushed through the terror and used **[Cat-Scratch Fever]**. My claw sliced into the monster's neck, and its thrashing turned even *more* frenzied as I jumped free and splashed into the water.

[Badass Move! +1 Badass Point]
[Dramatic Damage! +1 Drama Point]

I swam for damp land as Tails counted down from five in my head; I only had that long before the creature's blindness faded and it started hunting again. Four, three, two . . .

I hit the workbench and pulled my wet cat body onto it just as the water behind me erupted.

WHUMP!

The explosion rocked the whole lab again, and sparks rained from the ceiling as conduits snapped from the shaking. The vaulted roof cracked, filling the space with dust, and the maneater lumbered toward me through the dust. The explosion had knocked it back, but it kept coming doggedly.

So, like the cat I was, I ran away.

I used **[Hometown Heroine]** to get the speed to jump from one platform to another, trying to angle the half-blind gator into as many bombs as possible. Explosions shook the room, and tables started to fall apart as bits of the ceiling collapsed onto them. I had no idea whether the church would hold up, but I couldn't stop. Fursona launched kicks into the monster's side whenever it entered a grenade-free stretch of water, then baited it back toward more bombs.

After almost a minute of fleeing and watching [**Cat-Scratch Fever**] tick, the monstrous megafauna shuddered and went still, floating in the middle of the room amidst the rubble and shrapnel.

[**Good Thinking! +1 Cunning Point**]

"Is it . . . dead?" Fursona asked.

I shrugged. "I don't know. There's a gap in the ceiling. I can fly us out of here, but we should hurry before the whole place collapses. I'll get into Understudy."

"Got it." Fursona waded toward the maneater as I spun. It lay there, unmoving. My back faced it, and as it left my vision, I saw its battered jaw snap shut around my sidekick's leg! A second later, it dragged her under!

It started rolling even as I landed on my platform, already spinning into a [**Limelight Barrage**]. The thing had my girlfriend, and it rolled back and forth, dunking her and dragging her to the surface as it spun over and over. Whitewater sloshed over the tables and benches. Then the [**Starlances**] started firing.

[**Dramatic Damage! +5 Drama Points**]

The gator hissed, letting Fursona go and thrashing in the water. It went still again as she hopped toward my platform, shaking. I couldn't tell if it was from the water or the maneater's attack. "Thanks," she chattered through our earpiece.

"No problem." I summoned my sailboard and launched us through the ceiling before something else could go wrong in the lab.

[**End of Act Two: Act Three in Three Minutes**]

As we broke through into the church's sanctuary, where the tank and maneater dunking chair had been, I angled for the door. The walls had cracked, and it wouldn't hold up against much more fighting—at least, not the minor-league kind or the explosives Sister Sly loved. Plus, if any more bombs went off below, I didn't want to be trapped in the rubble.

We blew through the door and landed on the asphalt outside, rolling across it. I recovered onto a knee and both hands while Fursona's tattered fursuit took three more rolls before she got herself under control. "You good!?" I shouted.

She picked herself up. "Let's not do that again. Swimming with the sharks is one thing, but the first rule of finding swimming holes in Tortuga West is that you don't mess with a maneater."

"Yeah. Jungle Jim probably would have told us that if we'd asked." I brushed off my Costume as a camera drone swung over the groaning church, recording its damaged facade. "So, all that's left is Sister Sly, then. Where is she?"

"Right here! Game over, Fursona!" A set of power armor crashed through the church's wooden doors and landed on the asphalt, its jet boots melting tar.

[Faith, Hope, and Charity: Act Three in Progress]

57

Melting Tar

I rolled my eyes; Sister Sly's head poked out of the power armor's helmetless torso, the fox suit's eyes staring back at me. A few pieces of cloth, almost like a nun's habit, hung from its bulk and covered the solid-looking steel armor, and attached to her left shoulder was a launcher; I couldn't tell if it was for grenades or rockets, but it looked a lot like Theseus's arm. "I'm so sick of people thinking it's game over. We haven't even gotten started," I said.

"You're right!" Sister Sly leveled her launcher and opened fire. Orbs flew from the Swiss cheese openings, slamming into the asphalt and exploding as Fursona and I scattered. Laser grids popped up, only to vanish as the barrage went on and on, grenades detonating and destroying the grid generators almost as quickly as Sister Sly could launch them.

I found myself pressed against the church's wall with nowhere to go. The explosions carpeting the street raced toward me, and I used **[Quick-Time Change]** for Lab Assistant Panic, rattling off a rap and launching myself through the fire and flames as **[Freeze-Frame]** ate the damage for me.

[Flashy Fitting-Room! +1 Flamboyance Point]
[Steel Yourself! +1 Grit Point]

As the bomblets ripped apart the church's facade, the whole thing creaked ominously, and I watched TA-1LZ and Fursona dash toward the power-armored villainess. She turned smoothly into Fursona's kicks, lashing out with a servo-strengthened arm and bashing my partner into the street.

A wall of tasers bounced off her armor, though one or two stuck in the gaps between the steel plates, and she flinched back. TA-1LZ leaped onto a dumpster and then a fire escape across the street from the ruined church. I nodded; the high ground would help here.

But all we'd accomplished was disrupting her; she didn't look hurt, and the armor didn't have a scratch. If we wanted to beat Sister Sly, we'd have to peel her suit like an orange.

Then I used **[Speed-Hacker]** to attack Sister Sly's suit from the inside. The green lines of code flashed by in my goggles, and a moment later, the grenade launcher started firing again. Its shots bounced off the asphalt at the fox nun's feet this time. She backpedaled hard, staring at me.

[Good Thinking! +1 Cunning Point]
[Playing with Powers Beyond Comprehension! +1 Drama Point]
[Warning: Hunting Dog Antivirus Activated!]

I'd seen this show before and stopped the **[Speed-Hack]** instantly. If Sister Sly had an antivirus set up, she knew what Lab Assistant Panic could do—either that or she was paranoid. Her armor's breastplate and leg armor were blackened and charred from the explosions, with marks burned into them where the lasers had sliced into them.

Fursona hopped back into battle, landing a crushing **[Double-Kick]** on the power armor's chest, and something buckled. Sister Sly cursed and spun to stomp after the kangaroo, firing a few more grenades into the street before a clicking sound cut through the explosions. "I think I got her!" Fursona shouted.

"Like hell!" The shoulder-mounted grenade launcher fell away, and a pair of blades popped from the power armor's wrists. Its boots lit up with fire, and she catapulted through the air toward Fursona as TA-1LZ pelted her with tasers in a barrage so thick their wires looked like bridge cables.

I went for another **[Speed-Hacker]**, even though I knew the antivirus would stop it quickly, and, shockingly, it stuck. Her boots sputtered for a moment—not for long, but for long *enough*. Her leap turned into a flailing flop, and she caromed off the asphalt and into the church's facade.

[Good Thinking! +1 Cunning Point]

The bell tower wobbled precariously, then started tilting over the street below. Fursona hopped away, and I grabbed TA-1LZ by the Gatling turret, dragging her away as a horrible creaking sound filled the air.

Something snapped inside the building.

Suddenly, the roof fell inward as the tower disintegrated, toppling down onto Sister Sly. Her armor slid up, covering her head in a makeshift helmet as the dust cloud engulfed her. I definitely wasn't taking the church for Lab Assistant Panic's lair! But the real disaster hadn't even started yet.

The collapse happened in slow motion, and I was sure Rocko would add it in for dramatic effect. Even when the tower was halfway to the ground, I could still see the shape of the old church in the bricks. They hit the road, shattering into shrapnel or bouncing like bombs. I rolled away from one, but another slammed into my back, driving the air from my lungs in a painful whoosh.

I tried to get to my feet, but something heavy drove me back down. Heavy . . . and fuzzy.

"I got you—oooof!" Fursona said as bricks rained down around us. The collapse lasted way longer than any building collapse had a right to, but when the last brick exploded to reddish dust around us, it couldn't have been more than five seconds—maybe ten.

Fursona pushed herself off my back, offering me a hand, and I took it before slowly transforming back to Understudy.

"Think we got her?" Fursona asked. She started walking toward the giant pile of rubble where Sister Sly's power armor had been, then stopped. "Nope. Not falling for that a second time this Episode."

I landed as the music and lights faded, wand at the ready and Tails trailing behind. "Let's check it out. She might be alive under there, and we should save her."

As we got closer, a few bricks moved, and over the sound of settling rubble, I could hear a slow beeping that gradually sped up . . . faster and faster. It almost sounded like a self-destruct beep. But she wouldn't do that, would she?

Beepbeepbeeepbeeepbeeeeeeeeeeeee!

I threw myself away from the rubble pile as a muffled explosion tore open a hole in the brick pile. From inside, a thin rope with a hook snaked out, and a moment later, Sister Sly flew through the air overhead. "Nice try, Fursona, but you've only beaten my first form!"

"Why do you even care so much about this?" Fursona asked as she hopped toward the fox nun's landing spot. "You're not my rival; you're a girl in a fox suit. You don't even care about the Poudre districts!"

A laser grid sprang into the air, slicing through the sky overhead to box off the camera drone and leaving Fursona and Sister Sly to fight one another. I relaxed on the far side; it'd fade in a moment, and I'd be back in the fight when it did. Until then, Fursona could handle unarmored Sister Sly. She'd done it before.

In fact, really, this was fine.

I didn't need to be involved in the takedown here because it wasn't my show. This was Fursona's, and the best thing I could do was play sidekick—both for her and, honestly, for me. I'd have plenty of time to take the starring role as soon as 3V1L took the bait here, so for now, I'd let Fursona have the limelight.

Still, the moment the laser grid faded, Sister Sly got the **[Limelight Barrage]**. Every single **[Starlance]** followed her perfectly, and her explosives' smoke covered their approach until they'd closed too much to dodge. Hit after hit landed, knocking her onto her back in the middle of the street as the camera drone dipped in for a good look.

[Dramatic Damage! +5 Drama Points]

Fursona landed on the villainess a moment later, **[Double-Kick]** driving the air from her lungs, and I circled around to cut off her possible escape route.

Then, suddenly, an explosion ripped through the air as the church's ruins convulsed again.

"That's my cue! Time to go!" Sister Sly said. She shimmered and disappeared. Fursona reeled back like something had punched her in the face, and a moment later, she hit the asphalt. She popped right back up, looking back and forth, but another invisible blow hit her in the chin, and she stepped back, looking confused.

I stared at the smoke-filled corridor, then **[Quick-Time Changed]** back to Lab Assistant Panic. I couldn't find Sister Sly, but I could make it impossible for her to find me. That way, when she made a mistake, I could take advantage of it.

"Careful, Understudy. 83% toward a villainous breakdown from your earlier actions," TA-1LZ whispered as she shimmered out of sight. A moment later, I joined her with **[Set Dressing]**.

[Good Thinking! +1 Cunning Point]

Fursona had weathered the rain of invisible blows. As TA-1LZ snaked left, I circled right, trying to find anything I could use to track down the villainess. Fursona's head whipped back and forth, looking for her enemy as she pulled herself back together. The dust and smoke from the collapsed church and explosives whirled in the air around her.

"Catch!" Sister Sly shouted, and a grenade appeared in midair. It flew toward Fursona, who threw herself to the side as it exploded in a burst of flame that scorched the street and melted its tar. I was hardly watching her, though.

My eyes were glued to the swirling dust where the bomb had come from. It was moving, but not with the breeze. Instead, it was heading straight for me!

I took a deep breath, trying to see the point where the dust and smoke parted, and threw myself toward it.

[Good Thinking! +1 Cunning Point]

I hit something, and we both crashed to the ground. My shoulder slammed against the curb with a splitting pain that superhero damage didn't fully mitigate. A moment later, Sister Sly and I shimmered into existence, and Fursona leaped through the air. Her feet swung around as Sister Sly looked up in horror.

[HP 1/13]
[Badass Takedown! +1 Badass Point]

She tried to push her invisibility button again, but even as she vanished, I wrapped myself around her legs, pinning her in place. Fursona fell like a wrecking ball, crashing down on Sister Sly with a bone-crunching thud.

[Episode Finished!]
[Episode: Faith, Hope, and Charity - PG-13]
[Penalties: N/A]
[Episode Finished! +3 of each Style Point]
[Winner Winner! +3 of each Style Point]
[Role Focus: Flamboyance + Badass - Goal Unmet]
[Alias - Understudy] [Archetype - Magical Girl] [Community Rank - 174/523]
[HP 1/13]
[Styles and Skills]
▶Archetype Skill - Transformation Sequence
▶Combo Skills - Power-Weaving
▶Badass (54) (Skill Roll Available)
▶Cunning (42)
▶Drama (58) (Skill Roll Available)
▶Bit-Part Barrage 2
▶Starlance 1
▶Flamboyance (58) (Skill Roll Available)
▶Signature Skill - Adaptive Armoire 3
▶Stored Costumes: (Rainy Day, Copy Cat, Lab Assistant Panic)
▶Solar Wing 1
▶Quick-Time Change 3
▶Improvised Ovation 1
▶Grit (44)
▶Freeze Frame 1

As the emergency sirens filled the air and Fursona talked into the camera drone, getting the final words in for the Episode, I switched back to Understudy and sat on a pile of half-shattered bricks. Sister Sly wasn't conscious, but she'd be okay—probably. More importantly, she was out of the picture, and in a very, very public way. That'd be ideal for Fursona and me. 3V1L would take notice; with their rival out of the way, it'd only be a matter of time before they overextended, and when they did, we'd be there to take advantage.

An officer picked up Sister Sly and carted her off toward a waiting patrol car, and Fursona hopped over to me. "Thanks, Understudy! I really appreciate it. Now, take us home."

"I just did what needed to be done," I said, summoning the sailboard and waiting for my partner to climb on. Then we took off toward Walnut Tower, and I rolled my Skills.

[50 Badass Credits Used. Rolling Skill!]
[50 Drama Credits Used. Rolling Skill!]
[50 Flamboyance Credits Used. Rolling Skill!]

[Rank-Up! Limelight Barrage 2: Each Starlance in the barrage has a 10% chance to remove a buff power from its target]

[Rank-Up! Doom Ball 2: Can use Doom Ball a second time per act]

[Rank-Up! Improvised Ovation 2: Duplicates low-rank powers, giving a second use of the power]

"You did a lot more than that, babe," Fursona said. "It felt great to be the lead there for a little, and to have a villain of my own instead of whoever you wanted to fight."

"It's not a big deal," I said, even though it was a big deal to her. I had to play it cool, at least until we got home. The camera drone was still following us, after all, and until it was offline and plugged into its charger, I couldn't say much more.

I could feel Bianca thinking it, though, as she turned on the sailboard and wrapped her arms around me, letting go of the steering bar. "I know what we can do when we get home," she said through my headset, and I groaned. I couldn't flirt back without the camera drone catching me. Even if it was an open secret that Fursona and I were a couple, confirming it on camera was too much for me.

So I didn't reply—at least, not how I wanted to. "Yeah, we've got to get to work on our finals. You and I are going to write so many papers!"

58

So Many Papers

TUESDAY, DECEMBER 16

We lay in my bed, the covers a jumbled pile on the floor. My breaths lined up with Bee's chest pressed against my back; I'd given up on ever being the big spoon, and instead just enjoyed the afterglow as Bee's hands played with my tummy. The smell of sweat and green apples hung in the air.

"Hey," Bee said. She kissed the back of my neck, and I shivered. "Morning, babe."

Damn, had it been a fun way to wake up.

I struggled out of her grasp enough to roll over and stare at her blue eyes, curly hair, and shoulders as she breathed just as heavily as I was. "Good morning. I should get dressed." But I didn't move, and she pulled me back into her grasp like an octopus. There wasn't much I could do but let it happen, and it's not like I wanted to get up, anyway.

"Okay, I'll stay just a bit longer."

"Good," Bee said, moving her hands to rub my shoulders as I melted into the bed. "We'll have plenty of time for that essay later, and who knows when 3V1L will make a move, but right now, you're all mine!"

"Sure am, honey." I grinned stupidly. My whole body felt like putty, like she was molding clay with her hands, and when I tried to return the favor, she laughed and pushed my hand away. "What?"

"Babe, you're not great at giving massages," Bee said. "You don't push hard enough in the right places."

She pushed against my shoulder, and I gasped as it popped. "Holy shit."

"Yep. So how about you let me do my thing? *You* already did enough." She rolled onto her knees to get a better angle, and I turned my head to stare up at her. Her muscles rippled under her skin as she stretched. I shivered again; I had a feeling in the back of my head that wouldn't go away, and even though most of me had melted, I couldn't help but worry.

"What?" She paused, looking down at my back, and her fingers started moving across it until she found the knotted place to the right of my spine. "Keep your head straight. It'll be easier to push on you that way and get things into the right spot. Now relax, babe. Let me do my thing."

"Nothing. Just . . ." I gasped as she pushed on my shoulder again, this time driving knuckles deep into it and grunting from the effort. The sound made me snort, and I quickly kept talking as quickly as I could piece thoughts together. "I don't know, some funny feeling."

"Something I'm doing? Or something I did?" Her hands danced across the knot in my back. It loosened, and I melted even more than I already had.

I shook my head and talked into the pillow. "No, you were amazing. It's . . . I'm not sure. Forget it. I already have."

"Liar," Bee said. She stopped for a moment, and I made a whining sound. "Fine, if it's really nothing, we'll let it go."

Her hands kept their dance up for another minute . . . two minutes . . . until I'd lost track of time and didn't even notice when they stopped. I'd melted into her again, listening to her breath tickle my ear, and everything felt right with her arms around me again.

So why wouldn't that feeling leave?

It took almost two hours to get partially dressed, and Bee still wasn't wearing anything but a bathrobe she refused to tie shut, but we'd finally started to work on our Team Compositions essay. Because everyone in the class was partnered with at least one classmate, Dr. Mays had let us work on a single essay together as long as we were okay with sharing the grade.

So Bee sat at my laptop, typing dutifully away as I cooked breakfast in my underwear and a T-shirt. The apartment's thermometer was a little low, but both of us were still too glowed up from morning sex to care, and *I* wanted to make breakfast for Bee *myself*. I could have transformed into Ramsey Fieri, but honestly, it was bacon and eggs, pancake mix, and orange juice—even I couldn't screw that up.

"So, heard anything from Vigilant Vow or Honeycomb?" Bee asked, leaning over the cushions.

I stirred the eggs; they'd become soft, pale yellow, and at this point, I just had to keep them from burning, and they'd be fantastic. "No, not yet. Do you think they're dating?"

"Obviously. That seems to be what happens when two supers work together." Bee grinned.

I rolled my eyes and went back to the eggs and bacon. She was right. I'd ended up in relationships with the first two supers who'd given me the time of day, and she'd landed on her first. "It's got to do with being able to be honest. The secret identity is a big secret, and sharing it's really intimate or something, so it's logical that you'd trust another super with it and not an unpowered one."

"Yeah, sure. Or supers are just hot."

"Uh-huh. That definitely helps, believe me, but my ex was—"

"A dweeb? I am aware." Bee rolled her shoulders, shrugging the robe off one, and returned to typing away on my keyboard. As she clacked away on our introduction, I shoveled the eggs onto two plates, added the bacon, and flipped a pair of pancakes onto each of them. But the funny feeling was back—or maybe it hadn't left—and as I called Bee over and she dug in with an appreciative sound, I thought maybe I'd placed it.

"Would you still love me if I was unpowered?"

Bee snorted. "That's what you've been weird about all morning? You're worried about *that*? I mean, really? Yeah, if you were unpowered, I'd still love you. You might even know about Fursona. But we'd probably have to hang out at my place because you'd probably be living in Ash Hall or Cottonwood's lower floors. They don't give places like this to Extras, and they definitely don't let them keep them for over a year. So, that might be a dealbreaker. It's so nice here, and I . . . haven't been keeping up with my cleaning."

"Thanks, babe," I snarked. The place *had* been cleaner before Bee moved in full-time, but I'd at least gotten her to keep her laundry in a single pile and put her dirty dishes in the washer every so often. Hanging out at the Outback Stakeout Zone or in her room—which I still hadn't seen—might've been a dealbreaker for *me*.

When I told her that, she laughed and drowned her poor pancakes in syrup. "Yeah, yeah. It's a mess, and I'll have to get it cleaned up so I can host parties every once in a while—if you call having Cam and Su-Bin over for games a party. They're not really the liveliest. Do we know anyone else?"

"You said you had friends after the window incident last year," I said. Then I set my fork down. "Wait. You said regular students don't get places like this. Su-Bin's been here, and she knows I'm not rich enough to afford it myself. Do you think she suspects . . . ?"

"Nah. We were friends before your whole drama with her, and she probably just thinks it's a bureaucratic oversight or something. Those happen all the time, honestly. There was one guy who lived in the dorms three years ago, even though he'd graduated. I think your secret's safe with the school."

"Okay." Bee kept eating as I stared at her. "You're sure you'd still love me if I was—"

"Is this like the worm question?" Bee asked. "You need to stop. If I was gonna ditch you, I'd have done it last year. You could retire, and as long as you let me keep superheroing around, I wouldn't mind one bit."

"Thanks again," I said, this time more seriously. But as I played with my food, the weird feeling didn't lift. If anything, it pressed in more and more.

Bee noticed. She put down her fork, popped a last bite of bacon into her mouth, and stood up. "Annie. Couch. Now."

"Come on. Finish your food first. This isn't going anywhere."

"No. I can't eat when you're moping across the table. It's unsettling. Couch. Now." She grabbed my hand and dragged me off to the couch, where I waited until she sat down. The moment she did, I flopped down, resting my head on her lap while she played with my hair.

"Okay. This isn't really about me, Su-Bin, or Vigilant Vow. That's not why you're moping. So what's up?"

I let her fiddle with my hair for a while until she cleared her throat impatiently. "Okay, it's the same problem, but in reverse. When we, uh . . ."

"Had sex?"

I blushed. "Yeah. When we were in bed this morning, I felt like Anika for a while. No one cared about my superpowers or what I did with them. You didn't ask me to be Copy Cat or anything weird like that, and I didn't need to run around as Understudy. We got to be Bee and Annie, and it felt really nice. But then, when we stopped, and you started pushing on my shoulder . . . it's tight because when I tackled Sister Sly, I landed badly. Everything I'm doing is Magical Girl Understudy, not Anika DuPont.

"I don't think the Third Power War is helping, either. It feels like the things I did freshman year to be normal, like going to Ilneat talks and the job fair or stuff like that? That's all work now. If we're not in an Episode, we're on patrol, or studying for the degree program. It's a lot to manage," I finished.

"And Dr. Ayers's resources aren't helping, huh?" Bianca asked. When I nodded, she closed her eyes. "Okay. How about this? We've got a week of finals and the big finish against 3V1L, then the semester and the season are both over. Let's finish strong. Afterward, we'll find three or four clubs we want to be involved with. No superhero stuff during break, or during club time. We try to make friends who don't even like heroes but aren't APPEAL fanatics. That way, you can be Annie, I can be Bianca, and we can see what being a normal college kid feels like. Deal?"

I nodded. Bee's leg felt warm against my neck. "Deal. Just one week. We can do one week."

"Yep. One week."

My phone buzzed. I ignored it because it was on the kitchen table across the room. Instead, I let Bee keep messing with my hair, shivering sometimes when she rubbed against the spot on my neck below my ear. Whatever was on it, it'd be more stuff to do as Understudy—more fights to win, more people to save—and I really, *really* needed to be Annie for a little longer.

Then something exploded outside. "I guess we should check on that, huh?" Bee said in a voice filled with fake lightness.

"Yeah." I got up and grabbed my phone. It wasn't a text, but it *was* an email from TU.

Subject: EMERGENCY: Power War Possible Campus Incursion
To All Students
A joint assault by several major-league villains is currently underway near Tokyexico
University. Drs. Mays, Jackson, Tennyson, and Mindstorm are responding. Due to the
interruption, all finals are postponed until further notice.
All unpowered students and superpowered students mid-minor and below:
- Stay indoors.
- Avoid contact with active superheroes
- Do not engage McHammer, Lord Destructo, or any of their subordinates
- Do not attempt to attend classes until further notice
All high minor and higher superpowered students:
- Be on alert
- Hold your current position and wait for instructions from the Council of Heroes or
Tokyexico University Administration
Thank you for your cooperation,
Helen Barber
Vice-President of Student Services
Tokyexico University

I sighed. "Guess there's one more thing to deal with?"
"Yep," Bianca said, heading for the green room. "Time to suit up."

59

Suit Up

"Lord Destructo and McHammer couldn't *possibly* be this stupid," Bee said as we stood on top of Walnut Tower and watched the "fighting" in the distance. Not that there was much in the way of combat. The Mays/Tennyson/Jackson combo kept shutting down Lord Destructo's lieutenants, and only the fact that we hadn't *seen* either of the big vils was keeping them from suffering the same fate. Instead, they had Mindstorm tracking them down.

A very, very angry Mindstorm.

I could feel the psychic rage bashing against me, and I knew every student on campus could, too. If Mindstorm found them before Mays and Jackson, McHammer and Lord Destructo were in trouble—and not the small kind.

I nodded. "Yeah, this is dumb, even for villains. There's nothing to be gained here and everything to lose. So why did they do it?"

"You're not thinking about an Investigative Episode right now?" Bee asked. Her eagle helmet was off, letting her feel the cold December air on her reddening cheeks.

I shivered in my dress. "No. For once, I want to stay out of it. Getting between Mindstorm and Lord Destructo is not in our best interests."

"No, it is not."

We went back to watching the fighting. It wouldn't be long; Mays and Jackson were slow in that they could only take out one supervillain at a time, but they were efficient. I watched them teleport in, shut down a lieutenant with a shield the size of a car, and teleport away with the shield. A moment later, a familiar blue-suited superheroine slammed into him, knocking him to the ground.

"That's Springlock! TUSSA's getting involved! Come on," I said, using **[Solar Wing]**. Bee pulled on the Eagle-sona helmet, and we took off toward the fighting.

[Casting Call]
[Episode: Power War: Back with Avengeance - R]
[Role: Campus Crusader! Do you accept the role? (Yes/No)]
[Role Focus: Drama + Grit]

We dove toward the fighting as Milo's red-skinned wrestling moves subdued a second lieutenant, who dropped her blue-glowing staff. I accepted the **[Casting Call]** and landed behind the formerly shield-wielding man, who started running.

[Power War: Back with Avengeance: Act One in Progress]

His flight didn't last long, though. As he wove through the trees toward wherever he was trying to go, Springlock flew by my head and crashed into his back. A moment later, Fursona landed in front of him, screeching. The fighting didn't last long after that, and the villains were both down within a minute.

"Thanks," Milo interpreted as Springlock signed. I could read a little of it, but Milo was way faster than me. "We've got other problems, though. Sara's trying to mobilize TUSSA. The Student Supervillains are up to something!"

"Well, let's go!" I said. "We've got to get back to essay writing and stuff, so if we can mop this up fast, that'd be great."

"You got it. We'll head toward Mister Felsic, and from there, we'll loop past the Grant Building. You two go for Roth Arena, check it over real quick, and we'll meet at the Perkins Building," Springlock signed. "The rest of TUSSA is rallying there— at least, everyone minor-league and up is. The others are holding position in their bases or at the TUSSA Cave."

"Why didn't we know about this?" Fursona asked.

Milo shrugged. "Did you check your phones?"

"No." My face flushed.

"Well, there you go." He grabbed Springlock's hand, and a moment later, the two of them catapulted through the air, leaving red and blue streaks for a moment.

Fursona grumbled through our comms. "I mean, seriously? How could we expect TUSSA to get involved in this? It's not like the administration didn't just tell us to stay out of it."

"When has that ever stopped supers?" I asked. "Come on. Roth Arena. Let's go."

The gigantic white dome and sparkling glass walls of Roth Arena loomed over Fursona and me as we flew toward the stadium where we'd fought Theseus and Gourmet last year. As we got close, though, I realized I'd much rather have dealt with the two minor-leaguers. A figure in a massive set of armor crashed through a window, hammer swinging wildly, and a second one followed. A moment later, the psychic anger I'd been feeling since Fursona and I got on the roof doubled in pressure, then doubled again.

Windows blew out across the whole building, shards of glass freezing in the air. And, through them, Mindstorm stalked toward the two major-league villains. The glass swirled around her, then disappeared as she waved with one hand. "Boys, you're in . . . over your heads. You're going to lose them for this, too."

Fursona circled the three major-leaguers from a hundred feet up while I hovered just above that. The air had stilled until I could hear every spoken word—and a strange whistling sound, too. Suddenly, the whistling increased in pitch, and more windows blew out. "You caught me at a bad time, so you're lucky. I'm . . . full illusionist today, so your minds are safe."

The two hammer-wielding vils started flinching and trying to defend themselves from an invisible attack, and I realized two things.

First, Mindstorm hadn't made the glass shards disappear. She'd just made them invisible with an illusion.

And second—as an invisible shard sliced across my cheek and I yelped in pain— we were collateral damage!

[HP 12/13]

"Come on!" I dove for the shattered windows, Fursona hot on my tail, as the whirling glass storm sliced into our superhero damage. My arms and face burned even through the shield, but we pushed through as the storm reached what felt like a crescendo, dipping through the shattered windows and landing in the stadium's atrium.

[HP 11/13]

I rolled to my feet; if Lord Destructo and McHammer were here, their lieutenants might be, too, and we'd be in for a fight. But I couldn't see anyone except for a statue of the school's ram mascot, and *that* wasn't trying to kill us. "What the hell?" I whispered.

"Let's check out the underground," Fursona said, picking herself up and checking her wings for damage. "Not too bad. [**Fursonal Furcefield**] is getting good!"

We hurried through the building, heading for the secret tunnels the student supers used—and for the subway entrance. That *had* to be how the vils had gotten here undetected. It *had* to be.

But a familiar face was waiting for us when we got to the subway station.

Two of them, actually. Kind of.

"Understudy." Iron Fist nodded once, glancing at me. "And Fursona. Just who we wanted to see."

The devil-helmeted woman standing next to him grinned. "We timed this perfectly. We can take care of business here and get out before the rest of the school's heroes know we're here."

"No. The deal was that you'd help us reclaim our spot on campus, and in return, we'd—"

I cleared my throat, readying my wand as Fursona spread her wings for take-off. There wasn't time to wonder why one of 3V1L's *V*s and the SSS's leader were working together. I had to take advantage and hit before they did. "You're here for me, huh? Well, I'm right here, so let's do this thing! [**Limelight Barrage**]!"

A handful of [**Starlances**] ripped across the subway station, punching into Iron Fist one after another as he spun to dodge. Fursona took off and screeched. The sound echoed and bounced across the battlefield and ripped across his armor.

[**Dramatic Damage! +5 Drama Points**]

Then, with a battle cry, he threw himself toward me. His fist punched into my stomach, folding me over it and slamming me into a wall. At the same time, a reddish-gray aura whipped out from the *V*'s hand, snagging Fursona by the wing and holding her in place.

[**HP 9/13**]

My partner's screech echoed off the tile walls hard enough to crack them and blast the *V* back toward the turnstiles. She slid on the floor, ending with one hand up and the other on the floor, and a wavering red-gray shield took most of Fursona's attack.

Then I lost track of the fight between Fursona and the *V*. I had Iron Fist to manage, and, yeah, I'd fought him before, but this was *different*. This time, help wasn't coming.

This time, I had to beat him on my own.

I used [**Power-Weaving**]. Either I'd bait a [**Combo-Breaker**], or I'd get a ton of free damage if I could execute right. Either way, it'd be another step toward victory, and I'd already hit hard with [**Limelight Barrage**].

Then, as the fist slammed me into the wall again, I used [**Quick-Time Change**] and [**Freeze-Frame**]. The force of the blow launched me into the tile, but then I slid right off the reciprocating arm, landing on the floor a full six inches below Iron Fist's iron fist, which I moved my head away from.

[**Flashy Fitting-Room! +1 Flamboyance Point**]
[**Steel Yourself! +1 Grit Point**]
[**Floating Points: 1 Flamboyance**]

I used [**Wind Front**], the force of the gust picking Iron Fist up and tossing him away from me—and sending a whirling cone of wind through the subway station. Over the wind's roar and Fursona's screeching, we heard a clattering, chugging sound. The train was approaching!

[**Badass Move! +1 Badass Point**]
[**Floating Points: 3 Flamboyance, 1 Grit**]

Fursona flapped across the battlefield, a gigantic red aura tendril following her. It crashed into a pillar, and shards of concrete erupted from its far side.

Then Iron Fist sprang at me. As he flew through the air with his fist reeled back, I used [**Ride the Lightning**]. Iron Fist ate the lightning and kept right on coming, his fist crackling with energy even as my electricity ripped through him.

[Electric Lightshow! +1 Flamboyance Point]
[Power-Weaving! +6 Flamboyance, +3 Grit, +1 Badass Point]

His fist slammed into me, sending me sliding across the yellow line, across the edge of the platform, and into the oncoming train's path!

[HP 5/13]

I stood up, stomach aching from the blow, and used [**Quick-Time Change**] to return to Understudy. [**Rejuvenation**] healed me up, but before I could use [**Solar Wing**] to leap into the air, the sound of screeching brakes filled my ears. I wasn't going to make it!

[Flashy Fitting-Room! +1 Flamboyance Point]
[Rejuvenation Active: HP 10/13]

So, instead of trying to fly over the train, I jumped toward it.
WHAM!

[HP 4/13]

Getting hit by the train felt like . . . getting hit by a train. The air rushed from my lungs, and my fingers scrabbled for purchase on the metal grate. I found myself hanging from the engine, a few inches above the screeching wheels, as sparks shot from the tracks. One slipup and I'd be gone, and I didn't think four superhero damage would save me from an entire subway train!

I'd only get one shot at this. I had to get inside, where it was safe, and right now, the train was definitely "attacking" me, right? So maybe . . .

I used [**Quick-Time Change**], this time landing on Copy Cat. She was the toughest Costume I had, and if [**Freeze-Frame**] didn't save me from the attacking train, I'd need every chance at survival I could get. I squeezed my eyes shut as the world stopped, and Tails and I merged.

[Flashy Fitting-Room! +1 Flamboyance Point]
[Steel Yourself! +1 Grit Point]

Then something big passed through me. I opened my eyes and locked gazes with a horrified-looking train operator, then whisked through the engine car's back door and into the first passenger one. Then, suddenly, I was solid, rolling down the aisle and bouncing off Extras' legs.

The passengers wouldn't stop screaming as I picked myself up, brushing off my fur and sprinting for the stopping train's back door. "Sorry, excuse me, superhero business!" I shouted, ducking and weaving as I used [**Hometown Heroine**] to push myself faster and faster. I had to get back to the fighting. I had to—

CRASH!

I burst through the back of the train, the whole world going slow-motion. Iron Fist was sprinting toward the train, fist already starting to rev up again. Behind him, Fursona had the *V* in her talons, though the entire train tunnel had filled with a red-gray aura that bashed against her repeatedly. She wasn't going to be able to hold the *V* much longer.

I launched myself toward Iron Fist with [**Leaping Leopards**], using [**Doom Ball**] before he could get a grip on me, and my claws ripped into him. He whirled, but as I went flying, my claw lashed out at his face, and I used [**Cat-Scratch Fever**]. He rocked on his feet, the blind effect giving me a window to get some distance, and I got ready to hit him again.

[Badass Move! +1 Badass Point]
[Badass Damage! +3 Badass Points]
[Dramatic Damage! +1 Drama Point]

He teetered, tossed himself over a rail onto a maintenance walkway, and collapsed. A moment later, the *V* yelled, "Fuck!" and sent a wave of red-gray magic our way. It rippled through the tunnel, and when it passed, she'd vanished toward the TU stop.

"Come on," I said, wincing as I popped my neck. It was time to put an end to 3V1L's ambitions!

[**End of Act One: Act Two in Three Minutes**]

60

3V1L's Ambitions

"What's a *V* doing here?" Fursona asked as we dashed back toward the subway station. Iron Fist was out; I'd collected his surrender, and he wouldn't be a problem anymore.

I grinned. "Probably playing right into our plan. I didn't think they'd try something like this, though. The professors will mop up the *V*s, and we'll be able to make a play on the One *L* when whoever's left runs away."

"But the professors are busy with McHammer and Lord Destructo, right?"

"Let's find out." I leaped over the turnstiles and headed up the stairs into Roth Arena's atrium.

Wherever Mindstorm and the hammer-wielding vils had gone, they weren't outside. The dead, brown grass was covered in shards of glass, and the trees nearby had shining slivers jammed into their bark. It looked like it'd be a nightmare to clean it up, but Fursona and I didn't have time to deal with it even if we'd had the powers to help.

"Okay. Wherever she is, she's not our problem right now. This whole thing's set up way too well. Using major-leaguers to draw off the professors, then swinging in. 3V1L's gotta be looking for us, right? If I were looking for us, where would I look?" Fursona asked.

[Power War: Back with Avengeance: Act Two in Progress]

"Walnut Tower? That's where Professor Panic went to find me," I said.

Fursona nodded. "Good enough. Let's go."

We took to the air and hurried toward my secret base. After all, if Peter had figured out where Understudy lived without ever visiting, it wouldn't be out of the question for the One *L* to know, too, and if that was the case, we had all *sorts* of problems. Twelve stories of student housing, and having my secret identity outed—all that was bad. But worse, Su-Bin still lived downstairs, even if she spent more time at Cam's place these days.

I wasn't sure I wanted to help President Pak, but Su-Bin was a friend, and I couldn't have *either* of them angry at me—at least not angrier than they already were.

So the moment I saw the *V*, whose number I still didn't know, closing in on my home, I opened fire. The first **[Starlance]** punched into her back, and before she'd fully turned to face us, my second caught her in the side, driving her to a knee.

[Dramatic Damage! +1 Drama Point]
[Dramatic Damage! +1 Drama Point]

She rolled as Fursona slammed into the ground where her head had been, leaving talon-shaped craters on the cold grass, and I continued strafing and firing **[Starlances]** for a moment. Then someone screamed from inside Walnut Tower.

"You got her?" I asked Fursona. She nodded, circled, and dove again, pulling up short and screeching. The sound blast ripped across the *V*, and I took off toward the roof.

I landed in a roll, rushing toward the stairs. There were twelve floors' worth of students between me and whichever *V*s were attacking Walnut Tower, and I had to keep as many people safe as possible. As I sprinted through the green room, passing the empty camera drone chargers, I cursed under my breath. "Rocko, you're getting your damn finale!"

Then I burst out the door and into the hall, punched a window to create a plausible way I could have gotten up here, and started running down the stairs. "Villain attack! Stay in your rooms! If they get above this floor, head down as fast as you can!" I pounded on the doors, letting students know where they'd be safest.

I made it to the eighth floor, still far above where Fursona was—hopefully—kicking the *V*'s ass. Posters lined the walls about practicing safe sex, not drinking on campus, and a dozen ones with information about clubs I'd never bothered signing up for. If I could get through this, I was going to try out chess club or something calm like that. Boring and relaxing; that was going to be me from now on! I took a breath and turned around—

—right into a squad of 3V1L henches. They leveled their weapons, but I fired off a **[Limelight Barrage]** right into their faces before they could shoot. Their front line crumpled like newspaper, and the rest turned and ran, yelling for help from a *V*.

[Dramatic Damage! +5 Drama Points]

Okay, so we had at least one more *V* in the building. I took a deep breath and followed 3V1L's henches; if push came to shove, I could probably evacuate more people with Rescue Girl Lucky Star, but I'd rather give it a good fight before trying that game. Protecting the Extras would be a hell of a lot easier than teleporting them all out of here one at a time—even if that'd be *so* many Drama points.

The elevator opened on the seventh floor, and out stepped a big man in an ill-fitting 3V1L mask. He looked a lot like Cam or Waterspout, a big hulking villain, and a few henches ran past him to get to the elevator, but they stopped when he grabbed one and shoved him back toward me. "Come on. The One *L*'s offering power to any hench who takes down Magical Girl Understudy, plus a big reward to the *V* whose squad gets it done, and we're gonna make it happen. Now let's go." He cracked his massive steak of a neck and stepped forward.

I started retreating to the stairs. "Why do you care so much about me?" My wand flicked out, firing a **[Starlance]** into the *V*, but he took it with a grin—a familiar one.

[Dramatic Damage! +1 Drama Point]

"I don't. The boss does. He really hates you." The *V* stepped aside, and a hench with a pistol took aim, but I caught him with another **[Starlance]** before he could fire, and he crashed back down the stairs, taking a few henches with him in a tangle of limbs.

[Dramatic Damage! +1 Drama Point]

But the massive *V* didn't seem to care. He kept coming, walking up the stairs like nothing I could do would actually hurt him, even though the bruises from the shots' impacts were already spreading. Then, when my foot missed a step and I stumbled, he closed the gap like it was nothing. "Come on! Let's finish this!"

His fist crashed into my nose, and I thought it was the end. Instead, it barely moved my superhero damage, even though my head recoiled back.

[HP 3/13]

He laughed. "That's it? This is going to take a while, isn't it?" Then he cracked his knuckles and kept coming at me as I backed up. Another **[Starlance]** caught him, and once again, he rolled his shoulders and kept walking—not running, just walking. I'd only met two Tanks this ridiculously tough, and one of them was Waterspout. So, if I wanted to beat someone as impossible to damage as Brick House, I'd need a change of tactics.

[Dramatic Damage! +1 Drama Point]

I turned and ran. How had Brick House almost lost to the Florida Maneater? He'd taken an incredible amount of damage, but eventually, he'd gotten worn down, right? So I could keep doing the same thing. But I didn't have *time* for that, and if he kept pushing me back, it'd mean his henches could take more hostages—put more people at risk.

That wasn't acceptable, so the next time I reached a landing with a window, I threw myself out of it and used **[Solar Wing]** to stop my fall. Then I turned midair and shouted back into the broken window, "You want me? Come and get me. I'll be downstairs!"

The moment I hit the ground, I slow-transformed to Rainy Day. I'd have a few minutes before he got to the bottom, and I wanted as much HP as I could muster to fight him. I used **[Virga]**, letting the healing rain down on me as the red-gray aura and Fursona's screeches filled the air behind me.

[Medic! +1 Cunning Point]
[HP 5/13]

Then, I transformed into Understudy. I'd have time, surely. The music and light show started, and as I spun midair, the hulking *V* slammed through Walnut Tower's double doors. He ran toward me at a pace that felt both glacial and far too fast. Choral music swelled, my tiara landed on my head, and my feet hit the ground.

[Rejuvenation Active: HP 10/13]

He hit me a split second later, before I could spin and fire a **[Starlance]** his way. It felt like getting hit by the train or a hench's white van. His mass drove me into the hard ground, and I felt my sore shoulder scream in pain, but the actual superhero damage was shockingly low.

[HP 9/13]

I used **[Improvised Ovation]** and grabbed him, somehow hoisting him over my head while still on the ground and slamming him down. He hit the ground like an earthquake, and we both got to our feet. I brushed the mud from my shoulder as a camera drone hovered to one side. "When we're done here, you can tell your boss you tried with your one phone call."

[Faker with Flair! +1 Flamboyance Point]

"When we're done here, you won't be in any shape to make one," he retorted. Then he rushed me, and I fired another **[Starlance]** into him. The increased damage to tough targets *had* to be hurting him, but he barely seemed to notice.

[Dramatic Damage! +1 Drama Point]

Then, as his arms closed around me for another tackle, I used **[Quick-Time Change]** and switched to Copy Cat. His arms passed through me and he hit the dirt behind me as Tails and I merged.

[Flashy Fitting-Room! +1 Flamboyance Point]
[Steel Yourself! +1 Grit Point]

Before he could get up, I'd already leaped through the air with **[Leaping Leopards]**, and instead of having a Magical Girl wrapped up in a bear hug, he had a very, very angry Copy Cat to deal with. I scratched, activated **[Hometown Heroine]**, and scratched some more.

[Badass Move! +1 Badass Point]

The *V*'s hand wrapped around my neck, and as his grip tightened, I used **[Doom Ball]** and scratched the absolute *shit* out of his arm from the elbow to the wrist. He grunted in pain and waved the arm—and me—around, but didn't let go. "You have no idea who you're messing with, do you?"

[Badass Damage! +3 Badass Points]
[HP 6/13]

"You're . . ." My vision was going gray, and I couldn't think right. I tried to suck in a breath and used **[Cat-Scratch Fever]**. He jerked back and let go, and the air hit my lungs in a rush, only to get driven right back out as I bounced off the concrete bike path below me. I gasped for breath. "You're just a *V*!"

"Just a *V*? No, Understudy. I'm much more than just a *V*. I'm the First *V*, and today, I've got all the power to tough this fight out."

My vision swam, wavering back to something approaching normal, and I saw the First *V* breathe in deeply, then set his body. His eyes stopped watering, and he squared his shoulders at me. "Now, Understudy, do the boss a favor and die."

He stepped toward me, and I got ready to fight as best I could without Costume switches. A moment later, Tails started going crazy in my head. *<Duck! Duck! Nya-ow!>*

I ducked, and as I did, something big flew over my head. Eagle-sona screeched and crashed into the First *V*, talons out.

61

Talons Out

With Fursona in the fight, I found myself full of energy. I'd been playing defense against the hulking First *V* since he'd shrugged off my best attacks, but now? Now, I had a real chance of meaningful damage.

Unfortunately, I was stuck in Copy Cat, and my best powers were down. But I could still chip away at him. I threw myself back into the fight, claws lashing out as **[Hometown Heroine]** activated, giving me a little more speed. I scratched across the big man's back, then kicked off, driving my claws into his shoulders as he whirled to face me.

[Badass Damage! +1 Badass Point]

"Did you beat the other one?" I yelled between Fursona's screeches. Her wings beat, pushing the First *V* away from me for a moment and allowing me to catch just a little more of my breath, though my throat still burned from his grip.

"Yeah, easy! Once I got her off-balance, she went right down! Almost too easy!"

"Okay, let's take this guy down!" I used **[Leaping Leopards]** and sprung through the air. The First *V* was ready for it, though, and a meaty fist hit my side just as my claws lashed out against his neck, leaving thin red lines that blossomed into bloody cuts. I bounced off a tree, rolled on the grass, and sprang back to my feet, dusting off my Costume.

[HP 5/13]
[Badass Move! +1 Badass Point]

Then, before I could react, the First *V moved* toward me. He lashed out with his fists and feet while I retaliated with scratches, looking for an opening. Blows rained down on me, and I kicked out at the big guy's leg, but he backpedaled somehow.

[Badass Damage! +1 Badass Point]
[Tough Kitty! +1 Grit Point]

[Tough Kitty! +1 Grit Point]
[HP 4/13]
[Badass Damage! +1 Badass Point]

As we swung back and forth, my head grew clearer and clearer, and suddenly, I realized something. I'd fought this villain before—and not once, but a couple of times. He moved like Jungle Jim, took hits like Brick House, and even had the same physique; the only thing missing was his age. The First *V* was clearly younger and maybe a touch faster.

But if he was a younger version of Brick House, that meant he'd make more mistakes than the real deal would. His massive, meaty fist swung toward me, and I ducked. An oak tree's bark exploded behind me, and I took advantage of his stunned expression to roll to the side—just as Fursona screeched at him.

[Good Thinking! +1 Cunning Point]

The constant attacks were starting to wear down the First *V*; the next time he went for my throat, I danced back, and he stumbled. That was all I needed; I lashed out and shoved with all my might, then pounced on the villain the moment he hit the ground. His massive fists lashed out at me, but Fursona hit the back of his head, and after another vicious exchange of blows, he went limp.

The fur and feathers settled, and I picked myself up, then helped Fursona off the First *V*'s chest. She brushed herself off. "Holy crap, they made him tough!"

"Yeah, he's almost a carbon copy of Jungle Jim." I explained what I'd seen fighting both of them up close, then switched to Rainy Day, used **[Virga]** at a safe distance from the unconscious villain, and rotated slowly to Understudy.

[Medic! +2 Cunning Points]
[HP 6/13]
[Rejuvenation Active: HP 11/13]

"Okay. That's two *Vs* down. Do you think they full-committed to this? All three *Vs*?" I asked Fursona as we took to the air.

She nodded. "Probably. We still don't know how they got McHammer and Lord Destructo involved, either."

"Lucky coincidence, maybe?" I glanced toward the Student Union Building, where the sounds of heavy fighting echoed over a wailing alarm. Judging from the volume and the eight Mindstorms hovering over the building, that wasn't *our* show. "I'm curious if the One *L* is on campus today."

"Sure is," a man's voice behind me said, and I whirled around, expecting to see a power armor-clad villain walking toward me.

Instead, I saw a woman in an 3V1L mask topped by the most enormous bun of platinum blonde hair I'd ever seen and a man with a staff with a pentagon on its tip. I groaned. "Okay, which one of you is the *V*?"

"Both of us," the woman sneered, undoing her scrunchie. "I'm the Third *V*."

"And I'm the Second," the man said, "at least for the moment."

"Until you get replaced?" Fursona asked. "What kind of life is that? And didn't we just fight the Second *V*?"

The woman's hair fell free, draping down until it hit the floor and pooled around her like that one cartoon princess. She snapped her fingers, and it separated into three sections, each braiding itself into thick ropes of hair. "It's the best life I've ever had! I get to be the Third *V* today, and in a couple of weeks, I'll be the Second or First when it's my turn again."

I couldn't remember any villains with crazy hair in the few articles we'd read, and we definitely hadn't fought a *V* with that power. Her braids snaked around, whipping like silver snakes as she walked toward me, and I fired a **[Starlance]** at the villain. It hit her, and she flinched back, but her braids whipped out—right at my wand hand!

[Dramatic Damage! +1 Drama Point]

At the same time, the staff-wielding *V* slammed it into the ground, and a massive demon shimmered into being in front of him. Fursona cut off her dive, swerving wildly to avoid the thing's outstretched claws. She caromed off a tree and hit the ground, rolling in a cloud of feathers, then took off again.

I backed off as the hair-powered villainess moved forward; neither looked like Grit vils, so we just had to wait for an opportunity to take them down. Braids thrashed out at me, and I returned fire. Every **[Starlance]** hit, and even though the Third *V* kept a braid back to block, I couldn't help but feel like she was a step or two slow. "What's wrong? Bad hair day?" I taunted, firing another **[Starlance]**.

[Dramatic Damage! +1 Drama Point]
[Dramatic Damage! +1 Drama Point]

"No, this is harder than it looks," she responded, slamming all three braids down onto the grass as I rolled to the side. They swept along behind me, and I used **[Quick-Time Change]** and **[Freeze-Framed]** the damage, switching to Rainy Day.

[Flashy Fitting-Room! +1 Flamboyance Point]
[Steel Yourself! +1 Grit Point]

She stumbled as the expected hit failed to happen, off-balance. Then, before she could retract her hair tentacles, I used **[Wind Front]** for some space and started up a **[Thunderhead]** to get a little more. The storm cloud built up as the Third *V*'s hair whipped back, jerking her neck painfully. I blinked at that; surely she would have learned how to manage her own power's drawbacks?

[Badass Move! +1 Badass Point]
[Pause for Effect! +1 Drama Point]

The demon summoner had, somehow, not managed to finish Fursona off, either. In fact, she looked like she was winning, outmaneuvering the gigantic demon and getting screeches and knock-backs in on the *V* himself. He summoned a horde of tiny flying imps, but Fursona shrieked, and they fell apart into wisps of . . . magic or something.

Meanwhile, the storm was building.

I ducked one hair tendril, then another, but the third slammed against my stomach, dragging me toward the villainess. She laughed. "Getting the *hang* of this yet? I sure am!"

"That's awful," I said as she squeezed me tighter and tighter. Another braid wrapped around my arm, pinning it to my back painfully, and together, they started dragging me across the quad's grass and cement. I tried to get another **[Wind Front]** off, but my arm was pinned too tightly. My face bounced off the cement, and I winced. Part of me wanted to switch to Copy Cat and give her more than she could handle.

[HP 5/13]

Instead, I let the storm build as she dragged me closer and closer. The villainess grinned. "Guess you're all hair-tied up, Understudy. Gift-wrapped for the boss and everything. I'll get the first permanent spot for this!"

"Hey, what does—" I slammed into the concrete, gasping in pain. "Ow! What does static do to hair?"

"What?"

"Let's find out! **[Ride the Lightning]**!"

[Electric Lightshow! +1 Flamboyance Point]
[Thunderstruck! +1 Drama Point]

The air filled with electricity, and I directed it all at my foe. She couldn't exactly dodge without letting me go, and the lightning ripped through all three braids, surging into her. She flew backward, hair frizzing out as the braids fell apart, and I **[Quick-Time Changed]** back to Understudy and fired another **[Starlance]** her way before she could attempt to recover.

[Flashy Fitting-Room! +1 Flamboyance Point]
[Dramatic Damage! +1 Drama Point]

"What's the matter? Too many split ends? I hear conditioner helps with that!"

She didn't move and said nothing except a groan. I watched to make sure she wasn't going anywhere, and when she stayed down, I turned my attention to the Second *V.* Fursona had it mostly in hand, though; he didn't seem any more familiar with his powers than the Third *V.*

Come to think of it, *most* of the *V*s hadn't been super-competent. I fired a pair of [**Starlances**] at the Second *V*, and a moment later, Fursona's screech knocked him to the ground. He didn't move, and the massive demon she'd been dodging faded away to nothing. She landed next to the vil, made sure he was out, and wandered over to me. "That's all . . . four of them? Aren't there only supposed to be three *V*s?"

[End of Act Two: Act Three in Three Minutes]

"Yeah. Something hasn't been right with the *V*s. The sword *V* was competent, but the martial artist one fell apart when things started going haywire. The cowboy gun-fu expert was solid, but the one with the robot just summoned the baton-bot and called it good. She barely did anything else the whole fight. Surfboard *V* wasn't that tough, either. And now these four. Something's off here for sure."

"What do you think?" Fursona asked.

"I think . . ." I wasn't sure what I thought. But in the end, it didn't matter. We'd beaten the *V*s, which meant that the One *L* was on campus without his enforcers. The war with 3V1L was over. We just had to corner him, and it'd be done.

A convoy of black SUVs worked its way across the quad, their wide bodies covering the entire bike path as they slowly approached. Fursona popped her shoulders; I could hear it through the wings. I grinned. "I think the time has come to end 3V1L."

"You got it, boss-girl," she said through our comms. My smile grew wider, even as something exploded near the Student Union Building and a super flew overhead, screaming.

The SUVs pulled to a stop, one after another, and the doors opened, disgorging a horde of henches. A moment later, a man got out of the middle one. Even in his 3V1L helmet, I recognized him. The three-piece suit was immaculate, right down to the lapel pin on its collar and name tag I couldn't quite read across its right breast pocket, and even as he snapped his briefcase closed and set it back inside, I realized exactly what had happened, and why there were so many goddamn *V*s on campus today.

"Well, well, well, if it isn't Magical Girl Understudy," The Agent said, lips stretched into a smile that was anything but friendly. "You've been a thorn in my side for a year now, but with Jackson and that stick-in-the-mud Mays distracted, now you're all mine. Henches, you know what to do."

Act Three started, and as the henches started showing superpowers all around me, I threw myself into battle. One way or another, The Agent was going down!

62

Going Down

[Power War: Back with Avengeance: Act Three in Progress]

There was a moment—one perfectly calm moment before the quad outside of Walnut Hall exploded in a tide of superpowers—where it felt like it was just The Agent and me standing twenty yards apart, glaring at each other. My fists tightened, and I could hear my heartbeat pulsing in my ear. This . . . this *asshole* had revived 3V1L, ruined the Poudre districts *again*, and now he was on *my* campus, hunting *me*, because I'd won a race for the minor leagues that *he'd* been trying to rig!

What was his game? Did he get some sort of satisfaction from messing with minor-leaguers? And what was he trying to prove—and to who? All these questions ran through my mind and out the other side, replaced with one crystal clear thought.

It wasn't *right*. And I was ready to do something about it.

I raised my wand to fire a **[Starlance]** his way, and *that's* when all hell broke loose.

As my wand fired, every super in the quad moved—and there were at least twenty! The pink-and-blue bolt sliced through the air toward The Agent, who took it straight in the chest. But I couldn't follow up because a pair of eye lasers ripped through a tree nearby, and branches rained down around us!

[Dramatic Damage! +1 Drama Point]

Fursona got airborne but found herself in a three-on-one battle against a bat-winged vil, one wearing a jetpack, and one who hung out on the ground firing beams at her. I couldn't exactly help, either, because everywhere I turned, a *V* was already there, walling me off, firing a wave of green-tinted water at me, and catapulting through the air like a bullet.

I couldn't stop moving to take a breath. I *definitely* couldn't stop to attack for more than a second. All these villains—so many powers—all directed my way. I used **[Limelight Barrage]** to fire into a whole group of vils, trying to carve a path to The Agent. They fell like bowling pins, scattering every which way. Some got up. Others didn't, but I didn't have time to figure out why.

[Dramatic Damage! +1 Drama Points]

A *V* in a red cape and spandex that let me see *way* too much of him landed in front of me with a sword; I ducked the first swing, ate the second, and used [**Improvised Ovation**] to copy the attack. My *two* swords hit him before he could parry, knocking him into a tree.

[HP 4/13]
[**Faker with Flair! +1 Flamboyance Point**]

My heart thumped in my chest, and I let myself grin. We'd taken out a half dozen *V*s already! We were making progress toward The Agent. I used [**Quick-Time Change**] and [**Freeze-Framed**] an eye-beam and two powered punches, shifting to Rainy Day with the Itsy Bitsy Spider dance. A series of explosions rippled across the battlefield, and I threw myself behind a tree as bombs rained down from above. "Fursona, you got that?"

[**Flashy Fitting-Room! +1 Flamboyance Point**]
[**Steel Yourself! +1 Grit Point**]

"Yeah, one sec. Kinda busy here!" Fursona dove toward the gyrocopter responsible for the bombs, screeching and slashing at the unprotected pilot.

The Agent laughed. "You can't possibly think you'll win this, can you? I've got numbers and another two carloads of henches where those came from. You should just give up and save us all the time and energy." I wasn't sure, but there almost seemed to be a tinge of nervousness in his voice.

The henches didn't give me time to process it, though.

I used [**Power-Weaving**] to build toward *something* that'd break the tide of *V*s pressing toward me, then launched a [**Thunderhead**] into the air. The cloud started spreading overhead, sparks of lightning hopping through it as it expanded, but before I could set up a proper combo, a pair of villains rushed toward me in near-identical suits.

[**Pause for Effect! +1 Drama Point**]

I blasted them aside with [**Wind Front**], knocking them across the quad, and whirled around, only to face a trio of attackers with nunchucks and sais. How many henches *were* there? Two of the nunchucks hit me, spinning me around and knocking me to the side.

[**Badass Move! +1 Badass Point**]
[Floating Points: 1 Drama]
[HP 2/13]

I needed to shift. I needed to activate **[Virga]** and heal Fursona and me. I needed to fight the henchman swarm.

But I couldn't do all three. I took a running leap, throwing myself toward The Agent. If I could take him out, would it shut down the henches? Maybe. But even as I used **[Quick-Time Change]** to switch into Understudy again, I realized what *had* to be happening. These *V*s were *too* easy!

[Flashy Fitting-Room! +1 Flamboyance Point]
[Rejuvenation Activated: HP 7/13]
[Floating Points: 3 Drama, 1 Badass]

When we'd fought one *V*, or even two, they'd usually been tough. Maybe not always on our level, but challenging enough. They'd fought like they understood their powers, and they'd had superhero damage to match. Even earlier today, the first two *V*s had been brutal, but the second set had barely been a match for us; they'd done damage but folded pretty quickly compared to not-Brick House and the red-and-gray witch. The Agent's power had to be spread thin with twenty on the battlefield at once.

So, when I landed, I didn't go for The Agent. Instead, I waited, dodging vils' attacks and waiting for the right opportunity. **[Thunderhead]** finished, and I fired an empowered **[Starlance]** toward The Agent, who ducked behind a Tanky-looking vil. Unfortunately for the *V*, she wasn't ready for the full combo and smashed into her boss then bounced off the SUV's door.

[Dramatic Damage! +1 Drama Point]
[Thunderstruck! +1 Drama Point]
[Power-Weaving! +6 Drama, +3 Grit, +1 Badass Point]

That still wasn't my window, though. I fired another **[Starlance]**, this time toward one of the ninja-themed *V*s, and rolled to dodge a blow from a Bruiser whose muscles bulged unrealistically out of their armor. Then, suddenly, I saw it: an opportunity.

An Elementalist near the back of the swarm was powering up some sort of watery tornado; had he taken the power from Waterspout or some other super? It didn't matter. What *did* matter was that I could copy it. I used **[Improvised Ovation]**, started up my own tsunami-in-a-tube—only one, sadly—and the pink-blue water grew taller and taller. Then, when I couldn't hold it anymore—and as *V*s rushed me from all sides—I released it.

[Faker with Flair! +1 Flamboyance Point]

The tide slammed into the assembled hench-*V*s, shoving them into trees and ripping dirt and grass from the quad as it exploded outward. A moment later, my feet touched mud, safely behind the exploding wall of water. The Elementalist's tornado exploded a moment later, and I had to use [**Solar Wing**] to dodge the incoming deluge. Then, almost as quickly as it started, the power stopped.

Not faded away or dissipated. Stopped.

A pair of familiar heroes had landed in the center of the chaos. Dr. Mays stood in his full glory, furiously reading a package of some alien product as fast as he could while Dr. Jackson strode toward The Agent in her salmon-colored pantsuit and shimmering silvery bubble. Every other hero, villain, and Extra unfortunate enough to be anywhere near Mays was stuck in place, unable to move a muscle, and every power had frozen, too.

Every power except one.

As Dr. Jackson reached him, The Agent's face changed from a sneer to a glare, and a similar silver bubble shimmered around him as his finger pressed down onto his name tag. I tried to gasp but couldn't; Dr. Mays's power was supposed to be unbeatable! Suddenly, The Agent's briefcase was out of the car, open, and a pistol was in his hand.

BANG!

Dr. Jackson went flying backward as the pistol went off. She hit the ground hard, convulsing and clutching a wound on her shoulder. The Agent closed his briefcase and touched his name tag. As he did, I got a good look at the Ilnean letters on it. "Emergency teleport for Thornberry, now!"

And, just like that, he vanished into thin air.

Dr. Jackson was down, and Mays couldn't stop the advertisement without releasing the swarm of hench-*V*s. And, to make matters worse, I couldn't figure out where The Agent had gone. He'd vanished without a trace; not even his pistol had been left behind as evidence. I tried to crane my neck to get a better view, but *I* definitely couldn't break Mays's power.

He stopped talking, and I ran toward Dr. Jackson, already shifting into Rescue Girl Lucky Star with [**Quick-Time Change**]. Powers froze around me, then started, a dozen supers bursting into action, but I ignored them. The moment I reached her, she wrapped a hand around my ankle, gripping it like Fursona's talons until I could feel her nails gouging my skin. Her eyes closed, but she kept breathing. Then Mays kept going, locking the battlefield down around us.

[**Flashy Fitting-Room! +1 Flamboyance Point**]
[**Steel Yourself! +1 Grit Point**]

"Okay, we're going to get this figured out," I said, putting my hands on the wound. I looked back, but she was still awake, so it couldn't be lethal, right? How had it even punched through her superhero damage? None of this made sense, and my head was spinning. I needed more information.

Dr. Jackson couldn't talk. I couldn't ask Dr. Mays. And no one else could move. That left me with one option. I had to get Dr. Jackson out of here and drop her somewhere safe so Mays could let us finish the fight.

I activated [**Noncombatant Teleport**].

Nothing happened. The circle didn't appear below Dr. Jackson. She didn't disappear.

I tried [**Audition Notes**], but they came back empty. And then, cutting slowly through my panic, I realized that her power made her immune to everyone's powers unless she allowed it, and while she was unconscious, she couldn't allow it!

I only had one option if I wanted to save her. So, carefully, I wiggled my hand between my ankle and her fingers until they were meshed in mine. Then I hoisted her over my shoulder as best I could and started running.

I ran for a long time.

For what felt like hours. Days, even, with Dr. Jackson bouncing on my shoulder and gasping painfully with every step. Was I doing the right thing? Or was I making it worse? I couldn't tell. A camera drone followed me, humming along and recording her pained face, but I didn't stop.

In the end, I probably only ran for a minute or two before I got to the Student Union Building. The glass windows were blown out—all of them—and a *very* angry Mindstorm stood in the ballroom, looking down as a pair of police officers escorted McHammer and Lord Destructo away. They both looked *way* worse for wear, covered in cuts and bruises, but I didn't stop to talk with them. They were lucky to be alive, after all.

Instead, I jogged through the field of broken glass, shards crunching against my boots.

I hadn't even made it inside when a *second* Dr. Mindstorm appeared next to me, looking less angry and more worried. "What happened to her? Get her inside. We've got a medical station going until the ambulances get here again."

"The Agent. He shot her right through Dr. Mays's power," I said.

Dr. Mindstorm's face shifted again, this time from worry right back to anger. "Where'd he go? I can beat him!" Her fists balled.

"He's gone. I don't know. Off-world or something," I mumbled. "He had a whole army of temps. They're by Walnut Tower."

"Got it." Before I could say anything, Dr. Mindstorm vanished. *All* the Dr. Mindstorms did. I tried to tell her about Fursona, Dr. Mays, or what I thought was happening with the hench-*V*s, but I couldn't. All I could do was stagger into the Student Union Building—which was shockingly intact—and join the line of injured students and faculty.

But somewhere in the back of my head, there was another thought. That the TU administration was going to pin this all on me.

63

All on Me

With Dr. Jackson safely handed over to the med students and professors, and the camera drone in tow, I headed for the Student Union Building's door. All I wanted was to get back to the action, figure out where The Agent had disappeared to, and end this Episode. I was still furious—no, I was *more* furious—with him, and minor league or not, I wouldn't stop until he was done. Not just exposed as a slimeball, but *done*.

But I hadn't even gotten to the shattered doors when that dream was dashed.

[Episode Finished!]
[Episode: Power War: Back with Avengeance - R]
[Penalties: N/A]
[Episode Finished! +3 of each Style Point]
[Call it a Draw! +2 of each Style Point]
[Role Focus: Flamboyance + Badass - Goal Partially Met: +10 Flamboyance Points]
[Alias - Understudy] [Archetype - Magical Girl] [Community Rank - 172/523]
[HP 7/13]
[Styles and Skills]
►Archetype Skill - Transformation Sequence
►Combo Skills - Power-Weaving
►Badass (26)
►Cunning (51) (Skill Roll Available)
►Drama (46)
►Bit-Part Barrage 2
►Starlance 1
►Flamboyance (43)
►Signature Skill - Adaptive Armoire 3
►Stored Costumes: (Rainy Day, Copy Cat, Rescue Girl Lucky Star)
►Solar Wing 1

▶Quick-Time Change 3
▶Improvised Ovation 1
▶Grit (63) (Skill Roll Available)
▶Freeze-Frame 3
[50 Cunning Credits Used. Rolling Skill!]
[50 Grit Credits Used. Rolling Skill!]
[Rank-Up! Virga 2: Rain produces additional healing for allies only]
[Rank-Up! Freeze Frame 2: The time-stop lasts two seconds instead of one]

It wasn't a win, that was for sure. The campus was trashed, and my stomach sank as I surveyed the damage. Between Roth Arena's windows, the fighting outside of the Student Union Building, and the now-finished battle at Walnut Tower, I had no illusions that this was the second most expensive fight TU had seen since I started here. Worse, it had definitely hurt the most people.

How had that happened? It wasn't supposed to have been like *that*. The fight was supposed to have happened in Mid-Town, not at TU.

By the time I got back to a tunnel and sneaked my way back to my secret elevator, I knew Fursona and I had miscalculated. But that wouldn't happen again. I rolled my skills as the elevator carried me to the green room.

I waited in silence for the elevator with the camera drone hovering in my face. Hopefully, Bee would be there. We had some serious strategizing to do, and we had to do it before Rocko called.

Because the Ilneat *would* be calling. A draw wasn't a win, and they'd be . . . a bit peeved . . . that we hadn't won our season finale. I needed to make a plan to handle that. I needed *Bee* to help me make a plan for that.

The elevator door opened.

"Is she okay? Holy shit, he used a *gun*! Heroes don't use *guns*! What the hell happened there?" Bianca said. She was halfway out of her Eagle-sona Costume, and I helped her with her buckles before untransforming myself.

"The Agent's got some sort of power-breaker. He cut through Mays's power like it was nothing. It felt a little like when Professor Bagges ignored Monologue, but that shouldn't be possible. We have no leads, no *hunches*, even, about where he went, and he tried to kill Dr. Jackson. For all I know, he set up McHammer and Lord Destructo so they'd draw the professors' fire, but he came here for me, and I don't know what to do about that. He came *here* for me. Not to campus, but here!" The words wouldn't stop coming.

"We've gotta deal with him, but we watched him try to murder Dr. Jackson. *Everyone's* going to see that. He didn't try to take her out with powers or in a flashy way. It wasn't good TV. It was just him shooting her! If he hadn't run away, what would have happened? He had everyone beat right there, and we couldn't do anything to stop him. And now we've got nothing."

"Okay. Deep breath, Annie. We got a draw this time, but we'll win the next one. The Council of Heroes will know he's not to be trusted; he'll finally be blacklisted from everywhere in Tokyexico—at the least. It's a draw, but it's really a win. Less than a half dozen of 3V1L's henches got away, and without The Agent, they'll be powerless."

"Alright." I took a couple of shaky breaths. "Alright. We've got another problem, though. Rocko's going to—"

My phone buzzed.

"—that," I finished awkwardly.

We both stared at the phone awkwardly. It rang and rang, upside down, on the table, then went silent. Fursona—Bee—spoke first. "We'll tell him it's a win. 3V1L's a long-term villain for us, and even though we've struck a blow against them today, defeating them wasn't likely. Even Golden Goose couldn't do it, after all. We're going to need more than a couple of months."

"What about The Agent?"

"He doesn't matter. He's not in our rogues' gallery. The One *L* is, and *they've* disappeared. If The Agent shows his face in Tokyexico City again, the professors will be on him."

"Yeah. Yeah, Mindstorm was ready to hunt him down just now. That's a real threat, even to a metapowered super like him. And he's probably the weakest against someone like her, so maybe she'll deal with him. But if not, we need a plan. We need something."

"We have something. We're dealing with The Agent's minions while he's gone, and that'll be a blow to whatever rebuilding he wants to do. We're going to beat him in public perception, too. We can put the whole assault on him, and even APPEAL can't say that Magical Girl Understudy caused all this damage—not when so many cameras saw Mindstorm do it. We're okay, Annie. Take some breaths. We're okay."

"I'll toss us on speaker when Rocko calls again, then," I said, taking those breaths and rehearsing the impromptu script over and over in my head. It'd work. It had to.

The phone rang again, and I picked it up quickly. "Hello, Rocko."

"Anika, what's going on over there?" Mom's voice echoed in the green room, and the plan fell apart.

As I finished explaining everything that had happened, Mom cleared her throat. "Your dad and I are driving over tomorrow."

"We sure are, Dot," Dad said.

Bianca and I looked at each other, and I broke into a smile through my tears. I'd finished ugly crying a couple of minutes ago, and now the tears were the quiet kind. But then I shook my head. "You can't. The Power War—"

"You know who I was. I'll have you meet me at the gate with my suit if I have to, but they won't stop me. Make sure there's room for us. We can sleep on your pull-out couch if we have to, but there's no money for a hotel, so unless you're paying for it, we're sleeping with you, Anika." Mom's voice didn't leave any room for argument, so I made a sound of assent as she kept talking. "Besides, we missed Christmas last year, and I'm going to guess you're not coming here?"

"No. We're going to be too busy after this." It was true; I was willing to bet I already had emails from TU's administration about my involvement here. I'd be up for suspension or on behavior probation again; either that or Mindstorm's unretirement had taken the spotlight off me.

"Well, your business will have to wait until after Christmas, Dot," Dad said. "We've been worried about you. You don't call as much as you used to, and it sounds like you've been superheroing a lot. Your career's important, and it sounds like The Agent's a ton of trouble. You're going to have to deal with him, but don't forget about your friends and family. Let's set aside your work for a couple of weeks."

"Okay, Dad," I sniffled. I wished this conversation wasn't on speaker or that Bee wasn't here. She looked worried about me, too, but *her* parents weren't coming up from Tortuga West.

I talked with them for almost an hour, expecting to be interrupted by Rocko at any moment. By the end, we'd caught up pretty well, and Dad was throwing his clothes in a bag like they were going to leave right this minute. It took almost ten minutes to get Mom off the phone, and she made me promise I'd have her super-suit ready, "just in case." I didn't want her anywhere near the Madame Shockwave Costume, but she was insistent like only Mom could be. Eventually, though, we said our goodbyes, and I was finally able to hang up.

"Well, looks like the apartment's going to be crowded," I said, laughing nervously. Bee had kept herself together the whole time my parents talked about coming for Christmas, but now I'd see her real reaction.

She smiled sheepishly and poked me in the side. "Yeah, maybe more than you'd expect. I was going to tell you a couple of days ago, but I came out to my parents. They know I'm a super now, and after this, they'll want to see me, too. So, uh, we probably need to figure out how to host four adults for a week or two."

I groaned. "I guess we can say goodbye to our bed."

WEDNESDAY, DECEMBER 17

We'd covered the whiteboard in scribbles and sticky notes as we furiously tried to avoid an inevitable conclusion. We'd tried every possibility and plan we could think of to keep at least one set of parents out of the green room, but the only option besides opening up my secret base to Extras was . . . worse. Doable, but worse.

But at least it was distracting. Sort of, in a horrifying way.

I hadn't thought about The Agent, Rocko, or superhero work once in the last three hours because I was too busy rooting through Bianca's pigsty of a room, trying to make it livable for the two of us for a week. I'd taken one look at my girlfriend's abomination of a dorm room and vetoed the plan to have her parents stay here. There was *no* way we could get it clean enough for other people; if we were lucky, we'd survive living there ourselves.

"No wonder you've been spending all your time at my place!" I complained for the fiftieth time as I shoveled dirty clothes from who knew how long ago into a hamper. "Bee, this isn't okay!"

"I know, I know," she said miserably from the sink. The dishes were a loss; she had a garbage can full of cups and filthy plates. "I've been doing better at your place, but I was going to eat the deposit here and—"

"No. We're getting it cleaned up and spending the next week or two here, and we're going to like it—even if it kills us." I wrinkled my nose at the incredible pile of sports bras and socks in the corner. All my work, and I'd barely made a dent! "It'll probably kill us."

"Oh, shut up."

I stretched, and my back popped loudly. "Fuck, that feels good. Okay, we've got our parents figured out, assuming we can get this mess in order before your folks fly in. They can have my couch, my parents can have our bed, and all the Christmas stuff can happen at Walnut Tower. That way, we don't need to make this spotless—just livable."

"Oh, thank god. I thought we were going to be here all day."

"We are."

"Har, har." The room went quiet as we both attacked our assigned jobs.

Then Bee cleared her throat. "So, we still don't have any idea where The Agent went?"

"No. And you know what? I don't care about that right now."

"Really?"

"Yeah. I think my parents are right. He'll turn up again. He's not done with me. But we don't have any leads, and we're not going to *get* any until next semester, so for now, let's focus on my parents, your parents, and 3V1L. They're leaderless, powerless, and ripe to be beaten. We'll make a plan, sweep into the Poudre Districts after the break, and wipe them out; maybe they'll even have a lead to The Agent. But for now, no more shop talk."

Bee laughed cynically. "When has *that* ever happened?" I tossed a filthy spaghetti strap shirt her way, and she ducked. We both laughed when it hit the wall with a faint slapping sound.

"I'm serious. Unless our parents or TU bring it up, we're not talking about work. We'll have to manage the administration, but I need a break."

Bee washed her hands and wiped them dry on a rag that wasn't completely filthy. Then she shot me a look and winked. "I know exactly what you mean."

I laughed and pushed her away. "Not until this place is cleaned up."

She acted disappointed, but I ignored it and focused on cleaning up my girlfriend's dirty laundry. As much as I hated to admit it—and especially as much as I hated cleaning up Bee's dorm room—I needed the time off. Winter break couldn't start soon enough.

Epilogue

Smoke from a hundred cigars and cigarettes wafted through the Ilneat Earth Network's cruiser high over Earth. Rocko sat with their conference-provided earbuds muted so they could only hear the closest few speakers. They couldn't take the cacophony anymore.

The Ilneat Prosperity Representative wouldn't stop talking, and Rocko didn't care whether that blathering idiot was cutting the Network loose because of the Earth situation, Thornberry's continued absence from these meetings, or any other reason. What mattered was that they were being cut off. There wouldn't be an incident coming, not from ProsComm. That meant Rocko would have to make their own.

A hundred studios' producers sat around the table, and Rocko finally—finally—had a seat near the head. The Ilneat chewed on a fresh unlit cigar, watching their comms tablet. It was close to three in the morning back in Tokyexico City, and if everything had gone right, they'd hear from Pataki soon.

If not, they'd hear from Prosperity Command, and that'd be the end of their career.

Didn't matter. The risk was worth it because Project Ultima had everything it needed to boost DuPont into the majors ahead of schedule, and if it did that, Marino would need something to help her keep up. Otherwise? Two shows? Rocko couldn't imagine running two. One was enough of a headache—they were already on medication for their stomach, not that it was helping. What Snowball had failed at and Cartman had only just started to accomplish before their untimely promotion, Rocko would do.

Major leagues. The big money. A year in the majors: everything they and Pataki had done, and would have to do, it was all worth it for that prize. But that wasn't Rocko's ultimate goal. They'd accept it as the barest minimum of success, but the Ilneat wanted more. So much more.

The representative's talking head disappeared, and Rocko unmuted the others' volume, keeping their voice muted for now. Snowball cleared their throat. "I think we should take this message as the warning it is and start making plans to get out," they said, glaring at the others.

Cartman rolled their eyes and stood up from their new chair at the head of the table, gesturing at the former most powerful heroine's producer. "Snowball, you're one to talk. Who are your supers? Oh, right. No one anymore."

"Excuse me, but let's keep the name-calling out of this. We've got a serious issue here, and if ProsComm isn't willing to lend us support or cause another incident to solidify our position on Earth, we should consider whether the Network can resolve this crisis." Snowball cracked their knuckles, and Rocko rolled their eyes at the gesture. "If we can't, and ProsComm won't, we should quit while we're ahead."

Rocko unmuted. "If I may, you're all idiots. What skills do you have, Snowball? A Human Studies certification, Advanced Human Interaction, and a couple dozen other certs, all about moviemaking and Earth. You're looking at a decade of retooling before you could get hired on a space opera or murder mystery, or longer if you want to be done with showbiz."

"And? That's not so bad," Snowball said from their chair.

"You've got better options, though—three of them. You could go big, spend your cash to grab an up-and-comer, try to break back in. It might take a year or two, but it's an investment in your future. Or you could cut and run. Enough of you do that, and the Network fails. If it fails, I'll be pissed, and our colleagues will be, too. So, I propose a third option."

"What's that?" Cartman asked, sneering.

Rocko told them. At first, the other producers laughed at the explanation. Then their hands started wringing—both pairs—and they started making excuses for why it wouldn't work. Then, one by one, they agreed. As Snowball reluctantly nodded, Rocko stood up. "Great. You'll all sit back, we'll return to the Hot Zones and get the smaller studios in line, and then we'll let the situation on Earth play out naturally. No nuclear disasters, no assassinations, and *no* running away. Got it?"

When the other producers nodded, Rocko finally let themselves relax. They lit a cigar and puffed on it, letting the smoke interfere with the hologram projectors in the center of the table; normally, it'd be rude, but since they'd taken control of the Network and its fate in one fell swoop, it didn't signal disrespect. No, the message Rocko wanted to send was much more blunt. "I own your fates, so listen to me."

A door on the massive conference room's far side opened, and a human—a *human*, on the cruiser!—strode in wearing a tan business suit. There was a moment of absolute silence. Rocko could hear the ship's engines thrumming in the background. Then the room exploded in shouts as every producer started yelling all at once.

The Agent had never been in space.

When he was a boy, he'd wanted to. Thornberry had crushed that dream—or so the Ilneat had thought—but he was nothing if not a plotter. Now, fifteen years later, he was finally there. The Ilneat Earth Network cruiser didn't feel like he'd imagined it.

If anything, it felt better.

Fifteen years ago, when he'd been given powers and Thornberry had started him on his path to the major leagues, he'd known he was special. One of a kind, in fact. There were other powerful heroes, but one Tank served more or less the same role as any other. But only he could grant powers to the unpowered, and only he could lease powers from his fellow supers. That alone propelled him into the top few heroes on Earth.

But The Agent wanted more—so much more. The real power wasn't in *powers*. It was in the studios. So, for the last ten years, he'd been trying to make the case to the Ilneat Earth Network that running a studio wasn't just for them. That *he* could do better, with less, than they could.

He'd been on the cusp of victory with Vigilant Vow. The boy had been a perfect test case for how *his* powers—not Cartman's incompetence, and certainly not Thornberry's complacency—could make a studio successful. But then, some worthless minor-leaguer had ruined his plans and reputation. And not only that, but when The Agent set his backup plan in motion, Magical Girl Understudy had been there to stop him again. That idiot girl was a nuisance.

He sat in an empty chair he *knew* was his, staring at the shouting Ilneats as their four arms waved cigars back and forth. His hand strayed to his breast pocket, and he lit a cigarette of his own—lights, of course—and waited while one producer slowly bludgeoned the others into some semblance of order. Though The Agent recognized Cartman at the head of the table, Vigilant Vow's producer didn't seem to be in charge. He filed that away for later; the one shouting the loudest was the one who mattered here.

The long room grew quiet, and finally, the Ilneat who'd taken control stood on their chair. "What's your name?"

"Penbrake. Roger Penbrake. But since that's not your convention here, you can call me Thornberry or The Agent."

"Okay, Penbrake, what are you doing here? This is a meeting of the Earth Ilneat Network's producers, and last I checked, you're not—"

The Agent cleared his throat and tapped his chest, where a name tag was pinned to the jacket. "An Ilneat? Your security systems disagree. They recognize me as Thornberry, and right now, Thornberry Studios has over twenty superheroes and villains under its umbrella. That makes me, I believe, the largest single studio in the IEN, correct?"

The room erupted into chaos again. This time, it took almost five minutes for the uproar to die. The whole time, The Agent sat back with his feet on the table, staring at the Ilneat who'd done the speaking. They were the key to his entire plan; none of the others mattered. He was willing to put his grudge against Magical Girl Understudy aside for now; there'd be time to deal with her later, once he'd solidified his position here.

"I propose a fifteen-minute recess," the Ilneat said. A green light appeared on the table next to their nameplate.

"Seconded," The Agent said before any others could. The light next to Thornberry's nameplate lit up to a murmur from the assembled Ilneats. As more and more green lights—and a smattering of red ones—blinked on across the room and the seated Ilneats started to stand and murmur with each other, The Agent strolled over to the main speaker. They glared over their cigar.

"Why are you really here? You can't possibly think you can run a studio," the Ilneat said.

The Agent smiled charmingly. "I already am. Right now, my villains are losing to your heroes. We just lost the season finale, but 3V1L's not out of it yet. Their boss got away, and as long as Understudy and Fursona can't find him, they won't be able to move up to the majors. Unfortunately, their boss isn't on Earth right now." He winked and pointed meaningfully at his name tag.

"Okay, okay, but listen here, *Thornberry*. You're the low hand here. You may have the most supers, but they're underpowered losers. Until you prove otherwise, if any studio needs something from you, you do it. Understood?" Rocko, still standing on the table, jammed their finger into The Agent's chest.

The Agent nodded. He was used to the Ilneats' bullying. Thornberry had been worse, but they weren't around anymore, were they? He'd deal with Rocko the same way when it came to it. After all, that was what the gun in his briefcase was for: dealing with problems his **[Temp Heroes]** couldn't. And until then? Rocko would be his most important ally. "I hope to have a great working relationship with you and the rest of the IEN."

"Whatever. Get the hell out of here and get ready for a teleport to Earth. We're going back to the Hot Zones. My orders." Rocko dismissed him with a wave and reached for their buzzing comm tablet.

As he headed toward the door and down the IEN cruiser's hall toward Thornberry's empty quarters, The Agent couldn't help but break into a predatory smile. Phase One of his emergency plan was complete. He'd take the teleport to Thornberry's backroom, get Reggie and Otto on board with his plan, and start working his way up to the top.

Then, the other studios could see what humanity could *really* do.

Mrs. N sat at her desk; it was almost three in the morning, and she hadn't seen her bed in Mid-Town in days. Her crazy sister was out there, villains were running rampant across Tokyexico, and the Council of Heroes wouldn't leave her alone about using her powers to help restore order.

She didn't care about order, though. Just about the kids.

So, for the hundredth time since closing, she unlocked the top drawer, where a black handgun sat next to a magazine—insurance, in case someone she couldn't stop decided to break in.

There were only three supers she couldn't stop with a word, and she didn't trust any of them. Not. One. Bit.

The front door squeaked, as it did. "And then whoever it was went home," The Narrator said, her voice the picture of boredom.

Nothing happened for a moment. There wasn't a sound. She'd just started to relax when the next door opened.

Her hand gripped the pistol, and she flipped the safety off. "Whoever you are, leave or catch a bullet. We're closed, and I'm not messing around."

"No can do," a smoker's voice rasped, and the office door opened. The Narrator leveled her pistol at the small, four-armed figure silhouetted in the doorframe, then raised it. "I'm here on business."

"Your kind's always here on business. What do you want?"

The Ilneat pulled themselves into a chair. "I just wanna talk. No smoking, right? Shame." They closed the pack of cigarettes in their pocket, shaking their head sadly. "Name's Pataki. Listen, my boss, Rocko—you've worked with a couple of their heroes before—they need your help. We're working on some new super-suits for Understudy and Fursona. Understudy's is coming along nicely, thanks to my . . . less-than-legal, let's say . . . efforts. But Fursona's? That suit's a mess."

"And you need my help why, exactly?"

"Because of the kid. The girl in the dino Costume. How does her power work? What makes it tick? I can't figure it out, and Fursona's gonna need something big if she wants to keep up with—"

"You can call them DuPont and Marino if you want. I've known for a long time," The Narrator said tiredly. "So you want to understand Kaiju Kid's power? And what do I get in return?"

"Easy. Rocko should be in charge of the Network by now. They give the word, the other studios leave you the hell alone," Pataki drawled. "You get a good night's sleep—that is, after you work all that coffee out of your system."

She rubbed her eyes with her free hand, the pistol's grip heavy in the other. "You don't want anything else to do with the kids? Just to understand Kaiju Kid's power?"

"Word of honor, may I lose my job if I'm lying," Pataki said, holding up their grasping hands.

The Narrator sighed. Then she stood up, gun still in hand. "Come on. I'll show you the suit. You can have fifteen minutes with it, but when you're done, it stays here. Intact."

"That's plenty. You won't regret it," Pataki said, grinning widely enough to reveal their gorilla teeth.

Mrs. N already did.

Albert Clawson watched in disgust as Toll Publishing's printing presses roared to life. As Senior Editor, he'd argued against this. Toll shouldn't be a political weapon, he'd said. The truth could be handled better than this, he'd said. But in the end, the board had overruled him, eyes full of dollar bills and gold coins. He couldn't blame them. His had been that way, too. At first.

The machinery kept running, filling the silence with hums and cha-chunking sounds. Paper rolled through the machine, Times New Roman font filling page after page in the white-lit room as a few Toll employees watched the process. Word by word, sentence by sentence, Toll Publishing carried on with its motto: The Truth, No Matter the Cost.

And it would cost.

He'd been all for publishing. When the email came in explaining what it was, he'd been all for publishing it; the profits would be massive, and it was a guaranteed bestseller. But that was before he'd actually *read* the damn thing and realized what it was—and by then, it was too late.

As the papers piled up, another machine swept them into order, forming books; the thin, hundred-fifty-page manuscript had been heavily edited at Clawson's insistence, but even that short, they weighed heavily on his mind as he watched from the glass-plated production office. Toll Publishing had crossed a line, and the only thing stopping him from making his stand about it was the hypnotic rhythm of the printing presses as they rolled out page after page.

The binding machine stitched all the offset-rolled pages into one and folded them perfectly into a small paperback binding. On the cover, at the Board's request, a thirteen-year-old girl with undercut blonde hair and a wide, beaming smile stared back at Clawson. She looked happy, but he could only see accusation and contempt in her eyes—eyes that stared into his soul. Albert couldn't meet her gaze—at least, not for long. And she was way past listening to his apologies.

"Fuck this," he said, turning on his heel. He'd picked his hill to die on, he'd died on it, and the Board had run over him anyway. His letter of resignation was all typed up. All he had to do was send it, gather up his things, and he'd be on his way to something better. He stepped into the elevator, and the door chimed closed behind him.

The thin paperbacks fell into cardboard boxes on pallets on the publishing floor, and a forklift carted them into a warehouse. They'd definitely be a bestseller, the first one of 2043, and that'd be good enough for the Board. For now, though, they could wait like land mines in the dark, sitting silently until someone stepped on them and blew up the world.

Toll Publishing would send out *The Diary of Golden Goose* when the time was right, and not a moment sooner.

Author's Note

Hello, Aest here! Thanks for reading Magical Girl Undergrad: *Rise of 3V1L*.

One more book is coming in the series, but if you can't wait for the Kindle or Audible versions, check out aestbelequa.com for more of my work.

Please leave a review; it means a lot to me.

I'm usually on Discord in Aest Belequa Books (Discord.gg/xvkfnNMzfe).

Come say hello, tell me your favorite superpowers, and meet the fantastic community!

You can find the work of several talented authors at linktr.ee/coteh.

If Discord isn't your favorite, you can keep up with LitRPG through these Facebook groups:

LitRPG Books

LitRPG Forum

GameLit Society

About the Author

Aest Belequa is a LitRPG and progression fantasy author, play-by-post RPG game master, and former teacher from Colorado. He grew up loving fantasy and science fiction and tries to bring that same energy to his writing.

Podium

DISCOVER MORE

STORIES UNBOUND

PodiumEntertainment.com

www.ingramcontent.com/pod-product-compliance
Lightning Source LLC
Chambersburg PA
CBHW020643120726
47906CB00001B/99